CW01643397

HANNIBAL MARKS

An Epic Saga of a Cornish, Smuggling Family

Prideaux Skelton

Copyright © 2018 by Prideaux A.M Skelton.

All Rights Reserved. No part of this book may be reproduced in any form or by any electronic or mechanical means including information storage and retrieval systems, without permission in writing from the author and publisher.

Published by Cornish Publishing Company

www.prideauxskelton.co.uk : www.cornishpublishingcompany.co.uk

Prideaux A.M Skelton asserts the moral right to be identified as the author of this work in accordance with S.77 Copyright , Designs and Patents Act 1988 (U.K)

Historical characters in this book died well over 100 years ago. Other characters are fictional. No character is based on any living person. Any names that may be of living people are co-incidental and they are in no way connected with the story.

Captain Hannibal Marks 4th, 1819 – 1879.

One of the last in a long line of smugglers in Cawsand and Kingsand. Overlooking the two villages as they are today, much unchanged from his time.

Contents

Introduction

Intrigue, daring, tragedy, murders and more befall the Marks family on their journey from labouring for a living in Devon and Cornwall in the early 1700s up through to the senior ranks of the smuggling fraternity in the notorious free trading communities of Cawsand in South East Cornwall.

Brushes and friendships with the nobility, gentry and clergy of the day lead to a series of adventures that continue through four generations.

It is over 100 years before decline sets in as the Preventative and Coastguard services finally get a hold on smuggling in the area.

In the villages of Cawsand and Kingsand, prominently featured in Hannibal Marks, little has outwardly changed from the era in which the book is set. The windy narrow streets of the villages remain in the same shape today as they did in the mid and late 1700s. Ancient harbours, fish cellars, farmsteads, wealthy estates, local churches too, all remain to form the backdrop to the book. Similarly, many of the other towns, villages, farmsteads, country estates, churches and landscapes in the book also remain much as they did.

Trilogy preview

Hannibal Marks is one of a trilogy of novels, that are based on the lives and times of three Cornish families from the sixteenth to the nineteen centuries.

The other two books in the Trilogy tell stories based on the more gentrified and noble side of the family. Many of their fine houses and estates remain today, providing a continuing reminder of life as it once was.

Dastardly deeds and epic events such as duelling to the death between the powerful, royal pardons and favour, travels with the Court of the exiled King, form part of the books.

All this and more make the settings and lives of these extraordinary characters a contrast to those of Hannibal Marks, but, as readers will experience, all three do come together in the end.

The writer, Prideaux Skelton, has a rare permission from the past to tell these tales of deeply rooted Cornish families and their remarkable lives. Running through her veins is the blood of the principal characters in the books as she remembers well the folklore and history passed down as family stories, making the past seem not so long ago. Works of fiction they might be, but woven with real characters, events, folklore, rumour, speculation, all within the settings of towns, villages and homes that for the mostpart are with us today.

The novels were originally intended for family publication only, to pass down, that they might provide inspiration one day for subsequent generations to explore the lives of their family that went before them. To understand them, their surroundings and their times. Not to be forgotten.

Prideaux reclusively lives and works in their houses, where, to the rear, are sections of the ancient village, now hidden from the public eye. She walks their streets, uses their harbours, their old sinking stones as anchors, their oil lamps, utensils and other artefacts. The past is never far away from the present. The views to sea are very much as they were. The moors and islands in the distance, the beaches where the contraband was landed, the seas, beaches, rocks and coves that were the battlefield between the Preventative Revenue Cutters and the Smuggling boats. This is her back yard. Readers need not leave this world behind when they arrive at the last page of the book, for it is there, in our times, to visit and share.

Dedications

To my parents, grandparents, and all those before them.

To all who gave up the richness of their pasts and for whom the books have given them life again.

A special dedication is to Pearl, who was always determined to pass on folklore and snippets from older family members, who too had had them passed on. The memories of the towns and villages she had known before change and destruction came. These gems came flooding back to intrigue and to fascinate. Frank too, who was much closer again to the people and places of yesteryear, was always there with tales from long ago.

Also, to those not yet born for whom these tales were really written, before it was suggested they should reach a wider audience. They set out to provide a tunnel for them, through which they can travel back to the time of their forbearers.

May these books enable them to hear them, to touch them as well as provide a desire to look differently at the lands in which they lived their truly larger than life lives.

To Pimmy, who encouraged the writing of these tales and proof read.

Prideaux A.M. Skelton

Chapter 1

A Lucky Escape for Hannibal 4th

"Stop, in the name of the King. Stop. I hold the King's commission, the service flag, the ensign." The shout was shrill, timed to break through the silence that accompanied those few seconds between the shingles of the beach moving with the incoming tide and those moving on the outgoing. The noise created by the movement of the sand and shingles created an intoxicating rhythm that drowned the voices of those close to the beach. This was the voice of a lone Customs man. A Preventative man. He was addressing the folk on the beach below him, those in the small boats that plied between beach and the large boat offshore, the Smuggler. The smugglers, or free traders, as they preferred to be known, operated in one of the great hotspots of the trade in Cornwall.

It was 1840 and the Preventative man had been on duty with several others, employed to stamp out the smuggling trade that had become rife in this previously lawless part of South East Cornwall.

This was that lump of land perched on the very eastern end of South Cornwall. The peninsula had on its seaward coast the twin smuggling villages of Cawsand and Kingsand, sheltered from all but easterly winds, littered with coves, islands and estuaries in all directions.

The villages built some of the best of smuggling boats as well as providing some of the most experienced, competent smugglers and seamen to be found in the whole of Cornwall. This was an important coastal area to the smuggling trade for the entire south coast of the County. They were close to the big markets of the town of Plymouth and the towns adjacent to it. The villages had grown considerably as a result of smuggling. With all the facilities and activities of a small town, they were often referred to as just that, the towns. From here, large smuggling boats could be unloaded, goods hidden and distributed to their markets, whether by sea, river or foot.

Waving his flag of authority in one hand, pistol held tight in the other, the Preventative man knew the other men of the Customs' service were much further off on the Cliffside. He had to do this alone or the smugglers, their crafts, men and goods would vanish into thin air as quickly and quietly as they had arrived. He could take the glory of apprehending this group. Bounty and prize might be his. Recently appointed to the job he was so drunk on the prospect of glory, the risk to his safety of doing this alone failed to cross his consciousness.

His group had split up to cover the coastal stretch along the cliffs of Whitsand Bay as far to the east as Rame Head that night. They were doing this by foot. In amongst the bushes and copses in pairs, they could avoid being easily seen. He and his partner Preventative man had separated. As he went a bit further eastward alone and dropped into the isthmus of land that led to Rame Head, his eyes had popped with the sight that befell him.

A large Smuggler ship, just offshore, fully laden with fast rowing boats unloading her. These could be his for the taking. The others would soon be there when they heard his shots. They could run it within minutes. He would not be alone on this job for long, but it would be he that would claim the biggest prize, a slice of glory. The boat the Customs had out that night would come in to encircle and apprehend the smugglers from the sea. They would catch the haul of smuggled goods as well as the smugglers. It would be all down to him. He found them, and he would hold them.

Discharging his weapon, he would warn those smugglers plying their trade off the beach that lay about one hundred feet or so below where he was stood, to stop and do his bidding. This lone officer was perched precariously in the dark on the top of an almost vertical cliff face on the approach to Rame Head, a mile or two from Cawsand.

As he stood looking down onto the scene, the Preventative man suddenly felt the flat side of a cold blade, slide along his throat slightly nicking the skin under his chin. He felt the blade turn, the sharp end now running the width of his throat. The holder of the weapon was bearded, and it bristled against the back of the officer's head.

"One move from you without me telling you to move and you're gone. I'll feed the bits that I slice off you to the seagulls. Now, where's the rest of you?"

Bringing his knee up against the pit of the Preventative man's back he let him know it was not just the knife's blade on which he relied tonight. This was a big man, a man tougher and more desperate than he. The smuggler asked him again, "Where are the rest of you?" He pushed the knife against his skin with increasing pressure, but not enough to bring on his final breaths.

"They are further over the cliffs to the west. About two miles from here by now."

"And any of you coming in boats?" There was a long pause as the Preventative man thought how he should answer his captor.

"I thought so. Where are they?" With that the man took the gun from the Preventative man with his other hand. In doing so, he loosened somewhat the tight grip he had on the throat of the officer for a mere second. The Preventative man felt the slackening of the smuggler's grip. Thinking this was his chance he made a grab at the man's arms to move the knife away from his throat. The smuggler tightened his grip once more and the officer felt a trickle of warm blood run down his throat onto his chest and shirt. It was a mere graze, but the man was ready to finish him off if needs be.

"I told you not to move. Where are the boats? How many of you?" With that the smuggler placed the knife into his other hand whilst continuing to hold him tight around the neck in his vice-like grip. He took the knife down the line of his back unzipping his uniform with the sharp blade as he went. He paused as he took the blade further down towards the rump of his trousers. "No, No," pleaded the Preventative man.

"Quiet. Where's the boat?" With that the Preventative man's legs started to tremble. He had lost his footing on the cliff. As the whole of the Preventative man's weight fell on the smuggler's arm so his grip gave way. The Preventative man slipped away in front of him.

His cries were few as he tumbled down the cliff face, smashing against the rocks on his descent to the beach below.

The men working the Smuggler had taken little notice of the gunshot neither the sight of the Preventative man above them. They knew that their guards, their batmen, as they were known, were scattered at the top of the cliffs with enough manpower to stave off a good number of Preventative men if they had to.

The smuggler hurried down the steps cut into the Cliffside following the descent of his released captive. As he jumped the last few feet onto the sand, he saw the Preventative man lying, contorted on the beach, from his fall. Lifeless but warm, he was bent over a rock that protruded from the sand, his limbs splayed at angles to each other, broken and twisted. He was not far from the water's edge. The smuggler dragged him the final few yards and kicked him into the lapping water.

"Come on, spread the word that they'll be coming along Whitsand bay cliffs now and from the sea. There's a dead man, one of theirs."

He addressed the unloaders of the rowing boats and the oarsmen to get message to the Smuggler. The Smuggler was anchored in deeper water but getting as far in to the rocks as she dared go but leaving enough space to escape quickly if needs be.

"Let's get this Smuggler in sail and off again. We'll then get our boats away and tucked safely into the usual places. We haven't got long. Silly bugger was waving their flag as if he was the ass end of a revenue cutter. Bloody flags they've had, chopping and changing them over the last years. They should stay more interested in their bloody flags and ensigns. Worry about their colours and leave us alone to get on with our business. Red, blue, crowns and all the bloody rest of it. They may as well have one person on each cutter who does nothing else but change the damned things. Blue with a crown, red with a crown, any other colour you like with a crown."

The Customs flags and ensigns, symbols of their place, their status on the water, had changed over the last few decades as the service was put in the hands of different public and crown bodies. Under the Customs Board, under the Navy, under the Coastguard. So, it went on.

Among the village boats offloading the Smuggler was that manned by Hannibal Marks and Richard Cock. Hannibal was the fourth generation of Marks' smugglers in the Village.

The Marks had done well from the trade and after a hundred years or more in the business, owned several large smuggling vessels plying the English Channel to purchase their stocks of contraband. They also owned fishing boats, cellars too, where the fish were pressed for their oil and fish salted in barrels for sale.

The real money was in the dangerous smuggling runs to and from Brittany in northern France and the subsequent distribution of the spirits, teas, and silks to satisfy the insatiable demand for cheaper luxuries.

They had also started to invest with others in the larger smuggling boats and in doing so spread risks. They ran drinking establishments too, from where they could sell the spirits direct in the busy villages.

Hannibal 4th, as he was known, had barely hit 20 years of age. His friend Richard was about the same.

"Come on Richard. We have had the nod to get out of here. The Smuggler is drawing up anchor." With that a loud crack of gunshot was heard coming from a seaward direction.

"Look Richard the Smuggler's sail."

"It's been hit. Where are they? Where are they coming from?"

"Look there. That crack, ours is returning fire. Hear her anchor. She's away while she can. They'll find that dead Preventative man."

"The anchor's up. It's time for us all to split up and go."

"We all want to get away from here now. When they find that dead Preventative, we could all be for the gallows."

Luck was with them as they saw the Regina passenger ship in the dim light anchored up eastward and to the inside of the breakwater reef in Plymouth Sound. The construction of the breakwater was still a work in progress. They had heard Regina would be ready to sail at first light.

Grandfather Hannibal, indeed, his Great Grandfather, Hannibal 1st, had made a few moves that had taken the family to Cawsand.

He had been in Launceston for some years, having previously lived with the family on their farmstead at South Tawton. South Tawton was just east of Zeal on the Devon side and not far from the landmark hill that was to become known as the Cawsand Beacon.

What would he, the intrepid Hannibal 1st think now? What would he advise the latest generation of Hannibal Marks to do in this situation?

Hannibal 4th, as he was known in the family, had not met his Great Grandfather, although he had lived a long life for the times. Hannibal 4th had arrived in the world about twenty years after his death. His Great Grandfather's older boats had survived him though and were still in use. Hannibal 4th had always doubted there could be many original planks left as she had been repaired and re-planked in many places, many times.

The two young smugglers exchanged views in low voices, deciding that this was their moment. Yes, they would go alongside the Regina and enquire for work and passage, but not now at night. So how and when?

Talk had been that Regina was off to New Zealand with passengers and cargo.

Pulling hard in the sixteen-foot rowing boat they had been using to ply to and from between the Smuggler and the beach, they reached the Regina. There seemed to be no one on watch and the commotion further west had not drawn the attention of the slumbering ship's crew.

Ladder down, they took their chance and boarded her quietly, stowing away under some of the sheeting that covered a small boat on deck. Eventually they fell prey to the exhaustion of the night, to be awoken with the sound of Captain and crew preparing to get underway. There must have been some additional provisions loaded late on board as they heard winches running as well as shouting about the shore boat coming back aboard. They then heard instructions going out to another provisions boat that was carrying additional biscuits. They could hear jokes being made about their quality of the biscuits and the worm-infested provisions that had come from the bakery on Southside Street on Plymouth Barbican.

The Barbican lay just a short distance away to the other side of the mouth of the Tamar river, from where Cawsand and Kingsand lay. They would need to get out and speak to the Captain about work, but should they wait until the ship was underway and out of sight of land for fear they would be put ashore?

Neither had worked on ships this size. Ships that could travel the oceans. They had spent all their lives on smaller boats and ships. They had been trained in the building of smaller craft. Both had fished in the large sailboats used for the pilchard seasons and been on smuggler runs to Guernsey and Roscoff.

They decided to emerge when the ship was likely to be in full sail but not too far from shore. A peephole in the sheeting that had provided their cover had enabled them to watch the village become a dot in the distance as the Regina's sails filled with the fresh wind that was starting to blow up.

They had left their small boat, Rowena, to float free, with rope and stone dangling in the deep water, unable to reach the bottom. They knew the direction and pace of tide would see her hold fast when she reached the shallower water off the black rocks as she drifted in to shore. Chance would be that she would then be found and picked up by the villages.

They were confident the village would piece together what had most likely happened to them. Although Rowena was her name, it was not sign-written on her. There were, though, tell-tale signs to indicate this was a smuggling boat. The anchor stone at the end of the rope on the Rowena was a stone commonly used as a sinking stone to weigh down kegs of contraband under the seas only to be retrieved later when they knew the coast was clear of Preventative men.

The reception they had from the Captain of Regina was not as hostile as they feared it might be.

Work was secured, providing a lifeline for them, with a passage to a new life. Regina with Hannibal Marks and Richard Cock had started on its journey. This was a journey for the two men that was to herald a new Marks' era on the other side of the globe.

"Well Richard. We've got a few months before we get to New Zealand, wherever that is, so I may as well tell you a few of the stories I've been passed down about how we got down into Cawsand."

"How long do you think it will be before we can get a boat back again?"

"When we know the dust has settled. Maybe on this one when she returns?"

"With a bit of luck there's nothing much to connect us to the other night. Let's hope everyone got back safely and the Smuggler was not recognised or caught."

"How will we get word back home?"

"There will be someone heading back who can get a message or we can write eventually."

"Well we'll have to see. They'll find the Rowena and guess, if she's not wrecked, that we're somewhere, alive and well, but where?"

“They’ll know the Regina was close by and maybe think we joined her. They’d guess news would come from someone soon enough if we’d been killed or caught.”

“You’re a good writer Hann, so write. Tell them we are well. Tell them where we are. It can go when we get there or pull into a port where a letter can leave from?”

Hannibal put his hands behind his head, lurched back, looking heavenward at the clear sky. With a shrug of his shoulders he told his friend he had three months to listen to his stories.

“My grandfather was good for a tale or two, even three, four or more. He would tell us about the free trade and how we came to Cawsand all those years back. Lots more beside too. Much he wouldn't ever say but said more as I got older. Although here and there the tale might get bigger. The fish that got away!"

“Well, knowing Hannibal the fourth, three months will be needed to tell these stories, so you’d better get started I suppose. If nothing else, they’ll help me get to sleep!”

Chapter 2

Launceston, The First, Big Stop for Hannibal 1st

The Marks' family had ended up in South Tawton a long time before Hannibal 1st had arrived in the world around 1720, but before that, many generations had worked around the ports of North Cornwall and Devon, especially in Barnstaple and Bideford. At the time, these were successful port towns in Devon County, with strong shipping links to Ireland and the Americas.

Hannibal 1st brought his family to Cawsand and Kingsand where they had settled and made good their lot. Hannibal had not, though, come down to Cawsand without some stops on the way. Before Cawsand, he had mostly lived and worked in Launceston as well as the St. Stephens area near

Saltash. He had first moved to Launceston in Cornwall, on the occasion of his marriage to Joan Warwick, who was a Launceston girl. They had got to know each other when Hannibal 1st had taken up employment there. It had become clear that the farm could not keep them all and there was a declining amount of work he could do in the area. It was not too far, and Hannibal had often made the walk back to return to see his family and friends.

He had first worked at carting in Okehampton, about 5 miles from the small, South Tawton farm he was from, a walk of around an hour and half. He would sometimes return through South Zeal, a few minutes from South Tawton where he could see his friend and do a little extra work to unload ankers of spirits into the village Inn, the Oxenham Arms.

Ankers were usually in a tucked away place. There were no questions asked, just paid work available to move them into the Inn, mostly under cover of darkness. Sometimes Hannibal had seen the tubmen carrying the ankers slung around their necks, front and back. He had heard that the ankers had travelled up the nearby river Tamar from the coast with no duty paid. As the river became impossible to navigate by any means, the goods would make the remainder of their journey by land. The tubmen, sometimes walking long distances with these heavy loads, would deposit them at safe houses along the way, where they were stored. Some goods would arrive by packhorse, carriage or cart. The chosen mode of transport depended on the state of the tracks and whether they were safe to travel on unhindered. He had heard tales of boats travelling to France from the coastal villages further south to buy contraband. These boats were laden with all manner of uncustomed goods that bore no duty, making them considerably cheaper for ordinary folk to buy. They carried goods such as tea, cognacs, fine cloths and more. There were places Hannibal had heard talk of that he felt he now knew but had never been to, such as Cawsand and Kingsand from where many boats left. These villages faced the open seas but were wrapped around by the river Tamar, its inlets and tributaries.

He had often climbed the beacon outside of South Tawton, the tallest for many miles around, from whence he could see far into the distance, straining his eyes and staring hard to try to see out to the south to these places. He had heard tale of the legendary Sir Francis Drake, defeater of the Spanish Armada who would stay at the Oxenham Inn a hundred years or more before, whose lands had been not much further south. Drake's lands extended to the other side of the moorland where South Tawton lay and stretched down and on to Plymouth. Hannibal 1st knew there was money to be made further south, on the coast, for hard workers like him. Men who were prepared to take a risk and keep their mouths shut if troubles arose. Men who could resist the temptation to turn King's evidence to save their skins if caught. Men who were not tempted take any rewards on offer by the authorities to disclose information. Some of the finer spirits had been introduced by Hannibal to the South Tawton Inn. Other free traded items too had been offered to folk living in the area, including teas that found their way into households that could never otherwise have afforded them.

Although the inland smuggling activities were dangerous, they were in no way as dangerous as those on the coast where most of the preventative measures were concentrated. Once goods started to be moved well inland, those involved in their transportation were comparatively safe. It was not though without hazard. The high moorland areas were less wooded, with large tracts of exposed barren land where activities could be spotted for miles. Goods were usually moved at night by those who knew the territory well. This additional movement of goods inevitably put the price up but still made the goods substantially cheaper than they would have been if they had passed through the customs' houses.

This was though an uncertain, fickle trade, relying on punitive levels of duty levied on popular merchandise that in turn created markets in smuggled goods. Tale had it that when Hannibal 1st was a young man in his early twenties, the market for smuggled tea had a temporary lull when the authorities reduced the duty on it, leaving the heavier more difficult to move tubs of cognacs and genevas providing the bulk of the profit for those involved in the trade.

As Hannibal had got increasingly involved in the free trade so he met more and more folk in the area and spread his wings within a radius of about twenty miles from the farm.

This, a clandestine trade, built friendships, trust and camaraderie, often without any names used other than nicknames or Christian names.

Nicknames were commonplace, and all involved would know whom each other meant but without identifying them.

Occasionally, Hannibal would stay at friendly houses, farms, Inns and their work buildings as he did more and more work with the smuggling trade.

One of these was the Bell Inn at Launceston, close to the old Castle walls on the western side, just up the hill from the Church. The Innkeeper also had a carting business in the town. Hannibal would sometimes work for the carting firm doing all manner of jobs. He would care for the horses and repair the carts. He got to know a lot of folk in Launceston town from his carting work.

And so, it came that Hannibal 1st eventually moved into Launceston, securing his living and more beside in the Cornish town. Residing at the Inn had some additional benefits for Hannibal who soon made several friends amongst the townsfolk who would regularly go there. The Innkeeper took him into his family, providing him with friends and company to keep. This was fortunate as they soon put him wise about the folk in the town, those to watch out for and those he might trust. There were also many travellers passing through as well as regular townsfolk. Numbers would swell on the market days to sell or to buy. In amongst them were cheats, vagabonds, thieves who would lie and had not a trustworthy bone in their bodies. Hannibal learnt to distinguish one from the other.

Carting took Hannibal in and around all parts of the town including the immediately surrounding area, helping him get to know the outlying settlements as well as the town.

When going out of town their carting would often take them on the turnpike roads. These were considerably better kept and less likely to get them get stuck in the ruts and muds that plagued most of the old tracks, especially so in the rainy periods. If they were carrying more delicate wares, these were the preferred routes if goods were to arrive safely. The Innkeeper and other cartmen in his employ had made sure that Hannibal knew the ways onto the turnpike road from the old cart tracks to make sure where possible the turnpike road was accessed away from the Toll Houses and the vigilance of the toll collectors. This would reduce the costs of delivery.

Sometimes these accesses had been seen by the toll-keeper and blocked off, but this was rare. The lot of the toll house keeper could be an easy one if he turned a blind eye here and there to those who evaded the toll fee but ensured there were sufficient toll fees collected to satisfy the landowners and trusts whose responsibility it was to maintain the road.

There was little protection for travellers on the roads, but the turnpike roads at least had the benefit of being better used by larger carts and carriages which were often armed for their own safety.

Highway robbery was not common in the area but was nonetheless a risk for those in the carting business. This risk was sufficiently great that some basic weaponry was carried to make sure that the carters were not completely defenceless in the event of a hold up. Although never held up themselves, Hannibal and his carting mate, Luke, were on the scene of a hold up when once taking goods to Bradstone.

They had just crossed Greystone Bridge that spanned the Tamar, thereby joining the counties of Devon and Cornwall at this point. Bradstone Hall was not far on the Devon side. No other carts nor carriages were on the bridge this day, so they had crossed without giving way and with no one in the cornices waiting for them to pass.

They were in good spirits, despite the inclement, misty weather, that had fallen around them. They had joined the turnpike road further back and had not paid the toll. The Innkeeper would be pleased when they returned that his costs of the trip had once again been kept down.

"Luke, Luke, what's that noise in the distance? Slow the horses." They had the larger of the carts this day, drawn by two of the strongest horses in the pack. On board was a piece of furniture destined for the Hall alongside a crate that sat neatly inside it. Talk was that there was a family gathering at Bradstone. The heiress sisters were there accompanied by their respective spouses to discuss the future of the Hall and its large acreage complete with farms, hamlets and villages. Luke knew quite a lot about Bradstone as his grandfather had been a groundsman there and lived on the estate. He had only recently died. Luke had been a regular visitor to see him, as the walk from the town was a relatively short one. He also knew the other staff at the Hall.

Bradstone was an impressive estate with all the trappings. Luke's grandfather had said that the family had been lucky to hold onto the estate and not have it forfeited after the war. The war Luke referred to was the Civil War, when the then incumbents of the Bradstone seat ended up being a target for the Parliamentarians and the Commonwealth that followed it.

As the noise from the cartwheels stopped and the horses calmed, they could hear shouts in the distance. Fearing they might be confronted about their presence on the toll road, Hannibal said he would dismount and go on cautiously to see what was going on further up. Otherwise all had been quiet. There had been no other travellers on the road that they had so far seen.

With that Hannibal went off the road into the woods that conveniently lined this section of the road. There were no adjacent houses on the next stretch. They were now entering the Bradstone lands. As he trod with great stealth from tree to tree, giving himself cover from sight, the noise became increasingly clear.

The next tree stop revealed what was going on.

"Come on and hurry about it my fine Lord and Lady."

The rather grand carriage Hannibal saw had the two carriage men sat on the ground by its horses, hands tied, mouths gagged, with a man stood watch over them. His head was covered, making him unrecognisable. The other, who was talking, remained on horseback with a pistol in his hand, poised, ready to fire. He was politely spoken. He sounded more of the gentler classes.

“Empty your pockets and throw that which they contain before the hooves of my steed."

The authoritative, clear voice was unforgettable for Hannibal. This was not the voice he would have expected of a common thief, a Highwayman, nor was the way he sat on his horse suggestive of anything other than the demeanour of one brought to higher station.

His boots were gleaming, jacket and shirt well turned out. He wore a neckpiece that appeared of recent fashion, a jacket that sported a wide collar and gleaming buttons.

What was this all about ... a prank being played out, a jest? He was brought to his senses as he saw the highwayman point his pistol at the carriage only to jerk the gun heavenwards at the last minute into the air suggesting it was about to be discharged, but he did not empty the pistol. With that a small carriage trunk was thrown out of the carriage door, landing a few yards from the hooves of the highwayman’s horse.

Hannibal returned to Luke and their cart more quickly than he had taken to get to his vantage point. Blurting out what he had seen the two had quick decisions to make. Did they abandon their load and take refuge in the woods until the robbers had gone? Did they stay with it and trundle slowly up the road to see the stricken carriage party? Or were they to try to apprehend the Highwaymen by releasing their nags and giving chase? They decided quickly that they should continue their journey to meet the party and offer help.

As it happened, events overtook the pair. As they moved down the road, taking a sharp bend, so three horsemen galloping at speed came towards them. One reared up, unable to stop abruptly or pass. Hannibal and Luke responded by moving their cart to block the road. The horsemen veered with their steeds heading to the woods.

Hannibal jumped to with his pitchfork raised and faced the horses. Could he dismount them before they had a chance to prepare their arms and fire at him?

Luke too distracted the horses, making them veer and rise more into the air above as panic took a hold in them. The horsemen chose not to raise arms and fire but to get their horses under control and escape into the woods. Nothing more transpired. They got no good look at the men.

As the two peered into the woods after the horsemen, who disappeared into the distance in no time at all, they saw a small clump of items.

As they neared them, they realised that these must be from the highwaymen's haul. As the horses had reared the items had been released from the small carriage trunk secured to the side of one of them. They gambled that they would not be back now and would be well into their escape.

Picking up the dropped possessions, they turned them around and side-to-side carefully, just staring at them for a while. A few pieces of jewellery, coins, silver snuff box, two gaming cards and a scarf. They picked them up and continued on the road until they came to the stricken carriage where the carriage men were being untied.

The Lady and Gentleman were now outside of the carriage and all were clearly shaken by the experience.

"I knew we should have kept a firearm inside the carriage. Could have blown that rogue's head off if we had."

With that Sir William Noel poked and jabbed his stick sharply and aggressively at the carriage-man who remained tied up.

"Would have been better to have kept a weapon inside than outside with you two damned fools. What do we pay you for?"

With that he took a running kick at the carriage-man releasing his irritation with the events and himself.

"Should we stop, Luke? After all we found these things in the woods. There's no saying we would know they are to do with any of this. We could always put them back where we got them from."

"No, I think we should stop and when we hear the tale, explain how we came by these. Tell them we picked them up planning to try and find the owner."

They were within sight of the carriage party and had quickly made up their minds that honesty should prevail. They would stop, tell their version of events. Relating their story was daunting. Sir William was a barrister at law and an M.P for West Looe. He was travelling to Bradstone Hall with his wife, Elizabeth, who was one of the co-heiresses of the Bradstone estate.

Elizabeth Trollop was one of the three sisters who had inherited the estate. The Cloberry family had been at the estate since the Norman Conquest. There had only recently been heirs of a changed name, but this was the first time there would have been a sale of the estate out of the family since those ancient times.

The fate of the Hall, with its fine mediaeval gatehouse, associated church, surrounding lands, farms, villages and hamlets lay in their hands.

In all the estate extended to over one thousand acres to the eastern side of the adjacent Tamar river. The Noels had been to Tavistock, detouring to Bidlake Manor, on the way. They had stayed in Tavistock before returning this day.

Elizabeth knew the Bidlakes well. It was only about 8 miles away and she had often been there with her father and mother. They had some common interests with some of their landholdings neighbouring each other. Sir William had business in Tavistock. Whilst there, he had arranged for them to stay at the Bedford Inn. The Inn was situated next to the Higher Abbey Gate of the town.

"It would have been easier, speedier and safer to have travelled on our horse than use the carriage driven by these two," he repeated.

"Should leave them here tied up for a few days."

"We found these Sir. The thieves must have dropped them. We tried to stop them by turning our cart in front of the horses as they were coming at speed from the bend in the road. They reared. No-one was hurled off but we found these afterwards, partly trodden in the mud."

Hannibal and Luke produced the jewels, snuff box and cards.

"These are my Lady's favourite jewels. This snuff box was purchased especially from the snuff makers who arranged the box to be engraved with our crests. They are the most valuable things to us in that box."

Elizabeth, now composed, turned her head from the carriage to address them.

"To whence do you travel?"

Hannibal with bowed head responded, "We are travelling, your Ladyship, to Bradstone Hall, to deliver the crates in our cart."

Elizabeth, taking control of the conversation, requested that when they had made the delivery they come to the house. They were to tell the servants that Lady Elizabeth had asked them to come there after they had finished their business. She would instruct them to receive Hannibal and Luke of the Bell Inn carters.

Sir William took the snuff box and jewels.

"Keep the cards, they are no use to us now but may bring you good fortune in your lives. There is an omen associated with them. If by chance you re-unite them with their missing cards, come and see me again, and well rewarded, you will be."

They got into the carriage and off it drove, the one untied carriage-man taking control of the reins, the other, still waiting to be untied was next to him.

"Which card do you want Luke?"

Luke took his chosen card. His had a diamond on it and a picture of the sun smiling in between two men dressed in strange clothing. This left Hannibal with a card with the King and a heart. Centred was the King's crown.

"Would have had more luck if he'd given us the snuff box or the jewels," laughed Hannibal.

"Chance of finding the rest would be like finding a needle in a haystack."

He had brought this saying with him from the farm at South Tawton where some of the old folk had also used the saying, needle in a meadow, for anything lost that was nigh on impossible to find again.

"What if they ask at the Toll House about those horsemen, Hannibal, and it comes out we hadn't paid to be on the road."

This put a cloud over the whole episode. All they could think of was how they might respond by explaining that they were travelling on a lower path when they heard all the shouts. How they had gone onto the turnpike road to find out more. Both knew this explanation wouldn't bear any closer examination of the facts surrounding it. With that surety they continued, hoping nothing further would come of it.

As they turned off the turnpike road it was not long before they saw the mediaeval gatehouse of Bradstone Hall in front of them.

Towering high and over four floors, it was a massive structure. They could not easily see the main house that stood a short drive on, until they went through the gatehouse, which was manned by staff that also patrolled the walls that came off from it.

Word had already reached the Hall staff that they were to be helped to unload the cart and prepare it with the horses for the return journey.

They were also offered facilities in the servants' quarters to clean up, ready to be presented to Sir William and Lady Elizabeth. The full story had not yet though fully emerged.

Everyone from the gatehouse staff to the porters and stablemen wanted to know why Hannibal and Luke were to join Lordy and Lady at the main house.

The two said nothing, despite being pressed by the estate workers.

Unloaded and more presentable, they were then taken to the door of the main house where they were greeted and taken inside to the smoking room where they sat, waiting.

Sir William and Lady Elizabeth entered. As Hannibal and Luke rose from their seats, they assured them to be seated.

"Your bravery and honesty should not go without reward."

With that a guinea piece was given to each of them and a letter to go back to their employer. "Should you ever identify these scoundrels and provide such information to me that brings them to justice, there will be more to come," uttered Sir William with a steely determination exhaling through his pursed lips.

He was known as a man not to take being thwarted lightly. Today had seen not only his purse, but his pride injured too.

Hannibal and Luke bowed, murmuring quietly that they would do their best to remember anything they could about the men and return with that information.

With nothing further said they took their leave and headed back to the town. They would have to make tracks quickly if they were to catch the light, although the night sky was clear, and they knew the road backwards. The talk on the way back was of nothing else. Who recalled what? Were these highwaymen persons they might know or know of?

They would need to hold the pictures of the men in their minds forever. "What about the horses Hann?" Luke suddenly blurted excitedly. "The horses might give it away. You remember things about horses better than men." As they drew into the town, stabled the horses and cart, they knew they were much delayed. Hurrying into the Inn they sought out their employer that they might quickly explain themselves and present the letter.

Chapter 3

Joan Warwick & Tetcott

Sometimes the carting would involve trips a few miles north towards the town of Holsworthy, especially so to the big estate house there, Tetcott. Tetcott was less than 10 miles away. The southernmost Tetcott lands were reached within an hour of leaving the town. The house only another hour further on.

"I reckon you hold a candle for that Joan up at Tetcott, Hannibal," his workmate said as they were doing a delivery in Launceston. Joan was the cook's help at Tetcott. She lived in the servants' area there.

"And that Thomasine as well – they are both fine maidens."

Joan Warwick and Thomasine Spry were two young ladies in the employ of the Squire of Tetcott. Hannibal always lit up when they had a job to do at Tetcott and hoped he would see them. Thomasine worked as a maid-servant to Squire Arthur. She was about the same age as the Squire's son and heir, John, and she became a special friend to him. The friendship was frowned upon, but tolerated, by John's father who failed to understand the attraction of it, especially as it continued and developed over the years.

Unlike Joan, Thomasine had been born on the estate. Her parents, too, had been trusted workers to the previous Squire. The two girls were great friends. Thomasine was a little further up the estate hierarchy than Joan. They had spent much time together from the time that Joan had arrived to work at the house when they were both about fourteen.

By the time Hannibal was carting to the estate the girls had become young women. They too looked forward to the times when Hannibal, accompanied by either his friend William or Luke, would arrive, laden with goods ordered for the Arscotts or the estate. Collections were sometimes transported from Launceston by the Tetcott estate workers using their own estate carts. If the Squire was in town with his carriage, the carriage might be used for small unobtrusive items that did not interfere with the image of Squire and his fine carriage.

No, the Squire did not want his carriage and presence to be blighted with the spectacle of hauling and carriage of ordinary goods.

For the carriage to transport anything other than the Squire, his family or his guests, the items had to be of a value, a favoured spectacle to the eye, so much so that they deserved to be seen returning with the Squire, and in a befitting style.

If the Squire was in town everyone had to know. His carriage was one of the finest in the area. Before it entered the town, it was stopped to clean off dirt and scuffs from the journey. It would arrive, as did the family, in pristine order.

The Squire was always seen in town in his finest garments. Should he arrive on horseback, he was an imposing figure, always in his best riding garments, signalling the wealth, prestige, position of Tetcott and of the Arscott family, who had owned it for centuries.

Squire Arthur Arscott was a man to be reckoned with. Of high influence, he was connected by marriage to the ancient Trefusis family of Cornwall who were later to become Barons Clinton. His wife, Elizabeth had been a Trefusis of Mylor in Cornwall but had sadly died in 1714. His son and heir, John Arscott, was by his second marriage.

The Squire was not often to be seen at the buildings where deliveries were taken at the estate, but sometimes, he would be spotted and, if luck had it, he would be seen astride his horse. Long wig donned, immaculately, correctly lodged upon his head, the observer's eye would be drawn down to his lengthy coat, which was complete with engraved silver buttons denoting the Arscott coat of arms of two bucks. His feet would be adorned with the best of blackened leather boots that shone with a slipperiness that the mud and dirt of the fields and lanes would not dare stick to. The young man, his son and heir, John, was often at his side. He would be on a steed of similar gravitas and dressed to match his father. He was the Squire in waiting and often known as the young Squire John.

John was the same age as Hannibal. If father was away from the house doing his duties as Squire and "Lord" of the Manor, young John would seek out Hannibal and William if they were carting to Arscott, discharging Thomasine and Joan from their duties in order that the group of them could spend some time walking and talking together.

The young Squire was developing into a man who knew his own mind, what he liked, what he didn't, how he was prepared to live his life, and by what values. These were to be his values. They would not necessarily match those expected of him nor dictated by what he was destined to inherit, both in terms of possessions and status.

"Come on all of you, I'll get some horses saddled up and let's go for a ride. Joan, tell cook I want food and drinks to take with us, enough to go into the saddle bags."

"I can't tell Cook that Sir," exclaimed Joan.

"Leave cook to me." With that John went off to seek out Cook, telling her that Joan was not to be available for the afternoon and to prepare refreshment for him and his guests.

John's will and generosity were to be neither questioned nor disobeyed. His will stood, even if it might result in dismissal or reprimand from Squire Arthur should he return to witness this frivolity and mixing of the classes on the estate.

The other servants were of mixed feelings about it, but generally thought no good would come of this sort of thing.

The Arscott lands encompassed much of the upper sections of the Tamar river area. The group went through these, the village, the Church and back.

"It would be good to take you all up to see Dunsland House and its grounds. It's very grand," panted John who had raced ahead for a while.

"Grander than Tetcott," replied an exhilarated Hannibal who had not gone as far up at the other Arscott family estate.

"Much grander. It's owned by the Bickfords who married an Arscott. They came by the house and Park with the marriage." I think my father would like to think that the two estates were more bonded again with a marriage between me and one of the Dunsland daughters." With that Thomasine looked away.

John said no more on the subject but quietly reflected on the bluntness of his father's wishes that were not infrequently raised with his son and heir.

"You are coming towards a marrying age, John. Our lands have been separated from those at Dunsland for some years but tied by blood which has been watered down. Yes, watered down, much like the Cognac we get brought here sometimes. Watered down to a level where you can scarce taste the Cognac in it. For that matter the lands are tied to each other as well. They nie on run alongside each other for miles. It's up to you and one of those Dunsland girls to give it new strength.

More Arscott's needed I say. Give it more Arscott John, there's my boy. More Arscott is what's needed around these parts! A bloody good shafting of Arscott is what it needs I say! Shaft them all with a bit of Arscott blood. That's what we need, John. That's what we need."

With that the old Squire banged his tankard of Ale down hard onto the table in front of him. The table had been well prepared with his favourite ale and range of wines, cognacs with other spirits at the ready. So hard in fact was it slammed down that the whole of its contents jumped together as if fleeing in fright from the tankard. Fleeing indeed into the air only to break their bonds of unity and to slosh unseemingly onto the table, from whence they found the path of least resistance, and fell with the grace of a waterfall to the floor below.

"A few more years father ... to establish myself."

"Establish yourself! You don't need to establish yourself. You're son and heir to Arscott, every last sod in the ground of it. You're not an apprentice or clerk coming out of your time boy. You're an Arscott and heir as well. You can still have one of those pretty maids if you really must but think of the Estate. Think of the family name, its standing, it's land and possessions. Think of that finest Arscott cognac coming back to full strength and pumping through every vein in the arteries of the two Counties making everything around it grow in abundance and strength, John. Don't you forget that those Arscotts at Dunsland are amongst our most ancient. Back to the 1300's, remember. You could do it, John. You, yes you! It is only you now that can do it John. Arscott of Arscott again. All as one. All as one....."

Little did the Squire know that the woman for his son, by his son's own choice, was none other than his servant. John would not be accepting her as a mistress and mistress only. She was more than that and everyone, but the Squire, had seen this coming since their childhood.

As they cantered back towards Tetcott, Thomasine spoke her thoughts and dismay out loud knowing that her words were for her and the wind alone.

Had it meant nought that they been born under the same stars within hours of each other? For a short time, they were equals entering the world with nothing but hope. This was until the reality of birthright reared up its head, their differences in station stealing away the naivety of birth. For much though she loved Tetcott and with it most of her life, it was all it stood for that drove a wedge between them. In those quiet moments at night she dreamed of a life where all the trappings of what divided them were stripped away from John leaving the pair alone to face the world as it came to them.

Tetcott, despite the security it gave of a decent home, food in plenty, also represented the wall that kept them apart. For that and that alone she also loathed it, whilst at the same time, she loved it. She did not dream of being the Lady of Tetcott, only to be at the side of John, wherever that might be. John was fun. He saw the staff as not only servants, there to do his bidding at his whim, dispensable commodities if they did not please him, but, moreover, he saw them as people. They loved him for it, not out of duty but out of respect, kindliness and the care he showed for their wellbeing.

John's antics kept them all amused arming them with plenty of yarns and tales to tell about life at the big house at Tetcott.

"Get that damn fool toad out of here John. And while you're at it, tell that other damned fool, that Jester of yours, that Fool, that he'd better find something to amuse me other than his damned fool size and leaping around or he can keep out of my sight. What do we pay him for anyway? His damned fool talk? Yes, that's it, his damned fool talk!"

With that Squire Arthur deftly gave the Fool a strong tap in the ribs with his stick followed by a stout kick that sent him a good three or four feet away from the hearth.

Air-born for a few seconds the Fool wasn't too sure if he should make a joke of it or not. Squire Arthur was not a predictable man, other than to say his predictability was to be unpredictable.

The Squire did not suffer fools gladly and this Fool had been trying his patience ever since John bought him.

"John is there any need to have this dwarf under your feet all the time and following you around like a hound after a bitch?"

With that the Squire showed his kinder side and threw the remnants of the meat left on the bone when his meal was done, straight at him. It was an excellent shot, most unlike his usual way of dispensing with his surplus meat and bone after a good meal. This was to toss it heavenward, with a skill and practice that ensured that not only would it fail to hit the heavily patterned, ornate, ceiling above, but would also defy any unpredictable descent.

An unpredictable descent to the Squire took place in circumstances where the shape of the bone made its flight earthward to resemble more the random fall of a sycamore leaf with its seed.

On this occasion it presented neither problem for the Squire who had taken aim instead at the Fool, hurling it at him with the accuracy of a Greek Olympic discus thrower.

"Ha, perfect shot!" His shout of success pleased him as he saw the bone hit the Fool square on his forehead. The Fool, deciding to seize the opportunity to please his masters, caught the bone as it ricocheted off his forehead, leaving as the only evidence of its visit a slow drip of blood that rolled down the Fool's face.

On catching it the Fool stood upright, held it high, bowed and started to bite into the remnants of meat.

This was not an ungenerous gift as the meat was prime venison on the bone and the Squire too liked to gnaw at the bones after his meal before he summoned Thomasine to fill his glass that he might give it a good washing down.

There was always meat left within the crevices of the bone that the Squire could not get out no matter how he sucked at it.

Teeth were in short supply in the Squire's head and those left were in the wrong place for gnawing at animal bones.

The venison was usually from a good day's hunting with traditional archery used for the kill. A good day or two for the Squire was hunting, followed by more hunting.

It was made all the better if, when hunting the fox, the Squire had his favourite company with him and they'd had a good rampage over the Rectory gardens when following the hounds, field to field.

To see the Vicar storm out only to be shouted at, "Can't stop the horses and hounds when they've got the scent in them Vicar," gave the Squire immense pleasure, rivalled only by the pleasure in the sight taken by his son, John.

The Vicar had heard it all before, from both Squires. The young Squire John loved his hunting too. He would usually follow on by shouting as he passed,

"Pray for an ungodly fox, Vicar. One that keeps clear of Church."

Unlike his father, the young Squire John, had a light- hearted disposition, one that enabled the Tetcott Vicars to take it all in relatively good heart, giving back to John what he gave, in good spirit and banter.

The dwarf Jester then, with a deftness of hand, took the bone by its long stem, threw it in the air, making it somersault many times on the way up and on the way down, only to catch it cleanly again, although this time in his mouth. Saying nothing, he knew this would please and entertain the young Squire John, with a good chance of also giving some amusement to the Squire. This might, with some luck, instigate a turn in his mood. How right he was. The Squire's mood changed. The dwarf was again in favour.

Taking his bone outside, like a dog under the kitchen table that had been fortunate enough to be dropped a bone by the staff, he dropped to the floor and gnawed the remaining meat off the bone. With that a shout went up from John.

" Show father your new trick."

This was just what he could do without. His small belly full, the thought of a string of mice going down towards it was more than he could take.

But the Squire was in a good mood and this was no time to protest. Besides, the mice would be attracted to the smell of the venison lurking below. This would encourage them to straighten out their bodies with all their might.

With that he went outside and down the path to the small dwelling and area that had been specially made for him with everything changed to fit a person of his size. This amused John who had wanted a dwarf jester and manservant ever since he had had seen a dwarf couple entertain them when he and father had been visiting Great Fulford further eastward in Devon, in the Parish of Dunsford, some years back. They had been there as guests of a grand hunt.

John Fulford was similar in age to John Arscott, a little older. John had been enraptured by the full time Motley Fool in their employ. On discussing Fools over dinner, the men concluded that they knew of no other full-time Fools in the employ of the great houses of their time. These unique factors had led John Arscott to set about on his search for a Fool of his choice. He found John Black. He took Black John, as he had become affectionately known, into Tetcott's employ with the indifference of his father.

He had since become very fond of him. In turn Black John had become very fond and loyal to the Arscott household, save the Squire.

John had ordered his tailor to equip Black John with motley in traditional colours and another in the colours of Tetcott. Black John's role as Fool gave him a good status, provided he remained in favour with the quality and variety of his jests and quips.

He could speak more freely than other men, even to the Squire, albeit Black John was always far more reserved with Squire Arthur than Squire John.

Black John returned from his Fool's house and parlour with a string of small mice tied strongly together with thin twine. This was a favourite trick he had picked up in the travelling show he had worked with before he had been bought by John and taken into the employ of the Arscotts.

It was a trick that was almost guaranteed to never fail to entertain. It was a show that Squire Arthur and his son relished in displaying to guests. As he entered the room, smoke from the pipes that were sitting firmly between the jaws of father and son alike, alongside that billowing from the large, imposing hearth, faced Black John and his mice full on, as a wall of choking mist.

As the Squires ensured their smoke billowed elsewhere, so as not to interfere with their view of the show, that was imminently to proceed, nor would hinder the quality of Black John's performance, so too emerged the impressive sight of the fireplace with its fine accompanying surround.

It was this sight, the sight of the Tetcott Arms displaying their lineage in all its grandeur, that provided the stage curtain for Black John. The stage was now his. Like jesters of old that had amused successive generations of the holders of the British Crown, here was Black John, complete with his mice and best Motley to perform the very same function: to please his masters.

How would Henry VIII or his successor and favourite daughter, Elizabeth 1, have reacted to the trick he was about to perform, thought he? With that he took a bow before the Squires and the hearth, spun on his pointed bell adorned shoes, came back to his starting position, held the mice on a string high above his head, which simultaneously leant back to reveal his tonsils lying in the dark abyss of his throat.

The mice were lowered in. Down and down they went, wriggling on their stomach muscles only, but not able to do him any harm. Trussed firm, down they went until only the cord could be seen. The Squires were quiet. They then arose to look more closely at this trickery to make sure it was real and, as usual, real it was.

With that Black John jerked upwards and firmly at the cord and up the mice rose from the depths of his throat. He took a bow, made the string of trussed mice bow too by deftly jerking at the string then forcing it downward. The mice were clearly disappointed by their failure to grab any of the prime venison lurking in the belly of Black John, nor its remnants, that remained twisted amongst his teeth. They had to content themselves with its sweet smell.

Their expression of disappointment was known to Black John who stroked and comforted them, assuring them that they could nonetheless look forward to a reward when they returned. This would be a reward of yesterday's bread that had started to harden in Black John's cool area of his Fool's House.

Black John spun around to the clapping and laughter of the Squires. With that he skipped to the door, turned again facing the them, front on, bowing all the while, pushing open the door, to take one final bow before exiting the room.

As soon as the large oak, carved, panelled door groaned to a close, he untied the mice, putting them into a small wooden box that he had left outside waiting for the end of the act.

The box lid had breathing holes in it. He knew his trained mice were valuable to his act. They all knew what was expected of them. Black John was now off duty. As he danced down the cobbled section of pathway back to his home, he made a start at the job of disrobing from his motley.

Disrobing after a mice act on the way home was an art form in itself. Black John would toss the mice box as high as he could into the air, testing his ability to lift away a further section of the robes before the box fell back earthward to his clutches.

Maybe he should offer this as an act ..... and to get the motley back on again in the same way. His masters would like that one, but better perfect it first. Taking in Black John as Jester and Fool to the house was only one of the antics of John, the Squire in waiting, that started to bring colour and life into Tetcott.

John Arscott's passion for wildlife, alive or dead, extended to a range of pets, including ravens, toads and more beside. Taming his toad had gone well in the end. The toad liked food. John had food. John liked the toad performing for the food. Toad soon caught on to the deal. The toad comes for the food and takes it from John. John laughs, gets more toad food. Toad takes food again and so the ritual goes on until John laughs no more. The toad then disappears until food appears once more in the outstretched hand. Repeat performance! Happy Master, happy toad.

The same ritual went for the raven, until it flew down onto the table out of turn one day as toad was about to get his food, stole the food, pecking right through the toad who bled profusely, became comatose after a struggle for breath and life, then promptly died.

There were more toads and only one more met a fate as violent as the first "Old Dawty", for all the toads trained by the Squire John had the same name, which gave ease to all.

It was Old Dawty 3rd that too met an untimely fate, albeit not this time at the beak of a raven.

Old Dawty 3rd met his fate, moreover, at the end of a stick wielded by a guest at the Arscott table. On seeing the toad appear for food, the guest took one look at it, raised his stick and whacked it as if he were aiming at a ball. The hit was a resounding success for the guest.

Old Dawty was taken right on the arse, so square on, with such unforgiving force and velocity, that he lifted heavenward off the table.

With this, the guest took great delight in swinging his stick well back behind his head, coming forward to strike the toad yet again.

Full on the arse he hit him once more, seeing him hurl heavenward up into the rafters of the room, onto the Gallery above. The toad landed with a grace befitting his stately role at Tetcott, for he landed symmetrically, slumped over the rails of the Gallery, where he remained motionless, legs straggling the cross rail and slimy form limp, with no sign of life whatever.

The toad was dead. Black John had been curled up under the table as was often his wont and invitation, ready to amuse. On seeing this, such anger overcame him, that he emerged, leapt onto the table, stretched out his arms out to his sides as far as they could go and pushed his neck forward. He then bellowed and cried for the master's toad, much to the surprise of the guest, whose laughter was now drowned by the cries and whales of Black John. Suddenly and without warning, Black John crouched onto his knees and propelled himself towards the guest, knocking him onto the floor whilst pushing over his chair as he went, arms smashing into his back and causing great pain and discomfort.

"Get your dwarf off me Arscott," he bellowed. With that the astonished Arscott turned to look away. "I see no dwarf. I do see a dead friend and companion."

The guest was escorted from the room into the Hall and out into the night, followed by his trunk and manservant. The door drew shut and as he looked back, he saw the Fool jumping up and down in the large lower window gesticulating rudely and unseemingly with his hand.

"Damned toad got what it deserved, but so did that damned fool Piers. Damned fool Piers got what he deserved from a Fool.

Ha!" With that and an accompanying satisfied grunt, the old Squire shuffled from the table, helping himself to another glass of their best, muttering as he went "damned fool Piers made a fool by a Fool. Ha!"

Chapter 4

A Marriage at Launceston

"This is the third time of asking. If any of you know cause or just impediment why these two persons should not be joined together in Holy Matrimony, ye are to declare it." The Vicar of St Mary's Church in Launceston read from the Book of Common Prayer. It had been well thumbed since its arrival in 1662.

He need not have bothered to have the book in front of him as he could recite these banns in his sleep. This was the last reading of the banns before Hannibal and Joan were to marry on the 2nd January 1746. They had blossomed since he had asked her father for her hand. She had returned to the town of her birth and upbringing for her marriage and life with Hannibal. Life at Tetcott had gone but was not to fade from memory. Joan had made friends at the estate. Thomasine was the closest of these. They shared the bonds of friendship that only holders of mutual secrets can have. As Hannibal and Joan were preparing to take their vows before God, so she, Thomasine, would silently make hers. Her vow was that she would remain at Tetcott for all her days and be available to care and comfort John. She would even suffer silently the pain that would rain down upon her, day after day should her John marry for the future of the Arscotts.

She knew that no matter what wealth a good marriage might bring John, it was she, only she, that could bring him what would make him truly happy.

Squire Arthur would only be content to give his approval for a marriage that improved the position of the Arscott family, their estates, their standing. This would be especially so when it came to the Dunsland estate and daughters. John was expected to consider the family name, property and station. But this was John and John had not yet married in accordance with the wishes of his father. Indeed, he had not married at all.

Squire Arthur was becoming increasingly infirm. The gout had kept him in his room a lot of late and he rarely took to a horse or walked the parkland around Tetcott. Would John marry in the way that would meet with his father's approval? Would he do this as one last deed for his father before he died?

John and Thomasine were there at the wedding in Launceston alongside several of the Tetcott workers. This was a rare sight and many at the Church squinted and looked from the sides of their eyes to see the Squire's son at the wedding of a pair far beneath their rank.

There were only a few present at the wedding who knew how the very special bond between the four of them had been forged and the secret that Tetcott now held. The attack on Thomasine in Launceston when they had gone there with the young Squire a little while back had left its mark.

Thomasine had continued to be cautious on days of celebration, frivolity, drunkenness and foolhardy behaviour that went with these events in the town.

The attack had left its mark on the young Squire, bonding him to Hannibal in a way that defied rank and station.

John Arscott had planned to go to the town at Fair time, taking both his best hunting horse, Black Bird, and a carriage with the personal attendance and assistance of Joan, Thomasine and his horseman George. For Joan it was an opportunity to see her family and Hannibal. For Thomasine it was a chance to enjoy the bustle of Launceston, taking the occasional moments with John alone.

The Fair had filled the town with entertainment for its inhabitants and those from all around in abundance. Travelling theatres, acts with fire swallowers, walkers on the high wires, grotesque persons barely recognisable in human form ... and ..... dwarves for sale.

Black John would keep close to his master. So too would he keep the company and protection of the Tetcott delegation to Launceston. He was a desirable asset to the felons of the Fair. A temptation for thieves, he was, when alone, at some risk when walking through the dim of the windy, hastily formed aisles of stalls, makeshift tents, carts and displays of the show. If taken he would most likely be sold at another Fair many miles from Cornwall and Devon. Life with the Arscotts was good for him compared to the cruelty of the Fair and who knows what a new master could be like.

The young Squire had requested the attendance of Thomasine from his father.

"Alright John, take her to attend on you as well if you must." John planned to stay in the town to enjoy a night of ales, cognacs and merriment. He would take his fill on the best fayre the town could provide him with.

Holsworthy was his main stomping ground, but he was looking forward to seeing some of his old kind at Launceston, who doubtless would be viewing some of the events of the Fair and merrying afterwards.

They all had arrangements to hunt over the following days at Squire Coffins of Lawhitton and Hexworthy. John was looking forward to seeing Richard Coffin, a man similar in many ways to himself in age and position and with good lands for hunting and always a good table.

They were all planning to meet in the Tavern, stay over so they could take as much ale, food and entertainment as their bodies could ingest, and digest, before retiring. They would then travel to Hexworthy the next day and spend a few more days there before heading on back to Tetcott.

The Tetcott entourage arrived on the North Road, with a pomp and style that drew attention. They entered through the gate set into the ancient walls that had once defended the town to stable their horses at the Inn and take rooms for their entire party.

The young Squire took a room for himself, with others for Thomasine and Joan, George and Black John who shared respectively.

The Fair offered a chance for Black John to get some new ideas for acts and shows that might please his master. With that in mind, he stole off with George, to methodically navigate the Fair, scouring it for fresh ideas as his master took ale and food on meeting up with Richard Coffin.

Joan and Thomasine went off in search of Hannibal who they knew would be around the Fair or in the area of the Bell Inn. The town was too busy for carting today.

"There he is," whispered Thomasine to Joan as she spotted him in the distance by the fire eater. Hannibal's shape was quite unmistakable from whatever angle he was seen. He had been busy the previous day when the Fair came into town. Additional labour was always needed to help prepare for events of this size.

"Shhh Thomasine, let's go around, come at him from behind and surprise him." With that, the two went around the shows, making their way through the bustling crowd of onlookers that encircled every performance on offer.

As the pair meandered their way ever closer to Hannibal, they were pressed tightly together by the crowds making any progression towards their target difficult. Eventually they got to within twenty yards of the unsuspecting Hannibal when Thomasine said, "You go now .... alone. I will meet you outside of the Inn before twilight."

"No, come with me, we were not to part today." With that, Thomasine started to take another route back through the crowds to get behind them and be able to move more freely around by the old castle walls. It was more peaceful there. She could stroll along up and down the walls before returning to take another look at the shows.

Joan, in the meantime, came from behind Hannibal, putting her hands with their slender fingers tight together, in front of his eyes. At first, he started and instinctively was going to grab those wrists that had taken his sight when, in a split second, he felt and recognised their gentleness, taking in the sensation of the swell of her bosom on his back as she breathed deeply, then more rapidly with excitement.

This told him that this was she. Gently taking her by the wrists, but leaving her hands over his eyes, he responded, "I need to know the owner of these hands before I can decide whether to move or leave them."

A giggle of laughter came back at him. As she released her hands, he swung around to face her. With excitement in his voice he asked, "shall we go up the castle hill and then come back by the castle walls?"

With that, no more said, the pair escaped the thronging mass, making towards the inner area of the old walls. Thomasine had kept to the path, expecting the three to meet later a bit further along.

They did not hear the screams of Thomasine. They could not have been expected to, for these were muffled by the wart infested hands of her attacker, as they bled, weeping puss onto her, from older wounds which had opened after scuffles at various locations throughout the Fair.

Close up to him, she could smell his breath. It stank of the cider and ales of the hostelries that were well stocked to supply anyone who had money to part with. The sweet smell of hay that surrounded them thinly disguised the odour of the rotting teeth that remained in his head. This was topped off with the smell of the remnants of cooked pigskin that was his favourite. The event had ample open-air purveyors of his favourite dish. The hand was missing the ends of two of the fingers but remained strong and determined.

He had, in his stupor, wandered from the central area of the fairground and seen Thomasine strolling towards one of the old entrances that went through the wall. She had not seen him as she strolled along, taking the odd alternate skip. He had entered the recess of one of the old fort entrances and waited for her to return down along the path.

The tunnel entrance-way he waited in was blocked further along but still went into the hill quite a way. Straw and hay were piled high along its meandering pathway into the hill. There were further channels off the main pathway that allowed less and less light to enter that would give visibility to the surroundings.

He reckoned there were few folks that would come down here anyway and any that did would be unlikely to progress on through this dark area, into the maze of channels. Should they do so, it was unlikely they would come in far. Certainly not far enough to hear anything. Besides he would be quick with her.

She wouldn't see him anyway as darkness in the tunnel came quick with the straw piled high. Little light passed through the further in they went. Just a few yards in, well maybe a few more yards as well, and he would scarce be recognized by her after. She struggled to get free but hand over her mouth and with a strong arm pulling her in by the head she found it impossible to shake him off. She was not strongly built, and her struggles went unheeded when met with his strength and determination. Her attacker was fuelled by insobriety and lust.

As he threw her down onto the straw that lined the ground a good way in and let go his grip on her lips, she screamed, to which he laughed and mocked that no one would hear her now.

Thomasine didn't get a good look at him again for he was in the shadows, but his outline was full of menace. She would refuse to give into this. John had never taken advantage of her despite the many chances he had.

She would not succumb to this creature's lust and violations. He'd have to use force or kill her first. As he shouted in a blurred tone, "I'll do that as well if I have to Missy", Hannibal and Joan were walking above. The man was right to assume that sound did not permeate well through the straw and thick walling, but the ears of the young are sharp. Hannibal and Thomasine started as they both caught then sound of something untoward.

"Let's go Hannibal, I don't like this."

"No, let's go and see what it is."

With that Hannibal scaled down the wall, leaping the final few feet to the pathway below where he saw the tunnel entranceway. Toes tipped, he went in, through the straw flung area, until he could see the shape of two bodies lurking in the dims. He hadn't been noticed, thinking for a while he should go, leaving these lovers to their bliss and time together without interference from him. Thomasine again shouted through her attacker's hand that was now closing her jaws sealed. A muffled shout was enough for Hannibal. The sound was enough for him to recognize it as someone in distress. There was a familiarity to it despite its distortion. He could not be certain.

He knew he must go in further to see what was going on. He would go carefully though for fear that this was an act with legitimacy on its side. The hulking form that had Thomasine in his grip was not in such a stupor that he was unable to hear anything through the haze that an excess of cider had created in his head.

It was Hannibal's next move with his foot that alerted him that they may not be alone as he stepped onto the floor, crushing some small twigs below as he wen

The attacker let his grip on Thomasine go in response, but before doing so, held his fist at her, mouthing that if she valued her life, she would keep her silence.

As she nodded, so she also waited her chance. As he moved a few paces on from her she shouted, "Get me out". With that Hannibal knew it was her and gave the surprise of his whereabouts in the maze away by shouting her name.

With that, the attacker did not wait. His eyes had taken the benefit of enough time to adjust to the near pitch black of within. He lunged with all his 20 stone towards the shape that was Hannibal Marks, flying at him.

In the brief seconds that followed, Hannibal had decided his course of action should he be able. The man had grabbed him from the dark, front on, wrapping his hands around his throat. Hannibal fell back bringing the man with him.

As they landed the man's grip loosened and Hannibal, dazed but not spent, grasped the moment for them both. Summoning up the strength of his neck and stomach muscles to lurch his body upward he took the man's face and nose with his hand from under, forcing his fingers as far into his nostrils as he could take them.

The temporary limpness of the man as he jerked and rolled to one side to drag himself away from the pain, enabled Hannibal to push the rest of him off and raise himself up.

He expected now to be able to push the attacker face forward down and fall on top of him to the straw below and smash his elbow into his head to gain the advantage, but the man recovered too quickly, turned, falling back on him again.

He was too heavy, too powerful for Hannibal. As Hannibal grabbed the back of the man's head to pull him again towards him, thumbs ready to take his eyes, his life if he could, he felt a sharpness in his chest in two places. With this the man seemed to start to lose his strength and his weight got heavier.

He pushed him off and as he rolled the body away, he caught a glimpse of Thomasine's form stood in front and felt a warm, wet sensation hit and roll down his now bared chest. It smelt of stuck pig. This was a smell familiar to him from his early days at the farm in South Tawton.

As he rose, he could pick out a pitchfork lying on the straws that must have been used by Thomasine to impale the man. He grabbed it and rammed it towards the man's throat and head. Wide between the curved metal prongs that it was, it was not too wide for one of the prongs to miss the man's thick neck.

In went one prong and Hannibal was aware of the death of the pig. Again, and again he thrust on the prongs, finally skewering the man by the head to the wood that lay below the straw in places. He could hear the breath leave the man and they could both smell his foul smell exhaling from his body for the last time.

With this they staggered towards the entrance, emerging to see Joan further up the small lane. They all ran towards the quiet of the escarpment further around the old castle walls. Joan, aware only that something awful had happened, went along with them asking nothing until they caught their breath.

Hannibal and Thomasine lay breathing heavily, pale, unable to speak. Neither had killed before but this was they or he. The story came out and Joan, more able to be measured in her response than the other two, took Hannibal's shirt that was drenched in blood from the punctures that Thomasine had inflicted on the man when he toppled Hannibal. She squeezed out the blood, rolled up the shirt and pushed it to and fro along the grass and earth to dry it and take the colour from it as best she could.

Quickly she used it to rub down his chest, smearing any remnants of blood all over, so the colour left just blended into his skin. She then took it, tightly rolled, under her cloak.

"This must go. You will need another and quickly. Go bare chested and take part in the hurling. It is soon to start and then find another or take that of another. Calm now and we will all go to the hurling together."

When they arrived at the hurling green, they saw Black John and George. Should they tell them what had happened and ask for help? The more that knew, the more likely that this could come out. Who knows what might happen then and who would be believed or not believed.

Black John and George were having a fine time. They were waiting for the hurling to start. It might be best to confide in only one of them, ask just one for help. It was Black John who knew best of the master's affections for Thomasine. Black John was the most committed to his master. Yes, it would have to be Black John. Black John alone. Taking him to one side, it was Thomasine who revealed to him the events of the past hours. The revelations sobered him. Black John would have seen no harm done to Thomasine. He knew his master would approve of his helping. He must not though know of anything of these deeds. This was Black John's chance to repay the kindness he had been shown by his master. He, Black John, would take control of this. His master need know nothing unless he felt he had to tell him. He would not know, at least, not yet.

No time for jest or merriment now. His master would expect him at the table tonight to entertain and entertain he would. He would need to hide this body or dispose of it. It must be now. No delays. It must be done before there was any chance this man might be found. Anyone might steal in there and find him. Opportune lovers, he who used the tunnel as a barn to store the hay and straw. Anyone. Anyone could find him before he had a chance to deal with this man, this dead man.

He needed to wait until it was pitch black. He would then take the body. He may be small, but he, Black John, had the strength of a young buck. He would take this man with any blooded straw and bury him. He knew where. His lair at the edge of the Tetcott estate would forever hold the secret.

He knew where no one would think of it nor care. His earthen floor would keep counsel to infinity. This man was a killer and harmer of women. He did not deserve the burial rights of the churchyard.

He needed to use a horse and cart to do the deed. There were plenty here and a dwarf could manage if he had to.

Had not he, Black John, run around every track and knew each one like the animals who had made them?

Had not he, Black John, the eyes of a hawk and could guide the horse and cart by the moon safely to his lair. It was not far.

He would wait, hope and speak to Hannibal to arrange the cart. Hannibal must stay, so must Thomasine and Joan. They must distract and amuse his master, so he did not send out a search for Black John. With his plan at the ready he spoke with them all and they were all ready. Light was lost apart from the fires and torches.

Quietly he took the rolled shirt from Joan. This was it. Black John left the town by the unattended castle gate, hurrying through to the tunnel. Finding it, he entered, cautiously going further in, feeling his way, letting his eyes adjust best they could. Stumbling on the man, he took a deep breath and prepared himself for the deed ahead.

Dragging him with all his tiny might towards the entrance, he peered out, and, seeing no one, loaded the body onto the cart. Covering him with sackcloth, he made off to the lower reaches of the Tetcott land where his lair awaited.

The floor was earthen, and with his basic tools, Black John prepared the grave. He pushed and shoved the man into it, covering it over. Returning to the town he pondered these events over, and over, again.

Should he burn the contents of the tunnel so there was nothing there? No one would suspect. The fire would soon be through with no time to put it out. All trace would be gone. All trace that was of the blooded pitchfork, the blooded and gore ridden hay and straw, all that he could not see properly when he took the man. All, all would be gone. Gone too, the smell of death that had met him when he entered the tunnel. He would not forget. Yes, he would ready the fire and then go to the Inn to please his master and his master's friends. He had come prepared with some of his newest tricks to entertain all. He would make a spectacular entrance that would look as if his belatedness was deliberate to please his master and his master's guests. His garments were clean enough. He had been cautious in how he handled the man. Meantime the fire would burn. If seen the worst would be that he had set fire to it as part of his trickery.

Yes, he would think of a reason why it might be part of the trick, in case he might have been seen or were otherwise discovered.

* * *

The day had started well for Joan. The grey dress that she had used for work on the Tetcott estate, for Sunday Church, best occasions and all else in between, had been decorated for the wedding. Flowers, tiny offcut strips of silks and coloured materials had been tied into love knot bows and other bride lace shapes to adorn the dress, to lift it from its forlorn grey into a vibrant, colourful garment worthy of such an occasion as this. It was prepared beautifully, with tenderness, just so, and ready for a bride.

She took a wedding garland made from rosemary and roses by her friends. This treasure was carried with them on their short walk to St. Mary's Church.

"I, Joan Warwick take thee, Hannibal Marks to be my wedded husband until death us part and thereto I plight thee my troth."

With that Hannibal presented her with a half of a gold coin, the other half remaining with him. She placed the garland carefully on her head and the pair walked to the exit of the church.

When outside Hannibal lifted his bride high in the air to the delight of those attending. Most knew them, but there were some who had just come into the church to view the spectacle.

Hannibal and Joan Marks were halted in their tracks as if met by a brick wall when they reached the oxygen of the outside air. They stopped, breathed in deeply, and took in its purity. They started to skip together down the path, skipping that is, within the limitations imposed by Joan's dress and the restrictions it made on her movement.

They continued the short distance through the small churchyard back to the Bell Inn where celebrations were about to commence both inside and out. The dress had been slightly modified at the same time the flowers had been placed on it, just for the day. It was this work that had made it look the part, but made it less easy to move comfortably around in.

Small cakes had been made to accompany other little treats that had been prepared for the occasion, indelibly marking it for this popular pair. The best they could do came out today with plenty of ale to wash it down. The wedding entourage followed closely behind and soon they were all there. The order that those attending the wedding had occupied in the church pews, the Squire and his company in the front, Joan's father and mother, her cousins and others just behind, were all now discarded. It was time for merriment. Others too joined in the celebrations to make it an afternoon to remember.

The wedding had taken place in the morning as was customary, leaving the rest of the day to celebrate.

In the corner of the Inn sat a very finely dressed man with his helper. A silent observer, slightly obscured by the dense smoke he was largely responsible for creating, was gradually revealed when the smoke lifted to the ceiling. As it did so, his face took on an increasing clarity, becoming strangely familiar to the Squire.

The Squire watched him closely for a while as he pulled out an equally finely boxed pack of playing cards and dice. This was music to the Squire who was drawn to them as if the man had been a Pied Piper.

The Squire was indeed piped towards him with the right music played by the man to attract. Soon his friend that he had also arranged to meet here would arrive. In the meantime, John would look at this pack of cards and engage the gentleman in discussion about himself and what had brought him here.

The finely dressed man introduced himself as a former ship's Captain, by the name of Charles Caesar Rosquile, gentleman. He told them a story of his mixed fortunes at the mercy of the merchant vessels that plied the high seas on the Merchantmen spice runs, his times serving in the British Navy with more besides. He told of his misfortune when the ship in which he held shares with some of the greatest and wealthiest families in the land hit one of the biggest storms he had encountered in Pacifica.

"The waves were looming high above the boat just yards away. As I stood on the high deck controlling the vessel, I felt well satisfied that she would ride the storm as she went into the waves, seeing them off, breaking over the top of the boat, the water spilling away over the top decks returning from whence it came. But then there was the crack, the crack of a mast under immense strain from the weight of water hitting the sail and wood.

I saw the mast split from the top, the split moving down until it was ready to shear off a sliver of the mast. As more heavy water spent its fury thrashing against the bow of the ship, sending plumes flying vertically upwards, smashing against the now weakened and flattened mast, it finally cracked and fell, bringing with it rigging, sail and increased strain on the remaining masts."

The small gathering around the table grew as folk hearing more and more snippets of the story drew closer to hear more. Adjacent tables started to pack, with folk taking standing room as the tale of the sea Captain's woe and that of his damned ship and crew intensified.

"As we lolloped around with little control of the ship, waiting to meet our fate, we saw a dark shape loom from the swirling depths. This massive octopus, a sea monster, hit the ship with its tentacles coming up alongside to the top deck. As it rocked the helpless boat our gun carriages alongside other deck armament moved. The next thing we knew was that the ship was capsizing."

The noise that had previously filled the tables came to an abrupt halt as the seafarer paused, conscious that he had captured his country audience.

The celebrating wedding party was in the other section of the Inn continuing to make merry, leaving the gentry to their private tables and merriment.

Hannibal's attention was drawn to the conversation that was getting going on the tables. Soon, many more ears were straining, that their owners might catch some of the story that was now gaining momentum.

It was a tale more intoxicating than the effect of the alcohol being consumed by the wedding party.

"And what ship might this be?" Asked Sir William, cautiously.

Sir William Morice had joined the company of gentry latterly at the tables. He had not coiffed the ales and cognacs in such quantity as the others, nor indeed with such a relish as his fellow countrymen.

He was nonetheless, whether sober or not, up to hearing a good yarn from an old salt. He had only a short distance to travel from his estate at Werrington about a mile or so north of Launceston.

"The Nassaw, Sir," was the immediate response, one made without any hint of hesitation. He continued to describe the ship and her payload. With tears he described further the tragic unfolding of events and tale of the three survivors, of whom he was one, clinging to the floating debris as the monster slid down with the bulk of the ship. His hands started to gesticulate in a wild, uncontrolled manner. The veins in his arms swelled with excitement as he clenched his fists, raised his arms, whilst simultaneously throwing his head backwards with great drama and effect. Again, and again he looked heavenward whilst doing so, seeking grant of divine peace from the agony of his recollections.

Returning his head, then lowering it until his chin met his chest once more, he fell silent. His audience seemed unable to respond, their words stolen from them. As they waited eagerly for the next instalment, their quiet was disturbed by an anonymous shout from the other side of the Inn or had it come from outside.

"We knows he's in there. He, who dug up our folk with no care for em, all so he could play bowls without having to hear the Church bells and see folk to and froing there in front of his big house."

The shout was met with loud jeers. There was again difficulty in identifying the callers amongst the general throng of folk gathering everywhere. Sir William and the rest of his company knew what this concerned. He called for the Innkeeper to find the fellow and apprehend him.

Sir William's company said little, for they had doubted his wisdom over the demolition of the mediaeval Church that was next to his estate house, Werrington, to make way for the bowling green he had wanted there in its place.

"They got their Church back, just a bit further up that's all. Stone by stone it came down and was rebuilt. And with a new inside that'll last them for years."

With that he took a loud, defining and authoritative slurp from his ale pot, slamming it down on the table as if this spelt the end of the matter.

Fact was that what had embittered the folk of Werrington village and the surrounding area the most was the treatment of the churchyard. This too had to be moved to make way for the Bowling Green outside of Sir William's Manor House. It was the rough treatment of the dead that had sparked indignation, distress and anger. Bodies unearthed and re-interred any old how. Bones from long past mixed and damaged. The villagers thought this was sacrilege. Some early interments were too far down and would remain under the Green whereas those more recent were unearthed from the peace of their graves they had lain in quietly until this day.

Everyone knew of the curse the villagers then placed on him and his family that was working through.

"Witchcraft, stuff and nonsense," sneered Sir William, who, positioning his rump to the rear of the chair, pushed back slowly and cautiously to shift the centre of gravity in a vertical line from the rear legs of the chair, eventually pivoting its entirety on the freshly shod heels of his finest boots. This enabled him to stabilise the two of them together and slowly rock to and fro in a beat to suit his mood.

The mood and beat were one of impatience, an intolerance of this attack on his will, wishes and good judgement of right and wrong. How dare anyone question him. He, the Lord of the Manor of the prominent seat of Werrington whose lands and holdings spanned the two adjoining

Counties of Devon and Cornwall. Moreover, he, whose grand house and lands lorded above to the north of the ancient capital of Cornwall with its magnificent, albeit ruined castle, of the ancient Kings of that land.

Placing curses on him and his family. What next? "Bring back the witch hunters and burn them at the stake," he muttered, "hanging's too good for the lot of them."

They would pay for this. They who chose to humiliate him before his peers. Snarling inside, he returned to his table and to the colourful Captain Rosquile. A more convivial way of spending his time in the former capital of Cornwall he would now have.

"Should take a private room in this establishment to rid ourselves of the rout here, play our cards and take polite society," he sneered, agitated that more might be made of this around their table now. There would be no private room though as the others in his company did not want to interrupt the flow of the tale.

"Did you catch that Hannibal," whispered Joan, her mouth close to his ear. "Did you know about the curse at Werrington?"

Whether Hannibal had heard the tale it or not, Joan was going to recount it. The party huddled around to catch her whispers. It had been told many times and had spread throughout the area, but it was still enjoyed every time it was told.

"Well, it all started when Lordy at Werrington decided to move the Church from outside his house to make way for his new bowling green.

Worst of it was the way he and his working men moved the churchyard and the village folks' remains. 'Twas no Vicar there, nor no churchmen. In they went with pick and shovel ripping and ravaging. Stones damaged that had been there a generation or more. Bones everywhere. Tom Bawcock swore that some of the bones were his Granfer. Anyway, folk were very upset and vowed to seek their revenge. Was on a Sunday night after the evensong that they met, led by Sam Thatcher. He said it would be a curse blessed by all right-thinking folk of the Church as well."

"Go on, go on, yes go on", said Hannibal. "There's new things here I haven't heard before."

"Trouble with yarns, Hannibal, it is in the end, difficult to get the truth," whispered Tom in his ear.

The villagers had gathered down by the woods late at night when the full moon was at its largest. They swore allegiance to never tell of what they were about to do apart from in and amongst their own kind.

A circle was formed by them around the large tree that was uncannily at the centre of the woods. Holding hands, with heads covered and bowed, they started to slowly turn, first a full circle clockwise. They ended where they had all started, then proceeded to make a full turn anticlockwise. As they arrived back at their original positions, they uncovered their heads, pushed them back as far as they could go, looking to the face of the moon above.

The eldest female of the village then broke the human chain, going to the tree, pushing her arms around to the back of it as far as they would reach, starting to chant as she turned clockwise. The village chain started to turn anticlockwise in time with her turns giving a low monotone hum that gently filled the night air, disguising her words to anything in the distance that might remain in earshot.

She had a natural elegance of form and voice, learning well from her previous employ as a servant of the house. Usually disguising the eloquence, she had developed, she broke from these shackles and embellished the words without detracting from their time-honoured meaning.

"We meekly come, our Lord, as obedient Christian believers to ask for the curse of childlessness and poverty to visit one William Morice. He has brought, through greed and disrespect for his ordinary folk of the estate, the surrounding area as well as to the forbearers of their names and heritage, such contempt and disrespect for the sanctity and peace of their existence after this world, that thine justice must be wrought upon him. He hath desecrated their final places of rest and thy house, our place of worship to thee, that we humbly beg your retribution and lesson to him and what he desirous most on this earth."

With this, she took a blade, cast, fashioned, cleaned and polished by the smith. It had then been blessed secretly within the remains of the Church, before those too fell and were moved.

With deftness the blade struck and drew blood from her arm. One by one the village chain broke and reformed, broke and reformed, as the folk came one by one to be cut by her allowing the blood to spill together at the root of the tree in the same spot. With each drop that fell she repeated in a low voice, "This, the being of our people, joins together one for all and all for one in their plea to you our Lord and highest heavenly authority, master of all to serve justice on this, the earthly Lord of our Manor."

With that the chain moved again clockwise five times and then anticlockwise five times all heads facing towards the heavens with a final bow and fall to the ground. They stayed there to the count of twelve then left each other's hands and filed behind the village female elder who led them back towards their homes.

The wedding party had almost with exception gathered around to hear the tale. Straining their ears to catch every syllable of the whispered tones, the sudden silence had attracted the attention of the table in the other room, which too, had spent the odd moment straining, without success, to hear what had caused the silence of a wedding party.

This curiosity though had failed to displace that held by the Captain, and the Werrington Knight had thought little more of it all.

"So, Captain, prey continue. How did you and your company that clung to the wreckage survive to tell this tale? Why you?"

"By the Grace of God and Saint Nicholas we were thrown clear of the vessel into the raging seas. The section of broken and detached mast and bulkhead, alongside a row boat that too had broken away with entrails of the rigging by our side saved us. We grabbed the rigging and held on with all our might. As we were taken away from the ship and it went down to the depths with the monster wrapped around it, we continued through the swells and surf until the storm calmed. Our hands were almost to the bone as we had wrapped the ropes around them to secure us to the wood. This prevented us from separating and kept us afloat. The jerking movements, so violent, tore into our flesh. There were periods when we were completely submerged by the raging seas and thought the end was upon us.

As the seas calmed, it became easier, and when strength returned, we righted the row boat and got into her. The sweeps were lashed to her inside firmly around her ribs and seats. As we freed them, we knew that we might live to tell the tale yet."

"More ale and cognacs for our party, Innkeeper. Prepare this Captain fayre for his tale and a room for the night." The commanding cry came from Sir William, whose suspicions about the authenticity of their Captain, had all but been fully allayed.

Meantime, the wedding party had recovered from the recounting of the Werrington curse, only to once again tune into the Captain's tale. The Inn, so normally raucous and ribald, had fallen eerily silent once more.

"It's as if we'd have had a storyteller in our pay for the wedding, Joan," Hannibal said in a low voice still. "This will be a day and night for us to remember until our graves."

The Captain spoke not another word until his refreshment arrived, whereupon he continued, as if a fresh gust of wind had filled his sails.

"We untangled the spliced, broken mast and her rigging from the boat to free her, prepared the rowlocks and sweeps then looked around. It was as if nothing had happened; no ship, no debris, no bodies. What's more, no monster gentlemen, no monster. No monster at all, anywhere. He had taken them all down with him. Far down but we were for now saved. We looked far into the distance all around us but saw nothing. No ships, no land. I knew where we had been at the time we were taken but as for now, how far we had moved and in what direction, I knew not. We had no victuals and no fresh water. We knew it could not last long like this for us. We resigned ourselves to a premature fate in the hands of the Almighty. We decided to conserve our strength for a while. We would float with the currents and let God decide what our fate was to be. Feeling a bit less weak as time passed, we set to, making a sail and mast with the rigging that we had untied, a section of the main mast and the clothes on our backs. Poor that it was, it aided our speed and conserved our strength. It was the second night, as thirst was biting hard, that we felt heavy rain on us. So hard it was it drenched our clothes, our sail, filling our boots and the boat to its bottom boards. A tribute to the boat-builder and the caulker who stopped in the planks, for she hardly leaked a drop. We scratched a mark for each day that passed us. It was on the 13th day that we thought we saw a raised mound from the horizon in the distance and took to the oars. Night fell, and it was lost. In the morrow we saw it once more and continued again, hauling hard. Our fayre was the stinking flesh of a large dead fish that was floating close to us. All of us had had the cramps in the stomach after this meal but we all remained alive. It was that next day that we saw the land rise from the horizon and take shape. Excitement for our salvation was tempered by the sudden realisation that we knew not where this land might be, whether inhabited or not, friendly or not. We had little choice but to head there. It was surrounded by a reef with seas tumbling towards it, breaking over it to leave a lagoon of bright water. There must be a passage through we hoped. There was no sign of an entrance where we were and no sign of human form there. No smoke, no noise, just palms swaying. We decided to row around the Island. It did not take long for it was small and we could see a few other small ones not far off. Our draft was not great, and we decided that we would ride onto the reef with the next large wave and hope we could clear it and enter deeper water without harming the boat. Our prayers were answered and over we went, into the turquoise waters that lay in behind. The water there was warm to touch as we pulled our boat up on the white sands. There were no marks in the sand other than what looked to be crab claw marks and small holes into which fish had burrowed down during the receding tides. The water of the lagoon contained fish of all colours and sizes. As we walked up the beach, we trod through the husks of palm nuts, their decayed leaves and fallen trunks. Immediately behind the beach was dense palm. We saw a shallow trench that had been formed running down to the seas. The trench carried much welcomed fresh water.

We paused here to drink from the trench and crack open palm nuts for their liquid and flesh. We used the larger stones that strewed the beach here and there to break the tough coconut husks.

Some hours passed as we started to take in our new surroundings, expecting that this might now be our home until our final hours."

Pausing the tale, he gulped in air through his cracked lips, offering up a resulting loud whistle as it exhaled. The next breath was taken at the same time as the final sup of his ale. As the tankard lifted to roll down the last of the golden waters into his awaiting throat, he shuffled on his seat. This was to indicate that he was preparing to leave their company.

The impression he gave was that it was time for him to retire for the night, taking with him the nightmares of those days and what followed.

Almost as if it were a signal for his next tankard of ale, yet another duly arrived, but the Captain was in a lesser mood to continue than he had been.

"Enough of this story for now Gentlemen. What of a game of cards or dice or both?"

The table's company had been glancing occasionally from the fixation they had on the Captain's face as his story unfolded, towards the deck of cards he had been shuffling and fiddling with. Sir William's concentration on the story had momentarily lapsed, and, as he seemed to have adopted the leadership of the table for a while, he suggested to his company that the story did indeed pause to allow the Captain time to recover over a game of cards.

"Those cards have an ancient look Captain. Are they up to a game with a table like this?", he said as he looked around at his fellows.

"These cards have seen many years, it is true," came the response.

"They too were seasoned and preserved by the oceans. They were the only possession I had left when I was on the Eddystone light the night before it gave up to the almighty storm that ripped it from the reef. Another night there and I would have perished with the others and the owner of the light, in whose employ I was at that time."

"You were on the Eddystone light off Plymouth, built and owned by Winstanley?"

"Yes. I was in his employ on one of his ships as a young lad. I was there the night before the disaster that took it. I was one of his men who rowed him to the light where he planned to brave the coming storm. The seas were starting to swell heavily. We were expecting high waves. It was a job to tie up to the base of the light and get up to it, but we did and spent a short while there. As we left, Winstanley's keeper threw us some of his playing cards that stayed with me in my pocket and survived the shipwreck. They are well worn gentlemen but remain good to use."

So, what of it? Who will take on the old sea dog to help him earn a few guineas to keep him off the streets for a few more nights after this and to be able to stay in fine company here like that of your good selves until the morning calls?"

The gentlemen of the area left the room, conferred quietly for a while, returned to their spokesman's proclamation that they were all of one accord that they would all play and each would play for the Captain's playing cards, against a night for the Captain with full fayre.

The Captain looked them in the eye slowly and in turn as if he were inspecting the company of a ship or weighing up his enemy. He nodded to each in turn as he finished his scrutiny, until, that is, he came to the young Squire.

"But you Sir, I have seen your fine steed. Would you wager him not only against my cards but this ...."

As his voice tailed off with a long hiss for the "s" at the end of, "this" so he drew deep into his inside breast pocket, pulling from it a pocket watch, complete with a pattern engraved, which, on closer initial examination revealed the italicised words, "Deus Vault."

He threw it into the air high above the gentlemen's table, flicking it with his thumb as it was about to leave the palm of his hand, thereby setting it into a straight vertical climb heavenward, its gold hue catching the candlelight as it went. It sparkled in different spots around its circumference, only to fall earthward again when gravity proved too much for it to bear. They saw his chopped hand stay put from where it created the spin and go from clenched to open to clench and back, to open as it caught it, deftly and firmly.

"This watch means everything to me, he hissed as the words were again pushed wryly through his teeth. It was a gift following my saving of my master's ship against all odds in the northern seas."

He continued, "I will tell you the full story of this watch if you win it and take it from me, for the story must go with the owner of the watch, who will understand the meaning of the words. He must then also take them with him for as long as he owns the watch. Suffice it to say, for this moment though, gentlemen, that this watch is amongst the finest ever to come from the workshop of John Jefferys of London with the pattern work engraved by a Master Engraver of the First Degree."

The gentlemen stood aside to quietly confer amongst themselves. It was decided that the others would underwrite Squire John's horse in the event that the game should be lost. An agreement would be made with the Captain that they could insist in the event of a loss that Sir William would provide a steed of equivalent standard in place of Squire John's should he so choose. Such was the understanding between them all of what Black Bird meant to Squire John.

The challenge was accepted, and they sat to play for the timepiece or trusted steed. As the cards were being dealt, interest in the unfolding events was mounting from the remains of the wedding party, who had been continually straining their ears to gather more of the goings on.

Hannibal moved around to a point where he could see more of the events that were providing the evening's entertainment for the wedding party, or at least those who wanted to be entertained in this way rather than through the barrels that were rapidly emptying.

Equipped with but little knowledge of card games, he was though, fascinated with the proceedings.

Faro was the game of choice that evening, with the Captain taking the part of the banker. The Innkeeper produced a dealing box, designed to remove the possibility of fixing the deal by the banker. Hannibal watched the game proceed and with his long sight picked out that the cards were of the same type as the ones he and Luke had found two of that day of the robbery by the Highwaymen. He watched as the soda card was laid, then the banker's card. As more cards were laid down the dealing box reduced its number of cards.

Hannibal was looking for their card types feeling sure he would recognise the pictures, which were distinctive, but the equivalent cards he had seen were different in appearance. It suddenly dawned on him that this pack of cards might well have been missing their two and had been made up afterwards to complete the pack. They had been told when they were given the cards that they were unusual and no longer being printed and sold.

Could it be that the Captain's cards were originally those stolen by the Highwaymen that day, the day of the robbery. It was a while ago now. Even if they were, they had probably been made up with replacements for the missing two and then sold on as full packs. If they had been, how had this Captain come by them? He had said earlier he had been thrown them way back in 1703, off the Eddystone reef. Maybe he was the owner before they came into the possession of Sir William of Bradstone. If so, how would the Captain have got them back once more?

No this was fanciful thinking, maybe wishful thinking, as there might be a further reward if correct information about the cards could be passed back to Bradstone. If these suspicions were unfounded it could be the undoing of him and Luke though. How could it be proved with no doubt that the Captain was telling the truth or not? It was, though, odd.

He had no place to disturb the card game without another good cause. How would he interrupt the Squire and let him know his suspicions? And would he, in such ribald spirits, choose to challenge the Captain?

No, he must take a chance, say nothing and steal away on Black Bird. He would ride to Bradstone and hope the Bradstone Sir William would remember him. He would then leave it to Sir William to decide what next to do, if anything at all.

Black Bird had been brought down for the Squire to go hunting over the next few days. If he returned him safely without any murmur of his actions all would be righted. And if he did not, at least Black Bird would be safe from the hands of this Captain. Hannibal prayed that Sir William would be there at Bradstone or the Lady Elizabeth. Stealing into the stables, he quietly prepared Black Bird, unhindered, telling Joan he felt a little unwell but would not be long after he had washed away some of the effects of the good liquor that had flowed so well that day. He had not yet told Luke of his suspicions. This was safer with him alone for now. It was a short ride under the light of the stars, but he knew the way as did Black Bird, who was content to go with Hannibal. He remembered well and although sworn to his master, the Squire, seemed to understand the need to take Hannibal with him safely to where he needed to go. Through the byways and tracks he went, travelling the most direct route to Bradstone, crossing the Greystone Bridge and, with good fortune travelling with him, he saw no one who made any challenge to their passage.

Stopped at the Gatehouse, he was told that they were staying there but only Lady Elizabeth was at the house. Sir William was not far away. They kept Hannibal at the entrance while they went to alert the Lady Elizabeth and enquire should she want to see him at this hour, or any hour for that matter. Elizabeth summoned Hannibal to the house. Black Bird was taken by the grooms and prepared for the next journey. The story, accompanied by Hannibal's suspicions, were relayed to Elizabeth who called for help to don her riding clothes and off she went with Hannibal on Black Bird to see her husband at Kelly and take his counsel.

Sir William retained his fury at the embarrassment of the highway incident and held onto the straw that the cards might just identify his captor on the turnpike road.

"There is nothing to lose. We must head there straight away and act as if we know nothing. We must join the table. Hannibal has done what he pledged, and no harm must attach to him in this affair. Hannibal go ahead of us now with all speed. We will neither acknowledge you nor Luke when we arrive but may need to call upon you over the cards."

With that, Hannibal went with a speed on Black Bird that he didn't think he could ride at. When he arrived back, the wedding entourage and the table remained in full swing, with the Squire and his party coming off worse than the Captain who seemed to be very confident he was to win.

Hannibal now took the opportunity to catch the ear of Luke who sobered on hearing what he had to say.

"Sshh Luke. From now we must keep our own counsel and see what transpires tonight. I must to my bride who has patience enough."

The wedding party had thought nothing of Hannibal's absence. Attributed to clearing his head after a full day they were though pleased to have him back, unaware that he was elsewhere in his mind, albeit in the very same Inn. He could not get the night's proceedings, as yet without any conclusion, off his mind.

A wind whistled through the Inn as the door to the other side entrance was thrown ajar. In came Sir William. He had not managed to shake off Elizabeth, who, fearing there might be a scuffle, had not let him come alone. Irritated that he was, he gave up trying to order her not to go with him to these places, unsuitable that they were, he believed, for gentle-women.

After becoming more comfortable with his surroundings, Sir William stood overlooking the gaming table, and at the end of a round of one game, asked politely if he might join the party. Asking what he would put up as a stake he offered to double the amount of paid time at the Tavern for the Captain that the others had agreed to finance. When pushed he agreed to put his best stallion up.

The Captain's offer remained at the pack of cards and the pocket watch, but he threw in the last of the possessions he had that would not have removed the clothes from his back. This was an anker of the finest cognac to leave France. It was one he claimed that had accompanied him unopened since he acquired it from the cellars of a Duke's fine house following a game of cards. He had been sworn to secrecy about this game and therefore they would have to excuse him if he did not reveal the Duke's identity but a glass from the anker would swear testament to the authenticity of the tale and the spirit.

No anker of spirit of this quality could possibly have come from any other household than that of one of the finest gentlemen, or indeed, nobles of the land, claimed the Captain.

Sir William joined the table keeping his eyes peeled and planning to spot the two misfit cards. He did not have to wait long. One was dealt to him. He stared at it, staring again, straining his memory and holding below the table the card that Hannibal had returned to make the comparison.

This was still not enough to accuse the Captain, but the situation did not to him strike an accord of correctness. Elizabeth, who would not leave, had been staring consistently at the Captain from the sides of her eyes and straining her ears to pick up every syllable he used.

There was something strangely familiar about this man. Suddenly, some time in, she blurted out, "Bampfylde Moore-Carew. It's Bampfylde.

Bampfylde you have been to my home when I was, but a girl and you were at Peter Blundell's Tiverton School hunting whenever you were able. We saw you when visiting the Moores in the area of Cullompton. Your father was Rector of Bickleigh close by. It was before you escaped from Tiverton and went to live with the beggars.

"Bampfylde Moore-Carew ! ?"

The company almost in unison rolled back on their chairs, dumfounded, exclaiming with one voice the name that was gathering fame throughout England and the Continent, the name of the infamous master of disguise and proclaimed King of the beggars. Was this none other than Bampfylde Moore-Carew?

"Nonsense!" exclaimed the Captain.

"Anyway, who exactly is Bampfylde Moore-Carew?"

The Captain appeared unshaken and only mildly ruffled by this outburst. Elizabeth knew much about Bampfylde. Not only did she remember him from her youth, but it was only months before into the previous year of 1745 that he, the famous gentleman and rogue, had made publication of the stories of his colourful life. She knew of the publication, which, it was well known, was sweeping the country with its success. The nation had a pre-occupation with stories of rogues in the gentlefolk, of which there were few that came to light.

Bampfylde Moore-Carew though. Well...... he was in a class of his own. Racing through Elizabeth's mind were all the stories she knew of and had heard over the years about Bampfylde.

He was known to her family and his godparents too from whom his name had derived. Major Moore and Colonel Hugh Bampfylde both contributed to his name and he was too given his birth-right name, the ancient Devon family surname of Carew.

She remembered going to the rectory of Bampfylde's father, the Reverend Theodore Carew. She had also been to the homes of Colonel Hugh Bampfylde at Poltimore House as well as his later home in Somerset.

She had liked Bampfylde as a child and saw his rogue-ish activities as relatively harmless. She suddenly started to regret her outburst that might unveil him and see a chain of events that could lead him to transportation again, or worst still, sent to the stinking rat-infested gaols.

He was much older now. Besides she had heard that he had started to mend his ways with successful publications, an income to support his long-suffering wife and child with a stable home, replacing his roving tendencies.

This sympathy was tempered for a split second by the possible connection between him and the robbery. Her heart gave way in a flash of a moment and, to divert interest in this Captain, she challenged him, not choosing to raise the questionable origin of the two cards that might, by their incongruity with the rest of the pack, indicate a prima facie guilt.

"I remember as a child that Bampfylde had a long red stain and scar on the skin of his right forearm. It used to frighten me, especially the story of how he got it, fighting a long-jawed creature in the rivers of the Amazonia. If you are not Bampfylde then reveal your right arm Captain," said Elizabeth with a superciliousness that suggested she was so certain of his true identity that she would risk the escape of a man who had done her and her husband harm.

The Captain' s arms were well covered up and Elizabeth had taken note of this. It was unlikely that he would have such distinguishing marks by chance. This was a split-second decision to help him.

The Captain slowly rose from his seat, standing head high and jaw pointing outward and rigid. With great presence and theatre, he took a knife from the table. He tore at his garment that covered his right arm, holding it high, that the company throughout the Inn could not fail to see it and take in the drama of the occasion.

He turned slowly to ensure the audience would be able to circumnavigate his lower arm. He said nothing, leaving his silence to answer the question. There was no mark there. Elizabeth, overcome with apology, feigned a swoon and was helped to take a seat.

My unreserved apologies to you Captain. The Captain bowed in her direction saying it was of no consequence, but he would, after the game, like to hear more of Mr. Bampfylde Moore - Carew. The Captain lowered himself, ordering for a seamstress to be summonsed to make good his clothing. He then went to again be seated at the table when Sir William challenged him over the cards.

"Whether you are Bampfylde or not Captain, I would like to know more about these cards," retorted Sir William, by his tone almost brushing aside the relevance of his wife's outburst.

Bampfylde Moore Carew or Captain Charles Caesar Rosquile? It mattered not a jot to his need to restore his dignity and pride, both of which had suffered damage by the robbery affair on the turnpike road that while ago. His sense of justice though would not allow him to see the wrong man taken for it.

So, these cards, he thought. Let's have a look at them and ask again how he came by them. Were these the only cards in the Captain's pack that had been replaced with others that were at variance from the originals?

He would not yet perhaps reveal his hand over the two cards. No, better to just ask to see them, go through them and then make the challenge. He would though politely ask to see them now the game had been interrupted, especially as they were of fascination. The Captain responded to allow the game to continue to its conclusions before re-assembling the entire pack and handing it to him to peruse.

"There will be nothing there for you to find untoward, whatever your interest in these cards", the Captain said, displaying a cold air of authority in the matter. "Nothing is rigged. We are all on an equal footing, to rely on that combination of luck of hand with skill and resolve to win."

With that Sir William agreed and the game resumed.

Hannibal and Luke had been waiting in the hinterland of the Inn with breath bated. They had both expected to be called upon to produce their cards with a reason to the assembled Gentlemen having to be provided. They had been let off this for now and they too resumed to their own celebrations, temporarily forgetting the importance of the theatre that, they too, were in the midst of playing out.

Sir William did not want Hannibal and his wife leaving the Inn quite yet. Hannibal might still be needed to provide his evidence. This was though, his marriage day. The finest of Cognacs and fare were ordered for him and the wedding party, far above what they could afford to pay, despite the ankers that had been kept for this day as goodwill from the other free traders. Ankers not on view. Their contents were discretely emptied into the jugs of the wedding merrymakers.

The party then continued long after it had been expected they would leave and retire. An underlying sobriety remained with Hannibal and Luke. They knew as the final game of cards ended that their assistance might be called upon by Sir William.

Neither could now believe that the Captain could be the Highwayman. If he were, would he not have recognised them, and taken his leave? Maybe he would be so confident in his disguise that day to not fear them. After all, might they recognise only his voice? That would surely be insufficient evidence of guilt in this matter? Sir William had not recognised it.

No, the more they thought on it, the more they concluded this was not the man. It would be a strange thing to revisit the very area where he could be recognised and revealed of his crimes. Alas though, there was the matter of the two playing cards, but they would have to see whether there was a case to answer, and if so, how the Captain answered it.

As for Bampfylde Moore-Carew? Well, this seemed to reek of the same level of truth as maybe some of the Captain's stories. Best left alone and enjoy the occasion. Maybe he would have to tell his wife later as the first secret they would share?

Those fit enough in the wedding party to dance through the Inn and onto the street that led up to the town now took it on themselves to do this with a vigour.

Hannibal and Joan led the way. Off they went, hand to back and twirling around as they built up their speed. Those too old or infirm to dance the cold streets of a Launceston January were fortified with the sustenance they had received and grabbed more to take with them.

This helped them to continue their fight against the both the night air that was close upon them and the pain of their ailments that would have otherwise restricted their ability, let alone desire, to take to the streets in merriment and dance.

Snaking up, down and around the narrow streets, through the clearing of the centre they went, in and out of the old castle walled area, towards the south gate. The gate was neither attended properly nor locked these days. Through they went and back again until the first ones through were behind the last to go through. A motley gang were, they with all shapes and sizes and manner of attire, but with a common purpose of wishing the couple God's speed on their journey whilst also making the most of the festivity and the peculiar generosity of their surprise benefactor at the tables.

As the party came through the town and past the White Hart Inn to head downwards around the side of the Church of St Mary back to the Bell, those towards the head of the tail were astonished and sobered to see a lone rider jump onto a large black stallion with a long handkerchief as a rein. The man looking after the horse lay on the ground, bottle by his side. Shortly afterwards, following in force and in hot pursuit, were the members of the gaming table, accompanied by some others that had been watching close by.

What Hannibal did not know was what had transpired in the Inn since the party had danced away from it.

The game had finished. The Captain, as winner, prepared to take the prize of his choice. That prize was Black Bird, although the horse would be no-where to be seen. He had been asked to produce the cards for the players in order that they could examine them that they might ensure there had been no prejudice to fair play by virtue of any features of the cards known only to the Captain. He, with great conviviality, was happy to pass over the cards, doing so as he was about to leave and relieve himself outside. Other than Sir William there was no discontent at this, although Squire John was showing signs of agitation and considerable disquiet over the forfeit of his beloved Black Bird.

As soon as the Captain went through the door he took out and unfurled the length of material that had been folded in such a way as to project its upper section from the top pocket of his coat. The top pocket had been made especially deep to take the remainder of its length inside without several folds and making an unseemly bulge. This was a thin material. This was a material that when it showed itself above the pocket feigned to be nothing more than a handkerchief.

He flicked it out as if he were cracking a whip to reveal its full length. This was a material like the finest of silks. Strong, light, flexible, a material from which folds and creases fell away instantly to reveal a length of fabric with a design and purpose more than a mere handkerchief. This length of material, defined by its shape and texture, was to those who could recognise it better than the mere handkerchief it purported to be, was none other than the time-honoured tool of the horse thief. This was a material strong enough, long enough to provide an effective substitute for halter and rein on the largest of horses. One that would tie easily, unknot easily, whilst neither hurting nor hindering a horse when applied. He would get away tonight. There would not be enough time for any of the others to prepare and mount another horse, go after him and catch him up let alone hope to dismount him. And with that the Captain took leave of his company forgoing the hospitality that had been arranged for him at the Inn that night. His finely-honed intuition told him it was time to leave. Sir William's stallion was there stabled and released from the yoke and burden of his livery. No time to spare, the Captain mounted the stallion bareback and fixing his makeshift halter and rein was away into the night.

As their wait for the return of the Captain to the table continued, indeed continued to the point where it seemed the Captain was neither returning to his company nor retiring to his bed, his fellow card players went to look for him.

Nowhere to be found, it dawned on Sir William that he may now yet again be the subject of a fool's errand. For, should it transpire that this was the same person as their Highwayman, he would have been taken for a fool twice. Twice a fool at the hands of this man who proffered such disguise of attire and manner to deceive a man of his standing. He, a member of the distinguished and established landed classes. He, a knight of the realm, distinguished in battle and civic duty. He, being made a fool of amongst his peers and amongst the common rout in equal measure.

The Captain had made a fool too of the other players around the table. Squire John, although grateful for the safety of Black Bird, was growling with the others, threatening hell and damnation to the Captain.

The assembled gentlemen pieced together the story and decided they would hunt this fellow down. Was their man the infamous Bampfylde Moore-Carew? Or was he not? If he were not, then who really was he?

They had no evidence other than the suspicions of Elizabeth.

"Landlord, Landlord," yelled Sir William. "Saddle up your best beast here for me to get back to Bradstone. John let's get you re-united with Black Bird and set off to the home of this Bampfylde at first light. There's no point now. Where is the fellow? Curse and damn him!"

Elizabeth, almost afraid to speak, and with mixed feelings shared between fear of her husband's wrath and fear for the safety of her likeable, but rogue of an old acquaintance, heard her husband bellow. "Elizabeth, Elizabeth. Where does this fellow Bampfylde reside?"

"I don't know now. I have not seen him since I was a child. It may not have been him but just looked like him."

"Well Elizabeth, I would want to either count him in or out as our suspect. So, we want to see him, if we can find him, to ask of his whereabouts this day and hear him out for ourselves. He won't be fooling me again. If the Captain is indeed this Bampfylde Moore-Carew, he had better watch out for I'll be giving him a good whipping before he faces the court."

"Hannibal, Luke, I know this is your celebration, but I will need you to come too and give witness to this fellow from the day you saw him on the turnpike road to today, cards as well, if called to do so. Tell your bride it'll be worth your while. We'll be setting off at first light from Bradstone. Landlord, release Hannibal and Luke to me tomorrow. You too will be finely recompensed for your troubles. The young Squire nodded hoping he would not be expected to chip in to the mounting costs associated with the salving of Sir William's pride. If he had to, he would, but what a waste of good ale money. He hadn't in the end lost anything, and if nothing else, the Captain had provided his entertainment. He would tell the story for years to come. If it were the King of the Gypsies that they had encountered, in full disguise, with a quality and quantity of yarns to match, then what an eventful day and night it had been. Was it not worth a bit of pride in exchange? Yes, worth a bit of pride. With that the young

Squire effused sympathy, shared anger and indignation in equal measure with an accompanying intolerance but smirked to himself. "What a game of cards this had been." In the end the gentlemen decided to stay at the Inn and send their men back to get extra horses for tomorrow.

Sir William had quizzed Elizabeth further and at least now knew that Bampfylde was originally from the Rectory at Bickleigh. She had blurted this out earlier, but it had at that time been lost on their company. The hunting party would ride to Bickleigh. This was a long shot at finding out the truth, but it was all they had.

Bickleigh was a good thirty to forty miles away. Squire John knew the route. He had not travelled widely but knew Devon and much of Cornwall. They all retired.

Hannibal and Joan spent some time going over the day's happenings. What a wedding day for simple folk .... maybe not so simple. Now Hannibal and Luke would be travelling with the hunting party tomorrow and the evidence they might give could be crucial to Sir William proving his case.

"But this is our wedding night," exclaimed and protested Joan. She had expected that her now husband might be worse the wear for her today, but she would have him better the next day. As relative calm descended on them and the stories were told so they cared less and less for them.

Their thoughts turned to the nuptials they had yearned for. It was a cold night now, this night in mid-winter, but they were fuelled high with the alcohol, excitement of the day and finally, as the deep night fell, of each other's presence. Their moment had come. Often those rare times alone had proved a temptation, but Hannibal had refrained from exerting his will. In turn Joan had refrained from succumbing to the temptation she felt when he pressed himself against her in those moments of snatched embrace.

It had come close for them many times, but this was now their time. A first for them both, they forgot the excitements of the day and the early departure that was expected of Hannibal at first light. First light was not long off. There would be little if any sleep tonight.

Hannibal looked down at his new bride who by now had started to slowly remove the garments she had adorned for the day. Together they took in the cold night air deeply and, as it was expelled, made clouds of vapour that were caught occasionally and given shape by the streaks of moonlight that would appear through the window.

As their bodies moved and writhed, the cold air was taken in and expelled with increasing frequency, so the clouds of vapour caught by the moonlight danced its patterns tantalisingly before them. They would then leave as quickly as they had come. They left no lasting presence in any way apart from that engraved deeply into their memories.

The sharp pain Joan felt as she took Hannibal for that first time gave way to a desire for more. Yes more. He was not to sleep that night. No, not if she, Joan Marks, had anything to do with it. The Inn was quiet now but for them. They continued in the surety, that so intoxicated were the guests at the Inn, with the others sleeping in the adjoining stables and barns, that they were safe from the embarrassment of the expressions of pleasure that they could no longer contain nor prevent.

"Come to me again, and again", writhed Joan her heavily accented words, peculiar to those inhabitants of Launceston and its adjacent, surrounding countryside, softly and dreamingly drooling over Hannibal. Her few words, combined with her slowly and sensuously moving limbs, preyed on his every sense and sucked him in again and again until finally, despite their joining, they fell to slumber as one.

* * *

"Come on Hannibal", came the shout, as promised, and just before the first light descended on the town. It was Luke. "You'll be back in no time and with your pockets full for your new bride if you're lucky." The Squire was already up. Black Bird had been brought for him and he was ready for the hunt. Sir William too arrived complete with some re-enforcements.

Chapter 5

An Audience with Bampfylde

They all rode hard with the Squire leading the way. Sir William and the others were in hot pursuit. Keeping up was a difficult task. The Squire was not only an experienced rider, but he and Black Bird possessed a real meeting of the minds between them. Without prompt, the horse would compensate where necessary to make the ride for his master the more comfortable, sleek and fast. They were together, a well-bonded machine, comprising speed and elegance.

Stopping only when necessary to allow the horses to drink and rest a while, they approached Bickleigh from a vantage point to its west. It was the Squire who announced it, and they all came to a halt looking through the valley towards their destination. Their first call would be the Rectory to enquire of Bampfylde. Enquiries they had made along the way had suggested he was back at Bickleigh, the place of his birth and upbringing. As they galloped towards the settlement, the rush of adrenalin shot through each one of them. They had not planned what they were to say, but doubtless Sir William would take the lead, as he had throughout the events of the last twenty-four hours.

He had been fuelled and re-fuelled by his desire to track down his principal assailant on the turnpike road. The time was now at last approaching when he, that had so rudely deceived him, and taken his prized steed for his own, might be in sight to face his wrath and justice.

His whip had been freshly tanned and greased. Well rounded was the leather so it could cut through the air with an ease and velocity that when accompanied by the strength of Sir William's right arm would be capable of slicing right through this rogue's skin if he laid hands on him.

The inconsolable fury that had enveloped him since the encounter on the turnpike road had reached a crescendo, expressing itself in his hard riding throughout this journey. The feeling had been relentless. He and his steed would come up so close on occasions to the rear of Black Bird, that they had forced both horse and rider to go faster and faster. All roads now led to the highwayman and the Captain being one and the same person.

"Guilty, save he proves himself otherwise," muttered Sir William, unheard by the others, for the force of the wind took their clarity of hearing from them. If he were in fact guilty of these acts though, why choose the Launceston area to ply his trade, which was such a ride from his home?

If it were, he, Bampfylde, where was he when he was in that area? He would need harbour and succour. He would need accomplices. Who might they be? What was the gain for them? He wanted this to be their man. He had though, in those more rational moments, to recognise that it was the cards and the cards alone that now were the only common factor that tied the two men together.

They rode in and called at the Rectory. It was Monday morning and the Vicar was there. No Bampfylde. Bampfylde had though returned to his former home. He now sought out a living by writing about his past exploits and adventures. The first book had been published the previous year. By all accounts it was an almost instant success, taking away from him the urge to earn his living by roguery. This was indeed a tale of rags to riches for Bampfylde and his family. The respectability of his birth combined well with his long, varied and successful career in cheating his fellow mankind. A career that with adventure had taken him from poor man to rich man in a perpetual cycle formed an explosive cocktail for a readership hungry to know more of the life of Bampfylde Moore-Carew.

All was forgiven, just about in any event, by polite society ... although not by Sir William, not yet. The Vicar directed the party to Bampfylde's home and they walked the horses down to the house. Sir William banged assertively on the door, which was promptly attended by Bampfylde's wife. She told the party that he was with his daughter but was expected shortly. With that they asked if they could remain at the house awaiting his return, which they duly did. One hour passed and then another. Sir William had greater courtesy than to rigorously question the lady of the house on her husband's whereabouts in the previous twenty-four hours.

Eventually, accompanied by his usual confidence, Bampfylde walked towards them, a limp becoming more obvious to all as he closed in on them.

He did though, approach them bolt upright, his clothes immaculately presented on his robust form, long curled hair neatly falling to his shoulders, his pallor ruddy and healthy. Not a button out of place, he was unquestionably adorned with the finest of cloth that could be imported from the best of French mills. The colour of their vibrant dyes strongly displayed themselves to those who had the pleasure of meeting him.

Visitors would experience too, the casual glints from the golden hues of the rings adorning his hands. All these were for sure the marks and epitome of the city gentleman more than the countryman. A prominent figure he portrayed. One that might be expected to take office holdings suited to his rank and wealth in the nearby City of Exeter. Perhaps that of a Justice or a Collector of the Excise would be fitting. But no, this was Mr. Bampfylde Moore-Carew. Acknowledged gentle-rogue not gentleman. Confidence trickster extraordinaire was he, not a paragon of virtuous morality. Master of disguise acknowledged thief and cheat against his own class was he, rather than an upstanding member of the Gentry, Squirearchy no less, to which he was born and destined. He, Bampfylde Moore-Carew, walked, nonetheless, and with a complete oblivion to these inconsistencies, head high towards them, not only indicating that he was their social equal by birth, but he was, moreover, superior to them, as the crowned King of a people. Crowned King of the Gypsies by those travellers, the outlaws of Georgian society, who voted him into the role as a young man. He spared some thoughts for how he had become King as he approached his visitors.

The previous King had addressed his people at the ballot for a new King. He urged them not to vote for any of his children who put themselves forward just because they were his children. The criteria were to be based solely on the list of daring exploits that those putting themselves forward in the ballot could demonstrate. Exploits that demonstrated their miscreant behaviours. There was simply little competition that faced Bampfylde. His encounters and exploits of roguish behaviours across the land were both extreme and fully verifiable when compared to other candidates. The candidates' portfolios were listed on the wall of the establishment they had taken over for their gathering. The ballot comprised two boxes below to capture white balls for votes and black for the other boxes, indicating no vote.

Bampfylde won by an overwhelming number of votes and was duly crowned, King of the Gypsies. Amongst his most daring of exploits, the one that raised the most mirth, although it was not in itself the most daring of exploits on his list, was that involving trickery on one Madam Musgrove.

Madam Musgrove sought the help of an expert to discover the whereabouts of hidden treasure she was convinced was buried somewhere on her land. Bampfylde, holder of dark and mystic arts that could be summoned by him, and him alone, to identify the location of the treasure, was duly appointed, for twenty guineas, upon payment of which, he would be able to give her the location. With great ceremony and drama this he did. Madam Musgrove then arranged for the ground to be dug down the necessary twenty feet at a location four feet from the large laurel to the west of it. The dig was to be commenced on an appointed day and hour, this being after the handing over of the guineas. The overturned earth revealed only more earth and rock. The mysterious soothsayer was nowhere to be found. Now, not a young man, one in his fifty second year, he remained still strong and sturdy both of body and spirit. He still held himself well, well that is, other than the limp and slight twist in the lower part his leg. He was now getting used to sporadic callers. The book detailing his life published the previous year had brought personal fame as well as money. He was indeed a sought-after personality.

He did not always care for the visitors, being conscious he had become a spectacle of interest. Many of the upper, educated and literary classes had started to find his door. For Bampfylde it had been a matter of some concern that his fame and exploits might simply take their place in history, with no further tales to tell. But, what now, he asked of himself? What daring could he do that would not jeopardise this recent improvement in his current status in society, yet would give more to tell later, even if left as a legacy for his wife or his daughter to write about.

Standing now about six feet from them, he bid them good day, momentarily removing his hat, only to replace it again shortly afterwards.

"We are here, Sir, to enquire of your whereabouts during the last few days", asked Sir William, speaking with an authority that attempted to undermine the presumed Kingly status of the man he was addressing.

Unperturbed, Bampfylde responded that he had been mainly at home, with an excursion to the south coast to partake some sea air and to rest his damaged leg. Bampfylde queried the reasons for their questions and then bid them to take refreshment.

"How did you damage your leg?" enquired Sir William. Bampfylde explained it was in a fall a few years ago, adding that this had since robbed him of his old pleasures of hunting and horsemanship.

As refreshment was brought in and laid out before the company, it was Hannibal who felt that this man was surprisingly familiar but not the Captain, no not the Highwayman either. He couldn't put a place to it. It may have been fleeting and perhaps something to do with the running of free trade. Did this feeling of familiarity stem from the Inn at Zeal? Either way he was not going to raise anything that would connect him with this darker side of his living. Hannibal and Luke sat in the background but were too offered refreshment and took a small glass of cognac. As refreshment was offered and poured, he looked closely around him. He and Luke were then asked to see to the horses and as they left the house Hannibal shared his thoughts with Luke.

"That taste had a slight tang of the sea, Luke. I have tasted this before with spoiled goods that have been sunk and passed to us carters rather than delivered on. What is he doing with it? I have seen him before I swear it but in connection with the free trade."

The two said no more and would say no more. Back in the house Bampfylde heard that the company were trying to track down their Captain, as his wife had initially thought Bampfylde was in fact he, the old salt that they had entertained the previous night. He heard that they had come to satisfy themselves that he, Bampfylde, and the Captain were or were not the same person.

"I see gentlemen. Well, I will satisfy you, although I am offended that you feel such satisfaction necessary. What would you like to know or see?"

"Where were you at the coast and when?

" Budleigh Salterton at a rest house there. I can give you the name of the hosts and the whereabouts. If you so wish." With that he took to his writing desk and penned details.

Sir William took the paper and asked if they could see outside, the stables as well. Bampfylde agreed. Before leaving it was John who asked Bampfylde about his hunting and riding.

"Yes, I was so fond of the riding and hunting but can manage little now."

The young Squire had noticed his limp, and being an ardent rider and hunter, asked how he managed to mount and dismount.

"With great difficulty with some help required. I cannot ride rough for long and can be unstable in the saddle."

"I can see that", said John. With that their host rolled his trouser and showed them a swelling to the side of his leg and discolouration.

"This is the problem. The surgeon thinks that there is little that can be done to put it right."

The company looked around, especially at the stables. There was no sign of fine horses and certainly not any sign of their horse from the previous night. They had seen his packs of cards on the table and there were none of Winstanley's evident. They called Luke and Hannibal to show their cards to see the look on Bampfylde as he saw them. He was expressionless but enquired as to the rest of them and where he might purchase a pack of what looked to be a very unusual and interesting pack of cards.

As they left, the decision was made to not travel to Budleigh as they felt the story would simply be corroborated by those in the pay of Bampfylde. It looked as if they had drawn a blank here.

Hannibal though, keeping his counsel with Luke, was not so sure. There was something more to this Bampfylde. He was somewhere and somehow involved with the free traders. Sir William had a good look at that fellow and could not see him in the Captain.

"How could a fellow with a leg and limp like that ride away so quickly and be a Highwayman? Hmm, fool's errand."

With that they made the start of a slower journey back. They would stop the night close by before the dim January night started to close the skies.

They made it to the Oxenham Inn at Zeal where John and Sir William put away their anger at the other evening's events, taking to the card table and ales with other Gentlemen who too were seeking some entertainment to pass the evening.

Hannibal and Luke saw the other workers in the area that Hannibal had known a long time, especially since his days helping and delivering there with the free trade. Out at the back of the Inn, in the quiet of a small hidden room they drank and talked freely. Hannibal did not mention the cards but did talk of the card game at the Bell, the Captain and his escape. The other workers there listened intently.

One of them, known only as Patch because of the loss of an eye and the patch he wore to cover it, related that there were a few occasional visitors to the Oxenham who were always winners when they came. Challenges made about the integrity of the cards were always unsuccessful. They had never been there together which Patch felt a pity as a game between those extraordinary players would be something to behold.

There had, though, never been a Captain of this description at the table. Back on the gaming tables at the Inn the Squire and Sir William played more cautiously than the previous night with the Captain but took relatively heavy losses again, with one player taking most of the winnings, picking his moment and leaving with his winnings intact.

The party retired, returning the next day no further forward in their quest to find and bring their man to account. Sir William maintained his resolve to find the man who had made such a fool of him, ensuring that the Innkeeper was well compensated as he indeed had promised. So too Hannibal and Luke, especially so Hannibal, for the interruption to his wedding night and the next day. He presented Hannibal and Luke with further guineas and re-iterated his pledge that there was more to come should they be able to provide information leading to the apprehension of the person responsible.

Hannibal and Joan started their married life.

Chapter 6

Tragedy Starts a Move south

Birthing had been difficult for Joan from the onset. Joseph, their first child, was born a year after marriage. It was then that the rude reality of married life to the woman he cherished struck home to Hannibal.

"You ask for work at Tetcott if I go Hannibal. If the boy survives maybe you could call him Joseph after one of mine? No more free trading then. The boy will need you. He could be raised better at Tetcott and with Thomasine there too, you would have help. Or take him back to South Tawton. He could maybe have an education. Maybe put to a trade?"

"You sleep now. You won't be going home to the Lord yet." With that Hannibal took ale from beside the bed on which she lay, poured a little and pressed it gently on her lips beckoning her to take a sip. The water close by was used to mop her forehead and cool it from the fever. The blooded sheets had been cleaned and she lay with Joseph suckling her to the side to avoid the pain of having him rest on her. She was still too weak to rise and sit up. Pale and with a yellow pallor riding patchily over her already pale skin, she said she would sit up later and take a little chicken stew that had been prepared. Joan had not yet eaten.

A day had passed since the traumatic birth, when they thought there would be no ending other than one where both mother and baby would die.

Joan had struggled to do any chores for more than a month before the birth. She had been confined to her bed, unable to walk, unable to carry her child. Her limbs were bloated with thick veins appearing, looking as though they were ready to pop from under her thin, delicate skin, to burst, taking with them her life's blood.

"When is this baby coming?" shouted Hannibal to Joan's mother who was in their room above, comforting and encouraging her daughter.

"These men they're all the same Joan. They get their pleasures and we takes the pain from then on. First, it's the sickness, then it's the jumping and crashing inside and then .... well it's just pain all the way .... and all the time. Only thing I say is that it gets better. It will be better when there's another one. If there is to be another one after this.

Hear me Hannibal. This is all your doing! You men and your men's things. Cut it all off I say. I would have cut my husband's off when I had my first. Oh yes, if you'd given me that cleaver, he wouldn't have caught me again."

With that she banged on the floor with a stick her husband had hewn from a piece of fallen oak, especially to aid her mobility. It possessed a natural handle formed where a branch came off its small trunk. It was an ideal size for a walking stick. Down its length to its end it had many small twists and turns, each of which had uses. This time its use was its end which could clout the floor with a resounding thud.

"Hear me Hannibal. Leave her alone for a while after this!"

Hannibal thought better than to go up the stairs and stayed below listening hard.

"And don't think you can stay there forever supping with that Innkeeper and carting man of yours. Oh no. You can get ready to help somehow. If men can help at all with this."

"Keep clear of her Hannibal", beckoned Luke. The Innkeeper too saw his opportunity to impart some words of comfort and advice to Hannibal.

"She's always been a firebrand that one. But if anyone can help deliver that child and mother safely it's her."

The Innkeeper spoke with authority as if he had observed the birthing of many children at the hands of Joan's mother.

Screams pierced the air as the men below heard mother providing a mixture of encouragement, command and compassion, albeit not always at one and the same time.

"Here the child comes. What is it going to be? What are you blessed with? The worse is over."

With that mother eased the child out of her daughter, who was near collapse and running a high feverous temperature.

"More water. More water and cloths. Bring cloths. You've a boy here who'll want to see his father soon."

The command was directed at the floor and accompanied again by a brutal and defining bang of the stick on the floor.

Her mother was not coming down to get anything. The menfolk could play their part now.

"Sat down there supping their ales and the rest too. Baccy smoke everywhere .... when they can get it, steal it more like. Filch it from that hauling they do. Hauling that stuff, they shouldn't. I know, I see it going on here and everywhere."

Her complaints were heard, but with deaf ears, as she enjoyed the occasional fruits from the contraband hauling herself. Today though was a day when Hannibal would not be able to please her. It was a day when she saw her daughter come close to death. She had to place blame for this somewhere and expend the nervous energy that had built inside her during the last few days when her daughter had looked so pale and wan.

Joan's mother had always liked Hannibal, but, on this day, the day when her daughter looked so close to the next world, she saw him as the instrument of her troubles.

"Men, these bloody men. Poking it here and there. Can't he see she is a delicate child, not one for all that poking and thrashing about. Hear me

Hannibal Marks? No, she's not for all this thrashing about you like to do. You mind that next time. You mind it."

Turning to her daughter as she helped to clean her and removing the bedding, she winked.

"I know we can't stop these menfolk. I couldn't stop mine and I wouldn't have you if I had." She grinned at her daughter and her faced creased with pleasure to see her grandchild. "But I'll make sure he doesn't go near you for a while. Not until you're recovered besides. I'll stay in here too if I must. Let him try it then and he'll have this to contend with!"

With that she took the stick again and stroked its long and hazardous length. Hazardous it was, with its knobbly and sharp offshoots that had been trimmed along its shaft. She came to one close to the handled end, stroking that section for a while as if it were an old friend.

"I'll grab him underneath with this and from behind, just when he's not expecting. It'll come at him from between those great legs of his with me holding the end that is normally for the ground. The other end, this other, my handle, will get him sharp as I pull it up from the other end. I'll pull it so hard that he won't be going near you for nigh on a year I would say. I might then give it another good pull against him just for good measure. Then he won't go near you ever again!"

Hannibal heard this below. He winced, forcing the skin of cheeks and neck downwards to express his pain at the very thought. This thought, yes, this thought, of his fearsome mother-in-law in the same room was bad enough, but the prospect of her wielding that old stick of hers in fury was quite another.

Joan's mother must have thought in the ensuing few years that her son in law had taken notice of her for once and left her daughter alone, for it was a further six years before she was to go into labour again with another child.

"I didn't mean you had to wait this long," complained her mother after a few years had passed. "Where's a brother or sister for Joseph?"

Joan had many miscarriages well before she had a successful pregnancy. Many had happened since the birth of Joseph and it was not for lack of want on the part of Hannibal and Joan. Joan took a long time to recover from the coming of Joseph and the miscarriages made him the more special.

Honour was born next and this time the birth was considerably more straightforward for her. A small baby and a girl were a kinder gift.

"Look Hannibal, a sister for Joseph. He will be six years older than his sister. He can look out for her when we're not around."

The young Joseph was growing into a strong boy. He would often travel with his father on the carting rounds. Hannibal and Joan saw that learning to read and write properly, not just a few words, would be good for him. In a few years, they could ask Squire John if there would be work and an apprenticeship for him at the Estate. He had always promised there would be, and although they saw each other with less frequency than they had, they still would meet occasionally.

The young Squire had become the Squire with all its additional expectations on him, especially so those civic duties and the running of the Tetcott estate.

Joan had a family to care for with a boy to bring up. Nonetheless, Thomasine and Joan would pick up with ease where they had left off, tirelessly recounting the stories of what happened in their younger years, running through the various scenarios that might or might not have resulted.

What about those cards, what about her attacker, so many unanswered questions?

The Squire had not thus far complied with his father's dying wishes that he should marry well, and in choosing his bride, rebuild the Arscott estates in the area. There was no time left now to achieve this but still he looked nowhere else for a bride that would bring with her further estates to add to Tetcott. Thomasine remained his companion. Her status had risen at Tetcott since Squire Arthur had died. No longer was she a servant, but neither was she the Lady of Tetcott. There had been no children born to them either, whilst meantime, Hannibal and Joan had continued to build their family.

"Hannibal, Hannibal. Look it's Honour." Joan had a desperate and pleading tone to her voice, the final syllables of her sentence lifting, then falling, dragged out as if she had no other words to now offer. "No, oh no.

My child, my daughter. What is wrong? We thought you were going to get over the throat disease. She's gone Hannibal. She's gone. Don't go, don't go. Please don't go. It's not your time yet."

With this she took the little child to her bosom and cradled her cold and lifeless body as if she could nurse her back to the world she had left during the night. She stood with her and with a softness and intimacy that only a parent of a child just deceased could possibly understand, rocked her side to side, giving her movement, as if this movement could give her life once more.

Honour had been placed next to Joan and away from Joseph who was on the other side of the room they shared. He had not contracted the throat problems that Honour had on the previous few days. It had all happened so quickly. She had a very red throat and would cry a lot, not taking her milk without sickness. She had a racking cough. It was when the fever started, when they saw the lumps appear in her throat, that they feared the worst and prayed for her, falling asleep next to her, not thinking then that they too may contract this disease but that this was a disease of small children.

"Maybe we will all go together now. Maybe it is our time. Maybe we should all go together." Joan sobbed with desperateness and a wail that would haunt the soul of Hannibal for the remainder of his days. Joan then sang softly to their daughter as she rocked her slowly, in rhythm to the tune that was of her own making. "She's her Ma's lovely girl, her lovely, lovely Honour She'll soon wake from this sleep ...."

She could not complete the song and with tenderness she lay her down gently, speaking to her all the while.

"I wish I could be there for you to take you to the other side. I so wish you didn't have to make this journey alone. I live in the hope that you will have been met now by those who would have loved you on this earth. Those who couldn't be here long enough to meet you but are there for you in the next. Yes, I hope and pray they have met you there and will be comforting, you, for alas, I cannot. Oh Hannibal, how can we comfort our Honour now. She is so small. She needs us still. How can we do it? She will travel this journey without us. I don't think I can bear it."

The melancholy and desperate plea for an answer lost no intensity. It was one for which Hannibal could not find an answer that could help her. He bent over to take Honour from Joan. As he did so she rose and together they held her. It was first light, and the little Honour had been next to her in the bed they shared. Still she was. The colour she had once had with a delicate vibrancy to it, had drained away, telling her parents that she had gone. She had given a final sigh that they had not heard. A sigh that said she was little, she was tired of this. She had taken a final look at them that was her way of saying goodbye, a thank you for the care and life they had given for the short while she was with them.

A look that said it is goodbye .... but only for now. A look that said I will see you again and we will carry on where this has left off.

Hannibal lifted her high to him and faced her. Placing her chest to him he could hear no beat of heart against the wall of her little chest. They knew. Hope had gone.

They summoned Joseph to the other side of the bed but away from Honour and bade him kneel with them in prayer for her soul and journey.

Launceston had its toll of the disease and word had it there were several parishes around with it too. They had thought when so many children started to die that they should walk to South Tawton. Maybe they should stay there until it that it had passed. It had though, happened all too quickly.

Mothers had kept their children away from others who showed signs of the disease but to no avail. Several children had contracted the disease, and many had died within the last few weeks. The end of the churchyard was filling with the tiny mounds, their small wooden crosses above them, indicating a child was lying there that had been given up to God.

There had been talk of setting up a burial area outside the town, away from the Church, if more deaths occurred. The disease had taken a firm grip on the population. This would mean that the cart Hannibal and Luke used for their work might be expected to travel the streets and call for the inhabitants to bring out their dead to the cart for them to transport to the burial site.

Joan looked at Hannibal, distraught and wane.

“She must go to the Churchyard Hannibal while there is time. If this gets a hold, I would wish her to be at peace with all of hers and mine there and not in a hole in the ground with all the others on top all mangled, her little body meaning nothing.”

“We will do this now. I will take her alone with us to the place, but it must be the Church.”

They took Honour to a place they knew they would be able to locate again and again, one that they too might be able to have as their final resting place when that time came.

It was when it came to the arrival of their son, Hammond, that life was to change forever for the Marks. It was again, as with Joseph, a difficult birth. Hammond was to arrive just short of two years after Honour had come into the world. A year had passed since her death.

“It’s always these boys that cause the trouble.”

Joan’s mother was back and in full blaming mood once again, although this time the jocular tone did not last for long. Joan had ruptured and bled badly with infection setting in. She did not seem to have the strength to battle against this. Hannibal held her in their bed, which wept with tears of her blood as she slipped away to the next world. They had both fallen to slumber and said all they could. He knew that the end must be soon be nigh. She had been so strong in all the years he had known her and to see her strength ebb away, with nothing anyone could do but pray for her salvation, was more than he could take.

When, on awaking in the morn, he felt her cold, open jawed and with a colour unlike any other nature displays. He stayed a while, still holding her until he collected his senses a little, then gently prised his arm from hers. He remained, transfixed, just looking at her, closing her eyelids with a gentleness unexpected from such strong and powerful hands.

He knew though what now had to be done. As the coffin was made up at the carpenter's shop down the road, he helped her slip into it, the floorboards removed to take her down the coffin hatch.

The funeral was the next day at St Mary's Church where she had been baptised, married and would now be buried, joining many of her friends and family in the Churchyard.

The site was that where Honour had been placed. Hannibal knew where she was, ensuring it was unlikely more would follow before it was their turn. It was a place they had managed to reserve. An awkward little section of the churchyard not well attended and with saplings all around. He had gone that night to remove these to make room for her.

Joan was carried by Hannibal and her brothers to the Churchyard, followed by those who knew her that were in the town and available to attend. There was no time to alert the family at South Tawton or their friends further afield, such as Thomasine and the Squire.

Her wish was fulfilled. The burial was with her daughter, in a place Hannibal, Joseph and Hammond would always be able to recognise and return to.

It was a solemn day as her family and many friends trooped quietly into St Mary's, filling the pews and standing areas, then on to the churchyard.

Hammond was not to live long after Joan's death and her mother had looked after him while Hannibal was to work. His mother in law knew mothers with child who were happy to nurse Hammond, but it was as if he knew that his mother was not there for him and he wanted to be with her. The only way he could do this was to leave the world and leave it peacefully. Shortly after his mother had been placed in the ground, he too said good bye to the world.

"This is the second tiny box in as many years Hannibal that you have had me make. It is a sorry day, but the town has lost a lot of its children of late."

"Yes, but this is of a broken heart, I think. A broken heart for his mother, who he knew but for a short while, although long enough to know she was his and he was hers. But it was not enough for him, That short moment with her was not what he wanted. He wanted more of her and if the only way he could get that was to slip into the next world, then so be it for Hammond."

With that Hannibal took Hammond and saw him buried at the site where only a short time previously he had bid farewell to his wife.

It was never to be the same now she had gone. Joseph was nearing twelve Hannibal arranged with the Squire to have him apprenticed at the Tetcott Estate where his chances would be improved. Hannibal though was not to go with him and take work at Tetcott. Not long after Joan died, he made up his mind that the time had come to make the move further south where well-paid work was plentiful, as was the chance to improve the family's lot with a greater involvement in the riskier and better rewarded coastal free trading activities.

He could return for Joseph, maybe a self-made man, one who could secure for him home, property and business. His work for the smugglers had been to carry goods by hand, cart and mule to destinations in the area ,within the multitude of Inns and hideaways. Sometimes word had got through that more labour would be needed on a particular night or day. When labour had been short like this, he had got involved in bringing in trusted men he knew and getting message to them when they were needed. As he did more and more of this work, he had been trusted with the money to pay those men he had arranged. Hannibal would receive an extra cut in return. It was this additional responsibility that had brought him closer with those in the area who had lines of communication with the smugglers further south. They were in all manner of occupations. Some had enough work with the smuggling to do nothing else but smuggling. Hannibal too could have worked for no one else than the smuggling gangs but the cart, the Inn and the calls they made gave protection with cover to go with it. Hannibal continued to combine the two until he felt ready to move.

Work was arranged through the smuggling network he had got to know at one of the Skelton quarries which lay south of Launceston. These were part of their Stoketon estate with accommodation close to the Lynher River. The Lynher River came off the Tamar and fed into it. The foreman at the quarries was involved in the free trade and he was able to hire workers. Stoketon was close to St Stephen and Saltash in the border area of Cornwall with Devon. The village of Forder lay close by at the head of a navigable section of a tributary off the St. Germans river. This fed directly off the main Tamar river at a place not far from the open seas. The area was a complex litter of inlets, towns, villages, hamlets, estates and manors with routes connecting them by river, sea and land if you knew where to go. There was a considerable amount of smuggling here.

"You know this work and place Hannibal. You know Launceston and your family at South Tawton and son close by. Why go now? There's plenty of work with the carting. A home for you." The Innkeeper at the Bell had seen Hannibal, Joan and his family as one of theirs after so many years there.

"It's time for me to go and see if I can make more of it and there is more and more work and pay further south, they say."

"Well with that comes more dangers."

"I know but do it I must now, and work is arranged at a quarry further down."

"You have never worked in a quarry. It'll be harder work on you than carting and the other work down there will be full of that danger I say. Further down you go, further dangers. More fortunes they say have been made down there and more lives gone with it too. Are you walking down and leaving the things you have got now for your home?"

"Well I was hoping to take them. I've a little bit of money and was wondering if I could buy that old cart that hasn't been used a while and one of the old horses may be?"

"If you can fix that old cart so it takes you down you can have it, and we'll come to a fair price for that old horse. Mind you it will be two oldies together you'll be taking. So, take it easy with them both if they're to get you there. She can't have long to go but you could sell her and the cart then perhaps?"

Good byes also had to be said at Tetcott. When Hannibal went there on carting work, he had a chance to see the Squire, Thomasine and the young Joseph.

"I shall be saddened to know you are gone, Hannibal. There is always a living and home for you here on the Tetcott lands if you want it."

"There's more chances for me there now," Hannibal nodded, appreciatively.

"Well, don't you invite trouble ... and if you do, get word to me. I will never forget what you did those years back in Launceston. The debt has not yet been repaid in my mind."

"There never was one in my mind, Squire."

"Stay a little while. I will prepare a letter for the lady of the house, Ann Skelton at Stoketon. I would like you to give it to her on arrival."

Thomasine came in whilst John went to prepare his letter. "You are leaving Hannibal ... Joseph will stay here?"

"Yes, it is now time Thomasine. Things are not the same as when Joan was here. I need to make a new life. I can do better for myself and maybe for Joseph too if I go further south where there is more work, better paid work too."

"I know the sort of work that you mean Hannibal Marks. I know that you always wanted to make your way and make better of yourself. But all the talk is of the dangers that are down there with this work. They say it is getting more dangerous all the time."

"It is a chance I must take. Maybe I can find another wife as mother to Joseph one day?"

"Nothing will ever replace Joan."

"No, I know, but Joan, she isn't coming back for him now." With that Hannibal's voice quivered at the memories of them all, including those at Tetcott. She went towards him and hugged him hard squeezing his hand.

The large, carved, oak door, opened. The Squire bursting through it with his usual presence, letter in hand, looking rather pleased that he had done it and finished it with such fine hand. The ink had just blotted and dried ready for Hannibal to take. It was wax sealed with the stamp of Arscott. It was a true masterpiece of composition and presentation.

"Don't damage this on your travels. It is the best hand I can do and the best parchment we have." The two men briefly embraced and Hannibal lowered head in respect, turned and left. Thomasine watched him leave from the window upstairs. She thought what a forlorn sight it was. They had a few adventures those years ago, and then more ordinary life had resumed once more.

Hannibal had previously made the return trip to South Tawton to see his family, Conscious he might not be returning for a while, he promised he would get word to them all, so they knew where he was and that all was well. Similarly, he wanted word back.

A family of eleven brothers in total were at South Tawton and the neighbouring villages to see Hannibal. Two had died but the nine remaining had found work in the surrounding area.

The day came when, ready to go, he took the journey down to Stoketon. Part was overland, part down the Tamar River. The journey was only about 30 miles as a crow would fly but to get there with horse and cart would take some time and planning. The Tamar passed through Launceston but was not navigable that far north, so he would travel by land to the quays at Calstock where he would pick up a barge to take him down river. There he would pick up another to take him close to his new home, disembark the cart and horse to get there. He would hope to sell them both, maybe at the estate or maybe the quarry could use them?

Chapter 7

Stoketon Gives a Fresh Start

"I have a letter for the lady of the house, Mrs. Ann if it pleases," reported Hannibal. The door of Stoketon Manor was opened, letter taken, and the door promptly closed again.

The letter had been taken, without a word, into the house and up the stairs where it was presented to Mrs. Ann who was sat reading in her room. She was, at the time, gazing through its window to the view down the river valley beyond.

The Skelton quarries were below the farms, woodlands and Park that snaked around with the flow of the river. To one side lay the sizeable village of Landrake with lodgings for many of those folks who worked at the quarries below.

Breaking the wax seal, Ann read the letter silently to herself before opening out into a loud whisper as she spoke to herself.

"My Dear Ann, I hope that this finds you in good health, with the farm, land and quarries all providing for you well after the passing into the next world of your good husband.

You will have by now in your employ one Hannibal Marks, who has come to St Stephens seeking work and better fortune for himself after the demise of his wife. He has a son Joseph who is in our employ as apprentice.

Hannibal Marks did me good service at an occurrence of some violence to one of the faithful and serving folk of the Tetcott household for which I am indebted for his assistance. Should he ever fall into poverty of health, living or any disfavour whatever and to whomever, let it please you to let me have word of same, for I will do all to give him good guarantee and safety.

I am Ann,

Yours,

John of Arscott

"Well, well, I wonder what this Marks has done to win the favour of the Arscotts. I will have to speak with him direct as John is not choosing to share any more about it with me, at least, not for now."

There was a little row of stone cottages built from the quarry stone to house most of the Skelton quarry workers close by. Not quite as imposing though as the servants' house adjacent to the Skelton's Stoketon Manor. Stoketon housed most of the estate workers needed to keep house, farms, orchards and everything in between going. It was part of their wide Ellmere Estate holding. Comparatively modest as an estate compared to many that the Skelton family had previously had in the border areas either side of the Tamar. Their influence was waning from what it once had been. Despite this, there was enough though to live and enjoy the life of the gentry. At the Manor House and servants' quarters there were seven folk working for the Skeltons. In addition to this there were some let farms, boat making sheds down near the river and of course their quarries, all with their own workers. On the western side, the Skelton lands stretched into parts of Landrake and down towards the bridge at Notter where the river was little more than a big stream in places. From here they had some scattered lands and farms in the old settlement of Penquit. This Penquit he was told, bore the same name as the land held by Skeltons on the other side of the Tamar near Modbury and Ermington where they were part of the ancient Prideaux family. Hannibal had heard of the Cornish Prideaux in the north of Cornwall with their castle and extensive lands there. As he approached the quarry where his home was to be, he could hear its noise as stone was being hewn, cut, crushed and prepared for delivery, either by barge down the rivers or horse and cart by land. Hannibal would be doing anything that needed doing at the quarry and if required, work at one of the others nearby. Although new work to him, he had known the quarry workings in the South Tawton area where he originally had come from and where one of his brothers had worked.

If orders for stone were slack, workers would be taken to do some of the farm work or other work required by the estate. In the following months he got used to the working life of the quarry, alongside the night time work of the smuggler. The people he had got to know when he was part of the tubmen carrying gangs around Launceston were true to their word. He soon became part of them, taking tubs short distances over land and unloading small boats from the nearby river banks. The trade had been growing, and with it, came an increased demand for storage. It was not unusual for the number of tubs requiring carriage to exceed the number of tubmen available to carry them. This increased the need for more storage facilities along the routes they took. The quarries had developed hideaway areas that could take large numbers of tubs. Everything came in a tub that was easy for a man to strap on himself. Nothing was any different from what he had known before. It was one tub to the front and one to the back. The tubs weren't always carrying spirits. The less able men would carry tubs marked to indicate that they contained other, lighter items. Hannibal noticed how everyone who wanted the smuggling work got something to do and reward for it. Always paid in coin he hoarded his share out, making a few hideaways for it. Sundays remained a Church day or at least the morning was. The Church he and the other estate workers attended was that of St Stephens which drew on people from quite a large area of surrounding scattered hamlets and small villages. He would spend any daylight hours when not working, walking miles, getting to know the countryside and river areas around him.

Chapter 8

Christian Wyvell

Christian was a plucky, strong, young woman who knew the banks of the river network around the lower reaches of the Tamar like few others. She too had got involved with the free traders showing to them that she could handle a boat as well as any man, and alone. Showing them that she could provide hauling work to transport the contraband landed along the coast from Cawsand to Portwrinkle up through the rivers to safe storage, using her small, versatile sailing and rowing boat. Showing them, she was trustworthy and could keep the secrets of the smugglers.

Shallow drafted, wide beamed, sailed and oared, but capable of being handled by one, she had taken over the boat from her friend Sampson.

Sampson had helped her when, in quick succession, her parents had died. She was left alone to care for her younger siblings. Had she not they would have been forced on to the charity of the Parish.

Sampson would have been her lover, husband too, if she had so wished it. Often it was that she had been tempted, but he was happy to help them without that if she so wished. He was content to wait until she was older and knew her mind better.

Sampson was also involved in smuggling. Starting off as an unloader and tubman he graduated to working boats on the river. Before smuggling had given him a full-time occupation, he had fished from Portwrinkle, a nearby coastal village, from where he had often helped unload the larger smuggling boats, the Smugglers, that came in along the coast.

Using the extra money wisely, he had acquired the boat that Christian now used and given her the name, Night Sister. It was Sampson that had shown her how to handle the boat, how to look after her, teaching her everything he knew about the rivers. It was through Sampson that she had got to know more and more of the smugglers. Initially, some distrusting, they had developed understandings as she proved herself.

Sampson became closer and closer to her, to the extent that she was starting to think she should yield and accept his affections. Older than her but not by much, he eventually left Porwrinkle to rent a small and disused building near Sheviock on the banks of the St Germans river. near where it would split to the Lynher and Tiddy, all not far to the west of the main river Tamar. Christian and her siblings too had gone there to live, as he created a few rooms from the derelict old working building. It was safer for his small boat there than on the beaches that faced the open seas at Portwrinkle.

The boat would moor next to the building where he could work on her, taking her up a bit further onto the mud and shingle when needed.

"We are both alone but for each other Christian ... and your brothers and sisters. Folk talk, why we don't wed now?"

"They can talk all they like Sampson. If I was ready to be wed it would be to you if you'd have me. Maybe soon I will be ready." Her voice delivered the last sentence in a tantalising, teasing tone, slowing the words and raising its pitch towards the end.

"Your brothers and sisters, they would have you wed me."

"Shhh...." Her lips formed an almost perfect circle to make the soothing noise that beckoned him to be quiet and calm. She planted them on his cheek with a tenderness that defied the roughness of her working hands.

She had to raise herself up to reach his cheeks for he was more than Sampson by name only. He was of biblical Sampson strength and size. Dark complexioned, swarthy, Sampson was a bear of a man and stood there in sharp contrast to Christian who, though with a strength that in many ways could match his, also had a delicate, refined stature that did not mirror her work and capabilities.

Christian preferred to steer a course clear of this conversation.

Yes, her siblings would welcome a marriage between the pair.

Yes, if she were pushed for a yes or no decision now, this day, this hour, she would say yes.

She would, however, prefer to wait, wait until she knew inside her that the time was right, absolutely, unquestionably, right.

"I owe you everything Sampson, want to give you everything I can, including marriage, but wait a while yet?"

She looked at him longingly, but reservedly. She was imploring him with her eyes and the tone of her voice to wait just a little while longer.

A marriage meant children and she was not quite ready for that. She had taken over as mother to her siblings and would prefer not to take on more children, at least not yet.

As for Sampson, he could deny her nothing. It could wait until she was ready. He told himself that extra time would mean extra money to improve their position and prepare for a family.

He would return to Portwrinkle when additional help was needed to unload from the large sea going Smugglers. He was a trusted oarsman and tubman for the smaller boat owners in the village.

They would go out to the Smuggler to unload her, take the goods to the shore where there would be men, tubmen, waiting to carry the stocks to hiding places or start the journey with them inland and up the rivers.

The owners or their agents would be there to make sure their goods were accounted for and note their whereabouts. Sometimes these would be the boat owners, whether the owners of the Smuggler or the smaller boats.

His riverside building also made a good hideaway and store for the goods, especially those destined to travel further inland or to a point further up the river network, when the coast was clear.

Sampson and Christian were becoming a small but important part of the storage and distribution arrangements. They would receive good pay for this facility alongside some luxuries and no shortage of the finest spirits.

Close to the Tamar arteries, Night Sister was almost always at a state of readiness to carry goods further upstream or deeper into Cornwall. Sampson was always at the ready to take the extra guinea from the trade, whether as unloader, tubman, storehouse keeper, river transporter, it mattered not.

He had excavated down under the home he had created for them, to make a store that could be accessed by lifting boards, going through the joists then into a short tunnel that led into a good-sized store. The tunnel entrance could not be seen when the boards were lifted, and it was a crawl to get there. It went under the foundation of the wall and down a steep slope to get to into it. A large underground lair, it was well propped up with good strong timber brought up from the beaches where regular supplies were washed in.

Christian knew that the work unloading the large boats on the coast carried with it more danger than the work they did on the rivers. She would discourage it, reminding him that they had enough well-paid work with Night Sister and their storage depot under the house.

She would plead with him not to go but to stay, wait for the tubmen and carts to bring goods to them for distribution further on.

"There is always a first time to be caught, Sampson. We have come to rely on you now. If anything happened to you what would we do?"

"You know how to handle the Night Sister, just like me. No, better than me. You know the rivers like me, no, better than me. When you are on that boat it is as if the two of you are the same one. If anything should ever happen, and I did not return, you have the boat. You have our home. You will get work now. You know them all. You know where the coins are. Should anything happen to me you have it, have it all. Just take it."

With this act of generosity to her, she could resist him no longer. She went to him again and once more placed a kiss on his cheek. She lingered there close to him for a while.

"It will be you Sampson. It will be you." She spoke softly and directly to him. It was all Sampson could do to refrain from taking her in his grip and pressing himself to her. "Was this the moment?" he thought. "Was this it, the moment he had waited for? Was she beckoning him? Was she giving him the chance? Was now that time? Was the future here now and should he grab it? Should he push his will. Maybe that push was what she was waiting for?"

He held back. He could not run a risk that might change things forever. She had been prickly about any moment like this. There had been times when she had looked at him with that longing look but then turned to the side with bowed head. He had found this coyness difficult to interpret as well as to resist, but resist he had. Always pulling back from making a move on her that he might regret, she had therefore never had to reject him. She leant tantalisingly to him once more, gently pulling his head down to where his ear was next to her lips. Sampson could stand it no more.

As she whispered to him her promises again, he could feel a stirring from which he knew this time there might be no retreat.

"Wait just a little longer for me, please? I am coming to you. Just a little longer." With that he jerked back and turned the other way.

Speaking was difficult with his heart pounding so strongly. His words were stuttered, jagged, full of nervous energy, more so than he had ever experienced. He spoke towards the ramshackle door that divided them from the outside world and the slow-moving river so as not to show his feelings.

"I can do no other than to keep your wishes Christian. I have waited thus far and can wait for you longer to be ready. I have only to look at you, hear you, at any time, in any mood, to know there is none other and to know that, wait I will. The day you say you are ready for me will be my day and my life will be complete."

She felt the tear that had emerged from her eye to travel down her face slow as it reached the strongly featured protrusion of her high cheekbones. It was so cold she thought it might freeze before travelling further.

She did not have to worry for long. The flush that was coming to her face and the heat it brought prevented any of that. She quickly wiped the tear away.

Sampson turned, grinned and shrugged his shoulders at her. She did the same. Laughter followed and then followed the tears. They both knew it would be someday soon.

The fire now needed to be lit from the plentiful supply of wood outside, to warm them all and prepare the food. Enough of this for now.

* * *

"Sammy, look out !" Sampson was in a chain of unloaders on the beach. The Smuggler offshore was a big one for the times and had chosen to offload there due to the wind direction.

"It's the Dragoons. What are they doing here?" There were three. Dismounting, they called on the men to stop. Armed, they advanced fearlessly towards the smugglers who with only bats and hands rushed at them. The Dragoons were trained with sword and firearms. Behind them appeared two Riding Officers. Were there to be more? The smugglers had the power of numbers and determination, but the swords lashed around them cutting and slashing as they flailed, chopping through the night air before reaching the solid thud as they went through the flesh and sometimes to the bone of their attackers.

Sampson was in the front line of the rush, and as he suddenly felt the use in his right arm leave him, he was aware of something warm rolling down his back from the area of his neck. Then he fell.

The sheer weight of numbers of the smugglers on the beach as they rallied around, appearing from behind every rock, surprised the Dragoons and Riding officers. They had not seen this throng. As they started to beat a retreat it was too late, and they were overpowered.

"We'll take them with us out to the far seas and put them overboard," said one of them who was with the Smuggling boat off the shores. With that the men were dragged out and onto the boat. The Smuggler unloaded to the last item, then she sailed.

Sampson had been tended to as best they could, but they knew he could not live. His friend had stopped the unloading work and tried to stem Sampson's bleeding. It all happened too quickly. The random slashing of the swords to his body had caused uncontrollable bleeding. A doctor was too far away, it would take too long. Too much blood had left his body too quickly before it could be slowed. His friend comforted him and urged him to rest to get better.

"Tell Christian I will be there for her and watch over her if I do not get back. Tell her to do what I said."

With that he gurgled and spluttered, trying to hold back the choking on his own blood. His agony and distress were not to last. On the beach he had known, with the waves now starting to lap against his body, he took his final breaths, loosening the tightness his muscles had displayed during his ordeal to relax, finally dying in the arms of his friend.

"What is this?" Christian shrieked, falling to the floor as Sampson was brought into their dwelling. Her brothers and sisters woke. All together they surrounded him, fetching water to clean him, all the time praying for him.

The blood had stopped flowing. What remained had congealed, crusting along his body as it dried, mixing with the frozen cloth that was his clothing. When the men who brought him, slumped over one of the horses they had used that night, left, she spent the night with him, talking to him for the last time.

"I pray for you and thank you for everything you have done for me, my brothers and sisters too. We will never forget you for as long as we now remain on this earth. I should have given myself to you that night a few days ago when I could and when I knew it was right. Now, now I never can."

The following day Sampson was buried in the churchyard at Sheviock. His friends had returned to help Christian and attend the small service. For that night Christian remained there with him, by his graveside. She did not want any risk of interference with his body. As she packed down the earth of the grave, she lay on it, speaking through the earth to him softly wishing his journey well.

Christian then took her place as the only sole female operator of a small smuggling craft with a boat in that area. Women were involved in the trade but usually by hiding and disguising at their homes or by carrying smaller quantities hidden around them to the local Inns and Taverns.

She had now branched out alone into journeying the rivers. She would do this from where the Tamar flowed out to sea up as far as Calstock and a bit beyond. She would also work every tributary and inlet. The quarry where Hannibal worked by day had become one of the drop off points and hides.

Close to quaysides, with easy places to bring her shallow draft boat, she had become a regular sight at the right tides. Her boat had been named but had no name painted on her.

Night Sister's shadow and shape was distinctive to those who knew her. The carriers recognised it was her waiting for loading or unloading. There was less likelihood of preventative boats plying the smaller river areas upstream. Their larger boats concentrated more on the open seas where there were large hauls with commensurate rewards and prizes to be made. By land, many areas of riverbank were difficult to get to, especially so at night. Some riverside areas were sparsely inhabited, providing a favoured environment for smugglers.

If disturbed in their work by the Riding Officers, they were prepared to slay and dispose of bodies in the deep mudded areas and outworked mineshafts if they had to. The geography of inland creeks, woods, hills mines and quarries could easily disorientate those who were not fully familiar with it. She had spent much time getting to know the river on her own now, its estuaries, tributaries, the location of the villages, hamlets and farmsteads adjacent. She had worked out how and when she could navigate to them safely, considering tides, height of the river against the banks, winds, ice, snow and other features that affected the river. Christian had also identified escape routes should the need arise and places where she could trap and confuse the authorities. Places where she could lead them to their peril.

It was different without Sampson. She had learnt from Sampson, but it was he who would make decisions. He was her prop, her strength. Thinking through every move for herself was different. She was really getting to know it all now as an independent operator in her own right.

She had once worked where her parents had worked, on the Anthony Estate. The estate house was situated near the point where the St Germans river entered the mainstream flow of the Tamar, where the two mingled and forced their wills with and against the tides.

The Estate lay on the banks of the river overlooking Forder Creek close to St. Stephens, Saltash, with Trematon and Ince Castles opposite. Northwards lay the creek at Kingsmill, with Landulph to one side and Tamerton near Plymouth to the other. She therefore also had a detailed understanding of the layout of the estate, its buildings, who did what, where and when, who might be trusted and who might not.

These were all assets to her and would help determine the way she would conduct her business. She would make Sampson proud of her. He had left them the means to make their own way and a store of coins as their reserve.

This, a truly complex river and land network, was friend of the free trader and foe of those who were against their trade. Hannibal too was gaining an intuitive, spatial understanding of how these networks fitted together and soon developed a sense of it. He had seen much of Christian, unloading her boat and where time permitted, talked with her.

The horse and cart proved useful in unloading the small boat that Christian had and moving the goods it had brought along the tracks to and fro the quarries. Hannibal would also then join the carrying gangs that took goods further in.

Soon after meeting, Hannibal and Christian started to ply the rivers on runs together. He was keen to learn, and this was a starting point. Effectively apprenticed to her, Hannibal learnt mastery of a small sailing and rowing craft. He learnt to read the behaviour and mood of the rivers as well as develop an intimate knowledge of how they fitted and functioned together.

The two had an early understanding. Both had just lost people close to them and on whom they relied. Both were now looking to forge a new life. Both were involved in the shadowy work of the smugglers.

Working together turned slowly into what was tantamount to a courtship. It had taken her a long time to reconcile the death of Sampson with the possibility of a marriage to anyone else. There had, though, been one unforgettable incident that had sparked the romance.

"Hush, Hannibal," said Christian, "Lie low." This nighty's run was not the usual ferrying of goods from the banks of the St Germans River on the

Anthony, Polbathic and Sheviock side across to the opposite bank or up the rivers of Tiddy or Lynher.

They were to take the Night Sister, empty, to Kingsmill Creek, where they would be loaded near Landulph Church. This operation had required some planning to ensure the right tides co-incided with the right time of night. After this they would head up the Tamar to a quiet spot before they got to the main Edgcumbe Estate settlement at Cotehele. The estate lay on the Cornish side of the river. There were reed banks close by. Their rendezvous was a location that took them through the reed beds where they would be beached and unloaded. They had to keep eyes open for the sign as they neared, this giving the go ahead to veer close to the bank and pull through the reeds. If the sail were up there would be enough time to drop it and pull in by oar. They had heard that there might be a return load to be taken. This was unusual as these were usually one-way hauls. They understood that goods from Ireland had been unloaded at Padstow, travelling overland to end up at the Mill at Cotehele although some had been dropped off along the way. Whether these goods were Irish or landed in Ireland, they knew not. All they knew was that the goods were destined for the representative of a well-known family in the area. They also knew that the contents were the finest that could be bought, that they were small in volume and hidden in the containers they would receive. Both Hannibal and Christian were intrigued, but not enough to interfere with them nor enquire about them or their recipients further. They had a job to do.. They were not paid to question or know too much.

"Look! There's the sign." With that she lowered the sail knowing they were close to the reeds and would be taking the craft in to the spot very soon. Hannibal took to the oars, guiding the craft in towards the rushes. Stowing the oars once more and sliding out of the boat into the water as quietly as he could, he felt the soft mud below his feet intermingled with the small stones and pebbles that formed the bottom. This gave his feet a firm hold as he guided the boat in through the rushes by hand.

As they neared, with only the sound of the parting rushes and grasses within earshot, Hannibal felt the presence of horses nearby. He had an uncanny sixth sense for presence around him. The heat of their breath had cut quickly through the night air, meeting Hannibal as he pulled the boat up. He whispered to Christian, "they've horses to take the goods I can hear them." With that Christian started backing off and whispered back, "No there should be none. It is difficult to get them down here. They must be a bit further up. They were meant to be using carriers."

She had a feeling all was not well. They stalled the progress of the boat, making little sound, intending to make out back into mid water until they were sure of what was happening. The light went again.

"We are being lured like fish to bait – let's continue on up. Maybe there has been a warning." The Riding Officers occasionally came into the valley, but it was rare. They were few and usually in the pockets of the smugglers' paymasters. They could be expected to give little trouble. Maybe something had gone wrong, maybe not. Was there an informer in their midst? She was not taking any chances. Had they been seen coming into the rushes?

There was dark. There was cloud. With those thoughts and uncertainties, they proceeded gently by oar, hardly a drop of water leaving them as they entered and left the water. None, that is, that might cause any splashes, however slight. The same applied to the noise accompanying the strain taken by the thole pins. They must not now cause the pins to groan nor must they click or thud with the regularity that comes with the practiced skill of the oarsman.

Suddenly there was a crashing into the shallow waters next to them and they felt the boat veer bow to bank with the shout,

"This is the King's man. Ship your oars and come alongside." The night was ink black. None could see the other with any clarity. Hannibal instinctively lurched forward and brought his powerful hand down onto that of the officer crushing it onto the gunwale of the boat, coming back for more with the other until he felt the grasp go. Just as he was about throw himself out of the boat onto the man to finish him, he felt the boat rock sharply on the left and the brush of something hard against him. It was Christian. She had lifted one of the tubs they carried should it ever be needed as a bribe by its brace and was swinging it towards the man. It caught him solid to his face. He fell back into the water bending the reeds as he went. There was silence.

"That is for Sampson. My Sampson," she thought as she looked at the man as he fell, the light from the moon offering a momentary glimpse as it appeared from its hiding place behind the moving dense cloud above.

She could see nothing other than the man who might have killed Sampson slashing and running a sword through him. For now, he was that man. It was this thought that had given her strength and purpose.

Suddenly there was the increasing sound of splashing in the shallows and the rustle of reeds parting. It was the carriers they were meant to meet who, being just a bit further upstream waiting, had heard the noise and hurried down.

"We'll take care of this. Carry on upstream to the Mill now. They were loaded, and with that, the two punted back out and were on their way to the Mill at Cotehele Quay. This was Edgcumbe land. They were going into the heart of the estate. They did not usually use the landing point here but when they arrived, they saw no activity. As they pulled in there was just the Miller waiting for them with one hand. They were quickly unloaded, and Night Sister took on board some small casks and trunks with more arranged on a line tied to the stern, to float behind their boat.

"Hurry now," said the Miller, "the tide will be with you soon." As they went back down, they could still feel hearts pumping fast. They would hear what had happened back in the reeds in the coming days. The Riding Officer may have escaped with his life if he had not seen them all that he could identify them or was one who could be bribed. It was either that or he was drowned, and on the way to one of the older mineshafts that littered the area, never to be seen again. This was often the safer choice if smugglers were disturbed and could be subsequently identified. The riverbank close to the Inn at Polbathic was their return unloading destination. They were wary as they slipped down the Tamar and went westwards past the turning to the Tiddy river and along the flats. They need not now have worried. As they approached the small stone bridge where the waters shallowed, familiar shapes were waiting, and they were soon emptied. They kept their silence on the return to the other bank where Hannibal would leave to get home and grab some sleep, for it was a hard day at the quarry ahead. As he went to get out of the boat Christian looked at him intently and he her. They held each other for the first time. They had shared that night in a secret that would be scarce spoken about again. The embrace stirred them both and they knew that this was the start of something that would not end that night.

"I know you were robbed of your Sampson and I may never be him to you. My wife was taken from me untimely too but if you are ready for me now, I will be ready for you." Christian replied with her coy smile, head bowed and slanted slightly to one side, eyes straining up towards him, eyelids raised. The accompanying smile that gradually broadened said more than a worded reply was capable of. Heart beating as hard against his chest as it had when they were up in the reeds, Hannibal quickened his pace along the track to his quarry worker's home. The occasional jump heavenward combined with the hurling of his fist as high as he could into the air gave away his feelings of delight. He exuded a sense that all was good and well with the world and this permeated the air he walked through. He continued to hoard his share of night time work, for it might be needed if things were to go further with Christian. He was older than her but not too much and not too little. He could get them a bigger and better boat. He could get involved with the more lucrative sea runs to Roscoff,

Guernsey and others. She could stop taking these risks. All possibilities entered his mind as he conjectured on what life might be like.

The next day saw rare visitors to the quarry from the big house on the Skelton lands. It was Mrs. Ann, with her sister-in-law, the Miss Elizabeth. Ann had been widowed of late. Her husband, Richard, son of Thomas Skelton, had also died recently.

They had come to see how the quarry was running and to fly the flag with the workers there. The quarry stone was in demand for building and remained profitable. There were a few Skelton quarries in the vicinity as well as others owned by the larger estates. Around thirty worked all their quarries at any time. Several of their nearby homes were provided by the estate and built from the quarried stone. Building sand was taken from nearby beaches and washed for use as a component in the mortars. Lime was made at the nearby kilns.

Chapter 9

A Trematon Marriage

It was little surprise when Hannibal and Christian announced they were to marry. They had worked together increasingly and were frequently seen together. 24th March 1761 was the date set for their wedding.

When the day came, the Church at St Stephens was filled with well-wishers, including those who made it their business and entertainment to attend all services in the Church for whomever and whatever they might be held. Today it was to witness the wedding of Hannibal and Christian. There were estate workers from Anthony who had crossed the river, walking the short climb from Forder to the Church. Fishing folk and smugglers from Cawsand and Kingsand who had come around by boat from the villages. There were quarrymen from the Skelton and other quarries, with some of the Innkeepers too. The news had travelled with the jungle drums of the smuggling community, up and down the Tamar and across to Hannibal's home village of South Tawton. His brothers had arrived for the occasion, their first time this far south. The biggest surprise was the sight of Black Bird tethered outside of the churchyard. The news had reached Tetcott as well. Hannibal knew Black Bird right away. There had been a few Black Birds as the Squire's steed, always imposing. Bred to please the Squire of Tetcott, Squire Arscott's need for consistency with his horses was legendary.

The latest Squire of Arscott had made the journey down and brought Joseph. A full day's ride, he had planned to stay firstly with Ann Skelton at Stoketon, then onto the Anthony estate to do some hunting in their area. He had not forgotten the bond that had forged those years before and wanted to witness the start of Hannibal's new life. The wretched dress that Christian may have once worn for such an occasion had given way to a true example of the best in French finery.

Smugglers who worked from the coast at Kingsand and Cawsand had settled on helping the couple on their way with a few surprises.

"Try this on for size." The French merchant's man from Morlaix spoke in his broken English to his Cornish customer. At the same time, he wiped the beads of Ale that had dribbled down the side of his face when the rim of the pewter tankard holding his sustenance missed his lips. This was an understandable failure, for his lips were cracked and swollen from the brawl he had been in earlier at the Roscoff tavern where he had been waiting for the Cawsand boat. The boat was prepared and being loaded now for its return. Stowed well on board this time would be not only the uncustomed range of fine alcoholic drinks but also a cargo of even finer proportions. This cargo was a dress of fine silks and furs from the Paris clothiers. The Cawsand man leered across to the Frenchman as he started to take it from its protective wrapping.

"It's too good for you to handle for any longer than you need to. We don't want to take this back stinking of you, your whores and ale."

With that the two men shouted to the wench close by to fill their tankards as they slammed them down, drinking to free trade and the whores of Roscoff. The Frenchman replaced the section of dress he had removed.

The dress travelled back with the Smuggler, handled with considerable care when compared with the rough treatment of the tubs. Back it went to the Cawsand village where it went into the temporary care of the Spillers. Sarah Spiller took it on herself to open the crate, check it over and to make any small repairs as necessary.

Sarah was elderly now but possessed a deftness when it came to the use of the needle and thread. She had few competitors and was unrivalled in the locality. Her skills to patch and rectify were not to be needed here, however. This dress was in fine order. Even the putrid smell of the French merchant's man had lifted from the sleeve he had touched earlier. She held it against her.

"The Night Sister will like this," she stammered quietly, with a satisfied smile that showed itself as she rocked backwards on the rocking chair with the dress now carefully folded and balanced on her lap.

And the Night Sister did. The morning of her wedding Christian had put on the fine cloth with the help of her family and friends at home. They had made her a wedding garland to take with her and wear away from the Church after the wedding ceremony itself was over. The garland was mainly of rosemary and roses. The sweet fragrances would travel the pews of the Church and gently compete with those of the bouquets they had made too for the Bride's Maids.

Those attending were provided for as well. They would receive small bouquets when they came into the Church, to hold and provide colour that would contrast with the dark wood of the Church pews. Candles had been brought to provide a soft light that would complement the stronger light from outside that was determined to peep through the stained glass.

Predominantly yellow, the dress had been made in the latest fashion for the time. She had not expected this. It had been wrapped with great care by Sarah Spiller in some old, but well washed and clean, sack cloth, stitched around, to ensure the dress would stay as pristine as the day it was made when it was received.

"You take care of that," she rasped at Richard and the small crew who were going to row it around the evening previous to the wedding, along with a few other treats. By sea and river, the journey presented fewer obstacles, although not a direct route. As the crow would fly, it could be no more than a few miles and if it were possible to walk it in a straight line, a couple of hours might have done it.

It was an hour's hard row across the bay, past the fish palaces, tiny quays, the stretch of red sand beach towards and around the headland of Mount Edgcumbe with its Church at Maker standing high above. The boat then headed up the river Tamar turning in to the St Germans river inlet just before Saltash. The next turning was Forder Creek. Shortly afterwards the dress arrived safely at its final destination.

Yellow was the up and coming colour of fashion for those who could afford such things. Not seen much outside of the large town and country estates where the fashion news from London had made a successful migration.

Christian felt the Lady today. Lady Christian Wyvell was marrying her Captain - Captain Hannibal Marks.

"I should be Lady Wyvell of Wyvellscombe really Hannibal, and you, why you should be marrying her today."

"Wyvellscombe?" Hannibal had a puzzled look.

"Yes, you've been to the quarry there. We have used it. The estate house is up from the river. The quarry lies close by. It's up from the inlet there, you'll know, we've been past enough times."

His curiosity grew. "And why should that be?"

"It's been the family estate for generations at Wyvellscombe.

We stayed in the area not too far off when my family lost out in a will. I was told that a while ago now. Since then we ended up with nothing really apart from the name."

"Do you know them?"

Christian looked at him with a forlorn expression. "Yes, they know me and where I'm from, but that does nothing any good unless I should want to work for the estate. Then it might bring me favours.

"You'll have to tell me all about it sometime. So, I am marrying gentry and above me."

"Oh yes, Hannibal Marks. Can't you tell, I've inherited the breeding! Not quite a thoroughbred, but those ways can still shine through. You will see later!" Her wicked, nonchalant expression combined with the drawl her voice adopted, when she uttered those last few words, excited him.

With that she flung her head back, releasing a shock of shiny, auburn hair She looked in the Wyvellscombe direction. To see her now was indeed to see the Lady of Wyvellscombe. It was only on closer examination that the features of her day to day life shone through. To hold Christian's hands was to hold the hands, small that they were, of one who knew how to work. These were not hands that had ever known nurturing to ensure they were soft and smooth to touch. Soft and smooth were not words that could be used to describe the hands of Christian and she was proud of that. Hands that had been toughened and calloused from the ropes and rough wood with which she worked daily, hands that were not to be trifled with. The salt water, the rocks, the sands, had all played their part in moulding these, the most hardworking of her tools. Her face had a weather-beaten beauty that had given her a pallor of well-being. Her smile came with a few premature lines that ran across from the sides of her eyes into that shock of hair, revealing themselves fully only when blown back in a strong wind. Clear chestnut eyes shone through with a mischief that was not uncommon with the smugglers, blending but contrasting enough with her tanned skin. Her cheek bones high and chin only slightly squared at the bottom she was a woman with a natural attractiveness. Whatever trials life might throw at her to thwart this, nature's beauty, were destined to fail.

"I will be the Lady and you will be the Gentleman, the Gentleman in waiting for his estate by marriage, the Manor of Wyvellscombe, its lands and buildings."

"To the Gentleman and the Lady of Wyvellscombe."

"Captain Hannibal Marks, Captain-in-waiting for his Night Sister."

Hannibal, not sure whether to believe her or not, joined in on the game as they prepared for the short Church ceremony that would join them.

It was quite a walk to the Church from her home and when Christian left, she was followed by a small procession of friends and family. She stood out amongst the dark and light brown hues of the sackcloth that adorned most of those following.

The procession gathered strength as she continued down the tracks, paths and roads trying not to get the bright daffodil coloured dress too dusty or muddy. Several had handfuls of corn and seed that they threw over Christian along the way.

This was a happy day. As she approached and saw Black Bird, she knew that her husband-to-be would be happy. There was no other horse like this in this area. It could only be him, the young Squire Hannibal had spoken so fondly of to her. No longer the young Squire, but the Squire.

She had only heard of the Squire and his friends from the days he had been in Launceston. So too of Hannibal's family.

In many ways she felt she knew the Squire already as he and his antics had been the subject of many a conversation they had whilst on Night Sister. This had been his previous life and she was now his new. Her mind could not help wandering to what he might think of her by comparison with his previous wife.

Was she prettier than Joan? Was she taller? Was she bigger around? Who did he love the more? What would his son Joseph think of her? All these things quickly raced through her mind, but not for long. As she took her place next to Hannibal for the short ceremony, she wondered what he might have brought for her as a symbol of their betrothal. She did not have to wait long to find out ......"and I pronounce you man and wife" finished the Vicar of St. Stephens Church. With that, Hannibal gave her one half of a broken coin, keeping the other half for himself. This was though no ordinary small coin.

The gold coin, which was to symbolise their marriage, was a gold crown and would be hidden safely by her. For now, it would be tucked into her dress. She would with haste sew it in to keep it safe for now

Flush faced, the two left the Church to the low-lying gentle hum of the whispers of those attending. In the pew closest sat John Arscott of Tetcott. He would behave himself today. To Hannibal's delight he had brought Joseph. This was an added incentive to him to be the Squire and at least for one day, this day, to make Hannibal proud. No apples to throw at the Vicar if a sermon or ceremony bored him and no pet toads or ravens accompanying him. Food neither for the church spiders was he carrying today. Other than Joseph, he had, this time, come alone.

Hannibal had now left the employ of the Skelton quarry as fishing by day and the attraction of other work on the waters of the area by night had increasingly appealed as his coffers started to swell. Nonetheless, accompanying John Arscott for the marriage was Ann, widowed wife of Nicholas Skelton.

She had got to know Hannibal who, though working at the quarry would also work sometimes at the Stoketon House. Ann had never found out what had happened to cement the friendship of her worker with the Arscott house, but the wedding combined with the few days John had said he would stay at Stoketon would give her plenty of chance to find out. This time together might quench her curiosity that had from time to time visited her. How had it come to be that the son and heir to the Squiredom of Tetcott would so welcome the company of one of the lower classes and take him into his lifelong care. She would prise this from John in the coming days.

Hannibal could not help casting back his mind to his wedding to Joan in Launceston those years back and to Joan herself. She had been his first love, but Christian was too in a way. He loved her no less. If Joan had not died would he be here now and how might his fortunes be?

Would they have had more children and what now might they be doing? But no, this was not the time to ponder on such things that did not and could not now happen. This was their wedding day. The wedding of Hannibal and Christian, or he smiled to himself, Captain Hannibal Marks of the good ship Night Sister and Lady Christian Wyvell of Wyvellscombe.

Christian though could read his thoughts as they strolled down the hill to their new home at Forder creek and the location of their wedding celebrations.

"Is it the same as before Hannibal? When you were in Launceston?"

"Do you think of what might have been with Sampson when he was taken from you. Is this the same?"

"I asked you first !"

With that she laughed and started to run down the hill with her husband following close behind. Catching her up and lifting her high he looked at her hard. "Maybe today is the not the day to be sombre. This is the new life and we should respect those that we knew before but know that they would be wishing us happiness. We will all be together again soon enough." With that they spent a while sitting and looking to the valley below to their home. They were lucky. They were here to tell the tales and start again. She had never been to Launceston or Tetcott so other than what she had been told by Hannibal and the appearance of Joseph, it remained a life that had been and gone. One in which she had no part. This was indeed a new beginning.

The hill was a steep one to get down to the Forder hamlet. They had turned left from the Church, downwards into the fields and through the wood that ran up from the banks of the creek.

As the water began to peek at them through the trees so the sound of the peeling bells started to fade into the distance. Christian knew these bell ringers and they had turned out to give the couple a peel whilst at the same time honing their skills ready for the competitions that were ahead of them that summer.

The ringers believed they were in line to win and might walk away with a prize or two for their ringing. Stumbling over the tree roots that poked up randomly, often with little warning along the path, they could hear all the way, the hubble and bubble of the wedding party following behind.

The party had left a short distance between them to let the couple take the lead to the Inn and green where the celebrations would take place at the water's edge.

The couple's work with the smugglers was to pay off further that day as the drink flowed from barrels of some of the best that had been kept back from the latest runs. Teas and tobaccos too were in plentiful supply. The throng of happy folk making merriment included many of those from all the leading fishing and smuggling families in the area. The Dunstans, Chapells, Spriddells, Spillers, Cocks, Edmunds and Jagos were there to name but a few.

That night was a glorious one, remaining so into the early hours when eventually even the late revellers gave in to the need to rest, taking to the cottages, houses and Inns of the area. Others would sleep under their carts with the few gentlefolk there returning to their residences with their guests before darkness fell.

The new marriage, alongside a living coming now more from the free trade than the quarry, it had been the time to leave the quarry employ.

Leaving the quarry work had meant leaving the rooms Hannibal had occupied there. The little dwelling used by Sampson and Christian had been maintained. Christian's brothers and sisters remained there with one of her sister's gaining employ in one of the big houses in Sheviock where she went to reside.

Her brothers started to help Hannibal with the runs, repairing the boat and learning how to fish for the types of fish found in the lower Tamar regions.

Hannibal and Christian had taken a small cottage at Forder not far away by river from the dwelling near Sheviock to the west.

* * *

It was not long before the Marks house was to see a new arrival.

"It's time Hannibal. This baby wants to come and come now," she cried with beads of sweat pouring from her forehead.

The cottage in Forder had witnessed many births into the world before this one, and many deaths too. Hannibal's thoughts raced to the birth of Hammond and the death of Joan that day. He quickly went off to get Martha who had helped to safely deliver many babies in Forder and the surrounding area.

As the two hurried back down the Hill to the cottage and entered, they heard the familiar cry of a newly born baby. Leaping up the rough-cut wooden stairs, and jumping over some two at a time, he entered the room closely followed by Martha.

Martha had arrived panting, for she was a large woman who nearly touched both sides of the small stairway walls as she clambered up. They had heard no sound from Christian. All Hannibal could think of was that night with Joan. That last night.

The door flung open. There they were. Hannibal rushed over to her side. Martha came over to the bedside.

"Now come on Mr. Hannibal. Make way and don't crowd her. She needs rest and this baby needs to make its own way now in the world and cut this tie with its mother."

"It's a girl, Hannibal. It's a girl."

"And she looks healthy, as does her mother. Now go on with you Hannibal Marks. Leave us alone to get cleaned up. The poor dear has done this all on her own and so quick. A first child and so quick, so quick it's been."

Martha was surprised. She had expected a day and a night of it if not longer. There was though nothing for her to do other than to make sure mother and baby were well. Hannibal went below, singing the news through the cobbled pathways of the village, gliding along as he went. Out and back again. They were both alive. They were both well.

"Where have you been, Hannibal Marks? Get some water I asked. Hot if you can. Come along now." The two women smiled to each other upstairs. "Start as you mean to go on, I say. He may work hard but when he's here he can do something ... and while you are like this ... in bed ... he can do more than usual."

Baby Ann was followed in quick succession by two brothers, both healthy and well. William was named after Christian's father for whose untimely passing she lamented every day.

"How they would all wish to know them, Hannibal."

The next born was to carry the name of Hannibal's choice. Hannibal 2nd entered the world at 2.30 in the morning and was the largest child yet.

"This one is going to be like his father. Look at his jaw and the size of his hands. He is another Hannibal Marks alright."

Two years were to pass before Sarah was to arrive and another two before Hannah. It was after that when Mr. and Mrs. Hannibal Marks,

Captain Marks as he became known to her and Lady Wyvell as she became known to him, finally made their move to Cawsand. Hannibal worked increasingly alone as the children were reared and Christian pulled back somewhat from her position as the Night Sister of the smugglers.

Chapter 10

Call to Cawsand

The silence that came with that unique blend of some of nature's best, that dark curtain of night accompanied by a breeze so slight it bare filled the sails.

It was this that prompted the crew on the Cawsand Smuggler to fill their lungs with the salt air and raise their spirits with a rendition of a well-rehearsed song.

Mid Channel they were, well stocked, they knew there was little danger in this stretch of the sea of their being heard. Besides they kept a good look out and were part of a flotilla of three small Cawsand boats that had been loaded and left close on each other.

They had departed Cawsand and Kingsand, leaving at different times and arranging to meet close to the west of the lightship moored at Eddystone.

A new lighthouse was being built which would replace the temporary lightship but for now it served as not only a warning light but as a rendezvous point or bearing they could use for one.

To make the journey across to and fro Roscoff in sight of each other was to provide some added safety from pirates or others looking to disrupt the run. Staying in sight of each other they could keep watch and warn the others of anything untoward on the seas.

The run over had been trouble free and they hoped the return would be the same.

"Come on Hannibal, you must know it by now. You've been on a few of these night runs. It's about time you got that wife of yours and little uns out from that River and over to us and the open waters."

Closer now to the heartbeat of the smuggling industry in the area, Cawsand and Kingsand, but with easy access to the rivers and knowledgeable of them, Hannibal had started doing more first hand with the smugglers there.

With this came the chance and trust to go on more of the larger scale runs and meet with the dealers around the coast of Brittany and sometimes Guernsey in the Channel Islands.

One of the crew opened the first verse. It was Zacharias. His voice was the strongest, the lowest in tone. It had a growl that came from deep down. As the oldest member of the crew, Zach or Zachy, as he was known, had seen many things on the water and had been part of some of the early rowing crews. A tough old dog, he had completed several run-ins with the Excise and was known all down the south coast of Cornwall as well as North Brittany.

There were few Inns that didn't know the voice of Zachy and that small wide shape that was uniquely his.

'It's time to drop your sails lads, 'tis time to take an oar

Slide 'n through the rowlocks then take us to the shore

Give 'em a blink, if two come back, five counts then a three

We'll know the coast is clear for us as we scat to Penlee

As he finished on a long Penleeeee the entire crew launched in :

"No more lights, and quiet now, as we run in on the tide

Cut the ropes on the kegs we tow, and those along our side

Back we go, pull our boat, round Cawsand way and fetch

Our nets and pots for fishing, till nightfall hits our ketch"

With that Zachy returned :

"They'll all be there, my booties, ankers too, be damned

Customs men keep well away, or your cutters will be rammed

Like sinking stones, down you'll go, keep watch down in the deep

Have a good sup on us then .... if the kegs of brandy weep"

A dig in the ribs prompted Hannibal to have a go at taking the lead in the next bit .

"So, look lively, look quietly, no noise you must make

Muff your blades and be well sure you make no mistake

Then race to the beach, and hit the shores,

Before Hannibal could continue, a rasping voice finished the verse, shouting,

Legs at the ready for the Tavern's whores

The entire crew followed through then until the end of the song and with great gust.

"The kegs'll be well underground, looked after with tender care
Ready for our merchants, Inn-keepers, the usual pair
For we looks after our Parsons, for they looks after us
Lordies too deserve our best, Cognacs and teas a must

Excise will to Barn Pool, from whence the light did glow
Signs we use take us somewhere else for us to know
So, haul lads, haul, keep those leathers greased
No creaks no groans no letting up, its later you will feast

So bugger off you Customs men, don't come hurrying back
Leave the coast unwatched, and we might leave a sack
Full of goodies for you, your missus, father and more
Lots is there if you stay clear of our fishermen's store"

With that their pitchers were raised high, clashed together, creating and joining up the dents this rough treatment gave the soft pewter metal they were made from. The men, the comrades, yet again pledged loyalty to each other, drank to free trade, to the safety and deliverance of those who plied the seas for it.

"I think it's high time we made a move and made all your lives a misery now Zachy. So where are we going to stay if we move on into Cawsand? Can't be with you, not with all that smoke and smell you make?"

With that the ship's company took delight. Zachy was well known for his continual pipe smoking, from a pipe, the largest any had seen. They said its bowl could hold more, fine baccy than his tankard could fine spirit!

"Hssh now all of you what is that in the distance? Can you see it through the dark and as the moon catches it?"

"It's a way off, whatever it is."

"Remember a boat was washed up of late with no one on it and we have had a few come close. It's those Pirates. Those Corsairs."

"They don't dare come into the towns any more. We're ready for them if they do. They come ashore, that's the end of them. We'd let them have it."

"Yes, time was we have been told that they would come ashore when the towns were just a few huts, stores, small cottages and take off the men as slaves. Never heard of no more."

"They do it at sea now if they get half a chance. The boats are big and lots on them. If they take you, they chain you down they say, and take you off a long way."

"Grandfather told us of when they came once and went through the alleys and courtyards with clubs, swords and knives. Fire too. As they came through Grandfather's they were waiting for them. One by one they jumped them from the top of the walls and slit their throats. Grandfather brought his club down on top of one as he jumped down. He cracked his head right open. The other men were waiting too and when they were in the alleys came from behind and got them."

"I heard about that one. They took their clothes and went out on their landing boat to their bigger boat where there were not many of them, managed to get on board and killed the rest of them. They took the boat."

"What did they do with her?"

"Plundered her well. It's where those swords and knives came from you see here. You can tell them apart from their shape. The boat was broken and used to build cottages."

"They wouldn't come in far with the Navy ships here. Let them try it with a man o war in the Bay?"

"Shhhh. Sound travels on the water. Haul around and let's get from here. Send signal to the others."

"I can only make out one of ours. We lost sight of the other a while backalong."

A silence fell as they moved her around and headed as quickly as they could. The reef was in site now and with a fair wind they would be in soon.

"Look she is gaining water on us. Wonder what she is?"

"There's one of our boats. But her sails are flapping and she's lolloping around."

"She's towards that bigger ship. Should we go and see what is going on with her?"

"Best to. But be lively and quiet."

"There's no one on her and where's the load that was on her decks?"

"Be quick. Let's board her."

"It's difficult in this swell."

"Forget boarding her. There's no one on decks."

"She's empty."

"Look that boat is gaining on us. She's seen us."

"Make wind and let's away. Signal the others."

"I can see that ship making more water on us but still can't see what she's like. A bit closer and we might."

"I don't like the look of this. One of ours with nothing on. Heavy swell, no storm. Where are they?"

"That ship is something to do with it."

"Its shape is not one of ours. Whatever it is, I don't like it. This is trouble."

"I wager it's got ours on it. They would have taken our boat if it had been the Customs. It's not one of their Cutters. Look we can make out the shape."

"She's a slaver. That's an old boat. It's got oar holes down the side. I'll swear it."

"Ours are on there. What can we do?"

"Not much against that."

"We are near the reef. The lightship. Let's put out the light. There's a big swell. Can we draw her onto the reef? They won't see the start of the lighthouse, it's too small."

"We've got one musket here. We'll use it to take the light."

"Your shot had better be a good one."

The crack was loud, but it worked. The glass shattered in the night air and the lights soon fell to darkness. The large candlewicks gave in to the strength of the wind. There was no sign of any emerging boatman who would light and tend to the candles nor ensure the ship remained secured.

"Must have been those ankers we left them from the last run."

A smile, fuelled more by anxiety than good humour, went across their otherwise lined and haggard faces.

"Now we are on more even odds. We know this reef and seas better than most others. We know where we dare go on this tide and where we might have a chance of getting over or to the side but only just. We know just by looking at that ship, if she follows, she will catch the rocks."

"If she does, then what do we do?"

"If we're going to do this, we will have to get closer to her and sail her in with us. Outrun her, but only just, either over the reef at the east end in this swell and tide where we know we might just do it or move away from the reef last thing before she can turn."

The two boats converged, exchanging their instructions. They would sail close on each other and tempt this ship.

"Steer south west, then to the east making fast and straight towards the reef at that eastern side. Miss her altogether, I say."

"Will they take a chance in the swells and the high tides to go over?"

There was a place if they could get it right where, with their relatively shallow draft, they could do it on this tide, if and only if, they caught everything right. As they neared, they knew it was a pirate slaver.

"Our people if they are chained or tied could die in this too?"

"Here's the place. Pray for our salvation and their damnation."

The pirate slaver was close on them, but it was clear the Captain had decided not to launch a smaller boat. A smaller boat would now have little chance of catching them let alone successfully gaining control over the smugglers. Even if the Pirate had been armed with stolen canon, she would have been unlikely to catch the Smugglers with shot.

No, they needed to board if they were to take them and their kegs. It was them they were interested in. They would see them as easy prey. They would be thinking if there were three boats with potential slaves on, there would be more. This was a good hunting ground for them tonight. In their eyes they would have caught a shoal here, a shoal of men, a shoal of slaves.

The pirate Captain must have smelt the scent of the chase and on the reef his ship went. Luck was with the smugglers that night. The lighthouse not complete, the lightship able to be put out, both had worked to their favour. This combined with the right tides and swell of the seas had smiled sweetly on them. But what of the others? Their minds turned to their friends and accomplices.

They placated themselves with the sure knowledge that the life of a slave was a worse life than a death by drowning. Chained in the bowels of a ship to row until exhausted, then beaten until they rowed again or died, that was indeed worse than death.

The two smuggling vessels slowed, watched and listened. There was confusion, shouts and screams as they saw her twisting and lurching. The cracks in her wooden frame broke up the vessel further as the rocks went in. People were in the water. These were the slavers most likely, who were free of chains. They could not hold onto weapons and they could see as they approached that they were struggling in their heavy garments.

These pirates could not get on their smuggling vessels with any ease. The smugglers got their poles ready to dig them deep in the water as they picked out the exhausted ones.

"Look there's one trying to hold on to the rudder."

"He's for me," shouted Hannibal, as he went astern with one of the bats the batmen would use. Looking his foe straight in the eye, seeing his fear, he paused for a second. As the pirate lurched his body upwards from the sea, Hannibal lost his trepidation and humanity, swinging the bat with all his might catching the man with its thin ridge on the side of his head. His grip on the rudder couldn't hold and as his consciousness was lost, he slipped into the water once more, this time head down. More followed. They could see many could not swim and down they went, their cries unheeded.

"Any there clinging on, drag up over the gunwales and smack them like we do the conger, again and again until their heads are to atoms."

"But what of their companions?"

The ship silenced, the screams and shouting abating until there was no more noise from the lower sections of the ship. She was taking on water and lurching to one side. Feeling increasingly confident, they went closer and closer to the reef where the stricken ship lay. Pirate bodies were everywhere. Where they were struggling to swim in the cold seas, the smugglers went around and around gazing at them but leaving them to God's fate now.

It would not be long and very unlikely any would have the strength to swim to the shore or be washed up alive. There was little rock to stay on and the cold would soon get them.

"That's them. Look !"

There were six bodies lashed together, not chained but roped, hands and feet. They had enough space between the rope to tread the sea with arms, legs and feet. There were some others roped together too, not far off. They knew not these poor souls, but they would, after seeing to their own, go to them if they could.

The rope ladder was put down the side of the boat Hannibal was on and the sail having been dropped, the boat was punted towards them with caution.

Keeping a distance, one of the smugglers lowered himself into the water with a rope secured to the boat. He quickly got to them and tied the rope onto one which joined the hands of two of them. He proceeded to go around them, taking his knife to each in turn to cut the ropes that held them. With help, they clambered on board the Smuggler boat.

He could not get to the rope between the legs but had freed the arms. The men had little strength left in them. The pieces of driftwood they had clung to as best they could, went free. As the men tried to get onto the boat, they found that there was not enough rope between them to haul one man up, cut him free and then see to the next while the others bobbed by the side of the boat. Their strongest swimmer went down into the dark with his knife to feel the ropes and, with as much care and dexterity as time would allow, cut the ropes under the water. The knife was sharp, very sharp.

The men's legs were kicking, especially those furthest from the side of the boat, kicking to keep afloat. A more blunted knife would not have taken the rope. Sodden, tough and thick twine, knots having pulled together and tightened further, this was a difficult task. One false cut or slip might take a man's artery. One by one was released and pulled on board, shivering, pale, lips trembling and unable to speak, the boat lurched more and more. Finally, they were all freed, boarded and were made safe.

The other Smuggler had gone to the other men in the water who were fishermen from further down the Cornish coast. It turned out that they were Cadgwith boys and had gone out further earlier that day. Their boat was small, and they were taking in pots for crab and lobster when the pirates struck.

One of the six on this string of rope died. If he had died before he may have taken the other men with him, but he had stayed alive for long enough, despite his wounds and broken limbs. Thrown clear with the others he had not been so fortunate and had caught the full impact of a section of the Pirate boat as it broke away, crashing into the seas around the reef and into some of the men in the sea.

They told them that the others were chained below to row and there was no one as a slave that had been able to move free. Their chains were linked and chained again to the bulkheads of the ship. Those taken that day were roped together but not chained. There was most likely no further chain to be had.

The pirate ship was nearly full to bursting point.

"There'll be provisions and perhaps gold and silver for us if we go to the wreck and try to board her."

"We dare not. She is moving and breaking further. She will go down. She's full of water and even if she stays for a while ...."

They watched the ship slide and turn on the reef as they shifted sail to return to the Bay, keeping close to the shore and the rock line. The sign at the Pemberknowse was there as they came across the Cellars and towards the Girt beach.

They had lost a boat and a load in the end that night, but not one smuggler. They brought their vessel in close to the shore. The unloaders were at the ready. They had received the sign and knew no one was to interfere with their business tonight. Just in case they were going to bring the boat into the edge of the little cove that led up to the Inn on the hill. A tunnel went up from here. The tide was out so they could anchor up in enough depth of water. They could get close in so that the small ankers they had on board could be passed down on strings and dragged to shore, up through to the Inn from where they would be distributed in the village, hidden, just in case, and moved on the next night.

The men, who were wet and wounded from cuts, bruised muscles and limbs that had been pressed hard together when in captivity, were got off the Smuggler and back to their dwellings. Those who were not from the villages were given sanctuary until they were healed and ready to go again.

Anchored up, Hannibal walked through the village which in places was still awake, but for most, still in slumber. He had a lucky escape that night. Maybe he should stop now, return to the work he had done thus far. Maybe he was simply not really cut out for this side of the smuggling trade. The additional reward he could earn, was it worth it? Was it worth his life? If he were to do this work, he would need to go much further. Yes, take the risks but put the reward aside. Put it aside to own a share in the boat, maybe a whole boat or more.

The future was in armed boats. They were bigger, safer and fully equipped to store and transport large amounts of contraband. Yes, that was the future. He could set the foundation for his children and children's children.

Hannibal had a keen understanding of time and place and where he was within it. Not an educated man but a man who could perceive things. A man who could listen and learn. A man who knew this was his place in the scheme of things. He knew it was to be he who would take advantage of the times and opportunities being laid before him. It was his time to found and forge the future for the next ones. His time might not be for much longer, but it might. In any event, he felt as if he were a man much younger than his actual years. Yes. This was his purpose. This was why he was here. Yes, he could live here too. He was still strong and in good health. He might, God willing, have years remaining to take his chances and build his fortune.

There were piles of cut stone, uncut stone, lime, rubble and timber strewn along everywhere. There was a lot of building going on here. Pulling down of cottages too, making room for the bigger houses. Some of the little cottages were in behind the bigger houses now. They were starting to join up, forming lines of houses without a break at their fronts. The tiny cottages behind were still lived in. What would happen to these ...and the folk inhabiting them? Many of the old cottages were built into the cliffs where sections of cliffside had been flattened out for them to be built on with working courtyards in the middle providing security and safety. This was a time of change, a time of opportunity here.

Every other house was an Inn, Tavern, unlicensed premises or occupied by vendors of provisions of all kinds. It was early. No one much was about.

He was too old now for the pressmen to take an interest in him, so he was confident to walk the streets alone and unhindered. They would now have to be really short of sailors for the fleet to consider taking him.

The gauntlet was down. Hannibal and his family were ready to make the move or at least he thought his wife would be. She was from the St. Stephens and Saltash area so a move to Cawsand..... well she knew folk here and Forder wasn't too far.

If there were more boats leaving to return to Roscoff he was there willing and ready to go. That work carried the best pay. If not, he was ready for tub carrying the next night or work with the mules. There was always somewhere for Hannibal to rest his head for the night if there was plenty of free trade work around.

He could stay with Zachy, if he could stand his pipe, or in one of the barns on the edge of the village. The farms knew him now and occasionally he would be hired to put some work in there while waiting for work to move a run.

If conditions were right, Night Sister might be loaded as well and head up the river from Cawsand. Depending on the winds, he would either go from the villages and around the point nearing Drake's Island, or if his boat were at the creek at Millbrook, he would take her from there on the right tide. Night Sister was small, nimble and did not attract much interest, but she was large enough and designed in such a way that he could always sleep on her in the open if the weather was fair. She didn't make for a good night but if he was tired ... well he could sleep anywhere. Besides he didn't need a lot of sleep when there was money to be earned.

His pay for this run would come later when the Captain had done his business. It would go back with him to the new hiding place he had for it at their home at Forder. He would still continue to hoard his pay outs and shares. He would not see it all go back into the Inns, Ale and Whore houses just for the profit of others. He drank with them all but most of his money was kept. Hannibal had different things in mind for it. He could never have kept back money like this from any other work.

Chapter 11

The Marks Arrive

"Look lively lad, oars, stays, ropes and nets. Mind to keep them nets even." The young Hannibal, Hannibal 2nd, was now in his sixteenth year. He had woken to a booming voice calling to him from below. Looking out of the window, clearing his sleep blurred eyes, he saw a strongly built man with a lad of no more than twelve years of age in the courtyard area below.

The boy was gathering up items needed for the morning's fishing. Hannibal perched his hands on the window ledge, leaning out as far as he dare, to take it all in, ensuring at the same time that he did not make an unceremonious arrival at work by falling. A fall onto the pile of nets lying below the window might though have offered the chance of a softer landing than he could have otherwise expected from a fall onto the cobbles underneath and surrounding the nets. The cobbled courtyard was made of medium sized, well rounded beach pebbles broken roughly into halves. These were the cobbles. The flatter halves were pushed into the soft sandy, earthy ground beneath and packed tightly against each other in patterns. The pattern running around the edges of the yard, held in with larger stones, created a shallow gulley. This gulley allowed rain water, that had been channelled into it, the opportunity to flow, uninterrupted, along the cobbles to the street outside. Many of the local beach pebbles had formed from the very hard red volcanic rock, plentiful in the area. Smoothed or not by the passage of time and tide, these hard, beach worn, cobbles, would still provide a rough and uncomfortable landing to a fallen Hannibal Marks.

Hannibal was known to be a good sleeper as well as willing worker and as soon as woken would be up, ready to go. He had got to know the busy villages of Cawsand and Kingsand from a young age when he would accompany his father there. Cawsand and Kingsand were in fact still villages, and separate ones at that, but increasingly adopted the nickname of "the town" or “the towns."

Success in the fishing and smuggling industries continued relentlessly, pushing the villages to develop at a strong pace. There had been nothing like it since their expansion over a hundred years previously. It was then fuelled primarily by the strength of the local fishing industry. The high cost of local taxation to Plymouth based merchants had fuelled the building of the Kingsand and Cawsand cellars, the fish palaces, with the development of additional buildings needed to service their activities and provide homes for those working in them. Still in use to process the fish and build the boats, the previous spaces left between these working buildings and dwellings had mostly been filled in now.

Land close to the beaches, in ever reducing supply, could be leased at a premium. Dwellings, often with drinking establishments of one kind or another on the ground floor, were filling most spaces left between buildings.

Development was swift and uncompromising. As a consequence, the physical division between the two villages became ever more blurred. Those visiting could be forgiven for seeing an emerging small town. Kingsand and Cawsand still provided the boundary line between Devon and Cornwall. This, the arbitrary boundary forced by King and Parliament, continued to defy the natural boundary of the Tamar River that flowed just a short distance away.

Money was pouring in from seemingly ever-increasing naval activities off the shores. The demand for fish, and even higher demand for smuggled goods, raged with no sign of any abatement.

During his early years in the trade, Hannibal 1st had frequently speculated how the money from the free trade was distributed. He was determined, on reaching Cawsand and Kingsand, to work his way closer and closer to the main profit centres of the trade.

Determined was he to push his way to that centre if he had to, where the rewards matched the risks. The greatest reward went to those taking the greatest financial risks. These were the money men, those putting in the hard cash to finance the boats, the runs, the stock, the Investors.

Following close on their heels were those involved in the trading of smuggled goods on a wholesale and bulk basis, the Distributors.

Then came those facing at first hand the dangers of the open seas with responsibility for the large Smuggler boats, the Captains. The boat crew, tubmen, batmen, unloaders, they all took cuts.

Then came those providing storage and look outs.

Smaller boat owners daring the open seas were often many of these roles together, those working their way up to ownership of the larger boats or at least a part ownership.

Bribery, usually from the profits of the boat owners who would arrange and make the bribes, was not inconsiderable. Bribes were not always cash bribes, but the perks of receiving free contraband to bring life's luxuries to a household.

Zaccy had arranged rooms for the Marks family on their arrival in Cawsand, as he said he would those years back. It had taken a while for the family to make the move but it all eventually came to pass.

Night Sister brought Christian and their children down the Tamar to its mouth at Plymouth Sound, veering at the entrance to the west into the beach at Cawsand.

Hannibal arrived by horse and cart with the remainder of their belongings. They were now more at the centre of the operations. More opportunity. More risks. More money. Yes, more money for the family.

Here was their chance to take their enterprise and ambitions forward once again.

The young Hannibal 2nd was put to a trade to learn boatbuilding and fishing as well as learning to read and write well. He would have a good grounding to take on the growing Marks' smuggling and associated businesses one day. He was also going on more and more runs with his father and the others now, getting to know the smugglers and the secret network. Hannibal 2nd was indeed truly coming of age.

The Spillers were paid for the young Hannibal to lodge with them while he learnt their trades. The Spiller enterprises took in considerable breadth in the area. It was felt that it would be good for Hannibal 2nd to get a rounded education that would equip him well to take things forward from the point his father and mother had reached.

Some of the smaller boats were still built at the back of the Spiller houses. They could be carried when finished and taken to the beaches a short walk away. The stores and workshops at the rear also held some of the nets, pots and the like.

Smaller boats comprised the wide beamed strong twelve and sixteen footers, the day to day inshore working boats. These adaptable boats, though primarily for fishing and potting, would double up as the unloading boats.

These were the boats that would go to the large Smugglers that moored off the beaches and rock lined shores around the nearby coast. They would have returned from a run to France or the Islands of Jersey and Guernsey. These would be relieved of their goods, the contraband, as quickly as possible.

The long open boats, versatile in their design, equipped with both oars and sails, had been designed primarily for the early long-haul trips across the English Channel.

These stalwarts of the past fishing and smuggling successes had been giving way to considerably larger boats as the smuggling industry grew.

Insatiable demand consistently outstripped supply. The result was a prosperity that found its way into every household to some extent or other.

Every nook and cranny of the local economy was reached by the profits from smuggling.

Hannibal 2nd had been learning the boat building trade from ground up. He had started on the small boats and progressed to the larger boats.

The larger boats built by the Spillers were built just off the beach, originally outside but increasingly within the cellars that were adjacent to the water's edge, ready to be slipped to start their working lives.

These boats had become famed throughout Cornwall for their quality and design. The Spiller boats were ordered by prominent investors and smugglers throughout Cornwall. The cost of a boat could be recovered from the profits on its first run if all went to plan.

The demand had stepped up for boats that could provide innovative design that would fit the smugglers' purposes for the optimum efficiency.

The boatbuilders of Cawsand and Kingsand stepped up to meet this challenge and in doing so took the profits it could generate.

The reputation of the village for its smuggling vessels, the "Smugglers", rested on the design and quality of their boatbuilding.

Design that combined high capacity storage with cleverly concealed compartments, easily and quickly accessible.

Design that could provide a vessel capable of outrunning any Naval vessel or Customs cutter if the need arose.

Design that could carry armament as required to give a fighting chance when faced with conflict.

An uncompromising quality of build that outstripped the competition in Cornwall and its neighbouring County of Devon when it came to strength but with economy of materials should the boats be lost or impounded.

A boat, the cost of which was recoverable quickly in the event of loss.

A boat that could be replaced quickly if needs be.

This versatility saw boats introduced that could easily be used either as fishers or Smugglers. Boats that could be easily adapted when on the water to provide additional sail area that would give the cutting edge against any boat giving them chase.

These were the Cawsand boats. These were the Cawsand boatbuilders. These were the people, the Cawsand people who made the boats work hard and profitably in all weathers and conditions.

The young Hannibal Marks 2nd would soon Captain these boats.

He would have helped to build them, understanding them better because of his experience in design and build.

He would understand what design modifications might be made to make the future Marks' vessels that plied the seas amongst the best in their class.

He had been encouraged by his father to think, and think hard, as he was learning the trade. He challenged his son to think about the design of boats that the Marks could benefit from owning or having shares in.

He was encouraged to abandon no detail, abandon no ideas for improvement, however slight or far-fetched they might seem.

Hannibal 1st had always said it only took one small thing to make the difference in their trade and often it would be that which defined the difference between success and failure.

Hannibal 2nd had spent time learning all these trades and skills to underpin his future. Most of all he had learnt the smuggling trade, getting to know and build trust with people from the crews of the Smugglers to the unloaders, the batmen, the tubmen, then the forgers and the bankers who lurked in the background, underpinning the entire operation.

His education meant that he was a competent navigator, reader, writer. He understood currencies, exchange rates and had a smattering of French and Breton that could get him by with the merchants on the other side of the Channel in their own tongues.

He was getting ready to head up the second generation of Marks smugglers. It was the ability to forge these trusted relationships and know how to use, but not exploit them, that had enabled Hannibal Marks 1st to build their enterprise.

These were skills that were time served and had to rub off on Hannibal 2nd.

Hannibal 1st and his wife Christian had learned to cash in on the potential for selling some of the smuggled merchandise direct to the consumer through their own outlets and in doing so increase their margin of profit.

They had developed a keen sense of business and wherever an extra guinea was waiting to be made, the Marks were there, ready to trade and take the profit.

Things had come a long way since the days of South Tawton, Launceston, Trematon and Forder. Now, as the smuggling gold rush found its way to Cawsand and Kingsand, the Marks were poised, ready for their share of it, more besides if they could.

Hannibal 1st had continued to hoard the money they had made from smuggling runs and had enough to make a start with more of his own unloading boats running from Cawsand.

He could soon also make a start with a smaller but sturdy boat that could take on the Channel crossings and hold a good amount of stock.

With some luck and more cash behind him, shares in a larger vessel would be next and then his own. Maybe the Spillers could help to get a new boat built, to the specification of Hannibal 2nd and any credit extended could be repaid after the first successful run.

Father Hannibal 1st was now a spritely sixty-one years old, in good health and fitness, he was in his prime and poised to help move the enterprise on. He would promote the next Marks generation to take things much further again that he had been able to.

Hannibal 2nd emerged from the upper floor of the Spiller's house and was ready for the day's fishing. Everything was loaded in the Spiller boat ready to go. The stays were put in and the oars put into position and rested through them and inside the boat ready to pull away. The nets were put up the far end of the boat.

Another man suddenly appeared into view with two pots. "Don't forget these," he shouted at the boatmen. He deftly passed down the willow reed pots with rope and wood markers. They were placed precariously on top of the nets.

"Hannibal, Hannibal", was the shrill cry coming from the courtyard. Hannibal 2nd heard and hurried the few steps back to Spillers. The cries had come from Mary Spiller. Any excuse to catch the eye of the young Hannibal Marks, she had noticed he had left behind the spare thole pins for the boat.

All was very happy at Spillers' courtyard house where he lodged, from where he learnt his trades and skills. The time was fast approaching for Hannibal 2nd to return home. He had really learnt all he could from the Spiller enterprises. He was ready to take more responsibility for the Marks ventures which were growing quickly and spreading in influence. This was his time to take full advantage of the good times that had come to Cawsand Bay.

There was also the gregarious Mary Spiller to think

about. ....

Chapter 12

A Cawsand Marriage

"And what do you think you're doing here Hann? You know I'll be in for trouble if Mrs. Honor sees me here with you." Mary Spiller had been walking on the lower estate road collecting some wild flowers for the estate house where she worked.

The daffodils were out now, coming back every year in the same spot. The gardeners didn't cultivate here, and the mistress of the house was fond of some of the wild daffodils in her reading room. Mrs. Honor oversaw seeing to the flowers in the main house. She had entrusted the job of picking a small fresh bunch to Mary.

Hannibal had been across on the boat to Plymouth for his father and had seen Mary as they were approaching the Barn pool. On landing, he had jumped the stone wall that surrounded the estate to the seaward side. As the stone wall snaked around to the south of Barn pool it stared towards Drake's Island, eastward towards the Mewstone and to the open channel beyond. Rare was it that this side of the estate wall was manned or observed at this time of day. Here the wall was low-lying, and Hannibal went over it at its lowest point from the rocks below.

He moved quickly up through the woods making his mark in the bluebells as he went, coming to its edge where the daffodils were swaying in the breeze. There was a large tree at the edge, very close to the spot where Mary was busy picking her flowers. He stealthily crept up towards it, hiding behind its girth only yards from her. She was pre-occupied with her task, failing to hear the noise from a crack of a twig that he had broken underfoot on his approach. As she stooped to pick more for her basket he struck. Grabbing her round the waist firmly from behind he lifted her a few inches off the ground. The basket fell, and the daffodils scattered close by.

As she screamed, she brought her elbow crashing into his chest. Winded, he relaxed his grip and she turned towards him.

"It's you Hannibal Marks. I should have known. What are you doing here? You'll get shot if the gamekeeper's heard me."

They had nothing to fear from him. He was further up in the building near the big house where he kept his snares and equipment. He could steal a quiet moment there and some shut-eye.

Mary was a pretty girl. Hannibal had been very close to her from the time he had arrived to live with them. They had both been fortunate, escaping the outbreaks of childhood ailments and diseases. The freshness of their faces was testament to this good fortune and equalled by strong and fit bodies.

"You'll be walking home soon Mary, I'll wait and walk with you."

"You'd better get out of here now before you're caught. I'll be waiting for you at the top side." With that Hannibal dashed off as he had come. Over he ran towards the low wall and over onto the rocks. He covered the short distance quickly and in no time was on the beach overlooking the southern part of the Tamar. The previous night he had been in to Plymouth, delivering messages to some of the customers in the Taverns and Inns that took the goods smuggled into Cawsand.

It was part of the young Hannibal's job to make arrangements for delivery and collection to some of the Taverns that bought direct. They would sometimes meet up river in smaller boats. It was not too risky.

Wars with France had meant that much of the coast was not patrolled as it had been. Even if it were, bribery usually worked to stave off prying eyes. Nonetheless, he had been taught never to be too confident. For deliveries along this stretch of the Tamar on the Devon side there were several good meeting places tucked away and without the need for unnecessary risk taking. The Cawsand men would usually take the goods from safe houses in Millbrook at high tide, rowing the short distance. These buyers would normally take it in turns to meet the Cawsand boat.

Money would change hands on delivery unless other arrangements had been specifically made for the extension of credit.

A range of pre-agreed signals acted as warnings should either of them spot any danger that would abort the meeting. There were several boats in the area. Another small boat would hardly draw attention.

Nonetheless some care was called for. Smuggling remained a serious offence and rewards were still substantial when compared to the local subsistence wages.

Mary would be out soon. He must be at the ready to greet her at the top side and walk with her. With this he arose, brushed himself down, straightened his cap, collar and cuffs, such as they were, and strode, very upright, toward the agreed meeting place.

She was already outside the top gate waiting for him. The stone archway was a common meeting place that estate workers used. Mary did not live in as many did on the estate. Every evening she would take the walk up the hill from the main house where it joined the bridleway that led through the wood, then into the fields, which dropped down into the villages. Across the fields she would walk until the smoke of the village fires became so dense and pungent that it would fill her clothes.

From here she looked down on the rooftops of the village cottages. All peculiar shapes and sizes they were, piled onto each other, from the side, from the top giving rise to the labyrinth of little rough walkways, some cobbled, some not, that littered the villages, and joining everything together.

Tonight, she would enjoy her walk home, make it linger. She savoured these times and had run up to the archway, just a trifle worried when she had not seen Hannibal there on her arrival. The fine evening grew warmer as they quickened their pace over the tight grass of the fields. Rabbit holes were everywhere here, making a precarious time for walkers, whose minds were not concentrating on the ground in front them.

As they laughed and skirmished, Mary caught her heel, twisted and fell to the ground. They paused their walk for her to recover. Hannibal took his chance to get closer to Mary. They lay talking for a while, watching the sun disappear over the hills to the west.

Mary was in no mood to recover quickly from her fall and they waited, content to play along with the sham of the twisted ankle. They had a perfect view from here. The hills were not far off but neither had even been there yet. He had though been the length of the south Cornish coast on a boat with his father and knew every hiding hole with friends and safe houses from Prussia Cove to Lizard Point, from Mevagissey to Polperro and home again. He could sail and row now like any Cawsand man and was part of that clandestine club of Cornwall, sworn to secrecy and bonded by their trade. As they watched over the glowing sun arcing behind the distant hills, Hannibal looked seaward. He knew he could take his time tonight. No runs were planned, nothing expected in. Tomorrow was a different matter. he hoped for a change in the weather for the run. Rough seas, some wind and rain out there would be no bad thing. Tough conditions were often the best ones for the smuggling runs. After a while they continued the walk back. Mary's folk knew that he was walking with her and would not be worrying. They trusted Hannibal with their daughter. Hann as he was sometimes called was a village man now and they encouraged the match. They would not object to a marriage with the young Marks. He had always been welcomed.

* * *

The marriage was planned for the following month. It would be just short of Easter 1786.

It was an exciting time for both families. The banns were read to the tittering of the younger churchgoers and the smiles of Hannibal and Mary.

They would continue to live in with Mary's family first, just for a short while.

From now on the young lovers didn't miss a Sunday service at Church. Neither were they late. All eyes were on them at the little Church on the headland.

Two sides of the Church of St. Germanus in Rame stood overlooking the sea, to the west on one side and the south on another. Sundays could always be relied upon to sport a good turnout. Best clothes competed with the flowers in the hedgerows for their purity and diverse colours. Good fabrics were becoming as abundant in the village as were good brandies and could be relied upon to have come from the same suppliers.

Church was a time for most of the village to be together irrespective of age or interest.

The Vicar was a friend and at times more a work mate, well in a sort of way. The twin rooves of the church sat high and out of sight where they met in the middle and had been home to many a keg of spirit that had avoided duty. Even Riding Officers, mounted and therefore higher up, couldn't see into the rooves from any available vantage point.

They had fixed some anchor points to the side of the church building to which ropes could be easily fixed standing on the shoulders of another or walking up the side of the building on the short iron poles that had been fixed into the side of the building. These would provide some sure footing and hand holds.

Unobtrusive, they took away the need for clumsy and cumbersome ladders. In any case there were other places as well around the Churchyard and away from the sight of the Rectory. Some of the larger tomb tops, often a weight of granite or slate, if lifted, would reveal a large area they had excavated out to use as a store. Few Preventatives would run the risk of waking the dead by opening tombs. The smugglers thought differently, taking the view that those inside deep down would approve of their work and trade.

The big day came, and the little Church filled with well-wishers. There was only one amongst the village gathering who hid a falsehood in his congratulatory remarks. George Cock was there with his wife Jane and three of his children. He had a shine for Mary over the last few years and although well-hidden he had a pang of regret at the wedding. He was twelve years older than Mary and knew it was not to be. He was happy with Jane but being close to Mary always brought a shine to his otherwise grey and melancholy disposition. Her marriage to Hannibal was building a wall between him and Mary in his mind.

As the ceremony started his secret affections were blocked out completely. It was now cut and dried for him. She belonged to Hann and all would see that now. The bride came through the entrance of the church toward Hannibal. All eyes were turned except for his. There were no lights other than the altar candles and the building remained dim. The occasional beam of light would find its way inside, picking up the minute dust particles in the air as it went which would make a column of sunshine, picking out the colours in the stained glass as it travelled through on its way.

The light did not reach Hann. It came in through the West side at this time of day and year and lit up some of the old gravestone slabs in the western Isle of the church first of all. These were in slate and heavily engraved with names, dates and details of the accomplishments of the deceased whom they had entombed for eternity within the sanctity and due reverence of this ancient church.

They could not always be read in the dim of the church floor but when the light caught the slabs at just the right angle and intensity the detail shone through to remind onlookers of those long gone, their crests and inscriptions sometimes offering up an insight into their achievements. The full pews bristled with colour and life, much provided by the chatter that took the news pew to pew and back again.

The hustle and bustle continued until the Vicar called them to order lest they could not hear every word of his delivery of the marriage service as laid down by ecclesiastical practice and laws.

In many ways it was reminiscent of his father's wedding at St Stephens near Forder, Saltash and the celebrations that were held down at the riverside afterwards. The celebrations here started at the farm below the rectory. The farmers knew the couple as well as the parents. They too were part of that family of free traders.

Penmillard farm had at the ready a pig on a spit roasting slowly over the glowing pit fire that had been dug out for the occasion between the rear of the farmhouse and the cattle sheds. This was a prosperous farm held on lease from the Mount Edgcumbe estate.

It comprised several acres that surrounded the Church of St Germanus. This included Rame Head with its chapel on the top of the small promontory of land that poked itself into the sea. Steep cliffs on either side made it a treacherous journey from the sea upward but all useful to the smugglers. In a good year the farmers of the area would become share-holders in ventures.

At the least they were trusted and safe keepers of stocks of contraband. The areas under the cattle sheds were good stores, especially secure with a bull or two inside. The bulls provided a good insurance against too much interference from the riding officers. It was almost as if Browny, their old bull had an agreement with Edwards the farmer for a bucket of good fayre in return for acting out an angry bull part if unwelcome folk came into the barn.

The bull knew how to stomp his feet to great effect in the right places, away from the dung covered boards, under which lay the entrances to the stores.

He knew how to lower his horned head towards a visiting riding officer and give the evil eye that sent out the message that he was likely at any time and without notice, leave the control of the farmer to fix his prey on the end of his horns or with his immense bulk crush them on the side of the barn.

Penmillard's horses and mules were always at the ready in case the call came. There was usually some notice that they were needed the coming night. Always returned neat and tidy after a night's work this activity often paid better than the farm itself when times were lean.

Plentiful barrels of ale and tubs of cognacs were at the ready. Away from view the party started. There were few not there from the surrounding area. The Vicar too enjoyed his fill. He eventually returned home with a jug of the best spirit to warm by the evening fire. He knew it was ready for his taste and pallet when the earthenware jug was itself warm to touch. It was then ready to consume, alongside a good read, courtesy of the soft light that came from a selection of his church candles. The living at Rame was not a big one but this Vicar had income in addition to the living as well. There was also the added bonus of a keg and other small luxuries in return for a blind eye here and there to the goings on in the church and surrounding area. These were the goings on of the free traders. It was indeed reward for a blind eye rather than any active work the Vicar would provide for the smugglers.

Never money would he take, but goods enough to provide his wife and children with those luxuries normally highly priced and unavailable in the immediate area.

The next morning there was no sign of disruption and the tranquillity of Rame was restored.

The Vicar would also entertain the odd Riding Officer or other official as part of his passive role in the trade, providing them with some succour to hold them there a while.

There had been one time when his services had most likely saved the skins of several parishioners. Dragoons were rarely seen here at this time but sent fear into the smugglers if they were known to be on duty nearby.

There was only one way with these mounted, well-armed, often vicious forces of authority. They had to be killed and disposed of without trace. Bribery was not enough to ensure with any certainty that the secrets would be safe.

The night the Dragoons came to the rectory there was a big haul coming in. The outpost at Rame had picked up the signal. The goods were being brought up the cliffs, to then be taken onward into the villages. This haul would be taken in and hid in several different locations to be sorted for distribution.

The Vicar heard the Dragoon's horses draw up outside the rectory. As he looked out of the window with his wife and daughter, he knew they could take the folk scaling the cliffs by surprise, leading to much bloodshed.

As the door creaked open, he beckoned to his daughter to leave them and go to the cliffs. He and his wife beckoned them in, promising he would do all he could to help them in their quest. They accepted his offer of some sustenance before they continued.

The Vicar asked the Dragoons to whence they were heading.

"We are going to take the cliff paths from here along the Bay as far as Portwrinkle. We saw lights tonight which, although stopped now, have given us cause to believe that there will be illicit activities along these cliffs tonight. We have stopped to enquire if you have seen or heard any gangs of men, horses, carts, come past the rectory?"

"No nothing untoward recently. It has been a quiet time here. Occasionally we hear the rumble of cart wheels at night with no cart there, but successive Vicars here have heard the same thing for many generations."

“So, what pray is it?” The Dragoon spokesman asked the question with a dry and almost disbelieving manner.

The Vicar, knowing how superstitious folk were, replied, not at all unnerved by the question.

“The story was passed down by one of the Vicars incumbents here in the 1600s. There had been a terrible storm and shipwreck here at Rame in which all hands were lost. All lost that is, save two, who were washed in on a large wave at Queener and managed to cling to the rocks there as the tide was lower and ebbing.

When they drew strength again, they climbed to the top fields. One was badly hurt and had to be helped by the other. Their language was Breton, and they could not make themselves well understood in these parts. There were few left in Cornwall who could speak the native Cornish tongue this far to the east. The Cornish and Breton tongues were very similar.

Not being able to make themselves understood, they were feared as robbers. Part of a plot they were thought to be. So, it was they were clubbed when they stole into the farmhouse looking for help and food. That's the farmhouse just next to us there."

With that the Vicar pointed through the large window of the Rectory. He took a deep, saddened sigh, before continuing.

"One died, he's there now, buried in the churchyard. He was in fact not a seaman when the ship was wrecked but very much as your good selves, a horseman travelling with the vessel which was also carrying horses. We do not know now all the reasons.

Many were washed up dead on the beaches around here both men and the horses. It was a grizzly sight. Where possible the men were retrieved from the beaches their eyes all out and with mangled forms.

Most likely they would have been unrecognisable to any that knew them, maybe not even to their mothers. They were given a Christian burial together in the churchyard. Ever since we have had visitations here from the ghost of the murdered man whose soul is not at rest. Sometimes the men wail to be returned to their home shores."

The Dragoons were jaw wide at this tale and their spokesman asked if the Vicar had ever seen the apparitions. The Vicar looked heavenward with a big upward rolling motion in his eyes, caught by the light from the candles.

With slightly less movement in his head, he offered up a small prayer to his Lord and Master for all to hear in which he prayed for the release of the torment of these dead souls in his churchyard and for their eternal rest. He then bowed his head following it on with a silent prayer. In it he prayed forgiveness for what he was about to say. He prayed that it would produce a better result for mankind. Prayed that it would avoid cruelty, injury or even death by saying it rather than not saying it.

As he finished his secret prayer, he shook his head, which was an action followed by the Dragoons all together, as they immersed themselves totally in the Vicar's trepidations. "Yes, I have.

The one killed at the hands of the farmer appeared to me alone. He shook his mortal coils that he could not shake off yet, writhing, mouthing and gasping for help out of his predicament. I could only pray for his soul.

As I did so, his wails continued as he moved across the churchyard to the site of the other graves of his fellow seamen on that ship to seek help and comfort. As he hovered over that site, now unmarked, maybe deep under other interments, he pawed at the ground for them to rise for him.

The air produced a loud noise as the bones of those upper interments seemed moved by their spirits to provide a pathway upwards. It was then they appeared one by one, shaking their chains that were holding them to our land, the chains that were preventing them from returning to the soils of their homeland."

"How many were there Vicar?"

"It seemed like hundreds. Like an army, vengeful to take blood in return for their dismal state."

"Did they come after you?"

"They wailed their anger, wailed their lust for revenge. Revenge for their dead friend and, well, I cannot be certain, but against those of authority who had put them in an unsafe ship ... Yes authority, the symbols of authority, my friends ... it would seem that it is that which their blood curdles for .... and that, well, that could be us.

We rely now on their shackles to keep them from us. I saw some break and wondered if they broke what would happen. The sole murdered friend seemed unable to unshackle them nor though do any harm on his own."

"Have you seen them again?" asked an increasingly twitchy Dragoon spokesman.

"Yes. Every time more of the shackles are broken and they seem to become more able to move. Maybe their time will come or there will be folk that anger them so that the final shackles will break and free them."

"And what do you think, Vicar, might happen then?" This was uttered by another of the Dragoons who looked as if he were ready to take to his horse and flee that place.

"I do not know." With that the Vicar again looked heavenward, murmuring, in Latin, a prayer. Whilst toward the end of it, crossing his chest with the sign of the cross, then his forehead he observed the Dragoons were troubled and appeared twitchy and ready to leave.

"I think our quest Father will take us back down into the villages without further troubling you."

As they left, they looked for their horses, which were no-where to be seen. They looked at each other as the Vicar gave his parting words,

"Maybe they have taken these horses, maybe they have found a way of setting them free or joining them as ghostly horses who will run too with the dead horses, killed that night."

"How will we know, Vicar? How will we know if our horses are of the dead? How will we know if we mount them to where they will take us?"

"Have faith in the Lord and if they are indeed apparitions that you ride, ask for deliverance from your sins that you might not yet be taken to join them."

With that the men looked at each other and headed away from the Church down towards the villages hoping they might find their horses unsullied by the apparitions. But, how would they know? How would they be certain?

As they left, the Vicar's daughter re-appeared, knife in hand. She had cut off their tethers, riding reins and equipment. They would be re-united, eventually, but not ridden tonight. Maybe never again. They saw the Dragoons head off swiftly looking relieved to get away.

They stepped a pace up when suddenly they heard the clanking of chains close by. Their increased pace turned into a run. Superstition, stuff and nonsense or not ... they were taking no chances. Word had got to the local farmers from the Vicar's daughter.

They were making sure that loud, clanking noises would start when the Dragoons left and would continue as they went down the valley. They knew the night air combined with the echoes of the valley would make it difficult to identify the source of the sound and make it the more chilling. How right they were.

The Dragoons fled at a speed most like faster than the horses could have achieved.

The Vicar's mind drifted back to the present and the joyous occasion. Young Hannibal, he suspected, had too been drawn into these ways. He had warned him of the potential consequences but knew they had fallen on deaf ears. With that he decided without further thought on the moralities of the matter to enjoy his portion of roast pig. He would wash it down nicely to complete a good feast. The Vicar had drawn the line at participation in the dancing, preferring to sit and watch. Watch he did with an element of mild horror at the sight of his daughter who had entered into the celebrations, full swing. She had better enjoy it now for a while he thought for it would not last for long. There were other plans afoot for her future. The sight of Hannibal and Mary's marriage, their happiness at Penmillard, brought out much broodiness in the village girls, eying their partners, wondering too when it would be their turn.

The older Marks and Spillers had decided to stay a while. They would continue to enjoy each other's company for as long as the embers glowed.

They did not want to race back anyway. Let Hannibal and Mary have their time alone.

* * *

It was in the following winter that the chance arose that would provide a home of their own. The cottage was spartan inside like most. There were two rooms below and two above. They took it gladly and arrangements were made for them to move in.

The Marks had hardly known the previous occupant but as a sign of respect, and especially as they were going to live where he had lived, attended the funeral.

A few days later it was his immediate family that insisted on clearing all things out before they moved in. Every effort to go down and help met with polite refusals.

"Are you sure we can't do something", shouted Hannibal as he was going past the cottage one day and saw them inside working away in the dimpsy light.

"It'll be yours soon enough Hannibal Marks. Patience." Hannibal could make out that some of the floor planking inside was off the floor and up against the walls. They were all inside bottoms up and heads down into the under-floor space. It was difficult to see in and he had had to go up close to get sight of some of the goings on. Coming out from under the floor and from voids behind the fireplace arrived a variety of items.

This was the inheritance he had left for his children. Hannibal could see the glint of coins periodically as the flash of light refracted itself in through the cracks as he caught sight of them. There were quite a few. Surely the old man could not have saved these. He had lived poorly.

Suddenly the window shutters were slammed tightly together taking away Hannibal's glimpses altogether.

"You mind your own, Hannibal Marks," came a throaty voice with a tone of friendly displeasure at the intrusion.

Hannibal knew what was going on. The old man's legacy was from his share outs. Some things just had to remain private. Hannibal carried on down the street without a word.

* * *

Shortly after Hannibal had moved in with the Spillers a storm had blown up from the south east that brought the water, sand, stone and debris smashing in to the shores of all three of the village beaches. The storm had caught the village completely by surprise.

The fishermen, close friends and foes of nature, could all normally tell a storm was afoot before the storm itself knew. They would smell it and feel it. They could tell when it was going to start and from which direction it would be coming.

There were storms in summer, sometimes worse than those in the winter, though fewer. As the swell on the water rose, those boats already crewed and ready, left the bay for safer anchorage up river or around in Millbrook. When they left, the few remaining could be seen rising and falling sharply on their moorings. These were the smaller boats, but not so small that they could easily be hauled up the beaches every day.

Owners came out to check on their boats, drag them up further on the beaches before the tide came right in to take the beaches away completely. Through the gaps in the cottages the wind raged with ferocity few could remember the likes of. It banged shutters and doors on its way. It whistled loudly in its wake.

Hannibal joined some fishermen off the Girt Beach. Here the storm was making itself felt against some of the rickety cottages built on the rocks. The stronger more recent two- and three-story dwellings were braving it well but not quite so for the smaller cottages. So too the smaller boat stores that had started to take a hard, consistent, pounding.

Rolling in with increasing strength, the sea crashed against the buildings and rocks below them sending heavy water thirty feet in the air. The water came with a complement of stones, shingle and driftwood. Some of the stones were very heavy. It was these that could injure or even kill a man if he was caught below them as they returned to earth.

As they became increasingly powerless to intervene in the natural passage of the storm, the village onlookers started to talk amongst themselves. Some reminisced over storms in previous years, the damage to property and life they had caused.

"It's one of ours!" came a desperate cry from the crowd. Hannibal strained his eyes to see and his ears to hear more. Just south eastward of Penlee Point he saw a large oared boat well down in the water only to be tossed upward as if there were no ballast of men nor water let alone the stocks it was carrying.

There were several rowers, ten in all with sail down but he could not recognise them nor the boat. Hannibal knew where they had been. They had been out to meet a French supplier and were on their return when the storm blew up.

"Grab the ropes and out to the cellars that lie off the rocks. They might need help to get in." There were always boiled and seasoned ropes in the village. He ran across to gather rope strong enough to pull a man in on. He ran for all he was worth out of Cawsand and onto the track that made from the village toward Penlee Point.

Past the estate farms he went and soon reached the track that went down on to the rocks below. The oarsmen were holding on, despite sharp rises and falls that came from the relentless turbulence from both sea and wind. It looked as if some of them had lost those tools of their trade to the sea as a few of the oars, the sweeps, could be seen broken and bobbing in the surf.

The boat was getting close to the rocks further along from where Hannibal had reached. The remaining oars were forced into the waves by the men, whose strength and resolve united in the effort to keep the boat off the rocks and on a course towards the village beaches. Luck had also played a part in getting them thus far, before the storm had broken.

Cawsand beach was safest for their landing now. If only their oars could beat off the anger of the storm until they hit the beach, help would be at hand. When the storm had started to brew, they had used some of their illicit cargo to give them the warmth and extra strength needed for the final push.

They now looked a helpless sight though. There had been drownings before from larger craft than this and they all knew it. But this was a Cawsand boat, built for speed, carriage and strength against the elements. They knew and trusted these boats. This storm though, this was a battle the boats and their crews might not win.

Nature was, in the final draw of life, the one in control. Hannibal raced further up the rocks, through the spitting and lashing of the storm. He could now see the oarsmen clearly when they were on the crest of a wave and recognised them.

Despite all efforts these souls could neither pull the boat away from the rocks nor in toward the beach. None better than they. They all knew every rock, beach and landing place in the area. They knew the way the wind would turn and push the boats according to its direction and the state of the tides. They knew the effect this would have on their chances of landing at the different locations. They knew that this time they had a real fight on their hands. The strength of wind and wave was too much for them to fight against this day and slowly they headed toward the rocks. The best chance was to position the boat to come in toward the shallows next to the cellar. A small area but usually big enough for a boat or two to tie up and unload. It was now awash with the foam of the storm. It would be difficult to get men and cargo off safely even if they could get the boat in there. The rise and fall of the seas were ten feet or more within seconds.

Saving these men was now the most important task. The boat could be repaired or replaced and there would always be the next run. Hannibal could see what they were trying to do. He had now been joined by others. More men were waiting by the beaches ready to help as and when they could. Out at Penlee they could see that the boat was going to have to take its chances there. The cellars were the only real chance providing an opportunity to get off onto dry land. Most of this stretch from Penlee toward the Cawsand beach was almost sheer up towards the farmland above.

On the lower steps toward the sea there were some trees. This area could not be enclosed, and farmland was just left to fall away as nature desired. Dangerously steep for animals and humans, trees had established here that also obscured with their foliage the goings on below for most of the year.

There were nonetheless some ways up and down along the mile stretch that led from the village to Penlee Point. Tonight, the landing would have been straight on to the beach providing there was no signal indicating the presence of the revenue.

The weighted rope almost hovered in the air as Hannibal threw it out to the boat. The winds were strong but changeable and the stone was thrown off course slightly. Good fortune landed it inside the boat first time. Stone removed, the length of rope was tied securely onto the boat's bow end.

The oarsmen had already decided in the moment to take their chances by the cellars. The rollers were coming in heavier. They were close on the rocks but now was the time. Hannibal had been joined by village men. They all took their positions on the rope to haul in the stricken boat.

As the waves lowered, they pulled as ones possessed, allowing some slack as they crested and repeated until the boat was positioned ready as best it could to the entrance. The oarsmen re-positioned themselves and their oars in Polynesian fashion as their rowing space got less.

They knelt with their oars and on the crests used force and will to help push the boat a little further in. All their common strength was put together to prepare themselves for the final push. In they came against the rocks. The wood of the boat started to splinter so great was the force.

The waves took the stricken boat out, but the rope was taut. The oarsmen crouched in the boat as it filled with water. As the waves levelled for a short while on the start of the ebb flow, they sprung out onto the rocks two at a time. There were helping hands there to catch them for they could not rely so much on their strength this time. Most of the kegs were saved, whether from the boat or washed in to the shores.

There had been nothing else on this run that could have got damaged. No silks, no fine cloth, nor teas. The oarsmen sat quietly for a short while ashore as the other village men hauled up the cargo and salvaged the boat. The boat was secured just up from the rocks in between the trees and scrub. The oarsmen quickly gathered their wits again and their strength. Never far from death in these times, fear not only gave way to relief, but the need to finish their job. They were all soon up and back in the village to help distribute and hide the night's catch.

* * *

It was not long after this that the chance arose for Hannibal to take a lease on land next to his parents' house and build a house there of his choice with premises below, from which they could sell merchandise direct.

They could then build cellars further down again with storage, more perhaps. It provided the chance to build another bigger tunnel with chambers off that could feed into the ones built by father.

The Bloyes and the Bath family who were previously miners up river and further down into Cornwall would work with them to do this. They too were part of the smuggling gangs and were trusted to do this work.

Their quarters above, with access to the tunnels that would join up to others and especially father's and the hiding rooms off them would be helpful to them. The tunnel started here with access to other houses on its way down to cottages at the bottom, close to the beach.

This was an opportune moment. There had been a meeting of the backers and their agents to discuss the feasibility of joining the tunnels from Kingsand with the main ones at Cawsand especially the one that went from Pemberknowse up under to the Ship Inn.

From the Ship there were tunnels that went under adjoining cottages in a further labyrinth that joined many of the very old cottages built into the hills behind the more recently built houses. This would require careful planning and finance to achieve whilst ensuring minimal disruption. To do this un-noticed was a skill well-practiced by the honed engineering skills of the former miners.

This development would provide not only a good network to unload and store from both ends of the two villages from the sea and land but also close the gap between tunnels. This network gradually joining east to west and north to south with adjoining safe houses and ale houses, inns and taverns was increasingly providing the security required for what had become a large-scale operation.

An operation requiring dual purpose hides, storage and places to work. Areas big enough to practice the art of distilling the stronger spirit into weaker and re-barrelling or bottling it, ready to supply whether direct to their own drinking houses or wholesale to others.

The secretive convening of the backers and their agents went largely without names. The big backers and their identities could not be revealed but it was widely understood that they were of the gentle classes and did not want to be seen to have an involvement.

The profits though were too great for most of them to refrain from investment. Backing to put in the additional tunnels would benefit the Marks' enterprises and would come at lower or maybe no cost to them. This was the type of investment the Marks had learnt to exploit for their own gain.

Hannibal senior, Hannibal 1st, was now entering the lower rung of the backers. He had been continually and fastidiously careful with the money he had earned from the spoils of the trade. Those spoils had grown expediently as money put aside had been used wisely to invest in further facilities for the trade.

More boats, boatbuilding, storage, customers, unlicensed houses. The list of business interest with smuggling at their heart was developing rapidly for the Marks. Unlicensed houses meant maximising the profitability from sales of liquor of one sort or another and much needed cash to operate all sides of the business.

The Marks had developed their own moral code which they applied to their trade. They did not wreck boats, they did not take lives whilst there was another realistic option. The same unwritten rule applied to the other smugglers from Cawsand and Kingsand. Deaths were mistakes or a last resort, not part of the strategy.

As the eighteenth century started to close in though it became increasingly difficult to avoid skirmishes and hatred spread against the authorities as their powers and resources grew.

Chapter 13

The King of Prussia's Troubles with Revenge

"They were good years looking back Mary." Hannibal 2nd lamented as he spoke, lurching towards the centre of the hearth to take the kettle off the fire. He sighed as he reflected on the passing of the easier days he had known, when the coast was little watched with no meaningful preventative force based in any of the nearby villages and towns. Now, nearing the end of the century they had to take more care.

Hannibal, and his father by the same name, had gone on many smuggling ventures together. Close as thieves with the other smuggling families in the villages, the Marks had continued to prosper. They now had shares in some of the finest smuggling craft in Cornwall. Their interests included everything from boatbuilding, fishing, Inns, taverns, alehouses and now they had expanded into the provision of cash to pay for runs. The brokering of cash when in short supply was a growing part of the business. The villages had maintained their reputation for building the best and fastest boats in the decade or so since the marriage of Hannibal 2nd and Mary.

They continued to be well known for it. This unfaltering reputation was still prompting orders from smugglers further down the coast for their vessels.

These activities had extended their network, especially along the south coast. The network extended into the most powerful directly involved in the trade.

The days of beach landings with relatively little regard to checking the coast was clear, had now passed. Father had died just as things were starting to really tighten up. He had foreseen this happening when the war with France came to end but did not live to see the full effects of the government's drive to stop the trade in smuggled goods.

The village now had Ambrose Bowden, a Preventative Officer, stationed permanently in the heart of Cawsand. A house built for him overlooked Cawsand Bay. The houses of preventative officers had to either be provided by their employers or the occupant of the post would be required to already have a base in the area.

In Polperro, a few miles west of Cawsand by sea, Preventative men could find no lodgings and no sustenance from the villagers. There was simply nothing they could acquire on which to live. They were shunned and had initially to sleep on their boat.

Bribing this new breed of official still happened but became less easy. The bounty paid for catching a smuggling craft increased for the Preventative Officers. The position carried a wage and pension. Similarly, bringing in a smuggler was worth a lot in bounty money.

Them and us was getting stronger. More smuggling craft were caught and impounded. Smugglers ran the risk of imprisonment or even death. As these stakes rose so both sides increasingly took to arms.

With this Hannibal and Mary recalled the all too recent example of their father's friend, Harry Carter of Prussia Cove. Father had become good friends and associates of the Carters. 1788 had been the year. They had not been married long when the incident took place. It was bitterly cold although still and clear.

January weather was unpredictable, but there had been a few days of good fortune for the Carter crew and their 140-ton Smuggler, Revenge. Carrying sixteen carriage guns, she had been built for smuggling. She and the crew had innumerable successful runs to their credit. By the night of 30th January, she was moored off Penlee Point waiting to be relieved of the burden of her spoils. She had gorged on the fruits of Guernsey, so too the friendly ports of Northern Brittany, returning to fill their stores before setting sail again to reload, this time to deliver to Cawsand Bay.

Now was the time to see a profit for all those involved. They had traded well. Harry was guaranteed good quality merchandise at the finest possible prices, such was the regard in which he and the Carter family were held by the foreign merchants. There was never credit expected nor taken by Harry. Credit terms had been needed in the early days but now the Carter family empire was cash rich, operating from their fortress home at Prussia Cove. They would, in many cases, pay for the goods immediately on taking delivery of them. The Carter boats could be relied upon for the quality and measures of the cargoes. It was rare for a Carter boat not to keep good time and to a schedule.

This was a business empire and father Hannibal, Hannibal 1st, had aspired to build the Marks family business in the same way. Under cover of early nightfall, the arrival of the Smuggler had been expected. Harry took his spyglass and saw the rowing boats leave the shoreline. He could not make out what lads were crewing the boats this night but knew that he could rely on Cawsand men to offload the boat's cargo with best efficiency, safety and trust.

He had dropped anchor just inside the outer reach of Penlee point after having had the all clear signal from the Cawsand men as they came across Whitsand Bay and onto to Rame Head.

Signals were changed from time to time in case the preventative men should hear of them. Two blinks, one quickly following the other had been agreed on the last voyage. This indicated the all clear with long pauses until the signal was given again.

No fires indicating danger could be seen anywhere along the gawping sweeping bay that enclosed the villages from Polperro through to Looe and onto Rame Head. A little way along, as they turned in towards the coast, past the Rame headland, lay Penlee Point from where Cawsand and Kingsand would come into sight.

The entrance to Plymouth and the fruits of its lucrative markets for which much of the goods were destined, lay beyond. Two blinks they spotted about two miles out in the Bay from Rame. As they crossed due south from Rame there were another two and the same at Penlee. There would be no more now unless four blinks, to signal danger, came from the shores or were routed on to them from elsewhere, in which they case they would be gone again.

They waited and drew the boat round in a big circle. Coming alongside them as they turned the bows southward drew one of the Cawsand boats. It pulled to under the gun holes and one of the Cawsand men standing reached over to climb up the rope ladder onto the deck.

"It's all clear to drop anchor," he told Harry. With this the boat slipped away to return to Cawsand Bay. It would give the all clear to the other boats to row out to unload the goods. Unloading boats that were at Polhawn in Whitsand Bay and the cellars close by had already arrived and had started their work. They would take goods to hideaways in between Rame Head and the Revenge. The tubmen would take care of them from there and get them to safe places nearby. They could be taken into the village after she was cleared and gone. The whole village was ready to help. Tunnels had been opened and cleared and were ready to receive and safely secure the goods. Porters were ready to start their long nightshift to carry inland to Millbrook and other nearby places, where there were others ready to take in goods.

Speed was now essential to empty Revenge of her cargo and get it to safe places. The boats leaving Cawsand would bring the cargo they took back direct to the villages, into the corner coves of Cawsand Bay, into the corner of Girt Beach, into the narrow cove with the tunnel that led up to the Ship Inn and over to Kingsand beach. The tubmen would take over from there and soon get the loads to safe places, some straight into the Inns. The batmen would protect them from interference on their short journeys.

The openings, the opes as they were known, were manned and ready. The side doors of Inns unbolted and waiting. Sail lofts and their hidden hatches were open and ready to take the goods in. Tunnels were at the ready.

There would be six row boats servicing the now opening hatches of the Carter boat. There were no lights, but villagers were at the ready, their eyes had adjusted to the ink black of night that endowed the narrow village streets with their ability to conceal the goings on. They could see like cats.

Faye Dunstone was alert, squinting to see through the darkness of the room and through the crack in the shutter that went out onto the dirt road that passed by her house to Cawsand beach. The coves at the far end had the Cawsand row boats on the soft, mud like sand, known as the bargee, ready to be slipped into the bay at the far end under the fields and wooded areas above. From here they would keep close to the rocks until they reached the Carter Smuggler. Any sign of Preventative men and they would drop the goods in amongst the coves and small beach areas that littered the rocky area from Penlee Point to Widdy Cove at the extreme of Cawsand Bay.

The polished oars slid through the water with the only trace of their presence shown by the ripples in the water. Pins greased, leather wrapped and polished, they barely creaked as they took the strain of their oars, lest they be heard above the soft breaking of the waves on the shoreline.

This was a truly, precision trade now. They were all ready to leave the shore. A moon's shadow passed Lowenna Chappel's window and unnerved her. She went closer to the gap in the shutter to get a fuller look at the perpetrator outside. It was Bowden and his men.

"What are they doing here." Lowenna muttered under her breath, lest she be heard. She went to the rear door and up the path to the start of the track to the Penlee farms. She could scramble down here to the rocks below and to the boatmen that had not yet left.

Tom, her husband was down there. "Lowenna?"

"Bowden!" The other oarsmen looked at Tom. In the dark they could see a preventative boat leaving the shore. The Cawsand men were unarmed. There was little they could do.

"Where's the light?" Hannibal was there. "It's too late," said Tom loudly, there seeming no need now for hush.

A loud crack came and echoed around the bay they were in, as if a shot was ricocheting around the rocks that almost enclosed them. The crack was the mast of the Carter boat. A musket shot had taken the trysail.

Harry Carter had seen the rowing boats and had confirmed with his pilot that they were the Cawsand boats come to take the goods. Unloading had begun in earnest.

It was only when the Bowden boats came alongside following the hit their boat had taken that they all knew for sure they were under attack.

"Look over there. There's two Navy men o war. That's where the shot's come from." There was an increasing panic in the Pilot's voice. "Look there's a small boat coming from one of the men of war towards us. And what boat is that coming towards us from the Cawsand direction. It doesn't look like one of the unloading boats. The men on board ..... they're preventatives. They're armed. We are going to be surrounded."

Without words the crew cut the anchor loose and prepared to set sail.

The unloading boats cleared the area, leaving the partly disabled Smuggler to depart as quickly as she could. They would take the goods they had into safe keeping and get back to the village or take cover for the night.

"Over the side," Harry heard them shout. The Bowden boat had arrived first and with that the Bowden men boarded the Carter vessel.

"Take your muskets," Harry shouted to the crew. They scrambled for their weapons but there was too much confusion. They went below decks to consolidate their position. Harry engaged the preventative men head on and alone.

With no weapons save his own hands, Harry was turned upon with no mercy. His head was badly injured in the scuffle. He fell for dead on the deck. Realising that he could not now rely on the crew who were by now secured below deck, he lay as if dead for at least 20 minutes. He was taken for dead by Bowden as he himself boarded and assumed control of the Smuggler, Revenge. The Preventative service had taken control of the flagship of the Carter Smuggler fleet.

"Put him below," Harry heard one of the men say.

"What's the use, he's dead" replied Bowden, who gave Carter's body a deft kick.

Seeing him roll lifelessly on the deck he decided to finish the job by kicking the body into the waters below. Carter only went so far and came to rest, lifeless on the edge of the starboard side.

After a while, Harry, still conscious but feigning death, decided he was strong enough to make a break for it. He was a swimmer but had not much strength in him now, on which he could rely, to take on the short distance to shore.

Carefully, when there were no preventatives on deck, he slid down the rope that was at the side of the boat. He glided into the water and started to slowly swim towards the beach. It was difficult, and he swallowed much water in the attempt.

He got into shallower water when his strength started to fail badly. There were two ropes close to him that he had felt brushing his body as he swam. He grabbed one and hauled himself shoreward.

Seeing the white shingle told him that he was close to beach and gave him the extra strength needed to get to the safety of the shores.

The next few pulls came easily and as he felt the shingle, he stood up to walk from the water. Three men were close to him now. He could not run. Should he shout to them, turn himself in? He recognised them to be preventative men. Where were they coming from? There must have been an informer. The Navy boats had lent assistance. They must have had some advance warning. Who, who had informed?

The spirit that had made the Carter family so powerful in west Cornwall filled him in this his hour of need. He thought of this wife of only two years, Elizabeth Findel and his daughter of only one year, also named Elizabeth.

No, he would not give in. Give in to a hanging. Never!

As yet unseen by the Officers, he let himself slip back into the water. He remained there laying quietly. Eventually they passed on, walking up the beach and into the town.

He got up onto his feet once more, staggering onto the sand of the beach.

"Who are you?" The question was addressed to Harry. He felt two men either side of him. They grabbed him under the arms and asked again, "Who are you?"

He heard a man say, "Fear not, I am a friend. Come with me." With that Harry felt himself lifted from behind. Strong arms, fortified by the adrenalin flowing into every vein of their bodies, drowned out any fear or doubts that may deter them from their task.

They carried him into the town. Harry lost consciousness.

Dim lights and the smell of burning fish oil mixed with pipe tobacco greeted Harry as he came around from his unconscious state.

Through the blur came the first sight of his rescuers. Eight Cawsand men and his brother Charles were sat there. He heard Charles say with great joy, "this is my brother."

With that they stripped Harry of his sodden clothes and tended his wounds. There were deep cuts to his head. His nose was almost sliced into two. A doctor was called to tend the wounds, which was duly done.

Hannibal 2nd, often referred to as Boy Hannibal whilst the two Hannibals were alive, had been one of those eight Cawsand men. He could recall the incident well. "What's that noise?" Boy Hannibal had heard a rumpus not that far from them.

"Quiet now, we are well hidden here but we must keep the silence. All is not over yet. Mind, it's the door. Taking their weapons, they waited.

It was Francis Lobb, Boy Hannibal's brother-in-law to be, who creaked open the door to the small, hidden room. Francis came with news of outside and the noise they could hear that was gathering strength.

"They've sent more people from Plymouth and the Preventatives have locked themselves into the Inn. They took Harry's men they captured over to the man o war for safe keeping until they could take them in to Plymouth or bring them before the Justices. The Revenge was left unattended by the Preventatives and the man o war. I expect they didn't believe she could be unloaded any further and we would leave her go now. We did carry on though and got most off taking care to keep out of eyesight as best we could. She dragged anchor in the end and came in close to the beach, grounded herself. We managed to get some more off from there as well.

Most of the goods are in the Kingsand Inn opposite Prowse's and in Prowse's. They're in the cellars and on their way to the tunnels now so should be safe."

With that the door opened again and it was Hannah, Hannibal's sister.

"I have just been in the crowd that is around the Inn and Prowse's. More and more are coming. Bradley and the Plymouth men are here. They've got into Prowse's cellars but no talk of the tunnels. They're safe.

One of them blocked into the Inn is Felton. They are saying this is Felton's doing. The Revenge is down at the cove on the rocks. She drifted in and there's Preventatives there now, guarding what's left."

"Stay here Hannah. Let Francis return and be our ears for this. Go down and remain in the back of the Alehouse. It will not be safe anywhere tonight."

A groggy Harry Carter was not taking it all in but muttered on hearing the news.

"The Squire. The Squire. This is his stock. He must know. He must be told."

The Squire was Squire Edwards from Rame. The Squire was a big financier of smuggling runs. He had invested in the stock for this one, one of the biggest he had backed. He had taken full risk. A large advance payment had been made to the merchants with the remainder on credit, courtesy of both the merchants and the bankers.

The Carters, on this occasion, were mainly the shippers and handlers. The loss would predominantly lie with the Squire.

By the time Francis returned to the Inn and Prowse's, the assembled crowd were baying for the blood of Felton.

Felton, the informer, this was his doing. Felton was an Exciseman operating out of Plymouth but had until recently lived in Kingsand.

Not above bribing residents, Felton's tactics were despised. The knowledge of who would have given Felton his information stayed within only a few people. Felton himself and his informer. Felton was a man of the area and a traitor to do this.

"You Felton. You Bradley. I might have known." The Squire towered above them both. They were outside of the Inn and trying to get through the barricaded parlour into relative safety. They got there by walking in behind some of the houses and down the opes un-noticed. This way they arrived at the side door. They were though noticed, so quickly made off to the other side entrance, where they waited to be let in.

It had been too dangerous for the barriers to be released to allow them in right away, but seeing their plight, and understanding that there might be murder before their eyes, they released enough barricade to allow the door to be opened, just sufficiently so, to allow them in.

This was too late to avoid wrath and injury being inflicted from the Squire's sword. The Squire was brandishing his gleaming instrument of death from his aloof position on his horse. Not used for a while, he was ready to use it now.

Before they managed to be pulled in to the relative safety of the Inn, the Squire exacted a measure of sweet revenge, striking the pair of them. If he could, he would have killed or injured them on the spot and left their remains to the baying crowd to do with them what they pleased.

The crowd was behind the Squire. It was his money that had financed several runs. Although not alone as a provider of financial support, he had been prominent in the trade and a supporter of the front-line smugglers behind the scenes.

It was, in part, his money that contributed to better conditions for traders who had been caught and imprisoned. He would syndicate with others who were doing well from the trade to provide their own form of insurance to those lower down in the pecking order of the free traders of the area.

"Come on get a ram from one of those straight beams at the quarry. Let's get those buggers. Some of the quarry stone. Let's hurl it at them. We'll get in and let wo betide all of them.

That Felton .... why, that Felton, we'll tear him limb from limb and feed him to the seagulls."

"I want my goods," yelled the Squire.

"Come quickly. Let's get in there and get them out. Is the boat emptied?"

"Most is off, but she is heavily guarded now and from the sea too with the Navy boats just off.

The Squire's swipes with his cutlass at Felton and Bradley had achieved something before they were dragged into the sanctuary of the Inn that the Preventatives had secured.

It was Bradley who came off the worse. The Squire had slashed Bradley's leg and nearly torn off the muscle and tendons. As Bradley escaped into the barricaded parlour, dragged in by his fellow Excisemen, his agony was excruciating. He looked down to see the fractured and splintered bone embedded into the torn skin and fibres of his leg.

"May you never walk again, you blaggards. You bastard of mankind. I'll rip the other limbs off you before the night is out."

With that the Squire turned and went down to see what was happening at the cove where the beached Smuggler had been grounded and was now under guard.

Suddenly the crowd started to disperse as gunshot railed through the night and the smell of discharged shot putrefied the air.

The Squire had by now returned. He had been unable to salvage anything further from the boat. He was at the Inn parlour door continuing to try to force his way in when the Preventative re-enforcements arrived.

His status as a wealthy landowner in the area, one of long-standing and good family, well connected, was unable to save him from this one.

The armed re-enforcements eventually overcame the Squire who, red faced, and snarling like an uncontrolled wild boar, determined to claim back what was his, was taken and disarmed.

"Unhand me. Unhand me. Do you know who I am?" The Squire's efforts to save his skin even to the last went unheeded. He took much of the land from the Edgcumbes who knew him well. The Squire had interests in other land and farms widely spread around. He had amassed a considerable fortune from smuggling.

He had though sunk everything into this particular venture. It could now be this that could see the undoing of him and his family. This, this, all for that bastard of a man, Felton. He would see to Felton and Bradley. They were the main cause of this. The cause of his, his, the Squire of Rame's undoing. He would finish the job he had started on them.

The Squire was apprehended alongside many other rioters who were, for the mostpart, the Squire's men. They were taken to the Plymouth jail to await their fate at the old Bailey. For the Squire it could have been worse, could have been better.

He was unable to arrange his trial in Cornwall or even Devon. There was a fear he could nobble the Jury or the Justices. He was, after all, one of them.

Mary took a sup of her tea and asked Hannibal what had happened to the Squire then. She could not remember what had happened after he had been apprehended.

"No, this time he was for London. He was taken to Newgate before trial. Could have swung for it, but fortune shone on him alright. They gave him three years to serve in Newgate.

He survived, returning to tell the tale. Things haven't been the same for him since. Bankrupt they made him, and he never got back into the trade, as big as he was."

Harry was hidden in the village for some days before the doctor considered that he could be safely moved. He could not remain there for long. All villagers' houses were safe houses, but they were searched when it was realised that Harry Carter himself had escaped the clutches of the Preventative men.

The others were taken in for trial.

Harry was moved to Lostwithiel under the escort of the doctor and his brother Charles. They moved him under cover of nightfall. A safe house was provided until a reward was offered for Harry Carter. This was advertised in the papers.

"I know I can make this and with God's will live and fight another day. But what of the other men? Are they alive? Have they escaped?"

Three hundred pounds was offered for the Captain for a period of three months. Harry had to be moved. With that he left. He was spirited away with the blindfolded doctor, secured onto the fastest horse the village could muster and with riders to accompany and protect him, they left.

This was a journey riddled with risk and potential peril at every step the horses took. They all knew their lives were at risk. They were slowed by Harry who could barely hang on to his steed. He had summoned all his remaining strength to make the ride. Strapped into the saddle as best as could be done with ropes and cloth that only a seaman could arrange and tie to ensure Harry did not fall, they took the strain off the ride to some extent.

Scouts were riding far out in case of surprise. They too were armed, knowing they must be prepared to kill that night if disturbed by any authority. They must not be seen.

Harry must be kept from any view as they went through the settlements on the way. They would avoid them best they could even if taking these more convoluted routes slowed their journey. Harry was moved, deftly but cautiously. This was a precious cargo.

As Lostwithiel approached they knew that those scouting ahead might need to arrange for a carriage to come in which to hide Harry as he went through. It might be that they could arrange to take him by stretches of river where possible.

Although freshly clothed, he still bore and retained the marks of a recently injured man.

A safe house was made available at the house of a gentleman in Marazion. It was there that Harry stayed for three weeks until he moved to Acton Castle under the protection and care of his brother John. John Carter rented the farm. The family that owned the estate rarely interfered with whatever he chose to do there. Their rent was secure that was what they knew, and the odd present thrown in for good measure.

***

"Well yes we have had our fair share of troubles with the trade over the years, Mary." Hannibal continued his reminiscences. "Well yes and in between times we had a few losses too. Not of the money kind but with the children."

"I don't know if I can bear to think on that Hann. At the same time, I can't bear not to."

Mary's face painted a picture, for a brief moment in time, of the grief she had to endure, but tuck away at the start of every day. This expression of her grief for the loss of two of her children had also brought back to her Father-in-law, Hannibal 1st, the tragic deaths of his first two children. Both Mary and her father-in-law had lost a boy and a girl early on in their parenthood.

Hannibal 1st reflected on the triple deaths of Honour, Hammond and their mother Joan which had put into place a chain of events that had placed his life on a new course for the future. They were all here now because of those events. Mary had lost her first son who had been named Hannibal after his father. He was to be Hannibal 3rd. Hannibal 3rd had died at only 5 years old.

Hannibal 2nd and his father took it in turns to carry the small coffin with the little Hannibal inside. On the steep uphill walk to Maker Church few words were spoken. Occasionally they turned to see the village folk trailing behind. The burial site overlooked the open seas towards the Mewstone Rock, Bigbury and the English Channel. Hannibal 1st muttered in a low voice to his son a few words of comfort.

"He will look over us when we're on those seas my son. He will look over us now. When we look to the stars for our guidance and deliverance, we must always think of him, the first Hannibal 3rd."

"Yes, Hannibal 3rd, look over us and keep us safe as we have not been able to keep you. We will think of you always, especially when we look up to this place from our boats."

It was not long afterwards that Mary gave birth to Sarah and then again to Elizabeth. It was though, only a few years before yet again they were making the walk to the churchyard with a small coffin to bury Elizabeth.

She was buried on the site of her brother, the first Hannibal 3rd.

"This little coffin you can bear with one arm, Hannibal. It's so light as if there was nothing there. She was so small and so frail. Let me carry her a while. Please?"

Mary took the tiny coffin, weeping over it as she carried her daughter towards the Church.

"I can feel and hear her move, Hannibal. Her poor little body is hitting the sides in there. I must open it and set her right. I can't think of her hitting the sides and bruising her tiny self or maybe breaking her bones. I want to put her out of the world as she came into it. Perfect."

She placed the coffin down, pleading for help to open it and make her daughter more comfortable for her final journey.

"I'll take her Mary and make sure she is kept straight and doesn't move about. There's no need to do anything different. Come now."

Elizabeth had been born at Sheviock. Fearing the sickness that was prevalent in the village at that time she stayed until the birth, returning only for the baptism. She remained at Sheviock until the disease had passed through.

Hannibal 1st and Christian had kept the small cottage and boatyard that had been Christian's with Sampson. Her siblings had their use from its years previously and they had retained it afterwards. It still had its uses.

Mary used the little dwelling and store with her two children until it was the right time to return.

"Well Mary, that's enough looking back over things for one night. It won't get us anywhere.

The Lottery is due in and the boys will be unloading soon using all the boats we can muster. She has a big payload tonight."

"Are you going out there?"

"All our boats will be there. There's plenty of men with them. They are tucked away at the usual places. Expect the Lottery will be off Penlee near Lady Island and they'll be unloading into Polhawn or if there's any doubt, sink them around the cellars and we'll pick them up later."

"They'll send word here as soon as she is sighted, and the boys give the all clear to anchor up and start the unloading. I'll go up then. All our tunnels and stores are ready if they're needed but I expect for tonight it'll be the farms and the churches. It's a big load."

"Well, rest a while, it may be a long night to come."

Chapter 14

Lottery Brings a Wind of Change

"Hann, Hann! Come quick." Pascoe Spriddle had burst in hardly able to catch his breath. "Quiet now," said Hannibal 2nd, standing and resting his hand reassuringly on his friend's shoulder. "What is it?"

"It's the Lottery off Penlee. It's all gone wrong. There's shouting and screaming out there. Bowden's boat and men came. She's full to the brim. There are spirits, teas, silks and more. The boat is crammed and nothing much unloaded."

"Are our boats with her?"

"Some of them were. There hadn't been enough boats to unload Lottery quickly, so the Captain had sent Thomas George and William Rowe ashore to ask for more. I was on the beach. As we pushed more boats out, we saw the revenue boat leaving from the quay off Bowden's. We knew we couldn't get to Lottery in time to warn her before Bowden would get there. It was too late to get to the top of the fields to make a fire or send Lottery a warning light from a place they would see it.

We went up through the fields and wood above to see the Lottery from the high ground. I have just run back in to you. Our boats had left the Lottery. I could see them heading towards the coves between Penlee and Rame. I would be surprised if Bowden had seen any of them, let alone be able to say who they were or what they looked like."

With that, Hannibal tightened his boots and the two went in haste through the fields to Penlee Point, to a vantage point where they could make out something of what was going on.

Without warning the sound of gunshot ripped through the still night air. Shortly afterwards the silhouette of the six oared Bowden boat could be seen, making eastwards towards the Naval ship, which lay silent and anchored up towards Sandway cliffs.

Lottery had been anchored just between Penlee point and Lady Island. She was far enough off shore to keep clear of the rocks and far enough in so as not to be seen by the Naval vessel. Her position was such that she couldn't be spotted either from the village. Overall, the Captain had chosen a good spot to unload that night.

What could have gone wrong ?

What was the shot about ?

Richard Oliver, Captain of the Lottery had given a low whistle signal as the shadowy form of the Bowden boats came into view. He waited for the reply that would tell him these were the additional Cawsand boats that his men had gone in to obtain or that it was Thomas George and William returning. There were already three small Cawsand boats alongside the Lottery. They had been waiting for her over the previous couple of days.

Christmas Day had been a pre-arranged target day for the Lottery's arrival. The three boats and boatmen had spent their Christmas day tucked into the small hideaway cove just on the Point at Penlee.

The tides had been kind to their position and allowed the boats a small stretch of sand at the highest tide with a good space further back into the scoured out small rock cavern.

It was here that they slept, woke, looked out and waited in turn.

Expecting the usual response back to his call enquiring whose boat was approaching them from the other side, Richard Oliver was almost knocked over onto the deck with shock as a chilling reply was returned.

"We are the King's boat."

Ambrose Bowden, the resident chief Customs Officer for Cawsand, was now standing in the bow of his small craft. He had four rowers tonight who were positioned at the bow end and amidships with their oars. Six oarsmen usually manned the revenue boat but not tonight. Bowden was short on oarsmen but completely undeterred.

The colour of the flag and its detail were lost on all in the moonlight. Richard and the others knew it, whatever the state of light, whatever the distance it was away. The flag had a presence and a stench to those in the business of free trading. This stench could make itself felt like a wall of stone falling upon them. They knew it, they could sniff it out ..... it reeked of danger.

"Stay off you buggers, or we'll fire on you," retorted Richard.

Bowden held the revenue flag high and outstretched. He was precariously leaning forward as if he were a figurehead on an ocean-going vessel.

Swollen with pride in the office he held, he breathed in deeply, puffed out his chest and shouted to them to dare do it. He reminded them that this was a revenue boat. He reminded them too of the powers they had to board, search, arrest, detain the Lottery and its crew at will.

Despite the cold still night of winter and their vulnerable position compared to that of the Lottery smugglers, Ambrose Bowden, Officer of His Majesty's Customs, stationed at Cawsand as Officer in charge, cut a fine figure of a man.

He was indeed a figure of fearless quality. He would not be subdued by this lawless gang of smugglers who dared defy him and his commission. His uniform gave authority too, but even that was lost on its audience tonight.

The name of the Lottery painted on both sides was now within his view. Surprising all, three shots then rang into the air in rapid succession, lighting up the sky. This was so much so that it showed the faces of some of the eighteen crew.

The three small village boats had by now gone. They knew there was nothing more that they could do. The Lottery was well armed and with plenty of men on board. The small boats must go, before they could be clearly seen, and note taken of those on board and to whence they were heading. They must away quickly, give warning and prepare for what that night might further bring. They might have been seen but they had not been identified. The boats pulled up out of sight past Lady Island into a small cove.

Lady Island was no stranger to the smuggling and Naval activities that had been conducted near her small spit of rock that lie just off the rocky shoreline. Not really an island other than at very high tides she had witnessed not only the passage of generations of shipping but suffering, wounding and death that had come to those taking their living from her seas and shores.

Whatever she had seen happen tonight and whatever was yet to come would be on a small scale compared to some of the shipping disasters she could tell tale of. None though were on the scale of events at this very same site that had befallen her rocky outcrop just over one hundred years previously. Lady Island had then witnessed the death of over six hundred naval men on board the Coronation man o war.

The Coronation was caught up in one of the worst storm's men could remember. A mile off Lady Island, the ship had capsized, dragged onto the rocks around the Island where it was dashed to pieces, men with it. Much of its ironwork still lay in the shallows. Canon and cannonballs were still there. They could be seen at lower tides and in the seasons when the seaweeds were not providing so much cover over them.

There was much confusion over what then happened next between the Lottery and the Customs boat. The smugglers knew only that the Lottery was well armed, whereas Bowden and his men were outnumbered both by people and firepower. There was also, though, the Naval ship not far away to be considered. HMS Stag might be drawn into a scuffle, which could shift the balance of power away from the Lottery.

They had heard shots. Had the shots killed anyone? Who had fired? Had they come from the revenue vessel or had they come from the Lottery?

The men from the small boats as well as Hannibal then saw the Lottery sail past their position, heading westwards.

"They've cut loose their cable and are heading for home. They'll be there soon, sooner than we could get a message concerning these events to Polperro."

The Lottery was sailing to its home port of Polperro. Heading swiftly across Whitsand Bay, all on board were blissfully ignorant of the death of a Customs' employee from their shots.

They had left crewmates Thomas and William behind in Cawsand. They knew they would most likely make their way back when they could and take sanctuary in Cawsand in the meantime.

The Lottery had goods aboard, valuable goods. These goods were weighing them down. They had to be unloaded. They knew there was not much time and that the Polperro boats could have her unloaded before any revenue boat could come for them. They had the advantage of a good head's start.

In contrast, those on the Bowden boat knew precisely what had happened. "He's dead", shouted one of the Customs oarsmen to Bowden. They both looked at Glinn. He had most of his face and head blown away.

Glinn was an oarsman for Bowden. He had slumped forward as the shots were fired, coming to rest dramatically over his oar. A big man, he had to be carefully moved to the stern of the boat. Here he would be out of the way of the other oarsmen. They were now a man down on a rowing boat already short of two men.

This repositioning of Glinn would also allow Ambrose Bowden himself to take an oar. This meant moving the oarsmen around the boat with great care not to upset its balance. Previous injuries Bowden had sustained, in the course of his duties, had rendered him best able to row on only one side of the boat.

They manoeuvred Glinn's body into the rear of the boat, where, what remained of his head, was rested over the transom.

The water lapped against it as the occasional wave caught the stern, cleaning the congealed blood somewhat and revealing the extent of the damage to Glinn's head. As his companion oarsmen moved him, so some of the brain and gore that was hanging from the side of what was left of his head, broke away.

These macabre contents of Glinn's skull either spilled into the body of the boat, where they would slither on its bottom boards, slipped over the side, or placed themselves unwelcomingly onto the clothes and bodies of his former companions.

"There's nothing much left of him. Who's going to tell his family? They rely on his money and that boy of his, well he's only young. He isn't quite right you know. What are they going to do without him to bring in the shillings?"

With this they rowed back into the bay of Cawsand and across to the Naval frigate HMS Stag. Stag was fully equipped and ready to take to the High Seas on its next mission.

The revenue boat could now be seen by a growing crowd lining the roads and tracks that went through Kingsand and Cawsand. Bowden called up to the Stag from their rowing boat, announcing that he came as officer with the King's boat in the service of preventing smuggling. His voice travelled across the waters and sent a chill through the village.

He shouted that they had a shot man on board. Ladders were lowered. Glinn's body was recovered by the Stag men and taken to the ship's surgeon.

"He's dead alright. How did it happen?" The story of the night was given to the officers and surgeon on board and with that Bowden requested immediate assistance from the ship, which as soon as it could muster its men, took sail. "We know the boat to be a Polperro boat and she may have gone there."

In Polperro, William Johns was one of the men who eyed The Stag as she anchored outside the harbour, some of the crew taking to the rowing boat. He watched the rowing boat come in and round the harbour and tie up against the Polperro revenue boat and board her. Discussions were taking place.

William Johns knew now that the Lottery had been in Cawsand Bay that night and had discharged her cargo back in Polperro. He knew that there had been an altercation in Cawsand.

This had changed the plans of the Lottery Captain and the Lottery was now moored on the other side of the harbour out of view.

"Get word to Zephaniah boy," he muttered to his son. It was now coming to dawn. The boy slinked quickly through the maze of streets, opes and paths. Through the courtyards he went, watched but able to pass.

"Mr. Job, Mr. Job", the boy tapped on the shutters. "What is it boy?" "Father is watching the harbour and needs to speak with you."

For those who could read there had often been a concern as to how he should be addressed.

Was Mr. Job's surname pronounced Job or Jobe.

"Job by spelling, Jobe by pronunciation." Job would often say when first introducing himself to a new acquaintance.

"Off you go boy, run now and tell your father I'll be with him as soon as my legs can take me."

Job was an early riser. A bachelor, he lived for his work now. He had been up working on his ledgers since first light appeared. Zephaniah Job had been a St. Ives man originally but had moved into Polperro nearly 30 years ago. A man of education, he had taken to offering teaching in the village. He would teach the children basic mathematics, English and French. The classes filled as Polperro people could see the advantages in the literacy of their children. Similarly, they could see the benefits to their children in gaining greater competence in understanding foreign currency. Job was well paid in Polperro and soon became a trusted confidant. Polperro had a large, successful smuggling fleet now and Zephaniah Job had to no small extent contributed to this success in the last thirty years or so.

It had been Job who had brought an administrative structure to the trade in Polperro. Zephaniah had established lines of credit that extended both debit and credit in his weighty ledgers. Credit lines had been formally established with merchants in Guernsey and Roscoff.

Capital finance to build the boats and partake in large organised runs had been arranged by him, not only from within the landed classes of Cornwall but with wealthy bankers in London.

His web of twilight contacts had been spun around the entirety of the southern section of the country. Job's word was good enough for all of them. A signed promissory note from Zephaniah Job was as good as gold, often better, for a share in the profits of a boat or a run was highly profitable. It had fuelled the development of the landed estates in the area. Job was welcomed at their houses where meetings were held over several days in great secrecy. Zephaniah was the successful conduit between the smugglers and the upper classes.

As Zephaniah bent to tie his boots, there was another tap on his shutters. It was Hannibal Marks. The two men knew each other. Dealings had been done for a long time between Polperro and Cawsand.

Hannibal had travelled by horseback, daring not to travel in by sea at this time. Polperro had to be warned of what had happened that night. The horse had been tethered at the top of the village and he had hastened, firstly to Job.

Hannibal could walk, untroubled, through the lawless streets, as could any of the Cawsand men.

"Talk as we go to William's Hannibal. You must be the messenger for bad news to have ridden at night to get here. I heard news of your father's death. I am sorry to hear it. He did a lot of work with us and I had got to know him well."

"He remains at his house until tomorrow when he will be buried at Maker. In the meantime, we thought father would not mind covering the tunnel entrances for us in case Bowden and his men search it there."

"Clever, very clever of you to think of it, Hannibal. As I knew your father he would not mind. Indeed, he would most likely think that this was his last job. I hope he was watching these last hours and took relish in the part he has played in ensuring our safety. Yes, ensuring it from the grave... nay.... before he has even gone to the grave, but after he has left this world. I pray for his soul."

With that, they left the house, watched by the village as they went back through the maze of small cottages previously walked by Will's lad that same morning.

It was the quickest way. Eyes followed them and knew something might be amiss. What was Hannibal doing here with Zephaniah at this time of day? Best to look away. We have not seen him?

"The Lottery was unloading off Penlee when she was disturbed by Bowden and his men. One of his men was shot. We don't know who shot him, but the man died, and Bowden was last seen by me boarding the Stag."

Zephaniah pursed his lips. "They'd best make for Guernsey. Stay there a while. I'll get a message to our merchants to give them safe houses. There will be a price on the boat and the crew, that's for sure."

Zephaniah would make arrangements for their safekeeping, a new boat if needs be. William was back at the Polperro harbour, eyes fixed on Bowden. He was scouting the harbour's boats, rummaging as he went and now disembarking onto the granite harbour steps. The tide was high, and he didn't have many to climb before he was stood looking up at the dour maze of cottages that lined the cliff.

Thomas Pinsent had died last year. He had been the resident Customs House Officer since 1766. In all he had served for thirty years in Polperro and survived. Ambrose Bowden had known Thomas Pinsent well. His successor he did not know as well but he would rouse him and the men at the Custom House. William, Zephaniah and Hannibal watched from the vantage place at William's. After a short while at the Customs' House the men could be seen coming out in single file. Well-armed they were. They all looked purposeful.

"Where exactly is the Lottery lying?" Asked Job of William.

"Just outside the harbour walls. They'll see her if they set out and go west." With that, Hannibal, William and the boy left to get to the Lottery. Job arranged for warnings to go to the crew members' houses, should they be ashore. The death of a Customs official meant there would be serious onslaughts to face very soon. The village too must prepare. Crew that could not be identified must remain so. Hannibal thought too of Thomas George. He should remain in Cawsand now perhaps. Maybe he should work from there until the heat died down. Hannibal could return with his wife if she chose. They could stay openly in Hannibal's father's house. There was room at Hannibal's now. Any movements between the villages would be perilous soon and it would be more incriminating if he were found in the tunnels. If he were there with his wife and fishing with them it would be easier to explain. No one had known that he was on the Lottery. His friend was also in the village and could be there too. He was a younger man, another William, who at twenty-four years of age had no other family in the area. Cawsand would have had its searches by now.

Nothing found, things might be left to rest a while. Polperro would be another matter. This was where the crew lived, where the Lottery was based. They would return here to rummage the village time and time again until they found something.

Hannibal bade farewell, watching the Lottery slide almost out of view. Her fine large Cutter sail swayed the now empty vessel to one side, then the next as they tacked forward against the prevailing winds. He returned quickly to the top of town where Thomas's wife would be taking the long way around the lanes and fields. When he arrived, she already knew what had transpired that night.

"Thomas is safe with us for now Flora. No one but the trusted few know his whereabouts. To re-unite you with Thomas we should wait a while and go under cover of dark. Job will sort your house and things.

Richard Oliver now had twelve crew on the Lottery. In no time the sails were up, and they were gone. They went south west turning south to get out of sight as quickly as possible and head then eastwards in open channel to Guernsey.

William's son had been sent to pass word around the village that something was amiss and to make sure there was nothing about.

Stored contraband had been checked and made secure. Down tunnels it went, stowed behind the chimneybreasts, inside chimneys, even under the church alters. It was not, though, goods that were being searched for today. It was the Lottery crew. Bowden had taken a good look at many of them. They may not have seen the Lottery, but the men could be back here by now.

Searches for contraband in Polperro were known in the revenue service to be dangerous for those undertaking them.

Even the notorious Captain Bray of the Revenue Cutter, Hind, a man dreaded by the smugglers with a fearless reputation, had known fear when he had once searched the Polperro fish cellars for contraband. Bray was heading the search party when the Polperro folk gathered in strength to oppose him and his men.

"Move those nets and we'll out your livers," went up one cry. With that, a fight broke out. Bray and his crew were lucky to escape with their lives. They returned with military re-enforcement but by that time all had been moved to safer places.

It was therefore with some trepidation that Ambrose Bowden conducted the searches in Polperro that day.

Searches over, Bowden sailed into Plymouth to fully report on events.

Customs' House London announced a bounty and a pardon in an attempt to catch the killers.

Notices were printed. £200 was the reward. This was a considerable sum of money to the poorly paid for of these parts but not enough to break the chain of solidarity that had been forged around the southern coast.

As day broke in the villages of Cawsand and Kingsand the enormity of what had happened around Penlee hit the people. The dead man's body was taken into Plymouth for examination then off for service and burial. The villagers knew as the Dragoons came in that this was going to be one of their worst times since the area became a centre for the free traders. The houses had all looked to their tunnel entrances overnight, secured and obscured them. They had been emptied of any evidence, as far as possible, in the time available. Anything that could not be hidden well or was better out of the villages was taken out and scattered. This had been an enormous, risky task but word had spread quickly, and they all knew what they had to do. The tubmen had been busy that night, in difficult circumstances, but they had acted quickly under the mists of confusion. There was little time to spare. The death of one of the revenue men could see the villages almost taken apart, stone by stone, to find evidence.

Hannibal 1st was lying in state with the lid on his coffin now closed over. He would have to remain so a further few days to do his final act for the village and his smuggling colleagues. They had hidden Harry Carter a few years before when he was brought up the beach, given for dead aboard his ship. Now it would be one of the Polperro boys.

The two Lottery crewmen that had gone ashore to get further help to unload their boat had split the previous night when they realised, they could not return to the Lottery. Thomas George had gone to the Marks and William to the Mardens. Both would be hidden by the village for now. Their boat had no signs of the Lottery and was pulled up at Cawsand beaches along with other fishing boats. Down went Thomas George into the dank and dark of the tunnels. There would be little light and air for him until the coast was given as clear and the signal made that he might emerge again. A sole candle went with him with a means to light it for there was little light permeating through into the section into which he would be in hiding. Down under he went between the floors and ceilings. He was in a cavity that had been built between the walls of the house and the adjoining property. Behind here was the Marks' ale house to one side and another to the other. So thick were the walls he could barely make out anything of the noise created on the other side. Down he went until the tunnel entrance was before him.

Chapter 15

A Final Assignment for Hannibal 1st

Thomas George of Polperro settled into a store area off to one side of the main tunnel and waited and waited. Sleep could not come but eventually he succumbed to it and total darkness fell as the candle extinguished itself. When the shout was given for the all clear he came up through the tunnel system following the line of the rope that was there as a guide for that purpose.

As he approached the exit, he could hear the coffin being moved away. He knew he had to say goodbye to Hannibal 1st. They all knew Hannibal, or at the very least, knew of him. An old timer of the smuggling trade, they had all known of his rise in the trade. The coffin lid was carefully and respectively removed. Thomas took Hannibal's hand and thanked him for everything, especially these his last deeds for them. "Farewell for now my friend. I may see you sooner than we both think if I am caught. I may be the one to swing for this. Look over us all from the heavens Hannibal."

Whilst Thomas had been oblivious to much of the goings on up in the house from the relative sanctity of the tunnels below, the door had been unceremoniously thrown open at the house of Hannibal 1st. There had been neither knock nor shout to announce the coming of their unwelcome visitors.

The element of surprise was really no surprise, it was expected. In the front ale house, the serving wenches asked the Dragoons and the Preventatives with them to stay a while and drink with them. But no – there was no tempting these men tonight with a murder hanging over the village.

With no words exchanged, they pushed past and in trooped several of them, one after the other, running around the house allocating sections of it to different persons to examine. As they tapped walls, ceilings floors with their sticks and sometimes the handle end of the swords and forearms, two of their number raced up the stairs to ensure that they held the element of surprise.

The trump card of surprise, though, had in fact been held by the Marks family. Granny Marks had been up there keeping an eye on him, sitting dutifully and devotedly by the coffin. The lid was off, and the air was saturated with the odour of death with which everyone in the village, save only the youngest, knew and was used to.

As she rocked to and fro, they stopped and looked. They quickly went around the room not wishing to disrupt the dead nor inhale any more of the fumes of death that surrounded them. It was as if they had a premonition that the act of inhaling death would in turn cause death.

The coffin sides had been made to rest downwards, not yet nailed, but pinned lightly and they would have had to take the now rigid Hannibal by the hands and move him and then the coffin. They decided against this, choosing to examine the room around the body.

Fortunately, they had seen from below that the area in which Hannibal lay above was indeed the coffin slipway. They were satisfied that this could lead nowhere other than the room immediately below for the purpose for which it had been built.

They had not bargained on its depth and the structure of the joists holding the floor above. They did not think that they could be removed, thus making way to take a person crawling to get to the place where they could drop down into the start of the underground chambers.

The chambers were in any event clear and unlit. Nothing to be seen other than the odd rat bathed in the soft light of the candle or the wick whose light came from the pilchard train oil with its characteristic and unmistakably, pungent smell.

The smell permeated everywhere without revealing its source, so strong it was, wherever it went. When mixed with the smell of death it was overpowering to the Dragoons who were not displeased to make a quick exit.

It was the oldest trick in the book but rarely failed and there were in addition the subsequent layers of concealment. If one failed there was another, which could be relied upon. These were the clever concealments that would make discovery, even without the watchful, cold stare, of Hannibal, a very difficult task for the Dragoons.

The burial of Hannibal 1st had been delayed by a day and although the cold had been kind to what remained of him, it was really the time now. All of those who had wanted to, had said their goodbyes so the final nails were hammered into the coffin sides to enable him to be taken securely to his final resting place.

He had started off on a farm in South Tawton above the hills of Dartmoor with a number of brothers and sisters. His family had been in South Tawton for a long while and Barnstaple port before that. His journey had started a new dynasty of the Marks family and settled them in some comfort with property and boats, with trade to pass on from their base in Kingsand and Cawsand.

Hannibal 1st was leaving a legacy to the next Hannibal and any of the family who wanted a future in the free trade. They had the houses, alehouses and Taverns along now with cellars, boats and stores. There was the little matter of the cash inheritance as well. They knew where it lay hidden and that they were to build on this hoard if they could. This was the store of gold and silver coins for the next generations or whenever it was needed. The "Marks Bank of Cawsand" as it had affectionately been christened had been based right under the nose of the resident Customs officer Bowden.

The Lobbs' freehold house and land opposite the fish cellar in the centre of the village was the place. It was located but two houses down from the house and office of Ambrose Bowden.

The well in one of the old cottages in the back of Honour's house had been opened up by Hannibal to take the coins. Easily covered over or capped with stone the leaded boxes took the coins under the water deep below and could be hauled up and down by the secured chain that itself had to be hooked up from its resting place below the water line.

Hannibal did not need to leave a will disclosing all that they had. No, he would just die. All he had would simply be carried on and used by them as it was now.

Hannibal 1st had married twice, had eight children by both marriages. His first wife had died shortly after the birth of a third son with only one child, Joseph, surviving to adulthood. He had lived in Launceston, St Stephens, Stoketon, Sheviock and finally settled with Christian in Kingsand and Cawsand.

He had mixed with the gentry here and there, travelled to Guernsey, Roscoff and more, founding wealth for generations of Marks yet to come.

By the standards of this day, here lay a wealthy and self-made man. The villagers were all out for the walk to Maker where Hannibal was to be buried with a service at the Church held to respect a long, difficult life. A life that had contributed to the prosperity of the villages and its people.

Chapter 16

The Noose Tightens

The trees still standing within the village all took the thump of nails being hammered into their trunks, followed by the bellowing of a Crier on horseback announcing the presence of the notice that had been firmly fixed to the tree and its content. As heads turned, those who could read, drenched their eyes in the words, Reward and £200.00. Hannibal's heart sank deep.

The Crier rode through the village with characteristic pomp. He was over from Plymouth. His job was to bring the printed reward notices and nail them to every conspicuous place in the area.

The papers too were full of it. Only a few copies of the Sherbourne Mercury were taken and read in the village. The Doctor, Vicar and some of the merchants always had one. Its content was then spread quickly with some embellishment as it left the pages and travelled to a wider audience, mouth to mouth.

The Crier stayed on his horse when he stopped to make his formal announcements, one in Cawsand and one in Kingsand. He would be stopping on his return to repeat the whole exercise in Millbrook and St John before riding on to the crossing point at Cremyll back to Plymouth.

He had come equipped with sufficient notices and nails that other trees sited in conspicuous locations along his journey could be used to affix a notice and spread the word. He would not announce the notice at these places unless there was a sufficient crowd, or the likelihood of one assembling, to whom he might offer the spectacle of his presence and eloquence in the presentation of the written word.

Stopping at the Square in Cawsand, the large open space at the end of the village. The Square was yards back from the beach, the access to which was through a gap, wide enough to take horses and carts comfortably, two being able to pass each other with a measure of ease. The Square was not quite square, but square enough to have taken the title as the surrounding buildings had formed the shape around it over the years. There were three tracks that led into and out of the Square, all of which had dwellings of all shapes and sizes in now almost unbroken but jagged rows. Chimneys to their fronts, chimneys to their backs and chimneys to their sides. Rooves at different pitches, different heights and few with perfect symmetry. Some thatched, some with slate, stone and others wood. Local stone, nearby stone and some now brick. This was a motley collection and a fitting backdrop for the colourful Crier who blended with ease, indeed comfort in to the scenery.

Circling the Square twice, then riding up and down each of the tracks and roads, he called to attention all those who might be there in the dwellings, the ale houses, Inns, cellars, requesting they assemble in the Square to hear his announcement on behalf of the King and His Majesty's Commissioners of the Board of Customs.

Arriving back at the Square the Crier held himself high in the centre, waiting for the villagers and others there to gather.

When he felt he had attracted a big enough crowd, worthy of his announcement, he held his script well in front of him. With great poise and dignity befitting his position, arms outstretched, he unfurled the rolled paper, brought his head up high and looked to the crowd. He was nearly ready to begin. Clearing his voice, aided by a sup of the ale he had purchased from the large Inn adjoining the Square, he began.

"Oyez, Oyez, Oyez. Pray be silent to hear this Notice of the Commissioners of Customs on authority of his Majesty, the King.

Whereas it has been humbly represented to the King that Richard Oliver the Younger, Richard Barrett, the younger, William Swartman, the Younger, Philip Libby, the younger, Thomas George and Roger Toms, of Polperro in the County of Cornwall, and lately belonging to a smuggling vessel called the Lottery stand charged upon oath with being concerned with the wilful murder of Humphrey Glinn late a boatman belonging to the six-oared boat in the service of the Customs, stationed at Cawsand, on the 26th of

December late between the hours of ten and eleven at night off Penlee Point on the coast of Cornwall by firing from on board the said vessel called The Lottery with muskets at the said boat. His Majesty, for the better discovering and bringing to justice the above named persons is hereby pleased to promise his most gracious pardon to any one of the said offenders except Richard Oliver the younger, the Master of the said vessel and Richard Barrett the younger one of the owners thereof and the persons who actually fired who shall discover his accomplice or accomplices or be the means of any one or more of them being apprehended and committed to prison for the said offence. And as a further encouragement the Commissioners of his Majesty's Customs do hereby offer a reward of two hundred pounds to anyone of the said offenders except as before excepted or to any other person or persons who shall apprehend or cause to be apprehended any one or more of them the said Richard Oliver the younger Richard Barrett the younger, William Swartman the Younger, Philip Libby the Younger, Thomas George and Roger Toms whose descriptions are hereinafter mentioned which said reward will be paid by the Receiver General of the Customs upon the said persons or either of them being apprehended and committed to prison.

By Order of the Commissioners J.Hume Secretary

Descriptions

Richard Oliver, the younger, a dark complexion, long face, light brown, curled hair about 6 feet high about 26 years of age, rather thin but very bony and walks very upright

Richard Barrett, the younger a dark complexion, long thin face, black, short, straight hair about 5 feet 6 inches high about 32 years of age, very thin and rather stoops in his walk

Philip Libby, the younger, a dark complexion, round face, short hair about 6 feet high about 42 years of age very stout and rather stoops in his walk

William Swartman, the younger a dark complexion, round face, long brown, tied hair about 5 feet 4 inches high about 24 years age and of middling stature

Thomas George, a dark complexion, long, thin face and has a very wide mouth, short black hair, rather bald, about 5 feet 4 inches high, about 50 years of age of a middling stature and has lost part of the forefinger of one of his hands.

Roger Toms, a very dark complexion, long face, short curled black hair rather bald, about 5 feet 6 inches high, 45 years of age middling stature and has a rupture.

Hannibal's pulse quickened, then raced as he saw the poster and heard of the newspaper article. The missing piece of finger could attach Thomas to this. They must help him to leave the village unless there was another way to put anyone suspicious of his presence in the village off the scent. His mind was racing with thoughts as he returned to the house, sitting a while with Thomas.

"It's the finger Thomas, with the rest of the description, that implicates you."

"What should we do Hannibal, perhaps I should leave and take my chances?"

"I think you are safest here now until this has blown over. Best not to move. The notices will be everywhere and for an amount like that there is a risk you will be disclosed. But no one yet knows you are in Cawsand and no one yet knows you have lost the top bit of your forefinger. Lots of folk lose a finger."

"How about we get rid of it altogether or take a piece of another. I've never liked that little one at the end. Bloody useless."

"Let's not act in haste Thomas. Maybe you should continue in hiding for a while yet until this is over, or we could get you a passage to Roscoff and look after your wife here until things clear. You could start a new life here on your return?"

* * *

Meantime, events were taking place rapidly on the high seas along the south coast of Cornwall and west Devon.

"It's those Customs buggers! I'd recognise that rig anywhere. Quick take a closer look. What's the boat?"

The eyeglass was raised by the best sighted of the crew. "It's the bloody Hind. We'd better get out of here."

"It'll be that bugger Bray and his men." The shout went up and there were shouts from all quarters of the Lottery meshing into one cacophony of sound.

It created a haste and urgency in the crew.

"They'll take no bribe and show us no mercy."

"They'll have our skins for that death."

"We're travelling heavy but if we go west, we may be able to save our cargo and run them out and land our goods at the Cove."

Five months had passed since the incident in Cawsand. The Lottery crew had reached a stage of a quiet confidence that they had got away with it.

"Change course."

The Lottery changed course onto Bolt Head and the chase began.

"We've got cover of darkness coming if we can hold our speed and course."

On the Hind, Bray knew he was in with a good chance of finally nailing the lid on this, taking the prize of the Lottery and the smuggled goods she was clearly laden with.

5.00 a.m. saw first light with both ships off the Lizard sitting silently, becalmed.

"Of all days to not get a wind off Lizard Point. It's God's will doing this. The Lizard with no wind?"

Both boats were stagnant and moribund off the Lizard. Stirred by the occasional light breeze, but insufficient to fill the sails, they could not move.

"Come on let's try to row her."

The Lottery was far too big to row, but the men were trying to keep their distance from the Hind until they could get going again when a wind came.

The Hind had drifted closer and closer to the Lottery until Bray decided it was time to send a boarding party across.

"Take down the two best boats. Arm them well."

The two boats were sent across by Bray under the command, as they left the Hind, of Hugh Pearce.

"Look," said Pearce, as he gasped on nearing the Lottery and her name came into view.

"They have just covered up the name of the Lottery. The buggers. They didn't believe they could ever be caught. Come on lads, heave to and we'll get there and show them what for. Give it to them for what they did to Glinn."

The name Lottery had indeed simply been covered up.

"Any closer to us and we'll open fire."

"Back on your oars men, back on your oars," came the command from Pearce whose shrill voice cut through the air like a knife through butter. The shrill tone from this little, but stout, man carried over the water to the shore behind.

Pearce was not a man to back down from a threat issued by a smuggler, but this time he knew they were capable of carrying out their threats.

They had done so with Glinn. Now the chips were down they would be quite capable of doing it for a second time. After all, was there much to lose now? They could hang for what they had already done.

It might only be the difference between being cut up under the surgeon's knife when dead or being eaten by the Thames vultures when trussed up and left to swing over the river.... But death, well, death was death.

Lizard onlookers were gathering as the voices could be heard coming in with the tide. Each wave that broke gave a chance to listen to the dialogue. Lizard Point people knew the Lottery.

Around buzzed the talk over what they might be able to do to help her and the men. They didn't have to think for long when the wind started to spring up and the chase began all over again.

"Bloody waste of good grogs. Bugger Bowden, bugger Bray, bugger the bloody lot of them. Over they go one by one two by two. I hope they bloody well hole the Hind."

Eventually they were off Longships light when Bray fired on her.

"I don't want to be taken by Bray and his lot. Come on let's row in, we can do it. The Lizard people will get us away, maybe to a boat on the north coast."

Twelve of the smugglers got into the Lottery's rowing boats and rowed for shore, the others remained, waiting to be caught. This was a good day for Bray.

The Lottery had been captured after one of the longest chases ever known in smuggling days.

The Lottery was one of the finest built at Cawsand for the trade. Fast and sleek. Bray would welcome her into the fleet of Revenue Cutters if his superiors in the service agreed. Shame to cut up those craft .... at least yet. Let her catch those she was built for, thought Bray smirking to his colleagues as he gave the order to take his captives below and chain them up.

The Lottery was towed into Plymouth but one man on board had talked. Toms. Toms, was kept on Hind until all were caught but he escaped, managing to make contact with Polperro and arranging to meet his wife.

When Toms turned up at the agreed place to meet his wife, instead a number of the Polperro smugglers were there to greet him instead.

They had ambushed the meeting. Sparing his life, they stowed him away on a Smuggler to Guernsey.

He was unearthed by the Customs in April 1800. They took him back to Exeter Gaol under armed guard for questioning. Roger Mark also escaped.

He was not discovered, eventually finding his way back into the trade when things had quietened down. The identities of those aboard the Lottery that night, were disclosed by Toms. He was to turn King's evidence to save his skin.

The Customs had their key man, a prosecution witness who was on board that night, one who saw the shot discharged that killed Glinn. They had also unearthed Potter, their key missing person.

As for Mark who, although of Polperro, was related to the Cawsand Marks, well, he seemed to have escaped altogether. It was only the 's' at the end of the name Mark that separated them. The Customs had most of their men and certainly the key man.

The Admiralty were now ready to bring their case.

* * *

Job had been busy in the background. The men were looked after whilst in gaol with allowances for decent food and top lawyers appointed.

"This is at a cost, Hannibal. We are now looking out for the wives and families, the defence costs, as well as trying to buy off those who will condemn our men. What do you know of Ambrose Bowden? I would like a chance meeting with him."

Zephania had made an unusual visit out of Polperro. He had come up to Cawsand now the dust had settled somewhat to see Hannibal 2nd. Their meeting was in private at the top back room of old Hannibal's house.

There he saw Thomas, his wife as well, giving them some money that would enable them to lie low for longer, not working for the time being.

"He is a Revenue man through and through. We have tried cautiously to see if he may be turned our way like many of the others have. But Bowden ... no. Not Bowden."

"Mmmm, maybe when the time is right, he will take our money. If he values his life and that of his family perhaps."

"These are desperate times, Hannibal. Desperate times. Bowden is in the way. He could be replaced but maybe by one more, shall we say, amenable to discussions about their position."

Zephania decided he would look around the towns. Known only by sight and name to those who were in a position to make deals, those who were part of the Job circle, he moved around relatively unnoticed.

Ambrose Bowden's house was on the front overlooking the sea to the east and south. He had started rebuilding the house in front of the old one, but the work was not going well.

"Good morning to you," hailed Job on seeing him. He knew instantly who he was, although he was at this time un-uniformed, with no badge of office about him.

"Do you know if these fish cellars opposite that look a bit worse for wear are for sale? I am involved with the Plymouth and Polperro merchants. We could do with more cellars here to process the catches. Do you know of the owners of these?"

Ambrose Bowden looked suspiciously at Job who was inconspicuous by dress but possessing the manner of a gentleman, one of the merchant classes at that. He would see Job. His men were on creeping duties in the rowing boat and were well out of sight in the rollers that were coming in west of the Point. No signal of a crop as yet.

"Come through won't you," said Bowden who seemed eager to partake in a discussion with this eloquent and clearly educated man.

Job went into the part-finished building, through to Bowden's quarters at the rear that would eventually be demolished in favour of the new house.

"Costly business," said Job.

"Will be a good and prominent house when finished though."

Job was conscious as he looked out towards the track outside which served as the main road through the village, that no folk stopped outside the Bowden residence, moreover, they hurried past this house.

He had his man all right.

"Yes, the building costs never seem to end. The quarry stone, mortar, the craftsmen are all costing more and more."

Job's purpose was to open a dialogue with Bowden. He now needed to quickly build a level of trust and interest.

Chapter 17

Execution Dock

Tom Potter started to empty his last ale from the depths of his stomach as the cart carrying him and the Catholic Priest neared the hanging scaffold.

As was customary he had been allowed to have a pitcher of ale before his final journey to Exhibition Dock where the scaffold had been rigged, ready for use as low tide neared.

He had been paraded for all to see along London Bridge and the Tower of London. As he drew closer the crowds gathered in strength. He was today their entertainment. He knew that in the crowd would be some well-wishers who would remain in the shadows. He also knew they were there, praying for him as he took his final steps.

He thought he was reconciled to the inevitability of his fate, reconciled with his God. But suddenly the panic set in and he looked to how he might escape.

In a way he was now famous. He was being taken to the dock led by a procession, at the front of whom was the High Court Marshal. On horseback, chest swelled, head held high, taut he went forward. He carried a silver oar that symbolised his authority and that of the Admiralty Court over these proceedings.

Was there a way out of this, a way of escape, a last-minute bid for freedom that he could make? His mind raced, thinking of the options left to him. There were none. He finally accepted his position.

He was chained and held. No this was it. This was his time. He would soon be in another world where he hoped his prayers and penitence had been heard and would count towards his salvation.

He was in origin from an Irish Catholic family, settled in Polperro. In this, his final hour, he had turned to the religion into which he had been raised.

The Catholic Priest accompanying him to the scaffold continued to pray for him. He offered him redemption from his sin on repentance and prayer. Tom took this. Comfort it gave as the Priest beckoned him to look skyward and not at the crowds.

"He is your hope and salvation now Tom. Look to the Lord, not to this earth in your prayers. Beg and believe that they be heard. Are you a true penitent for the life you have taken?"

"I am Father."

With that the Priest delivered communion as best he could. He prayed for the forgiveness of sins and penitents.

Job had ensured that the Priest would be there to offer comfort to Tom on this journey.

He was allowed next to the scaffold as Tom was taken to it. He was not alone. Neither was he first to step forward from this platform to the hereafter. There had been others with him at Newgate Prison although Tom was fortunate enough to have had Job pay and bribe his way, ensuring his conditions were the best they could be.

Separated from the others, he could eat better food than the worm-infested crumbs and gruel thrown through the prison doors once a day. With him there were others who would suffer an even worse death than he.

There were pirates for whom the short rope was to be used. They who would dance on the end of the rope as their limbs twitched and writhed. These were the unfortunate. These were the felons who would meet death more gradually by strangulation rather than having a relatively clean death from a broken neck.

All the prisoners on the cart had taken their last quart of ale. For some it went onto empty bellies, helping to intoxicate them quickly against the enormity of what was about to befall them.

The Chaplains from Newgate and the Marshalsea that also accompanied them on their journey delivered last prayers for the condemned. This was a busy job and a full-time occupation for them.

There were few Catholic priests attending by comparison. Their rites were in a number of ways different. Some of the condemned pirates, fuelled by the ale, took little participation in prayer.

“It’s no good father, I am going to hell. I will at least be warm there for all I have done. No prayers on this earth will save me from the next. I can see the devil now. He stokes the fire. He waits for me. At least my shipmates will be there too, waiting.”

The Priest took no notice, continuing with his duties. The condemned pirates in his company could expect a difficult and painful journey into the next world. This was not only because of the agony delivered by the short rope, reserved for piracy on the high seas, but also because of the knowledge that afterwards they were to be tarred and hung for maybe a year.

They would be in chains up river, hung as butcher's meat, to serve as a warning to others not to transgress the rules of the sea and the Navy.

Tom knew he too would be receiving a final ending that did not bear his thinking of. There had been no bribery Job could arrange behind the scenes that might dissuade the Judge from passing that down as part of the sentence.

The Judge's words, as the twelve sworn Jurors returned their verdict of guilty of the murder of Humphrey Glinn, had burnt themselves onto his memory. They had taunted him as he woke in the night to a sweat, repeating them over and over. They would not let him sleep.

The Judge, in announcing to the Court the sentence delivered to him, had a tone of sobriety that had sent a wave of chill from head to toe.

"You will be conveyed to the place of execution on Friday next and there hanged by the neck until you shall be dead, and your body afterwards given to be dissected and anatomised."

There would be no burial in the churchyard back at Polperro nor in the seas he had known. No one would recall the good side of Thomas Potter.

Whilst languishing in the jail he had been told of the famous Captain Kidd who had been at that very place. He had swung from the gallows at Execution Dock nearly 100 years before. No one had forgotten him.

Even at his end he was saved for a while as the first rope broke and he had lived. He was not so lucky on the second attempt. He traced back in his mind the acts of that night of the 26th December last year to the day when he was hauled from his bed at night and taken to the gaol.

He should not have become so confident. He should have recognised his good luck and left Polperro for good. Maybe he should have gone to Ireland from whence half of his family had come, or America, where he could have made a fresh start.

But no, here he was at 26 years of age, facing an unceremonious death at this, Execution Dock, before his time had ripened on the earth. If there were a next world, he would not do the same again.

The assembled condemned were not hung on mass. The gallows took them one by one to the immense cheering of the crowd as the entertainment for them took longer.

He had to endure the noises from the pirates on the short rope as they gasped for breath, wriggling and dancing on the rope, to the cheers of the crowds on the banks.

His was at least to be a comparatively short time on the gallows. As the long rope was placed around his neck, a calm descended. He finally and unconditionally accepted his fate.

He could only hear the voice of the priest and those of his mother and father beckoning him. The noise of the crowds paled into the distance as the priest's voice soothed his soul as he prepared to account for his sin in the next world.

The other two Lottery crew that had been brought to trial for murder at the Old Bailey were William Searle and Thomas Ventin. They had been acquitted of murder but were to serve two years in the stinking hulks on the Thames doing hard labour.

They would eventually find their way back home. As they left the court to start their sentence, their minds turned to Tom Potter, their friend.

Was it really his shot that had done the killing or was it one from the Bowden's muskets? It would never be fully known. This argument had not been put by the defence. But they were there, and they knew the confusion.

This was all Toms' doing. They would find Toms when their time on the Thames was up. All the other men taken in who were on the Lottery were convicted of lesser, albeit still serious, crimes of smuggling. They too served their time on the Thames hulks doing hard labour.

They never did get to Toms. Toms, the informer. He was given employment as a Turnkey at Newbury Gaol for the rest of his days as he could not return to Polperro.

Toms often contemplated his knee jerk reaction to turn King's evidence that had put all of this into motion. On the other hand, he had saved the necks of many ..... including his own.

What was right, and what was wrong, might well remain unknown or at the least go, undecided, into eternity.

Was Potter indeed the guilty one?

Had justice really been served?

Should they have all hung?

Should the responsibility for the murder have been shared between them?

Whatever the rights, wrongs and what justice should be served to reflect the truth, Job knew that it was here his loyalties lay.

He worked hard to bribe those persons upon whose evidence the crew could face the gallows.

He had struck up a quick relationship with Ambrose Bowden and eventually, most cautiously, most guardedly, raised with him whether he should go to the Old Bailey and give evidence.

Should there be any doubt whatsoever over whose musket was responsible for the death of Glinn, Job was convinced he should not go.

"Oh, and by the way ……." as a conversation around the subject was ending over a meal in Cawsand, "that house of yours could do with getting finished.

I thought you might like a little help, so I am drafting some money to you as repayment for your courtesy to me as a host."

The association between the two actions was clear to Bowden as indeed it was purported to be. He didn't comment but took the Job draft for £106.00, the amount he said he was down on the cost of an early completion of the works.

"Let's say it is a little gift in appreciation," muttered Job as he left. It had the desired effect. It bought the men in the gaol awaiting trial a bit more time to live. It gave the defence a bit more time to get their case into position.

At their last meeting, their last dinner before the initial date set for the trial, Job had suggested Bowden might like to take a little stomach soother for the journey he was embarking upon by road a few days hence.

The journey was by carriage to London where he was due to give his evidence at the trial. Ambrose Bowden now knew what he was dealing with, and who. It was too late to pull out and it was too late to stay in.

He had accepted Job's money the previous day and this had to remain buried for his and his family's sake.

"Buried, yes buried," said Job with his dry and wry smile. "Buried in that house of yours, eh!"

On the coach to London he was sharing with others to give evidence, Bowden started to retch uncontrollably, just outside of Exeter. He continued the journey until he could no longer and was put off to rest a while at an Inn, where he stayed many weeks.

The trial had to be put off as Bowden was a key witness. Job had kept to his word and Bowden had not been given anything that would actually kill him.

The time bought did not achieve much in the end. Defence counsel had more time to prepare and Job to get his bribery machinery into position.

Still, even with the additional time, Job's banking and other connections in the City of London he could not reach the judge or jury.

Hannibal 2nd had travelled with Thomas George to get him and his wife away to safety. Guernsey was no longer safe but Roscoff, then further into

France, he could be safe. The network would take care of him and give him a new life.

The Admiralty had indeed tried the Lottery crew thinking they had the missing two crewmen on the Lottery that night, George and William, but they hadn't. They had, in fact, tried and convicted of hard labour two new crewmen.

Chapter 18

New Century, New Challenge

The meeting at the rear of Hannibal's house comprised the usual colourful line up of people with major stakes in the local smuggling operations. They were all there. The backers, their agents, owners and shareholders of the smuggling vessels.

Despite the jubilant talk that bantered and cantered in all directions around the room, of successful runs, of profits being made, there was a sombreness running through the company.

"Coming up to 1800 Hannibal, and things are far from where they were. We have the Customs preventative men in our midst now. Bowden in the middle of the village and his crew. Who'd have thought it just a few years back even. The brazen neck of it. They are a different breed as well from what we have been used to. Can't seem to buy their silence. What's it all coming to?"

"Polperro is going the same way. They all are. More places up and down the coast too are getting them. Preventative men stationed in the villages. What next?"

"We're losing boats at a rate we never used to, good boats. As an insult to us all, the Lottery is in the service of the King. The buggers even kept the same name!"

"Not being satisfied with taking a Cawsand built smuggling boat they are after our young seamen for their Navy now as well. Bloody pressgang!"

"Those pressgangs have got wise to where our seamen spend their time. The gangs from the Navy ships are sent ashore by their Captains to recruit seamen in any way they can. They're getting worse around here. They go to the Inns the seamen frequent and the fairs they enjoy."

"Hunting them out they are, snaring them, laying traps for them. Pop a shilling into their ale and when they drink from the pot, claim they accepted the King's shilling. They knock them out with any old makeshift stick that makes up a cudgel at the fairs and take them off. Next thing they wake up on the Navy ships miles away out at sea. Don't see them then for years if ever again."

"That's not the only thing that is taking our good seamen. If they're caught smuggling, lighting what they think are warning fires or anything else just about connected with our trade, we've got a more difficult job nowadays to prove their innocence. Even if we get them properly defended by an Attorney it's not easy to get them their freedom with a slap on the wrist. There was a time no court would send a smuggler to gaol or transport them to the colonies. Now they can end up in Bodmin gaol or be sent to the Americas or anywhere else for that matter."

"Whatever, it means that these men, good men, our men, are being slowly but surely taken out of the trade."

"And there are still those bloody people pirates, the Corsairs, stealing people, using them as slaves on those galley boats. They are still out there sometimes mid Channel waiting their chances."

"All these things are problems for us but the big one is the problem of these preventatives; their men and boats being stationed in the heart of our villages. I expect more will follow. We need to take steps now. Fight back before they get a hold. We need to be cannier than them, ahead of them, learn to think like them. Always be one move ahead, never one move behind."

"I agree. If we don't win this battle, we stand to lose boats, men, stocks all of it in one go. Being caught sees boats go, stocks go, men go. All in one bloody go. That is the business going. We must take steps to fight back."

"Question my friends is. What do we do? Where do we go from here? We all need this money that's for sure. I wouldn't want to try to live off fishing alone now."

The company all nodded, even the agents, who themselves would lose much of their income and status in the big houses without the profits brought in by smuggling.

Smuggling had fuelled the demand for the agents as well as given employment and opportunity to many others who oiled the wheels of the free trade industry.

"We need to take more chances when the weather is bad. Use areas dangerous for them, and their boats."

"Decoys have worked before. We could use them more, arrange new ones. Change them more often so they don't get used to them. Perhaps give them a little something at the end of it? For themselves ... and the King, eh!"

"Make it easy for them to catch something while we work in peace on the bigger hauls."

"Get them used to finding things somewhere else, even the odd big haul and small boat? But they mustn't think that they have been led to that."

"Oh no, they must believe it's down to them. They must be seen to have done their job well."

"So, where are the places going to be? How are we going to set this up?"

"Strengthen what we have, what is already working and trusted. Make it better."

Mewstone Island, Rame Head, the Churches. the Estates. Look at what we have first.

Hannibal drew a close to the shouts, the loose thoughts and made a proposal to the meeting.

"I'll go and speak with all our main people at the Islands, the Churches, see what we could work out.

I'll start with the Mewstone Island."

***

The entrance to Mewstone Island, surrounded by lower lying rocks, was easily caught in all tides by bigger boats. Many had hulls ripped asunder as eddies and currents combined with inshore winds did their worst.

The Island was not far from the nearest Devon shores, perhaps half a mile, and but a few miles from Cawsand. It comprised a few acres in all with a high peak. There were two rocks there, Little Mewstone and Great Mewstone.

Fyn and BJ, now the sole occupants on the Island, were brother and sister. They had lived there all their days. Father had been sent there on sentence of a court. It was like a banishment from the mainland for his crimes. Seven years is how long he should have been there, but in the end, he never returned to the mainland. He stayed until his death and was buried on the Island.

Fyn and BJ stayed in the house he had built for the family. Father had used any materials he could find on the Island, much of which had been washed up onto it shores.

They had done a bit of work for the smugglers before but this time the visit from Hannibal was to take a whole new meaning for their relationship with the Cawsand smugglers.

"Pull to, Hannibal Marks," came the rasping voice of Joan. Phlegm gurgled in her voice box. It was stimulated to clear itself by the salt enriched atmosphere of the Island. She breathed deeply to shout loudly to him again.

"Come on, pull to. Harder. You've been getting soft over there. You and all them Cawsand and Kingsand men need a good kick up the arse. You've been having it too easy."

With that she jumped into the water, grabbed the boat at the bow and pulled it up. It was only a very narrow bit of sand on this stretch of the Island. Hannibal jumped out. The two pulled the boat up the shingle out of sight and out of tide's way. He had come alone.

It was a hard row over, but he picked good conditions. The boat was big for one, but, rode the waves well.

"To what do we owe this visit?" "We thought you'd been banged up or transported." With that she laughed loudly, awaiting his response.

She was tough, weather beaten, hardened from a life with little luxury other than the spoils washed up from failed smuggling ventures. These were often the barrels, the half ankers, sewn by the smugglers onto the seabed for a later collection. They would sometimes break loose. The spirits that they could use, or sell were topped up by goods and money earned from helping the smugglers.

A woman of few scruples and determined self-preservation, Joan, Black Joan, or BJ, as she was known, was rumoured to have killed and disposed of a man who had come on to the island who was seen as a threat to their continued safety. She was said to have disposed of him by cutting him up and using him as fishing and crab pot bait.

The Island, for all practical purposes, was theirs. About five feet nine inches in height and at least fifteen stones in weight, BJ comprised mainly bone and muscle. She was well developed for island life.

It did not matter if the nature of the rocky terrain was difficult for most mortals to survive and thrive on, for she had developed a body for all conditions that the Island could throw at them.

An upbringing short on footwear and other niceties, she had grown up without many things to wear. The result of this enforced frugality was an uncanny if not unnatural adaption to the demanding needs of her surroundings. She was able to survive well on the bounties provided by the impact of nature on the Island.

Neither of the children had learnt to read and write but communicated well with the smugglers without the need for those skills. On the Island, keen long eyesight and powerful hearing were more valuable than being able to use the written word.

Her large, almost flat face, skin deeply lined before her years, broke into a large smile, creating further deep, sun drenched, crevices along her face.

Jet black, unkempt hair, tangled by wind and salt from the spray of the sea, here she was Queen. This was Black Joan of Mewstone Island. The pair were almost self-sufficient on the Island. Surpluses were bartered for other commodities. These also contributed to a cash income for use when it was needed.

The garden produced most of the vegetables they needed. The sea harvested plentiful fish. When times were lean there was an array of limpets and other small rock creatures on which to feast. Seaweed too had provided sustenance and she knew how to prepare it to make it part of a palatable meal.

Crab holes abounded, giving a plentiful supply of large eating crabs, sometimes lobster. There was usually no need to pot for them as the holes almost always produced a crab every few days. The days when they didn't, they would forsake the crude crab hooks used to hook the crabs out of the holes, for a pot or two. The pots would be sunk just off the island's rocks at low tide and be collected again at the next low tide. They did not need to go far.

Rabbits provided meat and they bred plentifully. The pair netted birds on the land, took eggs from the cliffs and high grounds. They took milk from goats as well as their meat at the end of their productive life or where there were too many for the Island to sustain. There was plenty of rough land for the few they maintained.

Her brother Fyn's appearance, similar in many ways to her own, but much leaner in stature. He was taller, his dark hair long and tied back at the pit of his neck. His face too, beaten and scoured by the weather, with deep grooves in his skin was largely hidden by his beard . These were the twins of the Mewstone that Hannibal Marks had come to do business with.

"So, how's that business of yours doing, Hannibal. Out for King of Kingsand are we ..... or King of Cawsand too now? Or both maybe?"

"Worse than they have been Joan, but we're still there and still prospering from it."

"We heard that father had died. May he rest in peace. And ... about Lottery. We heard the shots that night from here and heard about the chase. We saw some of it. We'd know the Lottery anywhere and those buggers on the Hind. We could pick them out from the darkness here when Bowden's boat went to the Stag. We weren't sure at first it was Bowden but when we heard of the night's happenings, we knew it was what we saw."

"It's all been getting tighter for us free traders. That Lottery business started to see change. Chance or not, since that business they have been getting onto us more and more. Bowden in the village is just a start. Polperro is going to have the same. Preventative men everywhere. We need to take stock Joan if we're all going to continue and not lose what we have all gained. We need to try a few new tricks, perhaps invent again some of the old ones too."

"Happen you think we might be able to do something to help for a bit of money?" Joan's voice quietened and softened as if she felt someone who they wouldn't want to hear this conversation was close by. Close enough perhaps to hear of their plotting.

"Fyn'll know it's you by now. He'll have got us the fire lit and some drink ready. Fresh water or spirit, it's up to you."

Fresh water was in good supply on the Island. Their house had been well sited by father and was close to a spring.

Their father had also dug a well close by which had never run dry nor tasted of the sea.

Not much escaped Fyn. He'd seen the boat coming their way. When Hannibal came into sight, he dropped his guard and carried on with his jobs as Joan went off to get him in.

On their way up to the house Hannibal wasted no time in telling Joan the purpose of his visit to Mewstone Island.

"So that's where we are now Joan. We thought that you could do more, more regular work. To be decoys, maybe. When the boats come in if we're off loading and landing around the villages. Also provide storage for us here until the coast is clear. Storage could be anywhere best, whether the caves, tunnels or sink 'em in the waters tight to the Island but in places awkward to see and get to with any safety."

"We have never seen Bowden's men or any of the others, whether Turnchapel, Plymouth or nearby, creep and trawl around here. We know some areas to sink the ankers that are close to the island. They are places where the water is sufficiently deep, but it is surrounded by rocks. Places where the low tide still hides the crop deep down, but the revenue boats can't get into. We could sew the ankers down there. There's also the caves and caverns we could use."

"Might be best to use them to store any empty tubs or broken up ones to make out that you have collected them when they have been washed up against your shores. Just in case they find them and go there. You could even sew these ankers off the shore in a place where the Preventatives could find them. Let them creep them up and take the credit for their discovery. Nothing needs point to you. All down to the Captains of the boats.

You also have a part to play in just rowing around with a light to put them off the scent. Get them off Sandways and out towards your island, whereas we'd be coming up around Penlee. Just keep nets on board in case you are caught up with. Your reason for being where you are seen and searched must always be fishing or some other lawful activity."

"We could plan a number of signals that change regular. Make sure you know after each run which signals are ours and what they will be. That way you will know what to do, when to go, the route to take and when to return."

"Maybe that old hermit over at Rame Head could work with us here and there to confuse them. That headland is almost like an Island at night. You could think a light from there was from out at sea. We could work together by the lights, maybe to give warnings to you or distract."

"Yes, maybe.

We are safer nowadays making runs in bad if not treacherous weather, at night or a mixture of all of these. Sometimes when the wind is from the west, running strong and perilous with much cloud and rain is the best time. Those keen eyes of yours would be able to see our signals in those conditions clear enough, but would you be ready to take a small boat out as a decoy as well?"

"Me and Fyn together can take any weather these island waters throw at us. So yes.... we could do with a stronger boat though .... bigger, with a good sailing rig and sweeps ..... and some spares ... just in case they get broken in all that bad weather you're warning us about. Anyhow, we could do a better job with two good boats. How about some nets and pots ...? To make it real like. Gift not a loan mind you, Hannibal Marks! We know you, always an eye on your money. Got to open that fat purse of yours. Open it up for Black Joan and Fyn. Go on. You've got it and we can help you make more."

With that they went through the signals. Hannibal promised them a Cawsand built boat that would be fast and able to be rowed by one or two, spars and sails with it.

"Anyway, I'd better be away. They'll wonder what's become of me and if I'm meat on your table tonight."

They went back down to push Hannibal's boat back into the water and with that he went.

Bolstering the role of the Mewstone Island now things were getting tighter in the villages was only one of many measures that Hannibal had proposed and discussed at the meetings.

On his return journey he pondered on the role of the hermit at Rame Head. It was a good spot to make use of and the hermit did work for them. What enhancements might be made to their working arrangements?

Rame Head, a promontory with a small chapel, high, isolated, but with a commanding outlook to the east, west and south, had long been used as a watch and signalling point.

Difficult to access from the sea with its unforgiving, treacherous cliffs, the smugglers had nonetheless cut deep steps into the cliffside that ran from the headland in to the beaches at Polhawn enabling them at various places to get up and down the cliffs from the beaches and rocks below. These were mainly tiny beaches crammed between high rocks forming a series of small coves, some with caves further in. These were accessible, depending on the tides, by the smaller unloading boats. The steps led into a series of paths through the high brackens.

These pathways gave them access to the farms and Church at Rame, with their abundant hiding and storage facilities.

All this made for a good area to land the cargoes even though it meant double handling the goods to get them into the villages.

Some pathways were deliberate dead ends or simply took those who did not know them well, and especially at night, in circles. Unsuspecting Customs men might be lured into these, sometimes to their peril.

The frequency of rough seas on this stretch of the coast made it a less favoured area to sink goods under the seas. Many strings of ankers had broken loose from their mooring lines and sinking stones or been dragged along the bottom to the rocks that waited to break them open, spilling their contents into the awaiting, thirsty seas.

Hinram the hermit of Rame Head, as he was nicknamed, was not really a hermit in the Celtic sense of a religious man, a solitary monk, one seeking solitude to contemplate the greater things, living a simple life. The small chapel at Rame Head provided shelter for him and a home of sorts.

In the past it had provided a look out point, a place to light warning beacons that could be seen for miles up and down the south coast. It had been the first place in the Country to have spotted the invading Spanish Armada coming to the shores of England. From here the first warning of it was given. It had always provided a look out point over a wide section of the English Channel.

The tiny chapel at Rame Head, at its highest peak, had provided generations of shelter for the watchers. Measuring no more than twenty feet by ten it had a lower and upper area. It was consecrated, a long time before, from the 1300's to the Archangel Michael.

Rame Head was therefore also a place of faith, a dwelling and look out point.

Now with Hinram it had been providing a look out point for the smugglers too. In return for some money and a stock of spirits he would keep watch and give warnings. He would light fires to warn incoming ships should he spot preventatives or dragoons in the area.

These fires were usually lit further down Rame Head on its southern side as it approached the sea so would not be seen by officers further back. They would not implicate him but provide the short warning smugglers needed to divert their boats. He kept some stocks of furze for this and fireforks down near the rocks and beaches.

Hinram had come into the area some years back and no one was sure if it was his real name, but he had chosen it. The rumour was that he had gone there to repent and spend the rest of his life away from the world where he had murdered and pillaged on the seas.

Originally from Bodmin moor he was rumoured to have once known a philosopher there, one Daniel Gumb, whose life of contemplation in a cave had given him peace, understanding and great insight into worldly things and beyond. Although living in the cave with wife and children as well he would gain his peace from the surrounding moorland and from the top of the cave that was exposed to the sky and stars.

This philosopher was visited by the rich and famous of the land, providing a place and person where they may take in his wisdom and consult on matters concerning their everyday work and lives. Hinram eventually chose to emulate the philosopher's life, at least by following a simple life that enabled him to repent his sins at Rame Head.

His newly found moral code that guided his existence fell short of preventing him from working with the smugglers.

These were free traders to him, living for the mostpart in accordance with the higher laws that governed mankind. Those that sought to thwart them should be stopped from doing so. Hinram had therefore reconciled his code of life with his work for the smugglers.

Hinram was in his usual spot when Hannibal arrived. He had ridden to the field that led in to the narrow isthmus of Land that would take him up the steep climb to the chapel by foot.

The increased pay for Hinram was welcomed. He scratched pictures as reminders into the stone walls of the chapel, describing to him the way in which he would receive signals that would indicate that he should light a fire or use his light to attract the authorities to the Rame Head area.

In front of him was a clear view of the wide expanse of sea. In sight were the Mewstone rock where Fyn and Black Joan were working from as well as Looe Island. These were all prominent outposts, poking well out from the mainland. They were now poised and ready for further deployment in the smuggling trade.

All the smugglers in the area could benefit from the use of these outposts and systems of operating. Hannibal was the co-ordinator but only one, albeit a prominent one, of those operating smuggling ventures. They had to pull together now more than ever if they were to stand a chance of succeeding against the resources of King and State.

Rame Church was not far away from here and was Hannibal's next port of call in tying the strands together.

The Vicar at Rame had turned a blind eye many a time. Maybe he could be persuaded to turn the other eye blind as well?

Could they harness better the advantages that the Church had with its position, space and sanctity to provide more regular, reliable, safe, interim, storage?

The use of roof gullies and sometimes tombs had proved effective, but could be moreso should the arrangements be better thought through and more reliable?

The Church also possessed fields that led down to the sea that raged between Rame head on its west side and to Penlee Point on its east. There were existing paths complete with ropes and pulleys to haul up the goods. Maybe they could expand their usage without interference from the Vicar.

"Reverend, I am here to talk about whether we could make a contribution to the well-being of the church and the churchyard. You may have heard that we are moving more of us to Cawsand from Kingsand to provide a larger home for my sister and family.

Many more of us will then be using the Church here at Rame."

"The generosity of the Marks! Come and sit with me in the garden room and take a glass. What sort of.... Mm .... contribution were you thinking about?"

"We were wondering about helping to secure the foundations that look shaky around the altar and the belfry tower ..."

"And ...... "

"Well the Rectory as well of course .... Perhaps some regular parish provisions? Maybe some for the poor too ... of your choosing, of course."

They both knew what this meant, some luxuries for the family at the rectory, which was not a substantial living.

"Make sure the work doesn't interfere with service times and all is restored for those."

"We will make sure there is no disruption. The men are prepared to work at night to keep interference with Church business to a minimum."

"Well, the Church can be bolted from the inside, so make sure you do so."

Taking his leave after further pleasantries, Hannibal headed back to the village, passing the farms of Penmillard and Rame on the way and then Forder stream before falling down in to Cawsand.

There would now be more options in a more difficult trading time.

The next meeting of all the interested parties and agents reflected on the progress Hannibal had made in pulling together a more resilient operation for the village.

"The increased use of the Churches is a good way Hannibal and through the incrimination of the Reverend in our activities it is unlikely he will do anything to reveal us. Maybe we can strengthen our position with the other reverends ... and perhaps bring Maker closer to us, perhaps?

I recall the last one at Maker moving a visiting Bishop out of the way of sight of our ankers of spirits when they could be seen from the top of the tower nestling quietly between the rooves below."

With that he let out the first ring of laughter the evening had witnessed. The others followed suit with deep sucks on their clay pipes to follow, filling the air with concentric rings of smoke until they broke up either on their own or by hitting the yellowed, nicotine stained, ceiling.

For a moment, just a moment, they forgot their despair for the growing losses they were incurring when runs had gone wrong and their mood changed.

"We are still turning in a profit. We live better than folk ever did before here. So, let's drink on the finest that we have and remember that."

Pewter tankards were filled, clashed together and for a while they turned to exchanging tales of past and present and of the Vicars too.

"So, about Maker. Hannibal, can you take a look at the Church and Churchyard and see if there is any more we can do there?

That overfed Vicar, so they say, has a few likes that maybe we could help him satisfy."

With that the smirks and laughter started anew.

“What likes would they be, I hear he likes all sorts that one.”

“We may need to get a special keg over for him. One in the shape of a fat, buxom, French Nun!”

“Or give him a keg with a fine woman inside. One that she could burst out of to please him.

That, or when the thirsty bugger is so desperate, he taps the keg and out falls her corks.”

“Wouldn’t make any odds to that fat old bugger. He’d have to wrap his guts around his back before he could get it out to use it.”

“Here’s to the Vicar’s pleasures. He’ll be ours soon enough.”

The tankards were slammed with their customary resolve on the table, accompanied by the equally customary spillages left by previous incarnations of this practice that had provided them with the red patterned stains that characterised and defined the meeting room table.

The Vicar was indeed a large specimen of mankind. Of short stature he was half as wide as he was tall. His garments were especially tailored to expand sideward to allow for additional girth he might develop, such had been his wont for many years.

The impact of the additional stones his body had added, had made him walk slowly, as upright as possible to avoid overbalancing whilst he walked to his trap that would take him the short distance to his Church.

It was a slightly longer route than walking the path from rectory to the Church. It was also more direct. Alas though, the stile had become less manageable as his girth continued to grow. The short hoist up into the trap and down again was easier than the walk to the Church. The trap therefore remained the preferred method of transport. His face was bloated with jowls that resembled those of a mouse that had stretched the sides of his face with a large feed that had not yet travelled the journey into its stomach.

When delivering his sermons, with their due passion and conviction, his jowls would shake, sometimes uncontrollably, affecting the sound of his voice, often to the amusement of the congregation assembled on a Sunday.

He was known to have a penchant for the ladies and especially so for the larger and more voluptuous ladies in his flock, of whom there were not many, but those that there were received special, more favoured attention.

Hannibal lost little time in setting about the task with which he had been charged by the meeting. He was sure that the Vicars of Maker and Rame would not discuss together any of the arrangements they had made. These arrangements were the unspoken.

It was a short ride up to the rectory from the village. He went on the steep track that led up to the view across to Mewstone rock where he had been only a few weeks ago to make the revised arrangements with Fyn and Joan.

From here he also had a commanding view across to Penlee Point. A short distance further up and he could take in the aerial view down to Millbrook, Anderton and the countryside in between. Across the river with its rich markets, stood the towns and villages around Plymouth. He paused a while and gazed at the sights, moving himself to take in the Panorama and consider again the strategy that would be needed to thwart the enemy.

He was looking at a battleground. He had to see it with the eyes and precision of a military commander as well as from the eyes of the revenue men. He needed to understand them, their resources, how they might consider their use and application against them and their business.

From there he joined the main track that led to the Church with the rectory off to the right a half a mile before. As he went down the track towards the house, he could see in his mind the smuggling run routes with their safe storage facilities spreading their risks, on the way

His mission today was to continue to strengthen and help secure, the network in this area. He had not long since walked this very same track up to the Church to bury his father, Hannibal 1st. He would visit the grave and church after seeing the Vicar as well to offer a prayer.

As expected, the Vicar was there. It was his mid-day mealtime and it was just ending. Drooling over his last pie for the day, he rose as he saw Hannibal arrive, took his pie to the door and greeted him. He bade his servant girl to clear the table and prepare another for his guest.

The Vicar received the odd tub of his favourite liquor, left discretely under the thicket that ran along the southern border adjacent to the main house. So, what would tempt the Vicar to allow more than to simply ignore the roof storage that they often used after a run?

Hannibal's mind had been racing with this question. More tubs, work to the Church, foods from Brittany? Maybe, but the Vicar had his likes and dislikes. He had no shortage of good, flavourful, food and English fayre in copious quantities to meet his desires.

His mind could not get off the jest about the French Nun. Maybe there was something in this? The Vicar did like the ladies and especially the flighty fat ones, or those mighty in bosom.

The Vicar's wife, in contrast, was a lean, austere, woman. There always existed a cool, indeed a detachment, between them. Both of good genteel families, this was a convenient marriage at the time it would seem.

Maybe it was different when they were out of the eyes of the peninsula, or maybe not. Maybe what was seen was what there was? They could do with an additional help around the house and Church perhaps?

Maybe a French woman could be engaged by them at Roscoff, one looking for a new start, some other luxuries for the Vicar's long-suffering wife, some of the latest fine foods from Brittany?

"Good morning Vicar. Could you spare me your time for a while?"

"Hannibal Marks! "A surprise. I hear you might be moving your parish."

"Not quite yet and not all of us. It is Maker that I have always known so well."

"Yes, we cannot do without bell ringing from the Marks clan."

"Well it was that on which I thought we might talk. Fishing and piloting are doing well at the moment alongside some other trade.........."

"Yes, yes, I know and thank you for the gift of the odd prime fish or two for the table, very good they have been. Very good indeed."

"Funny sort of fish", thought Hannibal, but he knew what he meant.

"Well, we could do with a little bit of storage here and there and were thinking if we could use any spare ground the church has, perhaps we could repay the favour in some way? Maybe do some essential repair work to the Church tower floors where the ringers and the bells are?"

"And what were you thinking of as the other favours, Hannibal....mmmm ?"

"Are you still in need of a servant maid to help you and your good wife around the house. Some of the Breton ladies, so we hear from the Breton fishermen, are seeking positions with good families here."

"Well it would help the family with their French language and help my good wife use her French. She doesn't get the opportunity now very often. And, and, ...neither do I."

His voice tailed off in a lamenting tone, designed to attract the interest of his surprise guest. The Vicar's jowls started to quiver unseemingly at the thought.

"What would you like to do in the Church tower for us Hannibal?"

"Well the central floors could do with strengthening. It is all getting old and the bells are very heavy .... If they should fall ....."

"Yes, yes, quite... well do the work quietly won't you so as not to disturb the dead. When do you think you might have a new maid arranged .... Sooner rather than later ..... ?"

"We will ask the Breton fishermen to pass around the word about the wonderful opportunity there is to join a prominent family in the area. I should not think it long."

* * *

Work started on the Churches very quickly afterwards. The backers met to decide how this could be best used and how to maintain the tacit support of the Vicars, or at least to buy their blind eye.

At Maker they built in a new floor under the level that housed the bells. There was plenty of height on the level below in the ringers' chamber that could be used. This provided a considerable additional space that could be accessed from the bell housing floor. It was difficult for a man to move around here, but nonetheless provided sufficient access with the reward of a very large concealed space between the bellroom floor and the ceiling of the bellringers area below.

The inside of the tower could not be seen, and the thick walls offered protection against too much noise spilling out. They were all cautious and a look out stationed on the top of the tower peering out from between the turrets went un-noticed from below. The lookout had a commanding view of the area, keeping a close watch to ensure work continued without interruption. Should they be interrupted, they had made plans to hide within the spaces of the tower.

Work was done in sections to avoid the risks associated with major upheavals that might attract interest. They knew that chances were, the Vicar, if called upon to open the Church and the tower, would take his time. This would allow them a chance to conceal themselves or tidy up and leave to continue on another occasion.

Candles kept light, the dripping wax occasionally missing its catch plate, falling instead to catch the men, burning the hair on their arms with an accompanying odour of burnt hair and flesh that added to the odours of toil in this confined space.

The decision had been made part way through, when they saw how many ankers the space would take up, that there may be a way of lining and caulking the storage area that could maximise its use. They could run a leat in the corner to the level below, discretely tapped as required. This would allow the kegs to be emptied into the space and the liquor drawn off from below when they were ready for it. This maximised the space and they could at night draw down and re-keg ready for the onward journey.

The timber had come from the beaches around. It was always being washed up. It had built the frames in many a village house. These timbers were as straight as they could be found. If they needed to lead the area in the end it would need to support the weight of the liquor. It couldn't be seen to leak below.

As far as possible the ringers would come from the smugglers own people. If they could effectively take over the tower it would be the best way. If it fell into use for signalling again, they would need to control and monitor the activity, but nightfall was their best friend. That and poor, difficult, weather conditions.

The old planks were used top and bottom. In the end it looked as if nothing had transpired there. At Rame the space below the altar was finished. They had dug down, well down, securing enough space to store many ankers.

They had to support the sidewalls, but the resulting chamber provided good storage. It was unlikely to be found. No one would move the altar let alone remove boards underneath it. Even approaching the altar was an act of solemnity, reverence and sanctity.

For those in the employ of the government of the day to disrupt a sanctuary was unthinkable. The work to the altar area was conducted with due respect and honour.

The smugglers were god fearing souls but were of the view that they had been forced to this by the actions of government that stood in the way of a higher right to free trade.

Hannibal felt he and the backers had made headway to help build on some additional strength for their industry that would take them forward, once again, into the ever-increasing turbulence being created by the Parliament's crack down on it.

Chapter 19

Reunion in Roscoff

"This is a good night to be taking the Five Brothers to Roscoff, Hannibal. Nothing too rough out there but a brisk wind and much cloud." The Five Brothers was a fast cutter done out as a fisher but ready to adapt to do the smuggling runs or to do some pilotage work. At about forty-five feet in length, kept light, with extra spar length available to her she had the minimal draft for her sail size. She had been able to out-sail most cutters built by the Revenue service.

Nothing was conspicuous in her overall shape that might identify her in the distance. No, her strengths lie in how she had been made. Subtle differences that would give her the edge if the race were on.

When full of heavy stock she slowed. The journey back would then be planned for rough seas when the Revenue cutters were less likely to be venturing far from safe port or anchorage. Off Roscoff the signal had been given to say who they were. The signal came back indicating it was safe to anchor and they would be met and taken in to do business. Those remaining on board would be brought refreshment.

As the rowing boat approached, they threw a line and it tied alongside. The men were greeted in the customary way. Hannibal and two others, armed, went ashore with them. English was spoken well by the merchants' agents and some of the seamen. Hannibal had received some tuition and had experience in using Breton and French.

Built in Cawsand, the 'Five Brothers' spent most of her time at sea. She worked hard for her living. The blackened hull and darkened sails she wore at night made her difficult to pick out, save as a silhouette against the moon's light.

This was a night when she slipped easily through the waters across the Channel to Roscoff. Roscoff was now starting to come to even greater prominence for the free trade industry. A main centre for storage and despatch onto the free traders' boats, the town was gradually becoming of even more importance to the trade than Guernsey. This shift was in spite of tensions that had been created by the wars with France. The wars were a disruption to trade that had to be overcome by providing safety to the smugglers when doing their business in Roscoff, coming in and out of the harbours and the like.

The Inn was on the water's edge with its own slipway running between its building and the ships' stores that adjoined. Run by the French merchants, it was a safe house but the tensions between France and England meant trips could still be hazardous.

The three from the Five Brothers clambered from the rowing boat onto the steps that would lead up and into the rear access to the Inn. Their host guided them up, through the short maze of passages and stairs to a room that sat two stories up from the drinking area below. Cognacs, brandies and gins were sampled. Prices, payments and quantity of different merchandise had already been agreed by the merchants back home with their French counterparts.

The Five Brothers had on this occasion, been commissioned to carry the goods and arrange offloading, storage too. Of some surprise, there remained a large amount of surplus space on board. Hannibal negotiated prices for enough merchandise to fill the Smuggler to its capacity, maybe more if it could be crammed in. The deal was concluded. The Smuggler would be brimming full on her return journey. Goods for the customer and for themselves.

Over the welcome drinks, Hannibal mentioned the arrangements with the Vicar. He enquired if there might be any Breton ladies seeking a position in England, explaining that the chance to be attached to polite society in the area had arisen with the Vicar's household.

This was met with similar explosions of mirth, albeit in the French style. Little different was it from that mirth that had been taken across the

Channel back at home in Cawsand when it had been raised with the backers.

"So, the Vicar likes our French ladies? Is it the accent or that they are prettier than your English ....? Non, Non c'est forms bien enchairs, ces ecclesiastiques ..."

"It is their shape. Yes, that's it. The Vicar knows the best shaped pears and they are the Breton pairs." With that the familiar sound of tankards smashing on the table could be heard echoing around the small room.

"We have your goods laden and ready in the store Hannibal. They will be loaded while we drink." Hannibal knew there was a man on board able to check the load as it was being carried by the stevedores, those manhandling the goods onto the boat. The men would have been preparing Five Brothers to take some of the cargo below decks into the spaces built for the trade. They would have opened her belly ready to fill, then nail her down again.

There was a moment's quiet when the assembled heard a familiar voice with a slight French accent come through the wall.

"Is that you, Monsieur Marks." Hannibal stared at his French hosts who started to quietly snigger.

"Is that you Monsieur Marks," now came the tempting voice of a French lady.

"C'est Monsieur Marks. Qui voulez connaitre," spoke Hannibal in broken French.

With that the door burst open. With lightening reactions, thinking this was an ambush of sort, Hannibal rose up and drew his pistol ready to fire at the door.

This was instantly met with more sniggers that rapidly fell into laughter and the smashing of tankards once more onto the table. Spirits were refilled into their awaiting receptacles.

As the face emerged at the door Hannibal dropped his guard. He placed his weapon on the table, striding swiftly towards his onlooker.

"King of Prussia!"

"Brother to the King of Prussia!"

With that emerged a second face. "Harry and Charles," exclaimed Hannibal. "It has been a while." It had been some years since Harry's boat, Revenge, had been surprised in Cawsand Bay. Some years since Harry had slipped overboard, taken for dead, washed up on the beach at Cawsand and dragged to Hannibal's home where his father had taken him in.

He knew of it well and the subsequent perilous journey to smuggle him onto Lostwithiel, then again to Marazion, finally to a farm in West Cornwall.

Harry had gone quiet for a while in the Americas until re-emerging again in Cornwall, appearing then in France, doing a bit of smuggling here and there.

"Look at the size of you," grinned Harry. "You've filled out with all of this sailing and smuggling. I was sorry to hear of your father's death, but he lived a long life.

I heard about your family. There is another Hannibal now who will come into the business?"

"Yes, we lost a first Hannibal. You might have heard? This Hannibal is our youngest and learning fast, he's picking up his knots already!"

Harry and Charles took their seats at the table and the conversation switched from the business, that had been just about done, to Harry and what had happened during the intervening nigh on twenty years or so.

"We thought you were a goner when you got tied up in the revolution here. We heard you were imprisoned."

"Many of my French friends went to the guillotine. I was there as they were dragged out of the cells and butchered. I got caught up in revolutions here, and in the Americas, but none so worse as here.

It was a good few years after the trouble in Cawsand with the Revenge. Off to the Americas I went and worked with slaves down west on the Islands, helping them to see the light with my faith. I came home to Cornwall after that thinking that the price on my head would have been forgotten.

I saw the Cove boys many times at Prussia but in the end somehow the Dragoons were tipped off. A raid at night meant that I had to go whilst I still could.

One of our boats brought me here. I still see the Cove boys who come out here, but still long to be back at Prussia. Charles here, my brother, he is in Roscoff much, but there is my daughter.... there is her family. I want to be with them more and more as I get older.

My wife died when I was in America. My mother-in-law wrote to me to tell me. I had to leave when I had only been married a year and my daughter was barely one year old.

Come, enough of me and my woes. Let's drink a while together. When will you be leaving? Where to?"

"We will be setting sail midday tomorrow. We're hoping for some stormy weather, some easterlies as we return maybe. We are using Mewstone Island as well to signal and store for us."

"Fyn and Joan! I was told they might be leaving the Mewstone for Looe Island, if they can."

"Well they're still at the Mewstone for now. We have had to look at other ways of distracting the Preventatives with decoys and new storage. Coming into the Bay, unless we are sure the coast is clear for us, is becoming too dangerous.

Never mind Fyn and Joan. Have you got a Vicar's wench for me to take home? What a price to pay for a storehouse!"

"Whorehouse did you say ...... Vicar's whorehouse or your storehouse!"

"It won't be a whorehouse at that house. They are a respectable family. It'll give the Vicar something to look at. Something to play up to.

His wife will most likely be glad of the break from his attentions, if she gets any. Silly old fool!"

"It'll give the girl a chance to meet good folk, marry well too. She'll be fed and looked after well in the meantime."

"We'll pass the word around Hannibal. Safe storage and at a good rent if you ask me!"

Harry sat quietly for a moment, not participating in the present good spirits. "Talking like this and going back over thing makes me feel I could do with going back for a while. See my daughter, Prussia and the Cove Boys but I can't stay there for long. Charles, it would be best if I didn't go back with you. You are staying a few days and have more business to do here. It is always more dangerous when I travel with you.

Hannibal, Hannibal, could you go into Prussia with me first? The Cove Boys are always on the lookout. They will see you on the horizon day or night whatever the weather."

Charles then ran through the signalling that was to go out as they saw and approached the Cove, from which direction it should come and what they could expect in return.

The Carters had large caves and a fortress above the beach at Prussia, tunnels which were dangerous to approach but well concealed. These caves led into a tunnel network that could be closed off.

The tramlines in the Cove rocks were still in use to drag large consignments into the cave entranceways using wheeled carriages that could be pushed by men or pulled by horse or mule.

High tides could render the entrances completely inaccessible. Above lay the cliff faces. Everyone was involved in the trade in this area. The King of Prussia, his family and subjects had reigned and lived supreme here.

Five Brothers had in the meantime been loaded up. It was time to go, Hannibal returned to the cutter that lay bobbing gently off the shores. Further down in the water than she had been, she was well prepared with all concealments complete for the journey. Tubs on top were not visible from a distance but were prepared with sinking stones and lengthy ropes should they quickly have to be jettisoned to gain speed.

They were also towing from under the waterline a string of tubs. It would not take much to jettison these either, if they had to. All they had to do was remove a few planks below and cut the rope loose.

These were last resorts, but they had to be prepared. As they rowed out to her, bustling Roscoff, with both its dangers and safety, a town that was always awake for trade, said goodbye to them.

They would soon be alone heading north to Prussia Cove just down from the Lizard.

Harry would be on watch and administer the signals when they arrived.

For Prussia Cove they wanted it rough but not too rough, for this was a tricky approach at the best of times with many a ship of all sizes floundering there.

The Vicar's wench, as she now was referred to, had not yet been identified but the next run would have the new rectory maid on board, they were sure.

A maid seeking a better life in return for pleasantries and attention from the Vicar.

Hannibal would see the Vicar on return to keep him sweet. There were some silks on board for him, best tea, brandy, cognacs and gin. Quite a stock to keep him happy for a while, stocks for the Vicar at Rame too.

"These costs are higher than they used to be under father," he sighed to himself.

The run back went smoothly. Rough, but the sea state did not prevent Five Brothers anchoring up within the relative safety of Prussia Cove as night fell. Harry had taken over the job of sending light signals to shore and guiding the boat in to its anchorage.

With the precision timing of the gunsmith or the watchmaker at their trades, the boats came. Donkeys pulled carts on the tramlines cut into the rocks, towards the great cave yawning in front of them.

Chain gangs formed to get the goods safely up into the cave. All means were used to get them in and stored quickly. There must have been fifty or more men there to unload the rowing boats before they even had time to slip onto the beach.

The unloading gang took to the water, waist high to meet the boats, passing the tubs one to another down the human chain until they were either slung into carts and rumbled up to the caves or thrown into arms into the caves one by one.

The whole unloading operation was done with considerable efficiency and speed. There was a silence amongst the men with the only noise breaking the silence being that of the cartwheels on the rails.

The shape of the cove did not allow sound to travel easily upwards, only out to the sea where it was drowned by the crashing waves that rolled in, even the calmest of sea states.

Harry was hurried up into the caves where he would continue through the labyrinth to the Carter fortress above and its safety. He was still a marked man.

The years could not disguise the change in appearance to his face that had been caused that fateful night when his boat had been surprised off Penlee at Cawsand. They had become the mark of his trade and of that night.

It was riskier now than before, but he was more prepared to take that chance to re-unite for a while with his daughter and friends in the Cove.

Some years had gone by and he was likely to be approaching the end of his days now. He would want to end his days here if he could. Be buried here, those were his wishes.

It was a rare occasion for a Marks Smuggler to be plying the seas back to Cawsand Bay without so much of a sniff of spirit to be had anywhere on her. Five Brothers could now be searched and searched again, it would be to no avail. Let the Preventative Cutters do their worse.

Maybe they should trawl some nets on the way, catch some fish to fill the hold. Let the Customs men rummage through a few tons of slithering, jumping, fish. A few congers eels and large crabs, bad tempered for being hoisted out of the depths and placed underneath a shoal of pilchards would give the rummage crew something to think about.

They might have a chance to taunt a revenue boat into chasing them, only to find this lawful cargo.

The day was good for sailing and they started back. This time no need for a watch, nothing to fear.

***

“Captain Bray, looks like a Smuggler to our west making fast.”

“I think it might have seen us, it’s turning. Mark it. On to it we go.”

Bray's boat had not been invisible to the Five Brothers either.

"That looks like the Lottery heading onto us.”

“Still around. To think we built her. She was used to carry cargos and now she’s been made to turncoat. She won’t be around long now, I don't suppose. We hear they are building new cutters for themselves.

We’ll give them a run. Turn south and then north again, keep going up and down.” Ditch the few ankers we have been drinking from over the stern and let’s fish. Slow her down. Let Lottery catch us.”

“Here she comes. Flying her colours. They are placing their flag over the side as well.”

“Stall the sails and ship up. Look your best. No laughing. Get about your work on the nets. Start gutting the fish.”

They waited for the boarding party to come alongside. They gave due assistance, unexpected courtesy was provided to tie their rowing boat up alongside, even helping the officers into the vessel.

The search began, nothing revealed. A man was sent under the ship in the freezing cold waters to examine in mid-water the keel and rudder to ensure nothing was being towed or kept down in the water.

There was nothing. The rummagers lifted some planks scouring in the belly. There was nothing for them.

Bray was a suspicious man but eventually exchanged pleasantries with Hannibal as Captain and bade farewell with the utterance,

"Either you are up to something Hannibal Marks or you have turned over a new leaf and are trying to adopt the lawful ways of making a living. Whatever it appears I would choose the former."

This was for him to guess at and Hannibal to know. They had been boarded not far off Looe and Polperro. A legitimate trip, they would pull into Polperro harbour and Hannibal would see Job, if he were there.

Job was in his counting house, as usual, maintaining his meticulous records of transactions. He put down his quill, replaced the stopper on his well of ink, discontinuing his correspondence.

Hannibal told him that it was one of the only times that they had moored up in harbour without fear.

He told him of the Roscoff sailing and Harry Carter. Job looked pleased about Carter. Usually expressionless, this news brought a smile that rippled along his face. A smile that could only be compared to one he could raise when counting money and bills on a good week.

"You heard about Robert Mark?"

"Yes, I thought I would pay him a visit while here. Talland Churchyard?"

"That's it. Did you hear all that had happened?"

"Some of it. We knew he was back on the Smugglers and had escaped from his punishment on the Thames after the Lottery trial." Hannibal had picked up most of the news about Robert, but this was his chance to be told the full story from Job.

"He did at least not get tried for the murder. He did hard labour on those Thames hulks but saw his chance to escape and did. He joined the smuggling ships when out, but it was that Bray.

They shot him. Put a ball right through him and killed him instantly. It was not far off here and he was brought back for a decent burial at Talland."

"Bray was in the Hind then?"

"It could be any one of our fates." Zephania looked to the ground momentarily.

"Come, let's go and see him now you are here. We can talk a while on the way."

The small trap was soon prepared with Job's help and off they went on the short trip out of the village to Talland.

"Everything feels free for a change, Zephania."

"Yes, we all have the yoke of what we do around us at all times. This time you are a fisherman here moored up with nothing to declare. For today at least let your crew make merry with the Polperro boys that are in the harbour and we will too in our own way."

As Hannibal related to Zephania the enhanced arrangements for storage and signals from the Mewstone to Rame and Maker, he could see that Zephania was listening intently and mulling over all possible outcomes.

"This with the Vicar at Maker. Could the wench speak about it?"

"Unlikely. She will know only that this is an opportunity to join a prominent and secure household working as a maid under the Vicar and his wife directly."

"So, nothing of us and our visits to Roscoff."

"No, chances are she will travel blindfold until we arrive. Then she will be taken to the Church or rectory to meet her new employers."

"Mmm, seems like it can work and keep him happy. The use of the belfry, so close to the markets of Plymouth and the river crossings are an asset to us. How long will he have to wait for his new maid?"

"Next trip. Francoise is going to arrange this in Roscoff."

With that the cart trundled up to the Church.

"Robert Mark, Late of Polperro, who unfortunately, was shot, the 24th day of January, In the year of our Lord God, 1802 in the 40th Year of his Age

In prime of life most suddenly,

Sad tidings to relate,

Here, view my utter destiny,

And pity, my sad state.

I by a shot which rapid flew,

Was instantly struck dead,

Lord pardon the Offender who,

My precious blood did shed.

Grant him to rest and forgive me.

All I have done amiss,

And that I may rewarded be,

With everlasting bliss."

"Well, here he lies Hannibal, our friend, Robert Mark." With that, the two men knelt slowly down to the ground, kissed the stone and rose again. On rising they remained silent for a short while, remembering Robert's bravery on several smuggling exploits. He had successfully bounced back many times against the odds.

"Come, a prayer in the Church and we must be on our way."

With that Job stepped respectfully amongst the headstones and mounds of grass that marked the resting places of souls buried beneath, until they arrived at the large oak doors of the Church.

As the doors dragged open, Job stepped to one side momentarily, inviting Hannibal to enter. The two men walked to the altar to kneel together in prayer for the fallen friends and comrades of their industry, going past several places that had been successfully used to store smuggled goods.

These had been introduced in the comparatively easy times for the coastal smuggling gangs, in the time of Vicar Dodge of Talland Church.

"Some of the old hides here are still in use Hannibal," Job reflected as the two men closed the doors, returning to the trap. His voice was lowered as if the very ground on which they stood had ears, ready to pass on the information to those from whom it had so successfully been concealed.

"We never had the honour of working with Vicar Dodge, Hannibal, but it is thanks to him that the Church has so many places we can use that are still used today. When I came, there were few smugglers around here who did not know him. Other folk were afraid to go anywhere near Talland Church at nightfall."

"I have heard many a story of the Vicar. Father knew his reputation as an exorcist up until the day he died. Wasn't he about ninety or more when he died?"

The colourful Vicar Dodge had been a good friend of the smugglers. Local folk would still not go near the Church after dark for fear of confronting the supernatural activities that took place there. Vicar Dodge was rumoured to still perform exorcisms there at night from his grave.

"Even now the Polperro boys continue to talk about his exorcisms to spread fear of it. He still walks the churchyard and surrounds. He calls up ghosts and chases them down to the sea at night, followed by his familiars in hot pursuit of all of them. People here swear they have seen this when overlooking the harbours or beaches late into the dark. The Church remains not well frequented because of the tales, not even during the day.

Anyone venturing close at night is likely to hear rumblings and groanings but more than often this will be the shifting of the stones inside to get into the tunnels and hideaways.

The present Vicar here is not a Reverend Dodge for us, but he is never seen in the Church or the yard at night. There's always something we leave for him.

You get your Vicar what he wants from Roscoff. Times are not so good, and we need to strengthen things on land as well as on the sea. Use this Hannibal, use this!" With that Zephania tapped his head with his forefinger to bring home the need to be cleverer than they had been.

Chapter 20

The Vicar's Maid Arrives

"What cargo's this Captain?" Jibes came from the crew as Hannibal helped the Vicar's new maid down the Roscoff quay steps onto the boat. "She's a pretty one. Is she here to do our cooking? Anything else she can do for us besides?" When are we loading up with something more valuable?"

"Mind your language with a lady on board. This is our only cargo this run. You'll get double payment for the next run. We'll be heading back as soon as we offload her."

"I'll be the tubman for her if you want to strap her around my neck."

Sniggers, laughter, lewd comments and more were hurled from the crew.

"So, you're Marie?"

In broken English with a strong French accent Marie acknowledged her name, tossing back her head in defiance at the remarks.

She had been blindfolded but Hannibal had been assured by Francoise that it wasn't necessary. This one was known and trusted. Her lips would be sealed, beside she probably wouldn't be able to distinguish the men easily after a few weeks.

"Yes, and I will be a good worker in England. My father, he was English, from Beer. He was involved with your trade. I know your trade. He came to Roscoff and lived with my mother who was from that area."

Whether there was truth in this they could not be certain. She knew about Beer and her English was quite good. She seemed quite educated. Why was she here. Either way, true or not, she was serving a purpose. It suited all of them. She had not been an unwilling person.

"That would explain your English.

Your new home and work will be with a good family. They are expecting you."

"Tell me about them."

Hannibal was out of earshot below deck and gave her a summary of her new employers and what would be expected of her.

"And this Vicar. You say he is big, like a fattened goose and his wife is small. Ha! Maybe I shall get him running around and get his fat off him, instead of him making me run around!"

They disembarked at high tide at the deep cove next to the old cellars and palaces just outside of the village. Hannibal had her take his arm for the climb up and the walk over the fields and gullies to the rectory.

Marie had little with her. Her clothes and belongings such as they were had been all rolled into a piece of cloth which had been tied at the top with a loop to make carriage easier.

Her petite form with sharp and wiry dark features had transfixed Hannibal's eye at times on the crossing. He looked for some plumpness that would please the Vicar and found ample as his eyes lifted towards the top of her thighs and heavily pronounced bosom.

She really was a woman of contrast. He had removed her blindfold when down below deck. Her eyes were light brown in colour against a pure white, piercing and striking. Long black eyelashes with sharply defined eyebrows. These were features that came with a warning that this was not a woman to be trifled with. Yet her lips were larger, pronounced, welcoming. The Vicar would more likely become subject to her will rather than the other way around.,

As they clambered up the narrow path that took them further into the fields from where they could see the rectory, he caught a glimpse of her shapely legs as she rolled up her dress and under garments so as not to drag it in the mud nor through the stream water that ran beside the pathway.

Not a lot of plump for the Vicar but it was there where it counted to please him best. Well he would have to await the Vicar's judgement.

"She'll be popular to court amongst the local lads when they get to know she's there, if the Vicar let's her out of his sight!" Hannibal hissed his words to himself.

They drew breath as they reached the top of the path.

"No regrets?"

"None. It was time for me to leave Roscoff."

With those few words they continued, past the Church of St Mary and St Julian. There was no one else on the pathways and they reached the rectory within less than half an hour, quietly passing the waking farmsteads as they went.

The rectory was an imposing building with additional stabling and workhouses adjacent.

The Vicar was having his breakfast whilst peering out across the lawn and turning area into the Valley. The drop down into the valley was steep with a stream at the bottom that flowed all year.

A small wooden bridge crossed the stream, providing a rear access to the house. from the track that ran next to the stream. The valley wall then formed again to rise again to a height well above that of the rectory.

Hannibal and Marie approached from the other side. They would only come into the view of the Vicar when they were almost at the front of the house.

"They're here," exclaimed the Vicar as he suddenly saw them approach. His jowls shook as was usual when he became excited. He stood up leaving his food behind. His attentions turned from food to his visitors.

He thought he would wait to summon his wife. She was in the day room where she could often be found reading or tending to her correspondence. If she was not doing that, she was usually reading a copy of the Cornwall Gazette.

Yes, he would wait until he had a good look at the new servant girl. If she wasn't what he expected she would have to go before she had arrived.

His plump hands had lined themselves with perspiration He wiped them quickly on his shirt to then sweep them through his hair to tidy himself. He spent a little time straightening his clothing to ensure that it felt more comfortable around his substantial form.

Duly preened and presentable, he waddled to the door to greet these callers himself. He wanted the first look and would need to make an instant decision. Was she to stay or was she to go?

"Come on in my dear." The Vicar's mind had been instantly made up as she bowed her head whilst simultaneously peering upwards to catch his eye.

The low cut of her revealing clothing was just the tonic that the Vicar required to add some excitement to his very predicable life in service of the Church and of his wife.

A deep breath from her swelled her bosom and the Parson's pupils swelled with them. The pupils rolled, heaved and swelled in time to their movement as his eyes strained to part from their sockets to get a close look whilst keeping his polite distance.

He looked her up and down. Just what he liked. A little bit of feeding up here and there wouldn't, though, go amiss. He kept a good larder. He had a good cook for the house. Feed her up they could, without difficulty, without changing routine.

Routine was sacrosanct to the running of his household and life within the Church. She too would need a routine. Almost ignoring Hannibal, finding only the time to bid him good day, he cocked his head to one side at Hannibal as a signal of approval. He hurriedly shut the door on him.

Hannibal was glad to leave and did so with a self-satisfied feeling of relief.

The Vicar busied himself making the introduction of Marie to his household and showing her to her room. The room had been prepared should the new arrival be satisfactory.

The large rectory had been equipped with several small rooms for servants which were at the rear of the house. There was a small door that separated these rooms from the remainder of the house whilst maintaining a working proximity should the master or mistress of the house require.

His eyes had refused to recede back into their sockets and frog-like they were watching her every move. Sniffing and snuffling like his terriers outside, he hid behind his handkerchief as her natural fragrances wafted past him as she moved in and out of the rooms. These fragrances were in fact blended from a variety of sources, not just her own. Like a good whiskey she had been unwittingly blended by her surroundings in the last few days. The hostelry at Roscoff, complete with its smells of ales, smoke, seaman's sweat and toil, had all come to be absorbed by Marie. These fragrances drenched the rooms at Roscoff and, with little dilution from the air outside, they wafted for a radius of some distance. It was absorbed by all who came that way and would leave not hurriedly but would only temper with time. This was combined with the fragrances of the open seas and the smells of the caulks and pitched ropes from her journey on Five Brothers.

This Vicar had a nose for finery. His could sniff out a good wine from fifty paces. He could then provide an excellent narrative about its pedigree. Little detail escaped his nasal senses, powers and prowess. These had been developed, carefully honed, tuned from years of indulgences and excesses. This was little different to him.

An odour of the rough dockside pervaded though, a seemingly uncomfortable bedfellow for the subtle, almost hidden, natural, poise of Marie.

"I would also like you to give me some French practice. I do not get the chance here in this Parish to use it often. Perhaps we could arrange a set time each week to parlez en francais et manges un peu cuisine de France? La guerre avec la France n'est pas notre concerne ici en la religion d'Anglais et l'eglise."

"Mais oui, Padre" said Marie with expression in her eyes as she approached him cautiously.

"Je desire travailer avec vous et la congregationale a l'eglise."

Her final drawn out emphasis on l'eglise was more than the Vicar could bear for one day. Her lips pouted wide to express the syllables at the end and to him the word lingered on and on as it rolled effortlessly off her tongue.

He took his eyes away for a moment, looked heavenward as if asking for forgiveness. It was but a fleeting guilt that the Vicar felt, soon giving way to the strong signals of a lustful lechery.

Marie drew back, hunching her back whilst drawing her arms closer together. As she did so she placed the forefinger on her right hand slowly to her lips as if she knew she had to silence his muttering.

This was too much for the Vicar's ability to maintain his semblance of composure any longer. He felt himself starting to shake with excitement. With that he arose saying he was taking his leave for her to retire and that he would go through her duties more fully the following morning.

As he arose from his seat, he withdrew from the room backwards exercising all the skill he could to open the door with a hand behind his back and guide himself through it. Guiding himself through the doorways of the rectory was not an easy task for this Vicar and navigation was made considerably more difficult whilst in one of his flustered backwards retreats.

With a radius not much less than the width of the doorways, negotiating the openings was well practiced, to perfection. His eyes though could not resist the opportunity to steal one last glimpse before retiring to his wife.

Duly, albeit briefly, introduced, she seemed to approve of the new arrival, showing an indifference to the diversion of her husband's attentions.

Marie was the key to unlocking a greater freedom for her to pursue her friendships and interests ,without interference and busy bodying from her husband. Marie was to the lady of the house, welcome indeed.

* * *

"My French has improved remarkably in the last few months Marie. It is all thanks to you and our little sessions."

Complete with his best robes and finery donned he was truly immaculate in his dress and demeanour when he had his practice sessions as he called them with Marie. He kept these robes in his robing room and it was here that he had his lessons and sessions with her.

He knew they would not be interrupted as he closed and locked the church doors from the inside, securing the bolts over once again. His finery was the only apparel sported by the Vicar and as he tossed them behind him to reveal the full majesty of his girth.

Marie knew what was expected of her. She had suspected that it might end this way but that this would be small recompense for the privilege she enjoyed in the house. Her workload was a light one.

She started to strut the floor, clucking like the chickens that were kept not far from the rectory to supply eggs and fowl for the house. Feathers were in plentiful supply in the chicken house for her to collect and use to make her dance more authentic. He would follow her around as the cock of the walk until he could bear the excitement no longer.

As she ceased her ritual display of feathers, she would turn from him, kneeling down.

She felt his sweat flung onto her back, rolling down her form in rivulets. Predictably by now, came the familiar weight of his surplus fat thrown up onto her buttocks to clear his way.

Their French language sessions had provided the Vicar with all that he needed to introduce her to his likings.

Marie had expected something would come from the Vicar's attentions. Well this was it. This was her new life, at least for now. Life was also in many ways good and better than before. She had the Vicar, her employer, where she wanted him.

The Vicar's wife was not interested in his attentions for her. Indeed, she seemed to relish the opportunity to see her own society. She was of a prominent family from far away and had started to travel now more frequently to see them, or at least, so she said.

On this occasion though, Marie and the Vicar were not as alone as they thought.

One of Hannibal's men was up in the belfry area under the guise of working there. He was in fact checking all was ready for a delivery. He had not heard any other person enter nor the locking of the door. Neither had the Vicar, pre-occupied with his forthcoming displays, seen any activity in the Church before he entered with Marie.

He would not have expected anyone to be in the belfry area. Hannibal and his men usually entered beyond nightfall.

The Vicar had therefore felt secure in his domain. His robing room was his sanctuary. It was his privileged area. His and his alone.

As Joe, Hannibal's man, came down the narrow tower steps, into the main area of the Church to leave, he was conscious of the presence of others.

With great stealth, club in hand, he gingerly made his way towards the direction from where he thought he could hear a faint noise. He had seen the locked door and thought maybe this was an ambush. He stepped onto the altar area and up on the stair to take a look through the narrow peep hole that went through into the chosen robing area.

In the dim he saw the Vicar and Marie.

Fortunately for Joe there was little light there apart from a candle they had lit in the corner of the room that made them shadowy figures.

There was though no mistaking the accent of Marie and even less so the possibility of mistaking the shape of the Vicar for that of any other in the entire region.

Both were shadowed against the whitewashed stone walls in the room. He had to contain his laughter but also some anger, for Joe had rather taken to the, flighty French, Marie of Roscoff.

Although much tied to the Vicar and his household, she did have times alone when she would walk the fields and paths that would take her to the nearest villages of Millbrook and Anderton.

Joe had walked with her a few times. He had learnt the routine she had for her walks, their times and places.

"I always come this way on these days unless it is raining hard or the weather is otherwise inclement. I usually stop here,"

She would leave Joe in no doubt where and when she might be found. The Vicar's need for routine was proving valuable. At services, she and Joe bade good day, but little more.

It was as though they knew that the looks they gave quietly and secretly to each other might reveal their burgeoning friendship. They did not want the unwelcome attention of either the Vicar or Hannibal. Neither of them would relish this turn of events.

Joe sat a while, his shock of fair hair moving from side to side as he shook his head in frustration at what he had seen. He was not angered at her, moreover he wanted to take her from this, but this was not the time. He needed to get to know her better, gain trust and bide time until the moment was right. Yes, that is what he would do. He would not refer to what he had seen nor that he had been in the belfry that day. No, just get to know her better and better.

Eventually he heard the heavy Church doors close and lock and he knew it was over. It would be safe to leave before long. He had climbed to the Church roof and could see them walking, strutting back to the rectory. Amongst his anger and hurt he felt a glimmer of amusement.

"What would his flock think if they knew of this? Their precious Parson strutting the floor, feathers where they shouldn't be. It's as if he were servicing the hens in the chicken shed with his maid servant and French teacher throwing seed on the ground for him to peck at."

Round and round this Vicar had gone, clucking, strutting, pecking until he started to peck at the back of his Marie. He had not waited to see all of this, but he could imagine how it had concluded.

The Vicar had eventually been thrown bread and provided with a sup of wine in a small bowl on the floor by Marie. He had greedily supped and slurped the wine. He gobbled fast at his bread. As his pecks turned to her, she had to tolerate and pretend to enjoy the Vicar's worst attentions as Cock in the chicken house. Clucking and pecking at her back, down her spine and flapping his false wings against her derriere.

Chapter 21

Hannibal 3rd Makes an Entrance

"He's too young to take the King's shilling!" The gruff, unshaven figure of a man had turned up at Maker Fair with a task to fulfil. The Fair was held on the green next to the Church as usual. "No, he's not, he'll soon learn. Better get him now before these rough necks here change his mind and turn him to the smuggling as well."

The fun of the games at Maker Church on the green had been disrupted by the Naval pressgang who had at first mixed comfortably and unnoticed.

The young Hannibal 3rd had gone with his parents to enjoy the sights and fun of the fair. The latest Hannibal had been born after his brother who was also called Hannibal. His brother had died at only five years of age. Now Hannibal was the youngest child with just his sisters. They were all there at the games. It would have been more correct to have nick named the latest Hannibal, Hannibal 4th but Hannibal 3rd he was to avoid any confusion.

"What do say lad, would you like to see the world and sail the big ships, learn how to navigate and use the stars? A girl in every port, eh!"

With that, the bigger of them grabbed Hannibal, who was almost alone. He had slipped away from friends and family to see more of the festivities, when he came across these men.

"Let the lad go, in a couple of years perhaps he can join up. Or .... Meet up with us again and join our way."

With that he let out a roar of a laugh that could almost be heard above the din of the occasion.

"No time like the present."

With that the larger man started to drag the screaming Hannibal 3rd down the hill from the Green and onto the footpath which led to Empacombe. Their row boat had been left there in the small harbour. Much confusion was now being caused by the gang. As others of their company revealed themselves, alongside their true purpose, and they set about their work, mayhem was created at the Fair.

Cawsand women were well known for helping to protect their menfolk from the unwanted approaches and violence of the pressgang. As they saw them clubbed and tricked into submission, so the women could be seen joining in to smash anything they could lay their hands on against the heads of the gang.

As Sal started to take out a further two of the burly Naval men, she kissed the pot handle watching the blood drip down the side of it.

She had, before administering her rough justice, looked towards the church spire asking God to speed her well and forgive her what she was about to do.

With that, and almost totally unnoticed by the Naval gang, she lifted the large iron pot she had been using to cook the stew that was for sale at the fair high into the air.

The stew had been spilled first to lighten the load, but the pot remained heavy, very heavy.

Her sinewy arms tensed with anger as she used all the might she could summon against the foe. Before the first man, who was about to face her wrath in full flight, could open his mouth in protest, she had smashed the cast iron bowl against it, removing and breaking at least six teeth clean away from his jaw leaving it hanging, limp.

As one of his kind saw what had happened, he lunged towards her, but she again swung the pot against his chest with such ferocity for a small woman that the man recoiled with a breathless gasp. This was so much so that he almost, immediately on impact, curled and slumped to the ground, shrivelling into a tight ball. When he was down, she promptly smashed the pot into his head. It was only then that she saw the young, unattended Hannibal being dragged off. Her stall had been near the path that crossed the green and went on down to the harbour.

The young Hannibal was easy prey for the gang member who quickly paced the path down to Empacombe. Shouting for help in the confusion as she was restrained by another gang member, she caught sight of his father and friends.

As they came to help her, she shouted, "Boy Hannibal ! Empacombe! Pressed!"

With that his father, Hannibal, who had broken free from the scrum of activity with the Navy pressgang, ran with two others, down the Empacombe paths, but took the longer route, travelling swiftly to cut him off.

"Quick up in the trees." They were not sure if they had beaten the man and the young Hannibal 3rd to the point in the woods where they could surprise them.

They had not long to wait as they heard the shouting and screaming from the young Hannibal. He was still being ruthlessly dragged by his captor. Joined by two others, they were carrying one of the Dodbrook men, who looked as if he had been knocked completely senseless.

They were brutes of men, specifically chosen by the ship's captain for this work. Merciless and with an eye to the bounty and favour they would cream from their Captain should they prove successful in swelling his crew numbers for the pending voyage.

Their ship was moored in the deep channel of the Hamoaze. She awaited the return of her prizes and would set sail when her decks were full of new conscripts.

There was no time to lose. These were tough, rough, battle seasoned men. Surprise would be essential. They had one chance. One chance to surprise them.

Hannibal 2nd took off his neckpiece that had been his father's. It had a story attached to it. He was told it was a makeshift bridle carried once, it was believed, by the reputed King of The Gypsies as a scarf. It may have bloodier work to do this day. He held the scarf briefly to his face and took in its familiar smell.

Inwardly he prayed for help to his father to give him the steel of mind, the strength of body, the fortitude for this deed. He asked that all thoughts other than that which he had to do now be taken from his mind. From his God he asked for both strength to do what was just and for forgiveness for his intent and actions. For this is what he had to do to release his son from these evil men.

With that, a calm descended. His eyes focussed through the branches, down towards the coming men. As they passed underneath the leafy trees, the men fell, in what appeared a remarkable and planned formation. Alas it was not, but they seemed to synchronise unlike before and tackled the captors.

Hannibal had his chance with the scarf and quickly used the advantage of surprise. Coming behind his boy's captor he lassoed his neck. He pulled with all his might. Quickly, deftly with his knee up against the thug's back he could hear the gasp.

The harder he pulled, the more he felt the arms quiver and body shake. He had no time to look around and be concerned for his accomplice, son nor the actions of the other man. He just had to hold on. The man dropped and Hannibal 2nd dropped with him, maintaining his hold.

The scarf was wrapped tightly around his wrists coming forward to be gripped by both hands. He fell with the man, crashing on top of him. He could feel the air being forced from his lungs. This was it. He pulled his elbows tight to his sides, lifting his bulk enough with the weight of the man on him to give him the extra few inches he needed.

He jerked and held it tight as he could feel his ribs crushing against the weight. He feared another jerk might release the man enough for him to get a hold and rise against him, but no. He relaxed his grip for just a second and jerked again and again.

As he felt the limpness of the man, he turned and saw his son using the fallen club of his captor on the head of one of the other men who had fallen to the ground.

Although he had barely the strength to call on for another onslaught, he knew he had to do it. The man had got the better of Hannibal's friend. As he was on top of him beating his head side to side, the young Hannibal had summoned up his last strength to take the nearby club and smash it into the man's head. He went still, blood seeping slowly from his ear. The third man had seen the plight of the others and ran to raise the alarm. All four gave chase and brought him down. He could not stay alive with the other two dead. In short time he too had gone.

Dusk was falling. There was no time to waste. They could be missed. The others would come his way, see the deed and raise the alarm.

They were not far from the little harbour, but they could be seen more easily there. No, they would have to go there. These men must go too.

It was a tough haul, but they met no one on the paths. The harbour was a small, private harbour of the Mount Edgcumbe estate. With a bit of luck, the workers there would still be at Maker.

They would not dare touch Lordy's men. They dragged the men, still warm down to the harbour.

"In the boat. Light her."

"No. It would be safer to out the men into the mud for now. Torch the boat separately or take her back and break her up before burning."

"Let's get her into the deep channel." With that they took the boat into the central channel and holed her. The dim of evening was settling on the pool and they hoped no one had seen what could change the course of their lives.

They swam ashore and started to drag the bodies around the path, past the workers' cottages and the harbour to the relative peace of the mud flats that appeared at low tide.

The mud was a very soft with a fine sand. Where the sea pushed its softer sands up into the estuary, so it was met by earth and other soft deposits washed down. This produced a very soft mud like substance at low tide. Very deep in places, it was capable of producing a suction that could pull heavy objects down far into its depths.

They buried the men in as deep a mud as they could, weighing them down. The mud had claimed many men before them. There had been occasions when the mud had given up its dead with a hand or foot emerging from it, telling something of the tale of its grizzly capture.

The Captain of the ship waited for his crew and their catch but as the time came to hoist sails, he chose to let them go. They were probably drunk and there was little time to lose. They would join another ship and be flogged for this, unless their reason was good. The Plymouth press had done well, swelling the Captain's numbers with experienced fishermen and seamen from there instead. These would do for now. "Leave the buggers there. Hoist the sails," went out the orders.

The two Hannibals would be safe that night, although they did not know the ship had sailed. The remaining men at Maker that were part of the ship would return to no boat and would expect they would be in trouble. They may desert now or present themselves to another ship.

Drenched in a mixture of blood and mud, Hannibal and his accomplices made their way back along the river's edge, choosing not to enter the town of Millbrook but take the track up the hill again, falling back down into the safety of Kingsand and Cawsand.

They had with them the men's clothes. They had resolved there would be little left of them against which they might be identified.

As the weeks went by, the mud, salt and fresh waters did their work in turn with the fish and worms to make these men unrecognisable to all.

They had behaved in a barbaric and ungodly fashion, but Hannibal was convinced they had no God on their side.

At the stream by Forder they washed quickly, returned to their houses pledging to keep the secret of what had happened. The boy Hannibal was sworn to the men's world of secrets if he wanted to live and see his father live too.

The bodies might yet rise from the mud in the coming weeks. The boat would most likely be assumed to have returned to her ship with the three pressmen. The deep channel would most likely keep its secret as the silt would weigh onto the hull and keep her sucked down. They might yet have work to do to finish this, but for now they could sigh in relief.

They had no need to worry about anyone else pressed. There was no ship or rowing boat. They would be safe now. As the press gang realised, they may be too late to return to their ship they would either take cover, flee or return to Plymouth, reporting to another King's ship for service and take any punishment that may be coming.

Chapter 22

A Trojan Horse in Cawsand

"You know what happened to Mrs. Andrew, at the Cawsand Bakehouse don't you Mr. Glinn? You were lucky it wasn't you. You worked at the bakehouse." The Surveyor at the Customs House in Plymouth sneered at his captive, a cousin of the unfortunate Humphrey Glinn, shot on board the revenue boat when it disturbed the Lottery unloading its contraband.

"Yes, Sir but I didn't know what was going on the other side of it, Sir."

"Of course not. You would never have wondered why smoke was still coming out of the chimney when your bakehouse fire was out. Baking all night, were you? Making sure there was enough bread for the hungry, day or night? Making sure that the stoves were ready just in case one of those fishermen fancied bringing up a plate of their best dinner for you to cook at 3.00 o' the clock ..... in the morning?"

The voice of the Surveyor of Customs rose up with a snarl as he spoke through his now tightly gritted front teeth, lips curled and pursed tight against them.

Few houses in the villages of Cawsand and Kingsand had their own cooking facilities. Bake houses were dotted around the villages with large brick ovens capable of cooking many village meals, prepared from fresh ingredients and brought to the bake house to cook. The bakers knew whose dishes belonged to whom, with no need to mark them.

Some of the best were so tempting to the baker as the aroma pervaded the bakehouse rooms, that he or she might have a quick slurp of them before they were returned to their owners. It would save the baker preparing his own food after all.

"Damn you man! Take me for a fool and you'll bake at the stake and with no mercy from me! Now, I know what went on. So too, do you. You have been spared the rope just because no one caught you in the act and it wasn't your business. Now Mrs. Andrew. Yes, Mrs. Andrew.

There she was when our man saw smoke at night from your bakehouse chimney. What did he see and what did he do? He decided to break down the door and check if there was a fire. That's what he did. Yes, he was concerned should the village catch on fire. What did he find?"

"I heard around the town, it was Mrs. Andrew, Sir."

"That's right first time. Well done. Mrs. Andrew. And what pray was Mrs. Andrew doing?"

With this the Surveyor at the Customs House in Plymouth, a senior, experienced man, started to impatiently stomp the floor. His fine leather boots shone to perfection. The metal corners on the heels so carefully crafted by the Plymouth Barbican cobbler, clicked on impact with the floor in time to his perfect pace.

It was almost a march. A march with precision accuracy of timing, faultless and falterless in its beat. The regularity of the clicking sound of the metal as it hit the flagstones of the old Customs House building reverberated around the room.

Though unnerving it also produced a hypnotic calm as Glinn tuned into its rhythm. A curious mix of emotions from Mr. Glinn pervaded the knife-edge atmosphere. Without relent it could be cut in two with a sharp knife.

This was not helped when the Surveyor took his walk around the back of Mr. Glinn, who was stood, hands behind back and straight upright. Glinn was very conscious of the noise of the heels clicking their way around to his rear and then stopping abruptly.

He dared not disrespectfully turn from his position to see what was happening, an action that would, maybe, have given him some advance warning of his fate and allowed him to prepare for it. The breath of the Surveyor both warmed the back of his neck whilst chilling it at the same time. This was an experience that succeeded in creating a range of mixed emotions in Glinn.

The Surveyor was playing a game with him. He was determined to get what he wanted. But what was that?

The rough rope used to tie the hands of Glinn was cutting into his flesh. This was made worse as his tendons and muscles flexed and contracted as a response to the nervousness in Glinn that the Surveyor had created. The expansions and contractions were not matched by any give in the rope.

The rope was an old, unforgiving example of the best the naval rope-maker could produce. It had been tied by roughnecks who had delighted in drawing blood from Glinn and seeing his veins protrude, almost popping in response to the tension of the rope as they drew it as tight as they were able.

The Surveyor was not a sadistic man but was growing increasingly impatient. His anger, partly with himself, spilled over. He could neither contain nor confine his irritation any longer to the controlled clicking and scraping of his boot heels.

Suddenly, without warning, he expressed his irritation by placing his metal boot heel against the achilles tendon of Glinn's right foot whilst facing the other way. As he felt the lower part of Glinn's tendon with his boot heel, he dug it in. Glynn did not flinch.

"She was stoking a fire Sir." Glinn came forth with this response as he winced with pain as the metal seemed to cut through the tendon and rest on the top of the back section of his foot.

The Surveyor released the boot pressure and continued to pace the room, coming to face Glinn inches from his eyes, eye to eye.

"Correct .... so far. What did she do with her roaring fire?"

Responding with speed this time, Glinn with a tone of sincerity spat out his words.

"I heard, Sir, that she was producing false coin, Sir. She also made blocks for the printing of notes, and had inks, fine pens to hand draw notes."

"Correct. So, she was a forger .... and she hung unceremoniously for it. Now I am here talking to you and you are here talking to me because I have decided to spare your ugly head from the gallows should you choose to take over her .... shall we say 'enterprise'."

His lips pursed closely once more, eyes squinting at the uttering of the words.

"Take it over, Sir?"

"Yes. Subject to certain conditions. Let me elaborate for you. We know your closeness to Mr. Humphrey Glinn and sorrow, indeed anger, at his death. Potter has swung for the murder he committed. There are more though who did not pull the trigger but who were culpable in his death.

We also know now that the Marks in the town and all those close to them have an involvement with Roscoff and the uncustommed trade between our two lands.

Furthermore, we know that the Roscoff merchants and their suppliers will want to be paid – indeed paid in the currency of the English, no more, no less.

Now what is this currency pray?"

"I wouldn't know Sir."

"Don't fool with me. It's coin or maybe notes… or both. So busy is this trade in your village you need lots of money. There just isn't enough to go around and around. So, what do you do? Not content with what money there is in circulation provided by our most noble Bank, the Bank of England no less. The Bank of England, London. No, she is not good enough for your needs in Cawsand. You need a mint. Your very own money supply. The currency of the Bank of England and the Royal Mint isn't good enough. Not good enough I say.

And we suspect you know the trade, Mr. Glinn. You could carry on her good work at a moment's notice… if you so choose.

We have, therefore, added these things all together. What do we get? We have concluded that you, if willing, could obtain important information about the manoeuvres of this money, where it goes and anything else to do with the smuggling in these parts. That is of course if you would prefer to carry on living amongst your own and make yourself an honest living, well, an honest living in a manner which I will come to Mr Glinn."

"But how would I take over the bakehouse?"

"Silence. It is for me to ask the questions and you to answer when I am ready. You have money, or we could get you some. Perhaps some that you had managed to conceal that has been forged. You take this money from your ill-gotten spoils. You then acquire the bakehouse, complete of course with its living. You continue to bake. You don't though continue at night. You do it differently. When we took Mrs. Andrew we did not find the second preparation and furnace area. No, we found out about it afterwards from her. We found the counterfeit still warm in the house when we saw the fire smoke and made our entrance. We also took a further look at that unearthly hour, looking for teas, cognacs and Geneva, perhaps even some baccy. It was then, a surprise, when we questioned her, that she told us all. All about the additional furnace area and shall we say the 'secret room'. The one with the furnace on the other side of the chimney.

This truthful disclosure did avoid her the more painful way of leaving this earth. But leave it she had to. You can return and take this up without anyone thinking any the different about what we know or don't know.

We wouldn't interfere. You can make your money this way and from us. But we expect to know all about who has this money, when it is ordered, collected, by whom.

Anything else beside that will help us.

You get to save your miserable skin, take some measure of satisfaction in your revenge. You will then see those against whom you bear grudge get what they deserve.

We get to nail those we want to get to who are behind the Cawsand trade. What do you say? Well, come on, come on. Is it gallows or gain for Mr Glinn and his family .... and family to come perhaps.

I gather your family once made money further into the west from mining and metal ore. Well here is your chance again. You be our ears and you can have the money you make from the counterfeit coin, notes and anything else, for as long as you are there doing it.

You shall be undisturbed. But you keep your silence about this or by God I will see you to the gallows like she who created and operated this Cawsand Mint before you. I swear I would walk you up to them myself. I would tie the noose. My knots are not the best.

You would writhe and squirm before you finally departed. You would have plenty of time there, wriggling away, gasping for breath. Plenty of time to listen to the jeers, the mockery of the crowds. See the surgeons below eagerly waiting for you, waiting to take you apart."

The Surveyor nodded impatiently at Glinn, prompting him to make his reply.

"The grudge I hold, Sir, against the traders from Polperro as far as Cawsand, is not well known. I harbour it alone. My cousin Humphrey Glinn was a good man and remained loyal to Bowden and those who employed him. I did not think he should have worked as boatman for the preventative service, but he did. Boatman was all he was. He kept his family from that meagre wage, with some fishing.

For his work, as just an oarsman like any other, he had his face blown off. I saw him in his coffin when he was released for a decent burial. A good man's face you have never seen like of, Sir. His widow would not look but bade him goodbye by reaching into his coffin and holding his hand. She spoke to him with tenderness of touch and of voice that would melt any man's heart, Sir. She asked of him softly what it would be that might now become of them whilst assuring him peace on his journey, saying that she would doubtless see him soon. She bade him in quiet whispers not to worry about them for she would raise her mettle in his name. She promised to raise his children well. They would not be separated she promised."

The Surveyor was moved by his disposition. He had moved around behind him again so as not to show any feelings. He believed this man's utterances. He knew Humphrey Glinn as well. He let him continue.

"This Sir, this, was, in spite of temptation from the traders to breach that loyalty in some way or another. That night a cough or splash might have made signal to the Lottery and they would have been prepared. If he had, he might have saved his life. Now he has given that life. Were it not for you and your kind, his wife would have been thrown back to their parish. Further, Sir, his son, who has an impediment of speech, would have not received the teaching and education he has been afforded, that he might be able to make a fair and honest living. A living that will keep his poor mother too without concern of old age. Keep her in adequate circumstances as well."

The Surveyor could bear it no longer and he interrupted.

"You will face trial and be acquitted. You will say that you baked and that is all you knew and did. The prosecution will offer no evidence other than you worked for the convicted forger who has since been to the gallows. The Bank of England will say no more on the matter. They have had their person, Mrs. Andrew. The prosecution will then convene to discuss their case. They will return with dropped charges in the light of no further evidence and that they believe justice to have been served already. Everyone will take you as the simple bakehouse worker who knew nothing of the night time activities of those to whom you were employed and to whom you owed your living. They will consider you as just the baker of bread and cook of meals. You will be sent back to continue that trade if you so will. The lease of the bakehouse will be provided to you after suggestions of the magistrates at the trial. You return to the village and continue to bake and familiarise yourself, if you're not already, with the other side of your previous employer's business.

Doubtless you will be asked to produce coin and note. We will collect this knowledge from you through the normal bakehouse activities and the purchase of bread. We will inspect your ovens like all the others in the area for a while until word goes about, we are satisfied that there is no longer any illegal minting in the town other than that grown in the garden. Ha! Yes, the only Cawsand mint to be found is the sprig on the smugglers' dinner plates! Ha!"

With that he laughed at his joke, inviting Mr Glinn to accompany him in the mirth, which he duly did.

"You will receive treatment no different to any other whose premises we inspect, but we will not find anything untoward. No, nothing will be found, nothing at all.

It is only known that we found the forged items, not the facility by which they were in fact actually made, that lay behind the bakery oven.

It will be no surprise to those engaged in the business of purchasing forged coin and note that the mint that lays behind could start up again, operated by a trusted individual ..... you."

Glinn felt uneasy about this offer but it would serve to avenge his cousin, enable him to get even with the illicit traders, whilst at the same time providing a fine living for him and his family, for his family to be .... for its duration.

He could still have a good living after they were done with him. Just become a baker only, but the money from forgery and favour from the authorities would give him a chance to secure the future for their family for a long time to come.

He would be eligible for a good marriage too. He had his eye on a few likely candidates. He could have children and have them best educated, out to a good trade, maybe move away when all was done. They had people in Turnchapel who could take his children as apprentices in fishing and piloting. Now piloting was the thing. He could have his sons, or at least one go to the piloting. Maybe he would have enough to buy a share in a pilot boat for them. Maybe the others could be recruited to the Navy as Midshipmen.

What fortunate wife and children he could have. This baker could provide a better life for them than most bakers could dream of. His mind raced through the possibilities that this arrangement could have to change their fortunes.

"Yes. I will do it."

"Wise man. Wise man I say." A satisfied softening of his jaw-line followed. He had not wanted to see this man tried and to the gallows. He was worth more to them alive, as the baker.

"Just take what comes and go with it and you will be at the bakehouse before long. Do nothing to see us, nor make any move to speak with us again. It will be us who will make moves to you. You will know it when it happens."

Glinn left under guard and was taken to the gaol, where he was treated like all others awaiting trial.

Glinn had in fact known of the skills that Mrs. Andrew had built with her husband, poor soul who had died a premature death. She had continued the bakehouse, using his skills in the melting of the metals and the moulding to produce the coins so badly needed by the free traders.

It was known simply as the Bakehouse to the area of the town it serviced. It was not the only bakehouse. The bakehouses would all keep their ovens alive and warm from early in the morning before many were up. They would be up early, stoking the fires for the ovens to rise to baking temperature. They all stocked the raw ingredients for their bread, which was brought in by hand cart, or sometimes horse and cart, from the Mills nearby and on the surrounding farms.

But the Andrew bakehouse also had another name known to those in the senior echelons of the free trade in the area.

The Cawsand Mint was indeed its name and the huge arched ovens looking so innocent as they baked the village dinners and bread shared the same chimney as the Mint that lay to the other side of the oven.

Here the alchemists had plied their trade, melting silver and other metals required for the traders to pay for their goods. So good were they it was difficult to tell them apart. The size, slightly smaller from the moulds that had made them, nonetheless took a trained eye to see.

A struck coin of the realm had a crispness but wore soon and these coins when cleaned and then roughed and dirtied with the smeech soon became passable for the genuine and used struck item.

As notes became commonplace, so they too formed part of the standard repertoire of the forging. By print and by hand they were crafted with suitable paper used for the genuine articles and provided by the smugglers. If they could obtain the finest of spirit, they too, could obtain the finest of papers used by the Bank of England. They would enter the money supply through the accounts in the Channel Islands of Guernsey where the merchants would accept them, bank them or use them to trade so they ended up elsewhere.

***

The "trial" took place as the Surveyor had said it would. Glinn found himself with relative ease back in the Cawsand bakehouse where he had previously worked for the Andrew family. The rest of the Andrew family had left the bakehouse industry now. The execution of Mrs. Andrew had made their decision for them. This was a marked establishment and they were a marked family for it.

From here he lived and worked, providing baking for the area of Cawsand within easy reach of his bakehouse when compared with the other bakehouses in the area.

***

"What time do you rake out, Sam?"

It was Hannibal who had put his head around the door of the bakehouse. Samuel Glinn's heart raced. Was this it? He had been fortunate so far.

There had been no demands on him. He had spent time working at the rear of the bakehouse to check out that he could, in fact, without the Andrew's experience to guide him, forge copies of coins work lead for print and copy notes himself.

He had enough raw materials to work with and was ready to work on the production of coins. Hannibal came in. The two men talked at the back together about everything and nothing for the best part of a couple of hours.

After the cordialities were exhausted it was Hannibal who got straight to the point.

"We could do with some activity again out of the Cawsand Mint, Sam if you're ready. I know it must have been a big shock when Mrs. Andrew was taken in but the Mint itself has survived without making itself known. You have the skills. What about it? Are you for us?"

"Yes, I'm for you Hannibal." They slapped each other on the back and got down to business. Hannibal agreed to get the raw materials to Sam and to guarantee payments per coin minted at different rates per coin to reflect their weight, material and complexity.

So too for notes, although coin remained the strong currency when trading direct. The banking system was increasingly using notes too, where trust had developed. Payments were now made using all manner of means of exchange, but coin when there was any doubt, now coin remained strong. It had a tangible value. Everyone could do something with coin.

Coin was still the King of currencies for Hannibal and his dealings. He had also developed some business in the brokering of coin for others who needed it. There was simply a shortage of currency to trade with.

Promissory notes and cheques were available for many but hard currency that could be traded was essential too for the smaller trader and those not so well established.

Establishing lines of credit remained an obstacle to easy trading. It also required good reading and writing skills as well as sound administrative ability.

This is where Job's credibility in the banking system at home, in the Channel Isles, Roscoff and more centres of the trade in Northern France besides, had helped to grow the industry.

Even Job though had need for good coin and note. The two men started thrashing out an arrangement, but it was easy. Hannibal had a lot of money to spend on this. He was not constrained by budgets. Credible, usable means of exchange was essential to oil the wheels of free trade commerce.

Hannibal would not be the only trader requiring this hard currency, but he was an important one. Now with shares in several boats and a few of his own he had large currency needs.

He would also broker and arrange shipments, finding himself at the front line of arranging financial transactions. How things had changed from rowing out to large smugglers that had moored offshore from France and other countries with contraband to sell.

Glinn took a deep breath after Hannibal had gone. He'd pulled it off and could make a start using the skills he had learnt with Mrs. Andrew and what she had left behind gave him the chance to do it.

Following the initial euphoria of his successful discussions, being treated as a fellow merchant, important to the free trade in the area, a cold wind in the airless still of the room flowed past his forehead, as the reality of what he was about to embark on struck him fully for the first time.

He would be betraying his fellow townsfolk and although he had a grudge against the trade that had seen Humphrey meet his end in the grizzliest of ways, he remained at odds with his own actions.

Death had been Humphrey's thanks for simply being an oarsman for the wrong people at the wrong time. He, Samuel Glinn, had few real grudges against the Cawsand folk. After all, was it not a Polperro man, indeed an Irishman by origin who had done the deed that had robbed Humphrey of his life as well as a wife and children of their husband and father?

He was now about to do worse than Toms had done with the Lottery betrayals. This was going to be two faced. One face to the authorities who would now control him, the other to the townsfolk traders. These thoughts kept him from sleep that night as he wrestled alone with his thoughts in the room in which he slept.

The room adjoined the chimney that ran up through the centre part of the bakehouse. It was always warm there. summer, winter, it mattered not. Whatever the weather conditions outside, this room was warm and soothing as he lay and slept. Not tonight though, and not for many to come, would he feel the soothing warmth of the bakehouse.

It symbolised everything that was now wrong. Warmth and security for him brought with it a cold wind for others. Could there be a half-way house? Could he satisfy the Surveyor and his lot whilst at the same time making sure that the traders continued with no more damage because of him than that which they might have suffered in any event?

Yes, if he could do this, he would again be allowed to take the sooth of the warm room and sleep again. There was no one but himself to talk with about these matters. He could not voice it for fear of being heard. He would have to plot this in his mind and his mind alone. Only he would know the real truths. This would be a lonely place. He had better get used to that. Maybe though, if he thought long and hard about it, he could work out a way through, a way that would line his pockets with gold, and, when it was all over, bear responsibility for as little harm as possible to others in the trade. Yet again his mind turned to the dream life he might have after it was all over.

He could then leave this place. He could set up somewhere else where no one knew him. Take a wife there perhaps, have children. His wife wouldn't have to be from those he had his eye on here. No, a fresh start was called for. Yes, maybe this would be his chance or maybe just settle here, bury the past and what had happened to Humphrey. Live quietly and well for a man of his station. More settled in his mind, he wrapped the sheet around him and fell to a much-needed slumber.

Chapter 23

Joe Gets to Know Marie

"Can't you control that man of yours Hannibal. That.................. that............. damned Joe." "What has he been up to now?" replied Hannibal with a tone of reluctance to hear what he knew he was about to hear. He had guessed what this was about. "He has been showing attention to Marie. Too much attention for my liking. She is an innocent lady of considerable culture and charm. Not like that uncouth example of mankind, Joe. I fear he may lure her into wrong ways. If it continues, we will need to consider a replacement for Marie. She would have to return to Roscoff. I cannot be doing with divided loyalties with the servants, if you get my meaning Hannibal. I don't want to smell that Joe in the room when we have our French lessons. No, not that Joe. No, not anyone for that matter."

Hannibal had been summoned to the rectory after Church. He was splitting his Church attendance duties between the two. With the Marks' residences and businesses operating from both Kingsand and Cawsand, he succeeded in doing this. The two were quietly strolling out of earshot through the small wood nearby. A slow stroll it was to accommodate the pace of the Vicar.

They stopped a while to look seawards to where the works were soon to start to create the Breakwater. An ambitious plan to break the force of the seas in a storm that would prevent the waves from coming full strength onto the sea frontage at Plymouth and its surrounding coastal stretches.

A line of submerged rock, manmade and capped off at its top. The works were planned over many years.

"He will often stay after service and walk through the Churchyard. If she gets a chance she will go in there too. I have seen them going down to the woods below. She returns with some flowers, bringing them back to the house. She then says she has retired there to enjoy the air after service and pick some flowers.

She never mentions Joe and I have not yet said that I have noticed these meetings, let alone that I have observed them occur with increasing frequency. I have not wanted to warn them. But you, Hannibal, yes you.

You could tell that Joe to keep away without mentioning the fact that I have seen them.

Nip it in the bud is what I say. Yes, nip it, nip it in the bud."

All had gone well with the use of the Churches for storage. Hannibal, for one, did not want to see any disruption to this. He also knew it was unlikely he would be able to control the hot-blooded Joe.

He would speak with Joe to see what this was all about. See if there was a chance it could be dealt with now and as the Vicar said, nipped in the bud. If not, it might be best that arrangements were made to obtain a new Marie for the Vicar. This might have the added benefit of keeping the Vicar with them. A new interest may well be a good thing.

"I will speak with Joe carefully to see what, if anything, is likely to be in his mind. If this can be closed now all is well. If not, then let us arrange a new Marie for you. I have been in Roscoff recently and there are some very attentive ladies looking for opportunity in a good household such as yours."

"Oh, and pray what are they like? Are they competent at French and English? Could they be attentive to my French requirements do you think? Perhaps you could have them drawn for me when you are next there and I could look and decide what one I may prefer to join our household?"

Hannibal could see that the prospect of a gentle stream of maids for him from France might be the only way to keep his good will for their trading requirements at the Church. Maybe there would be something else in addition that he could expect from the Vicar of Maker. No others caused him this difficulty, but Maker held now a good stock at any time for any one storage facility. The arrangement was therefore of special value to them. It was also relatively safe. No searches made, no disruption. If anything, they would like to see how much more advantage could be taken here. The Vicar's house and buildings maybe. There had to be more that could be done here, a place where the revenue would not dare go and interfere. The Vicar at Rame was much more easily pleased.

"My wife and I have the honour of being invited to the Earl's ball next week where I shall deliver grace. Marie is meant to be attending the carriage to help tend us as we alight. We are not arriving by trap. This time we are being taken from the Rectory by one of the Earl's carriages. It is too late to acquire a new Marie for the ball. I want to know we have a well behaved and unsullied Marie in attendance, using her French as we alight, holding my wife's gown off the dirt, if you understand me Hannibal. I don't want anything disrupting arrangements now. The Earl has expressed interest in improving his French. The arrangement we have is a good one that benefits all in different ways."

"Maybe change is called for after all. Are things doing well for the business Hannibal .... eh, are they?"

The Vicar seemed to have already made up his mind on a change. He just wanted to remind Hannibal of his obligations for continued good will. This might be easier than persuading Joe to change his course. With that the two men looked at each other. Hannibal dropped his head, raised it again, and bade farewell. The Vicar remained still, nodded and Hannibal turned to part. He turned again, responding to the Vicar's clearing of his throat which indicated he had one more thing to say.

"And .. all between us .. of course?"

"All between us of course, Vicar."

Hannibal nodded again and once more made his move towards the door.

Joe was just beyond the last Pilchard Palace, barking his nets, when he saw Hannibal approaching along the sand past the coves.

Barking involved the boiling of the nets in a preservative made from tree barks, usually that from the oak and birch, when it was available.

It produced a pungent and pervading smell that was fortunately lost into the air around the quiet spot used by Joe. The coves had been formed when rock was required to build the cellars and were now used to bring in the smaller boats to offload.

Hannibal, as sure-footed as he had been as a boy, could have walked it almost blindfold without catching a foot or falling. The tide was receding, and Hannibal crunched along the sand at the tide mark, which at the beach past the old cellars, was always strewn with the remnants of small shells, more-so than the other beaches for some reason.

As his boots weighed heavy into the wet sand the noise, with that of the tide, took the troubles off his shoulders for a few minutes. There weren't many about on this stretch.

The bark house was just a little further along raised up onto the hard rock by about six feet from the high tide mark. It could get cut off for the odd hour or two in very high tides and had been kept away from the main work building.

The stench from the heavy smoke was unwelcome there but Joe seemed to thrive on the job. He appeared outside of the barkhouse.

"Hannibal Marks at the barkhouse these days. To what do I owe this honour?" The two men grinned at each other.

"Your ear for a while, Joe?"

"That won't cost me anything Hann, so you have it."

"It's about Marie, Joe."

"I thought this might be coming around the corner, but not so quick. What's happened?"

"I can't say it all Joe, but I've got to ask if you will keep off Marie. There are so many local girls who would rush you down that aisle Joe. Why Marie?"

Joe finished off the section of net he was working on and faced Hannibal eye to eye.

"Let's take a walk Hann. Get some air." The two men walked down from the barkhouse, back across the sandy beach from where they walked up the grassed slope by the large, old cellar that led to the fields and up towards the Church. The footpath went through the edge of the Edgcumbe estate. The two men said little until they got to the high land.

"Problem is Hann, I have taken to Marie. I know there is this thing with the Vicar, but I think I can bring her round from that. I'm putting away my shares and hope to get enough to get a house, build a boat even, a boat that could be used for a living one day. A living that doesn't have the chances and risks with it that we all take. We've been starting to lose boats Hann. Up and down the coast they say the same. It's getting harder .... and for how much longer?"

Maybe we all need to start thinking about how we can put aside for an easier time perhaps. I see a life like that with her one day."

"Joe, I know what you mean, but this life, this one that has given all of us more than we would have had, this life is what we know. We've all worked at this and prospered from what we would have been. This with Marie is the sort of thing that might scupper some of it. At best, set us back a bit. The Maker facility works well. It might also affect Marie's situation here as well if the Vicar turns against the two of you. I know that the heart rules us at times Joe ... but can you lay off her for now, just while we see what we can do to sway the Vicar's affections elsewhere .... and this remains with us Joe. That includes Marie."

Joe paced around in circles, looking away from Hannibal. Without warning he threw out his arms to the sides as far as they would stretch and threw his head back. It was a violent jerk, bringing his arms to his sides, elbows bent, powerful fists clenched to control his anger, he turned to face Hannibal once more.

"Why's it got to be me Hann? You know what that Vicar is like to her. She is well fed and watered, can enjoy being at the large house .. but in return for all that there are the Vicar's pleasures she has to tend to. She may come to no harm but it's no life in the end, no life. What happens when he tires of her or what if it goes further and she gets with child? He won't want to keep her then nor take responsibility for a bastard. Certainly not face anything to do with bastardy. Not with his name. Not as Vicar. Then what for her. Back on the ships I expect, away from here. Convenient for him she is. From Roscoff and poor, she could be sent back without a murmur from anyone, anyone at all .... but me.

I'll do it though Hann and tell her that I'm going to be going off with the trade, won't be around much to see her for a while. That will be that until I get the all clear from you that she is free from him.

Providing you give me your word that you will try to steer his attentions. You try to free her without anything happening that would cause her damage."

"I promise Joe. It may take a while. Be patient." There was a good deal of trust here and Joe trusted Hannibal to do what he could. He did not want to jeopardise either the safety of all in the trade here by his actions or the position of Marie. He could see that.

Chapter 24

The Edgcumbe Ball Changes It All

The house at Cremyll, was the setting of the ball for local dignitaries, hosted by the Earl of Mount Edgcumbe. The prominent Edgcumbe family had recently joined the more elevated ranks of the peerage. The ball was hosted by Richard, the second earl of Mount Edgcumbe and his older children, Lady Sophia especially. She had become of an age to accompany her father.

Recently bereaved, his Lordship had thrown himself into his work at both a national and County level as member of his Majesty's Privy Council and the Lord Lieutenant of Cornwall. His passion for music and the opera was reflected in, and fuelled, the work on his book, which was very much a work in progress. He was resolved to publish it. Much of his taste in music would be on show at the ball. The house could accommodate many guests that had travelled any distance.

Others had made their own arrangements to stay close by. For those attending from the environs of the Plymouth area, the chosen crossing was that at Stonehouse, from which a ferry crossed the river to the Mount Edgcumbe lands on the other side.

Carriages met the ferry to transport guests on the ten-minute journey to the House. The crossing by rowing boat at Cremyll took at least an hour, often more. This was especially so when there was a horse or two to transport to the other side as well.

Crossing the river at this lower point as it met the open seas, made the crossing by rowing boat hazardous in some weather conditions. That day the river and open sea were calm. The journey had been easy.

Most guests coming from the other side of the river near Plymouth had chosen to cross by foot with carriages and horses left on the other side. Carriages awaited to take guests from the ferry to the house. Some had arrived by River and plied down the Tamar as the house was situated by the west bank of the river just as it opened into the mouth of Plymouth Sound. Planning and correspondence about the Ball had been arranged well in advance.

Extra staff had been drafted in from the area to provide additional kitchen help, with others available to help make the guests' arrival and preparation for the event as easy as possible. Grooms were available for those who had travelled by horse or carriage.

This came with the Edgcumbe facilities to store, clean, maintain and repair. All were at their best. All staff and trades people were on high alert to provide anything to make the guests' arrival, stay and departure as comfortable and easy as possible.

For guests who had brought servants and other assistants, arrangements had been made for them too, ensuring they were provided for as their station should allow.

This gave an opportunity for workers of all ranks to swap notes with those of the same rank, spreading news and gossip around the estates.

There were some absences as a result of feuds and fallen gentry, balanced by additions from the swelling merchant and professional classes, as well as from those of high rank in military service that were available to attend.

"Does that Mr Pollard of the Navy still reside in Cawsand or this area, Piers? asked a Naval Lord, who had travelled especially for the Ball. The visiting Edgcumbe family member replied that he knew not but enquired of his interest.

"He is the man credited with shooting dead that fellow who killed Nelson at Trafalgar. Modest sort of chap. His father put him to training as Midshipman and he has been making good. Family came from nowhere it seems, but young Pollard has been making the most of himself. All helped of course by his reputation as the man who avenged the death of our Lord Nelson.

To cap it all Nelson knew his waters well and stayed at Cawsand we understand. Ship Inn was his favourite ... and that of a particular friend of his ...." With that the old Naval Lord bent almost double as he coughed and spluttered, looking at Piers Edgcumbe as he did so. He clearly expected a nod of understanding.

The famous Lord Nelson had been well known in the area for liaising at the Ship to see his friend, Lady Hamilton where by co-incidence they were both staying.

The Naval Lord was pleased with himself at being the catalyst for some mirth which now was the solemn occasion of greeting and announcing the guests as they arrived.

He felt he had had an impact with a member of the host family and wasn't going to let it stay at that without going for an encore. Besides, he now had a small audience that had gathered to whom he could perform.

"The Ship Inn would have seen more rocking about on the upper floors those nights than Nelson would have had at sea in a bad storm. Just as well he doesn't get sea sick, I say ...."

With that he bent backwards as he brushed the tears from his eyes. His vision cleared, he saw that all the company had moved away, apart from Piers. The audience had spoken.

The Vicar had been collected as promised. He and his wife were in their best finery. This local bastion of the established Church was adorned with his finest of ecclesiastical robing, that he might provide the best of deliveries of Grace before the assembled ate and made merry. Lighter garments were cared for by his maid to ensure he could change and retire more comfortably after his role was satisfactorily completed. Not that he intended to just deliver an adequate performance. Oh no, a satisfactory performance was not what he intended to deliver. No, his would be an exceptional performance, nay an exemplary performance. One that would be unforgettable, short though it was. For its clarity, the depth of emotion and inspiration it provided to all those upon whose ears it fell. Men would talk of this grace long after it had been given, mused he.

The carriage had arrived through the upper gatehouse road. This wound its way down through the western side of the estate, past the tumbling water feature that had been directed that way, through the tree-lined avenue, off which the road to the house led over a small bridge.

As they arrived with house to the right of the party, the horseman continued past to make a sweeping turn around the large circular area that had been created especially for this purpose.

They were then correctly positioned to allow the travellers to alight directly outside of the main entrance to the house, taking their leave to the stable yard once their travellers had climbed the few steps to the house and were safely inside.

The Vicar's wife was helped down by the waiting footman followed by Marie, whose prime purpose at this point, was to keep her lady's gown from falling onto the road. She was then to follow behind with the gown carefully suspended from the potentially damaging stone steps, until such time as it reached the safety of the top step.

She then performed the same duty for the Vicar whose robes were at least of equal length and splendour. Her duties completed, Marie was escorted to the servants' quarters to await further instruction.

The Vicar spoke in French to Marie with an eloquence of tone and a volume that demonstrated to all of those nearby, his ability in the more complex use of vocabulary and syntax. Just as they were turning and about to leave, Piers Edgcumbe appeared, having heard a smattering of high-quality French.

Almost continual wars with France had prevented much free travel on the Continent and the language had not been as well practiced as much as it had previously been. Tours had to be more carefully arranged to ensure the travelling nobility and gentry were not endangered.

"J'ai ecourie plus de Marie a la place de l'eglise Maker." With that the young Edgcumbe bent his head briefly.

"We will have to practice my French with yourself and the Vicar one day. I do not get many chances at the moment and I hear you have been encouraging good French practice with him."

With that Marie curtsied, blushed and replied, "Enchante, Mon Signeur."

She had not before been addressed like this by a member of such a prominent British household.

The young Piers was taken with the beauty of Marie and her sense of natural poise. This was someone he would like as a member of the staff at Edgcumbe or one of the other Edgcumbe residences. His French could perhaps benefit too when he made his appearances at the estates.

With that thought in mind he swivelled, turned and went back onto the greeting area where the Vicar and his wife were announced.

The musicians played on the upper floor to entertain the select and influential gathering of worthies below.

The servants' quarters were alive too, feeding from the atmosphere. They made jolly to the music, which permeated down as well as up, providing pleasure for all those in earshot of it.

Marie danced the tables and around the floor. She had not had much merriment like this since she had arrived. As she went outside of the servants' area to get some air, she heard a rustle in the bushes close by. Startled, but thinking it deer or badger perhaps, she thought little more of it, but stared a short while at the bushes.

Without further warning, Joe appeared finger to lips bidding her quiet. She turned and saw no one there and walked further into the pathway away from any light. At the end, there was Joe.

"I haven't seen you because I am going to be away a lot with the trade. I won't be able to meet up after service for a while I don't suppose."

"Joe, our walks and talks have kept me going. They mean everything to me," she said with real sorrow coming through.

"When will be able to meet again, when will you be free Joe?"

With that Joe gave her a surprise peck of a kiss on the side of her cheek, looked at her with eyes that told her he did not mean this. He then stole away into the darkness as he came from it, saying, "Keep your counsel about this."

She felt, in a way, quite desperate. He had been a friend, maybe he would become a lover one day when all this was past her. Now all she had was her comfortable life, but with the lustful Vicar in it.

All escape routes seemed closed. Marie knew now that she had to plan a break from the Vicar but how? She ran into the darkness in his direction. After a few minutes she knew he was there. It was in the wooded areas between the rear of the house and the field at Maker Church. Suddenly she felt his arms around her waist and she grabbed him around his. She could feel him tight against her.

She knew she had to take him. She knew she was not with child from the Vicar. This was her chance. She would have Joe if he wanted her. She could feel the heat of Joe and his pulse running through every fibre of her body. The two pressed hard against each other. As they kissed, she held Joe even more tightly to her, pushing herself against him from behind, so he could feel her shapely form. She could feel him move against her and she gently slunk to the ground, waiting for him.

She did not have to wait long. Her excitement rose to fever pitch inside as she heard the rustle of Joe pulling off his clothing.

She then saw his shadow, cast by the near full moon of this clear night, momentarily dance against the large tree opposite to where she lay. This was how she knew he too was ready for her.

She rose up from the waist to pull him down and towards her. Her limbs were trembling. As he took her, he could feel her legs shaking against his, then they relaxed for her to wrap herself around him and pull him tight into her.

She brushed herself off and told Joe to go quickly and that she would work out a way for them if he did the same. He promised her his faithfulness as she ran back towards the house to the servants' quarters.

When she arrived, she was conscious she was flushed in the face and her shaking was starting again. She composed herself, entering through the door she had left about half an hour previously.

"You've been a while Miss Marie. Been taking some of that fine French wine from the cellar, have we?" With that the servants left in the room laughed.

"French wine. Good wine but not so much here since the war. We shouldn't be entertaining the French. Maybe Marie's working for the French authorities or maybe she works for the army or navy in France and is finding out our secrets.

She's not really a maid here from Roscoff at all!"

"Hey Marie – how about asking that Joe for a bottle or two of the French best. Reckon he'd do that for you."

"I don't know what you're talking about. How would he have any of that? Besides I hardly know him and would hardly recognise him."

"Oh, yes!" they all said in unison.

"Ask us to believe that and we'd believe anything. We've watched him on Sundays. Always sniffing here, there, everywhere. Always waiting for you."

"Better watch Joe Spriddle we say. Good for a good bottle or two or maybe an … anker!"

"I don't know what you're talking about."

"Best not let the Vicar hear, Marie." They looked at each other and laughed.

Marie wasn't too sure what they meant nor knew but she didn't want to pursue the conversation, so killed it dead when she retorted, "The Vicar will be very upset when he hears you've been talking to me like that. I wouldn't be surprised if he talks to your Lord and the young Lady about it."

The room silenced more. They clearly weren't sure about all this with the Vicar and chose to stop it there. They weren't too sure about Marie for that matter. If they had seen anything with Joe, they would have alluded to it now she thought. They hadn't. She gradually relaxed with them, awaiting her call to help with her Lady's gown, to make an exit from the Edgcumbe house.

The time came, late that it was, and off the rectory household went. The young Edgcumbe family member who had spoken to her earlier was there to bid the rectory party farewell. The Vicar made a great display of speaking to her in his best French for all to marvel at. The French were not the most popular in the Country now, but accomplishment in the language remained an accolade as it did for all of the main European languages.

The Vicar had been soaked in the best food and drink available in the area that night. As the coach lurched along the rough road so he could feel the delicate balance of his stomach acids change from a state of reasonable balance to turmoil.

He showed his appreciation for the fine fare on which he had gorged continuously all evening by a series of belches made from different parts of his anatomy. Made with such conviction, chorus and chord that their volume and variation of pitch could well compete with a peel of his Church bells. As his gases filled the little coach Marie saw her Mistress waft her fan in dismay and disapproval, though successfully shifting their potency from her direction.

"Come on you horses. Stop that noise. Stop that stink."

The horses looked as puzzled as the Vicar who heard the driver. In a slurred voice the Vicar shouted to the him not to blame a poor beast for his own lewd behaviour, but to refrain from feeding him too many of the fallen, maggot ridden cider apples that they had passed.

With his usual self-satisfied, superior look at his companions he lifted his arms, crossed them and brought them to rest on his expansive midriff. There they would stay until he felt he needed to shift himself on the seat to make room for a further explosion from the depths of his gut.

This had indeed been a good night, he thought. Grace had gone well, with his characteristic gusto. Yes, he was indeed the master of Grace before food and drink was served at the best of the local houses. With that his eyes shut until he was awoken on arrival back at the rectory.

The young Edgcumbe had spent an uncharacteristic amount of time talking to the Vicar, mainly so about servants. He enquired much about Marie. The Vicar, pleased with the attention, had agreed she could spend time at the Edgcumbe residence at Cotehele, where he was spending much of his time, that she might work there as a maid, using her French regularly to provide him and others with some regular practice. The Vicar had proudly sanctioned the sabbatical, under the influence not only of the intoxication of the liquor that had dulled his senses, but the occasion and the attention he had received.

It was only upon sobering, which only the passage of time can bring, heralding with it the next morning, that he did recall the promise and started to think better of it.

He would miss his sessions with Marie, and, who knows, she may not return. She might prefer the Edgcumbe House. Should they be satisfied with her they may provide her with an appointment there. An appointment at the Cotehele estate of the Edgcumbes would be more attractive than he could possibly provide.

Cotehele was more of an occasional residence for the Edgcumbes but visiting family members gave it a reasonable use. The Vicar did think afterwards, why there? Why not what was now the main house at Cremyll? Furthermore, what might she say about their little indiscretions when he was not there to monitor her conversations?

How could he retract on this arrangement he had been so foolishly drawn into? Surely, he the Vicar, he the intellectual superior, despite his more, lowly rank, could out-manoeuvre these Edgcumbes?

Time ran out when, next day, a maid from Mount Edgcumbe was brought to the rectory to replace Marie for the duration of her stay at Cotehele.

Damn that Edgcumbe, he'd thought of everything and pulled rank on him. He would have to let her go for a while and hope for the best. Maybe he should now see about a replacement for Marie anyway?

Yes, that was the answer to all of this. A replacement. Hannibal Marks, that was the man to see. Marie watched closely as her familiar surroundings melted away from her as she travelled up the river with a small bag of her meagre possessions.

The bag was the one she had arrived with, a length of cloth with her things in side, tied at the top in a way that made a carrying handle. There was little there but a few items of clothing and a momento of home, her life before this. Most importantly there was the little gift she had received from Joe. Not much she thought for her life as she considered the rectory and all the Vicar's possessions, let alone those of his wife.

As for the Edgcumbe House and this boat she was to travel on, well. Well ... what was her life about. She was a servant and would most likely stay one until she died unless .... Joe. Joe was the one who could take her from this. She may not live in a big house, but she would have no master.

She had taken Joe because she wanted him but knew that if she got with child from the Vicar then none may want her and then what. But if she knew a child were Joe's? Joe wanted her but just wasn't ready.

The Vicar, she was sure, had most likely a hand in the change Joe had shown towards her. What would he now think when he heard of her move away? This might be her chance. Break from the rectory forever. But why her? It couldn't just be because she could give practice in French. The Edgcumbes were well able to make their own arrangements for this, with someone from the nobility. That would stay whatever changes in France.

Well, she thought, dreaming a while, maybe they are getting someone from the French noble classes, coming to them with a quality of the French language to match her true station .... or maybe they are not.

Someone who has been dispossessed of noble rank and in the clothing and work of a poor maid I could be. Maybe .... Maybe that is what they see?

The sail up river took the daytime but there were stops along the way. This was a working boat after all. It had its usual business to do for the Edgcumbe estate. The boat made its way slowly up past the quays, towns and settlements that took their livings from the river and the land adjoining it.

The lower sections on the Plymouth Dock banks with their naval ships and boatbuilding, made the noises that broke the silence and tranquillity of the river. This combined with the noise from the hulks moored up close by, the noise of prisoners at work.

There was much activity to and froing in preparation for the new break-water that was being built that Marie could see on leaving. The taking of men and stone from different parts and from the Plymouth side further in the distance.

Much of the stone had come from the cliffs of limestone she had seen in the in the distance, some closer by from the Cremyll limestone cliffs that formed part of the Edgcumbe land.

Marie had truly mixed feelings when she left the rectory. What now would be expected of her? Either way she was away from him and probably had a while to see if she might be with child from Joe.

She would know it was Joe, given a few weeks. How could she then get word to him?

She need not have worried about news travelling to Joe. This was a boat that plied the river for the Edgcumbes regularly. It did so almost continuously. The boatman knew everyone who used the waters of the Tamar with its surrounding seas. Joe was one of these.

As they struck up conversation about life at Cotehele and people she had got to know whilst at the rectory, Joe's name came up. "Joe Spriddle. We all know Joe. He was brought up on the water and on this water too, Joe.

Knows every bit of both banks of the river as she goes up and down and snakes around, seas out there as well," said the boatman.

"Well if you see him let him know that Marie is at Cotehele. I have something of his to return to him that he kindly lent me a while ago and something small I have made as a thank you to him."

The boatman thought little of it, promising he would.

The river narrowed, taking on a greater peace and calm the further upstream they went. The boatman took care in the narrows as the barges passed that were bringing their surplus produce down to the traders gathered at the various small quays on the way.

The bigger markets of the Plymouth area were waiting for them as they finished their trip downstream, journeying out into the mouth of Plymouth Sound.

"We're not so far off now," yelled the boatman, as they negotiated the never-ending bend in the river. "It'll be work starting for you soon at the big house." As they drew closer to the estate quay, she could see much activity. She heard the whine of the Mill that was close by. The Cotehele quay was a busy place and, as their boat tied up, people seemed to emerge from nowhere to help, making a start to take off the few items she was carrying.

“You’ll be walking from here. Hey Tom, take Miss Marie up to the house, would you? She’s not been to these parts before. She will be working with us for a while.”

“We heard about her coming,” said Tom as he looked to Marie. “Frenchy,” he muttered under his breath. Marie wondered how word could have travelled so quickly but thought better of asking.

The walk up to the house was a steep one. Marie marvelled as they went past the manicured gardens, entering the gates to the house.

"To think this house is only lived in sometimes by its owners. Well I suppose those Edgcumbe visitors are using it and then there is all the staff."

“Well it must be Miss Marie from Roscoff?” The stern looking lady, who interrupted her thoughts, greeted her at the servants’ entrance. Jane Arundell created an atmosphere of her superiority, initially looking down on her with a grace that she had probably acquired from working under the nobility and gentry of the region. She, and her family going back, had worked for the estate for generations. Occasionally, they had travelled with the Edgcumbes as they toured. They had served visiting monarchy from England and beyond. They did though have their own claim to associations with royalty of a sort and were proud of it, keen to let any new arrivals know, stamping an authority and status in the pecking order of the servants.

"Did you see the Church at Landulph on your way?" she enquired of Marie, as the she walked with her to where she would be working and sleeping with the other maids.

"I can't say I did."

"Well, when you return, I will ask the boatman if he could stop and show you."

"What will I see there, Maam?"

"We're from Landulph. Married into the descendants of Theodore Palaeologus. Who else, of course? Can't you tell?"

"Theodore ..... " Marie struggled with the surname.

"Yes, there is a brass there in the Church to his name. Why, he was descended from the Byzantine Emperors. He came to Landulph about one hundred and eighty years ago. His first wife he married in Chios was Eudoxia Commena. She died and left him a daughter Theodora you know."

As she prepared to speak further, she grew in stature. She always liked a new audience for the story.

"Where is Chios?"

"Don't you know? Oh dear, well Chios is in the Mediterranean Sea of course. Your home would not be far away."

Marie fell silent, feeling confused and uncertain. How did this woman know so much? How had she come to this from such a prominence in this area? She was a servant, as she was, even if much senior to her.

Miss Palaeologus, as she was sometimes nicknamed by the other servants, when they remembered how to pronounce the name, continued, tongue in cheek, with a hint of sarcasm.

"She married Prince Demetrius Rhodocanakis at Naples. The Prince had several children with her including, Dr. Constantine Rhodocanakis of Rhodocanakis Castle which is on the Isle of Chios.

He, my dear, was an eminent doctor and friend of King Charles II of England. They met while the King was in exile."

The encyclopaedic information reeled off her tongue with the precision accuracy of the historian rather than the servant.

There was not much more she could offer.

This diatribe was almost by rote and well-rehearsed.

She omitted to say that when Theodore arrived, he led the life of a hermit in a wood for some time, near Tattershall. It was only an Italian friend of the nobility that persuaded him to come out of seclusion and return to society.

On his emergence from the woods he came to Plymouth, then Landulph. Here he held property and lived with his new wife. He had married her near Tattershall.

Mary Balls of Tattershall thus became Mary Palaeologus.

In Landulph their offspring married into the prominent Arundells before conflict had set in with the coming of the Civil War. One son had sided with and come out for the King, whereas Theodore, perhaps unexpectedly, came out for Parliament.

Time passed, generations died with their wealth and influence passing with them. This left many future offspring to take their chances in the world, making their way as best they could.

"Well Marie, anything you want to know about Theodore and all of these fine people, just ask."

With that she lifted her head high and walked ahead. Marie gathered quickly that the way to win over this new friend here was to treat her with some respect, maybe go as far as with reverence.

The truth of all this would remain another matter, but it was clear that Jane liked to relate the story as she knew it.

Yes, that's what she would do. She would keep her on her side by preening her. She may need her in this new place even if she was only to be here for a short while.

The weeks passed. Marie settled into her duties within the household at Cotehele seeing nothing much of the young Piers who had started all of this.

She breathed many sighs of relief but despair at the same time as she realised that she was with child. It could not be the Vicar. It could be no one else's than Joe's. But what now? What would happen to her?

What was expected of her at this household and to where would she return?

She had to see Joe. Had he heard of what had happened to her from the boatman? Her intuition told her that he would be there for her and when he heard this news .... Well, trepidation she might feel, but somehow, somehow, she felt things would end well.

"Master Piers would like to see you in the main courtyard Marie."

Nicholas, one of the upper Hall boys had been sent down with this message.

Marie was in the middle of her cleaning duties. Jane was close at hand.

"Well you had better go, Marie. I can't think what the master wants with you now."

With that Jane head high, her demeanour aloof, strutted off as if wrongly upstaged by an inequal.

"Marie, I expect you have settled in here now and thought it might be a good time to take the opportunity to practice my .... Francais artisian ou Francais de pays?"

Marie was bid to take a seat. Unsure on how to best behave, she curtseyed and took the seat, which was positioned in front of him. It was a safe, comfortable distance, she felt. A distance that avoided any very personal engagement with the attractive and energetic, young Mr. Piers.

She spent about half an hour with him practicing his French. She did not though feel able to correct him. He was interested in the ancient Breton tongue which was not her first. What he said in response to her very polite question as to whether he had visited Corquadille in Breton, actually referred to his attendance at the port brothels. She contained her giggles quietly until he continued to say, when translated, with great pomposity and presence, "I like to see many people at the brothel."

"Is my French so bad that you cannot contain your mirth, Marie?" he enquired. At this he rose and walked the room thinking maybe this should be the first and last French practice with Marie. He was perfectly capable of making himself understood adequately after all. He did not need to be mocked as well, especially by a servant of the household. He pressed Marie for an explanation. Marie now knew she could not risk failing to explain it.

"You are using the country folks' language to say how you know the brothels and would like to meet many ladies there."

Feeling good that she had got this out she fell into further uncontrollable giggles about it. These giggles were successfully rivalled by him as he digested the impact of what he had said.

Servants had positioned themselves as close as they could comfortably manage to the doors and windows of the room the pair were in so as to grab even the most meagre snippets of scandalous behaviours. In many ways this was enough. A new servant girl exchanging laughter with a member of the Edgcumbe family. There was a distance to be held and this had exceeded it. Why, they thought, has he brought her here? The other servants could only think of one thing. But if she was to have the ear of Piers, she was to be watched and not trusted with the servants' gossip.

"She isn't meant to be here for long we hear."

"Well, we'll see about that and what the others in the family say about it as well. No word from those quarters yet?"

No one had any information about how the senior Edgcumbes felt, if they knew much about it or what they might think of this latest exchange.

"Well, she is meant to be here for her French language as well as servant duties. May be true and is nothing more than that."

"Mmmm .... we'll see about that too."

Marie left the room, nothing untoward occurring as she had feared it might. It was, it seemed, as it had been represented to her, nothing more than practice in her native tongues. She had rather taken to the young Piers. He may have unwittingly been her salvation from the clutches of the Vicar. She watched for him over the next weeks, continuing to have practice sessions, usually unplanned, at his calling and whim. She was always there, always making sure she was ready and presentable if the call came. She would practice her own tongue and converse with herself. As the weeks rolled by, she wondered when the call to return to the rectory may come.

"Looks as if a new maid has arrived at the rectory to replace you, Marie."

It was the first she had heard of it. Despite her desire to break from that life, it still represented what she knew here and a measure of security in an insecure world. What might become of her now? Where was Joe? Would her position be kept on at Cotehele? And then ..... and then there was the child. She knew now it had to be Joe's but what would become of her if she had to go from Cotehele because of this and Joe was not there for her?

She had expected to return to the rectory by now or receive unwelcome attentions from the young Piers, neither of which had happened.

"Come on Joe, where are you?" She knew he went on the crossings. She knew how dangerous these were. What if her Joe was no more? Then what? What if Joe never came now? He said he would. Where was he?

"Joe, oh Joe," she sobbed into the white of her pinafore as she sat in the quiet of a small recessed area that caught the late sun outside the courtyard wall. It enclosed the blacksmith's workshop and other working buildings.

"What have I done coming to Cornwall? What am I doing here?"

Distressed, she took off to the quay, the white of her pinafore stained with tears. She clambered through the wooded area not wishing to meet anyone. On reaching the quay she started walking downstream, just carrying on and on. The tide was not high. Here and there where neither path nor bank existed, she could continue. She just wanted to walk and think about her limited options in life. She had been over and over these in her mind, but once more she went through them. Again, again, just one more time, once more, over and over ... and over.

Should she try and find Joe, get back to the village or try to get a message to him? What if he didn't now want to know her? She could not stay for long at Cotehele. When discovered she would have to go.

Could she throw herself on the mercy of the young Mr Piers? Would Jane help her? She did not know Jane well enough to ask but she was the only one she talked much with and the conversations were mainly speculation around the same story she had been told about Landulph, Theodore and the Arundells.

Should she now try and get back to Cawsand and Hannibal to ask if she might be returned to Roscoff? Should she return to the rectory? This was the Vicar's doing. He had a new maid now. Maybe she should tell him of her state.

He would not want her there but what if he thought the child was his and his followers believed this? Might he not then help her? How could she convince him the child was his? She would need to do this now and not wait any longer for fear he would blame the household at Cotehele or even try to put the blame on Master Piers. Now that would be a fine thing. Would he dare to do that? No, he would try to blame someone else. But what if she could say something about him. Something only those who had got close to him could possibly know.

She was starting to get desperate and anything, anything was worth trying to make sure she did not fall into destitution and be unable to return to France. Even the parish would not likely provide in any meagre way for her. She wrapped her arms around one of the small trees lining the banks and cried again out loud.

"Joe, Joe, where are you?" It was as if her cry had been carried downstream intact and unbroken by the wind. Maybe her Joe would hear it if he was on the water further down.

She felt better for this and the walk, although nothing had been resolved for her. She was no further forward. Perhaps she should throw herself to the mercy of the mud and tide and let it all be ended. Peace could descend for her at last. Everlasting peace. No one would know it wasn't an accident. She would be buried in the Churchyard at Calstock.

She continued walking until she saw the Church but a short distance away.

She walked through the churchyard into the Church, passing and peering at the several monuments to various people of the parish who had been buried there.

There would be more beside with unmarked graves. That would be hers. Unmarked. And there could be two there, but no one would know apart from her, her child and her God. Not even Joe if he ever came would know. Joe should know. How could she get word to Joe about it?

She saw some Edgcumbe memorials as she approached the altar.

She could not read all but was able to pick out the names. Francis Edgcumbe died in 1665. One to his father who died the following year.

She remembered Jane telling her a story of Francis when she pointed out the portrait of Mary Glanville, his mother, that adorned one of the staircases at Cotehele.

Marie had been cleaning the massive ornate frame in which the portrait sat. While Jane had been watching over the operation, she had told her of the tragedy the portrait told.

She remembered the story as it sounded such a tragic one in which Master Francis lost his life at only eighteen years of age just outside of Plymouth.

"So, you are Master Francis?" She muttered slowly under her breath for fear he might hear her and feel the question impudent.

"I suppose now you wish you hadn't started that duel to the death in Plymouth that took your life so young. A life so full of promise and privilege."

She grew more confident now that she would not be getting a reply. She could in her head hear the words of Master Francis reply to her and maybe these were words she wanted to hear.

"Don't waste life young Marie. Don't throw it away on a sense of honour. Find Joe. Find Joe ......"

When she got back to the house she entered as quietly as possible. She would have to wash her clothes and hope they would be dry for tomorrow's work.

"And what have you been doing to end up in that state." The voice was Jane's.

"You had better come with me and we'll get these cleaned now, right away. Come on you can't be seen like this. Now tell me, what have you been doing to end up in this condition?"

"I was just walking by the river and it was where the tracks stopped."

"Silly girl."

"I walked up to the Church as well to pray for my family who are all gone now."

"Alone?"

"Yes, alone and I saw no-one at the Church nor Church yard. I did though see the mark of the grave of Francis Edgcumbe the son of the lady in the picture you told me about."

"Oh yes." Jane stood taller at this point about to air her knowledge to her willing audience.

"How Lady Mary could contain her distress as the mother of Francis, I wonder. Maybe she did not. Losing a son so unnecessarily. You can see the anguish in her eyes, dear, if you look carefully. She would have been perhaps in the middle of her life when the portrait was painted?"

"Do you know much about how he died?"

"Oh yes, Marie. My family have been here a long time and they would have known the young Master Francis. They would have passed down the knowledge and what we know here of course."

"And ………."

"Well, it was all to do with that Master Skelton. Well, well …… nothing. This will have to wait for another time. It is a long and tragic story."

"Where are the Skeltons now?"

"They were at Landulph too and had an estate there, but they moved, and it was mostly eventually lost. There are some near where you were at Maker. Turnchapel is the main home of the Skeltons they say. They build boats there for the Navy and they are pilots. Our boatmen know who they are and the tales travel to this day. Some of the tales they tell may not have all the truth dear. Anything you want to know about Francis Edgcumbe and the Skeltons just come and ask me. When there is more time. We would know because we were also from Landulph and connected with Theodore, you might remember."

With that Jane did her usual dramatic departure when she was so fortunate as to have an audience. Her voice had lifted, her head took her eyes and nose upwards. She turned to leave, satisfied that she had been provided with another opportunity to air her knowledge.

She must leave and get to Joe. That is, assuming Joe was alive and well. He said he would come for her, but he may not know where she was as yet.

That means back to Cawsand. But where would she go there and how was she going to get there.

She would follow the river downstream to Cremyll. Provided she followed the river she would be alright. She would need to plan her move. Was there a way she could travel with the boatman? They would not hide her or take her without the knowledge of the house.

There was no time like now. She would have to leave on Sunday after the Church service. It was full of the townsfolk and workers on the estate, who filled the pews.

She felt a familiar breath of warm air pass her neck as she took her place in the pews. The smell was familiar to her and there was something, just something ..... The man behind her was bearded and had a hat running low. As he took it off, he winked at her and pursed his lips beckoning her to remain silent, to take no further notice. She knew what he meant. It was Joe. It was Joe! She could hardly contain her excitement. As they chanted, sang and gave responses, she heard his voice in her ear He sang to her to meet him later at dusk at the Churchyard. The words sounded like the responses and were all but lost in the throng of voices. They were softer, but she picked up on them. She knew she must not alert anyone. She had been brought there in the employ of the Edgcumbes, the most prominent nobility of the area. It had been at their request. She knew now what was afoot. Joe was there but few would be able to recognise him. He had grown a beard and was in smart clothing. His hair had changed. But this was Joe. She had known it. She could smell Joe's smell. The safe, comforting smell of Joe. That warmth that came from them that perhaps only they could feel. She nodded after he gave instructions, just once so not to be noticed and then just listened to her heart pounding. This was it then. What had he in mind?

Dusk came. Marie had stolen away to the churchyard. Looking around in the dim of the beckoning nightfall she saw a trail of vapour. Her eye followed the trail. It led her to her a horse. It was a fine-looking beast. By its side was Joe. With no words said, he mounted her onto the horse, leapt up, took the reins, turned the horse which gently reared and they were away.

She held tight as they travelled swiftly. She had no things, nothing, but then she didn't have much but had left behind the gift from Joe. It was tucked into a secret place on the estate where she could find it and look at it when she felt she needed to. There was little at Cotehele to remind anyone that she had been there. They went through small hamlets and towns, skirting them wherever he thought prudent.

Joe knew his way. He had worked the rivers and the land in the free trade for miles around. He knew the routes to travel unnoticed by most.

They stopped a short while and dismounted. They were at the edge of a wood with a stream, outside of Callington. He pressed her to a tree on the bank.

It took her by surprise. Before she could take a breath to fuel her lungs with air, he had pressed his lips against hers. As he took her arms and held them up against the tree, she was spread with all limbs outstretched.

She gulped in as much air as she could as he released his lips from hers. She took Joe again and again. When it was over, she wondered if she should tell him now or wait. She would wait until the time was right. All that mattered was here and now.

"We're off tonight, there's a Roscoff run. I don't think we should stay. We don't know how Master Piers will react, nor the Vicar, although he has a new fancy to play with now."

"But Joe, I came for a new life here and this is your home."

"Yes, but I am known in Roscoff as well. Although still dangerous, we can work from there on the trade. I can always to and fro and won't be linked to you leaving. It will soon be forgotten. We can return then." "Where did this horse come from?"

"The farm. He's a beauty, isn't he?"

"When did you learn to ride like this?"

"And you, you, Marie, seem more comfortable on horseback than I would have thought. You soon learn lots of things in the free trade," he chortled, summonsing her back onto the horse.

He took her leg to help her up and as he did so his hand again slipped towards her thigh and he firmly gripped her. There was no time to waste but Joe, excited by what he felt, its warmth, lifted her down again and they fell to the ground.

"Joe there is time for this when we get to Roscoff. There is a lifetime for this."

Her protests were not matched by her actions as her body welcomed him again and again.

As they resumed their journey, their bodies relaxed, rising and falling with a natural grace and harmony with the movement of the ride, her feelings of freedom showed themselves as she shook her hair to the wind.

She hadn't yet told him that all manner of horseriding in France, including bareback riding, was a thing she had learnt in her childhood. They arrived whilst still dark.

The horse was tied at the fields near Rame. He helped her down the paths that were cut into the rock but obscured. At night they could little be seen but he knew his way and helped her down onto the sandy cove below. The tide was just right. A small boat was waiting. He pushed the boat into the water, lifted her above the encroaching tide into the boat, pushed it out into the sea, took the oars. As they met the westerly rollers coming and were buffeted against the strength of the incoming tide, they saw the hulk of a Smuggler in amongst the mists and dark. They were waiting for them, but not for much longer. The boat came along side, was tied and they were helped aboard. Next thing they knew sails were catching the wind and they were gone

Chapter 25

The Surveyor Wants His Pound of Flesh

"So, what has the purveyor of fine coinage and notes from the Cawsand Mint got to tell me then?" The purveyor, Glinn, had been told that he must get himself onto the Barbican in Plymouth. His instructions were to enter the bakehouse situated in the street that backed onto the Customs House. There he would be taken through into the rear of the building as if doing normal business.

This bakehouse supplied provisions to ships moored only yards from the bakehouse. Their biscuits and other produce would also be taken out to large ships moored in Plymouth Sound. It was not unusual for Glinn's merchandise to be sold to these ships as well, servicing them from

Cawsand Bay. What was he doing in a room in the back of a bakehouse? At least he wouldn't risk being seen going into a Customs House. That might be the purpose, but what was a bakehouse owner doing to know the Customs?

Glinn felt out of his depth in this situation. Maybe he would have been better on the end of a rope than in the pocket of this Surveyor of Customs.

"Have you got any dates for when large amounts of your ill-gotten produce have to be delivered and to whom? Anything else known yet? About anything, anything at all?"

There was a silence and Glinn started to stutter. He was now sitting on one of only two chairs in the otherwise barren room.

"Well Mr Glinn. Well?" With this the Surveyor took his favourite position when interrogating people.

He went behind the chair upon which he politely invited his suspects to sit. He placed his hands on the sides and leaning over spoke into his victim's ear. Softly to begin with, then a roar which would make the interviewee jump or tense every muscle wondering what would happen next.

Today was no exception to this practice. Although Glinn had received a measure of it previously, the Surveyor's techniques still put a fear into him. Maybe he would have more in store for him this time?

"I have a large quantity to be delivered at a time I know not when yet Sir."

"When will you know and who pray is your customer?"

"Hannibal Marks, Sir."

"Oh yes the Fisherman .... Fisherman with the lifestyle of a merchant that is. Yes, a merchant .... A fine trader but in the clothes of a fisherman.

I have reports of him mending his nets ... landing fish .... Yes, and then fishing from the best class fishing boat known in the area. Oh and of course .... Oh yes, I forgot his taverns, Inns and the rest. Yes, a poor tavern in the town. Doesn't live in them now ... oh no.... not good enough for the wealthy fishermen now is it? Has built himself a fine house, another that is, and for three lives I hear," he said with a self- satisfied rasp in his voice.

"Seems to know a lot of people, people of some influence, rumour has it. Now I wonder who they might be ......? We need to know when this delivery takes place. As much as you can find out about any sailings and the repositories for their catch .... and who else might be working on these boats ... perhaps hauling in the nets and pots perhaps or ...... pots that is with a lining of silver .... Or the gold of best liquor. It'll soon be worth more by weight than the gold that pays for it."

His sneering laugh pervaded the atmosphere of the room. With that he went to the door quietly, sharply opening it. He put his head outside, turning it from side to side looking for prying folk. He didn't want any interference in this operation.

"Don't want anything to scupper things, do we, Mr. Glinn?"

The Surveyor returned to his station at the rear of the chair, to rest on the backs of its arms which protruded out a short way.

Sliding his hands to the two rear legs of the chair he pulled upwards and backwards with a sharp jerk. Glinn was successfully tipped out of his seat.

As he steadied himself, knees on the ground, head forward, the Surveyor gave him a sharp kick to the behind with the point of his boot.

Glinn fell forward, now face on the floor. He was sprawled out, unsure whether he would be wiser to remain like this to await more of a beating, or whether he should get up. Either way he might incur more of the Surveyor's wrath. It was difficult to predict his next move. Whatever decision Glinn made would most likely displease him.

The decision was fortunately taken away from Glinn when the Surveyor bellowed to him to get up and get out, returning when he had more information.

Glinn left by the back door that would lead him into the New Street that ran to the rear of the bakehouse. He had to go through a narrow opening.

The narrow ope ran adjacent to the side of a large dwelling with trading premises below before it emerged onto the street itself. The sound of the street had been muffled by the buildings. As he emerged, it was to the sight of a throng of traders, delivery carts and the noise of people shouting to announce their wares and their prices. Folk were hanging out of the windows, pouring out their night pots as they contributed to the noise and variety of smells running the length of the street.

The conflicting smells made for a curious, resulting odour, that was different from those back at home. Back in the village, if the inhabitants were fortunate, the rush of wind through the street whichever way you faced, cleansed much of the air, giving way to the sweeter smell of his baking.

Here in the dank narrow street there was little air to wash any of the putrid smells away. They simply had to co-exist together, competing for the attention and favour of those in the street.

Glad to get away, he started back. It was a risky business being here at all. He had already worked out what he would say if spotted and challenged in any way over his appearance on the Barbican. He needed to sample the competitors' products for ships supplies. He knew the competition in the villages but here it was a different matter and they had some customers in common.

The coin and notes may be able to produce the big money, but what if that stopped and baking was all there was. A village bakehouse made a living, but the supply of ships with the products they wanted, biscuits that would keep longer than others, bread while in port, these were all products he needed to be able to supply, and supply competitively. He needed to know his competitors ... and they weren't all in Cawsand. He remained safe for now, safe from both sides. His time could run out. He would have to deliver information. What was he to do? He had a change of heart occur a little while back and now it was crunch time. All skins would have to be saved.

How? If he told Hannibal or any of the others what had happened to him, he would surely meet a fate that could be worse than that of the gallows.

He had been over and over this same ground again and again. There was nothing new to think about, yet still he went over and over it, returning to the same options.

On his return, he worked through his plan.

"If I meet with Hannibal and tell him that I have just been done over by the Surveyor of Customs, told to inform on happenings, he will believe it and not think it has happened before. That will never be believed if I delay and don't tell him now. I must tell him today, but he must agree to working out a way in which the Surveyor believes he has valuable information. Information that can make a seizure, a large seizure at that. But, a seizure of goods and not people. A seizure planned and achieved in such a way, that all the traders get away and no harm is done anywhere. This could work. But when luck runs out or word gets around, he will need to get me away, forge a new life and bakehouse somewhere new.

That Hannibal was a rough trader when the chips were down. He just had a veneer of sophistication that he had learnt, on which he could call and rely upon when the situation so needed it. He had always seemed nothing but a fair man. He had the respect of the area. Hannibal Marks could arrange all of this. It would look like he was saving him and his men from the gallows. There was no time for this better than now. Whereas he had a grudge that needed fulfilling for the deceased Humphrey Glinn, he could not turn in his townsfolk. They did not kill him."

He started to rehearse his story. That nightfall he went to the residence of Hannibal and asked if they could speak ...... alone. They went into the back area and with a straight eye towards Hannibal he declared his position.

"I have had one of those Surveyors onto me Hannibal. He has threatened me with the gallows if I don't provide information on the happenings as I hear them."

"And what have you said?"

"I have said I will. He knows about the Mint. He says he and his men will leave it alone if I do this for them."

"What does he know at the moment?"

"Nothing."

With this Hannibal went towards Glinn, staring at him inches from his face, his facial muscles tensing as he spoke. His eye muscles narrowing the visible part of his eyes.

"Are you certain of this?"

"Yes, by God."

"We will turn this to our advantage. We will bring in this Surveyor, Bowden and his men like we would bring in a shoal of fish."

"One thing Hannibal. I want no bloodshed like happened before. ... and that means the King's men too. No bloodshed. No more. No more."

"No bloodshed. Wait here." With that Hannibal left the room to pace the house and think. He would make this decision without the others for now.

There wasn't a lot of time. He was off soon on a run shortly. The weather had encouraged much mist. This brought conditions, both good and bad, for smuggling runs. He would have time to think this through better before the revelations about Glinn had to be brought to the attention of the others and consider which of them needed to know.

Pacing up and down, Hannibal pondered quickly on the position.

If we get rid of Glinn we do not know where and when a Trojan Horse like this might re-appear. Whereas if we know where it is .... as now ... we have the advantage. We can feed it. We can nourish and train it.

At least now this was the devil that they knew. Glinn, after all, had come to them. This was a different approach by the King's men. There had always been the odd informant, especially where reward was large enough to tempt the weaker. These were though but isolated, rare incidents. This had taken more planning. This was a longer-term attempt at securing information and bringing down the entire network, not just claiming the odd success.

Returning to the room and the wary Glinn, Hannibal issued Glinn his instructions.

"You will go again and see this Surveyor. You will tell him that you must up your supply from the mint. You must store it ready for a collection on Thursday morning, at 4.00 a.m. dead. Tell him that we expect it to be ready, hidden in mawns and nets. We will come from the top path down and will leave by the side and down through to Girt where a small boat will be waiting. Say that you heard that a Smuggler will be returning three nights following and hoarding its haul of goods on the west side of the Mewstone island before all on board set off to the Churches next morning."

The inhabitants of Mewstone had now left to take up residence on Looe island. They had serviced the trade well from the Mewstone for a good while but had abandoned their home there for the larger, more productive, Looe Island.

They continued to provide their services to the traders from there. About thirteen miles away from their previous Mewstone island home, leaving forever the house they and their father had built, alongside animal buildings, wells and the rest, for a later incumbent to use.

The Surveyor looked pleased at Glinn. He enquired about the amount of money that was needed to supply and reckoned if this represented payment for one shipment at the least this was going to be a large haul. Glinn was not there long. He used the Barbican bakehouse to get a message through. The back room was again used for the two men to meet.

"Very good, very good. Go now, do your business here as you might be expected to and get back to your work."

The Surveyor had started to get what he had wanted. He had his man and was not now deploying his usual tactics to put the fear of death into Glinn. No, he could back-paddle now for a while and see what continued to come.

Glinn scuttled off. The Surveyor met with his chief men who would be stationed on the Mewstone. No boat was to be close that smelt in any way of the Customs services. Nothing must happen that might stop the Smuggler from coming in to this place as expected.

Instructions were given to ensure that neither boats nor men interfered that night with any lights they may spot. There would be a clean sweep allowed for the Smuggler that Thursday and Friday night onwards.

They would prepare to pounce. They would catch the smugglers in the act. Glinn had no information on which Smuggler it might be, nor her Captain and crew. Bowden and his men were not party to what Glinn had told the Surveyor, but they were given instructions to keep in the area of Penlee Point and Cawsand beach for the coming few nights and to watch the Mewstone. They were to await instructions from Bray's boat.

If they saw any activity, they were still not to leave that area until instructed to do so.

Hannibal and his men were preparing in advance and well before the Thursday night. The men had been told as much as they needed to know.

"Sew a big crop just off the island. Use those damaged and spoilt ankers we have left. Fill them with some spirit and water. Dilute the tea and get some other merchandise together that has spoilt. Get a good-sized load of these spoiled stocks on the Smuggler with her name covered over. Make sure it's loaded on her loose, not so loose to lose it, but at the ready to release overboard near the Mewstone when you get the signal. Keep your sails at the ready too, ready to sail off towards Roscoff. Bit of luck, tide and wind we can get the tubs to float onto the island."

The instructions had gone out to Hannibal's men who took the smaller fishing boats with their cargo stacked high. They were to conceal it both under water and in some of the redundant hideaways around the island. The next day, crop already sewn, would be the day they returned with the Smuggler.

"I reckon they will keep themselves well off the island, concealed but ready to get there quickly, giving chase if needs be. They'll also be on the island. Bowden and his men will probably stay there so as not to alarm us or to stop the Smuggler coming in. Probably use Fyn's old house for shelter. We've left them a couple of ankers stowed in the corner in there to keep them happy that night. They'll think they've found something already. I will be fast in my bed and so will the others that the Surveyor suspects." This would be a major test of Glinn and where his true allegiances lie.

"The Wembury Boys got news to watch and to send a light to let us know when Bray and his boat are seen anywhere their side. They will then send further lights to say where and when they are seen to leave. We can then let our boat know they are then to get away, with haste."

The crop of contraband successfully sewn a few days previous, the night came for the Smuggler to come in, when she got the signal.

"There's the light. They're there. Look there's another and another, three quick after."

"We've not long to come in close to the Mewstone, slip a row boat, ankers, chests and away."

"Ready boys, hold your tongues, brace yourselves and prepare to pull round, then go with haste."

"That bloody Bray and his men are good .... and their boat," whispered Elisha Edwards to the others.

"But we're better. Come on we know these waters and tides. Do as we have been bade and we'll be in the Roscoff Church for morning service!"

With that they approached the island from the south west and got as close as they dared. The light was just enough to send signals to release the ropes. The ropes were at the ready, goods and row boats slipped. As they saw them rolling to the island in the light westerly wind, so more went and then more until they were spent. The sharp-eyed Elisha could see the shadows of men clambering down the Island. They had seen the delivery. With that the smuggler turned, caught wind and raced southwards. They could see the Bray boat starting to move."

"I can see their sails flapping."

"Come on there's no time."

The seamen, some of the best, took the wind and set their course to take the fast Smuggler south to Roscoff. They had the advantage of surprise and time. They knew they must keep out of sight. Neither them, nor the boat, must be recognised. Bray would not know who they were nor what boat they were on.

The chase had started. Bray had the disadvantage of time and position. He had not expected this. With a frown, Bray brought lines to his entire forehead. Tightening his throat, he said with a resolute tone.

"They must have seen us or had signal. We were seen on the island. Those boys have keener eyes than most. They might have seen those bungling fools of ours. There's no missing their shapes. They would know. What would folk be doing there at night in any number. Hardly the missionaries saving souls? Give chase and stretch her all you can. Keep the sails full and tight."

Despite Bray's good seamanship, boat and men he was outraced. They lost sight of the Smuggler. With no sighting as they reached the Eddystone Reef they turned westwards.

"No knowing where they've headed for. We'll carry on west until first light. If there is nothing, we'll return." The smuggler boys hit mid channel and started to relax.

Next stop Roscoff where they would pick up the next load. The money, freshly minted, was following. Bray, Bowden and this Surveyor would not now be expecting anything further for a few days.

"These are their boats and goods. There's a lot of it. What a haul we've got"

"Best in a while."

"Wonder what made them throw overboard and take flight."

"They must have seen us. Look at these. There're hundreds coming in. This was a big haul. They've lost on this tonight. Collect them up and bring them ashore. We'll get around and look further at first light."

First light came, and more was seen floating and smashing against the almost continuous line of rocks around the Island. The Surveyor was aboard the Hind with Bray and on returning to the Mewstone, was taken ashore. This was a rare voyage as he was usually land based.

"What have you got? Is this it? Lots of kegs for us but no smugglers?" "Men have been sent around the Island to bring back any more. They will check around to see if any strings are there too."

"They left in haste. They must have seen you. Where were you when you heard the tubs splashing?"

"We were ready for them. The men were going down to the shore waiting for them to come in."

"Have your brains been dashed before getting employ with the service or has the service addled them? These men can see and smell revenue folk from a mile away. Your instructions were to wait your moment.

"We had been lying in wait. The moment felt right to make a move when we saw the Smuggler, heard her anchor and saw the small boats hit the water. She was preparing to unload."

"Looks as if the boats had no men or they had got back to the Smuggler when they saw you. Unless the blaggards got into the water and swam to shore or onto another part of the island?"

"We didn't catch them, but we have got their haul."

"And a big haul it is. Take it on board and get it back. Search this island. Some of them may be here. There's bound to be places on the Island they know that can hide a man. They would have been in the small boats. My bet is on them being on the island or across at one of the beaches near Wembury.

If they've got to the mainland, I doubt we'll get them tonight. Even here I doubt we'll find them. They're like crabs this lot, they can walk sideways into any nook and cranny.

Needs a bloody crab hook to get them out. A crab hook. Yes, a man hook maybe?"

With that the Surveyor looking satisfied with their success so far, roared at his own joke and then, despite the dark, took out his eyepiece to scan the horizon for smugglers.

"Well Bray, a good haul. Didn't get our men by the looks of it, but their gains are now our gains. This has set them back a while. I would wager on the coin and note having been passed over too for the goods, both genuine and from the forge. Either way it will have cost them. Next time we'll get our men. Now where is that Hannibal Marks and some of his main men. Out on that Smuggler I suppose."

* * *

As the bells pealed at Maker Church the following morning, Hannibal and his wife took a pew, preparing themselves for the ordeal of the Vicar's sermon. As he listened, his mind drifted. What had taken place out there? Word would come soon he hoped. If it were bad news they would have seen or heard something by now. Their boat had not been seen. Bray's had been seen alone alongside some activity around the island.

"And let us pray for those who risk their lives daily for our food and sustenance. Pray they be safe when facing the ravages of the sea and the uncertainties it brings. God save their souls. God save the souls of those who have been lost at sea. Where we know not where they are, let them be trusted to your care O Lord."

The Vicar again delivered his prayer and sermon from a lower plinth than the pulpit provided. Built for an earlier, more slender generation, it provided but slim width and steps and he did not want to risk its overturn.

There was a precedent for such instability when faced with the weight of the Vicar. To the delight of the worshipers but to his great dismay, it had since been fixed to the side now with the appearance of a sturdier version.

"May they be safe and returned to us," muttered Hannibal thinking of his crew and men who had risked being caught that night with all that could bring for them and their families.

Their fate was indeed uncertain at this moment, known only to them. "Good sermon and prayer for our fisher-folk Vicar."

"We always think of our good fishermen and the risks they take in the turmoil of the seas, Mr Marks. Please God to see you at Church. You and Mrs. Marks are well I take it. You're not on your boat quite so much now Mr Marks. Well-deserved rest at your age. Get the young ones to do something I say. Learn the ropes. Yes, learn the ropes."

"Oh yes, thank you Vicar. And how are things for you and your household?"

"All well. All well, Mr Marks. We have a new member of the house who serves for us and is just acquainting herself with her duties."

With that the Vicar turned to the next in the small line of parishioners who wanted to bid the Vicar and his family well on God's day.

"A new face here at Maker?

Welcome to our parish. And who prey comes to meet with the Vicar?"

"I am only here today Vicar. I am here on the King's business and seeing our Mr Bowden."

"Ah, he does not seem to be here today maybe his employ detains him. That is allowed, even on God's day. An exception for the agents of the King .... And the King is next to God.

And from whence do you usually come?"

"I am from Plymouth. From here you can almost see my parish Church, the Church of St Andrew's in Plymouth, up from the Quay."

"Ah yes, I know St Andrew's. A fine Church and one with many fine monuments to the good folk of Plymouth who have served it well."

"Was that Mr Marks and his wife I saw in the Church as well today? A break from his fishing on the Lord's day."

"Why, yes, he was just here and with Mrs. Marks."

"Ah I know of him only by his good reputation."

"God speed and be with you."

"Thank you, Vicar, and for your good sermon and prayers today."

With that the line of Vicar's well-wishers continued to slowly move along.

The Earl and his daughter, the Lady Edgcumbe had been in their family pews, that section of the Church positioned close to the altar. This area also gave a home to their private altar and prayer area. They had left first and been greeted by the Vicar. Their household followed so they too could return quickly and prepare for the remainder of the day.

The walk back took Hannibal to the view over the open sea, one of his favourite areas to contemplate, to ponder and muse on the business. It came with almost a half circumference view, including the Mewstone Island. He looked anxiously over to it. All was calm. No boats, no activity could he spot but it was a few miles off and who knows. He was to keep away and would have to wait for full news.

"Fine day. Fine day."

The Surveyor was on horseback and riding back to Bowden's.

"Yes Sir. It is. One of the best we hope."

"We hope indeed." With that, the Surveyor moved slowly off, down the steep slope to the Bowden residence where he hoped Bowden's wife or one of their children would be there to receive him. The heavy thud of the well-shod Surveyor's horse slowly made its way with his master held high displaying a stern disposition and authority that sent its presence as shockwaves entering every dwelling he passed.

His was not a known figure here but his presence, stature and piercing eyes that entered every doorway, every ope, every nook, these habits gave him away.

It was rare for the upper echelons of the Customs service hierarchy to leave the sanctity of their sinecures, or dirty their hands, for that matter. This Surveyor was different though. He had a personal authority to stamp out the free trade in his area and this part of his area was the most renowned. He had his spies now. They were on the ground. They were above the ground.

The Lottery incident had been before his time here. He knew of it only by reputation, but it provided the backdrop to his role and mission. The entire chain of command down to those involved in the day execution of activities was in this area.

It had them all. All in one rancid, stinking heap as he saw it. They all had roles to play. Here had been the wall of silence. But he, he, Geoffrey Benjamin Burke, he, yes, he, Surveyor of his Majesty's Customs' service, had broken this wall. The breach in the dyke was down to him and with his continued barrage of assault he, yes, he, would bring the rest of that wall tumbling down to reveal all that lay behind. Then it would be to the jails, the colonies or the gallows for them. Their boats finally smashed, with no use other than to keep them warm or build their houses. The Crown's coffers would fill.

He had the authority and now more means to achieve his objective and with good men besides. "Good day to you, Mrs. Bowden. Your husband has not yet returned but he will be here soon I expect with the cutter, Busy?"

With that, Geoffrey Burke scraped his boots, tethered his horse and entered the residence. This was the Customs outpost of Ambrose Bowden, his wife and children. The large house had been busy over the years with their thirteen children, although most had left now.

The two sat and Elizabeth called to her maid for some tea for the Surveyor.

"And a very good day to you Mr Burke. Yes, I am hoping to see him soon. He has been more in Plymouth than here since taking command of Busy. He speaks more of being pensioned off nowadays. Well, he is sixty-eight years now and has in his time received some rough treatment in the Customs employ."

"I know. I have heard of it. We would miss his service."

"He fears he will soon no longer be able to meet and satisfy the requirements of the position. Maybe he now deserves some time back at home and not to be exposed to these dangers. Maybe go back to fishing as was his business before he started to work for the Preventative service."

"Hello, Elizabeth."

"Ambrose. Come in and look who has honoured us with a visit."

"Mr Burke, Sir. I have just been brought ashore. Busy is at anchor here with the crew."

"A busy night indeed," laughed the Surveyor who again appeared rather pleased with the relevance of his own pun.

"Went well. Went well. Very well, in fact. Although, we didn't get the blighters, but we have taken their spoils of their trade, much of it, much of it. Our stores are crammed full."

"No but we might work out who it couldn't be from those that remained here."

"Mrs. Bowden and I have just been talking about your ending your service, Ambrose."

"Time is coming. I can feel it in my bones. They ache more and more. It's some of those old injuries, I do suppose." Ambrose drifted monetarily as he inwardly reflected and shuddered at the thought of some of the confrontations over the years.

The Lottery came to mind as the worst. Glinn's death and the subsequent trial had taken its toll on him. it had been a close shave. It could have been him with a head shot to atoms and not Glinn.

There had been other times when he himself had suffered serious injury, with lasting effects. He could see the scenes now. He could hear the voices. Clear as day they were, despite the passage of the years.

"Press the bugger. Squeeze the juice out of him." Spluttering, gasping for air and life, Ambrose, dutiful to the last, reached again for his Customs' Commission. This document gave him the authority to enter premises of any description and purpose for the work of protecting the revenue. Ambrose knew his Commission off by heart. As he could feel the air being squeezed from his lungs, he gasped out the start of it,

"By the presents hereby given to me by the power ......" He stopped as there was no breath left to get the words out. He had entered the home of the elderly, but irascible, Mrs. Spriddle. She resided in the street by the meadow and nearby the track to Rame. He had had reason to believe that goods bearing no duty were concealed there.

"Get out of here! Get out of my home! Bugger those old words of yours. They don't wash here!"

Having done what was required of him by law to enter the premises for the purpose of search and being satisfied that was good enough to guarantee his safety, he proceeded down the stairs into the basement area of the house.

He was equipped with some basic leverage tools to take up the floor boarding. His informant had said that there were joists that could be removed. If he crawled underneath, he would come out into a chamber that lay in behind. which, through a very low tunnel, concealed an area carved from the rock.

"You won't find anything down there. Let the devil be on you. Coming in here to an old lady's house, frightening her witless, what next. Damn you! With that Mrs. Spriddle threw an old stoneware bottle at him that was resting, minding its own business, in her larder. Bowden managed to put his arm up as a shield, but it caught the top of it.

As it fell to the ground it clattered on the boards and rolled across the room.

"What was that?" muttered the grumpy Spriddle son. He was down below with his accomplices.

They were watering down the high proof spirits into smaller containers ready for taking up when the all clear was given later.

"There's footsteps too. Best go and see who it is."

"That's the boards coming up. We're not expecting any tub carriers until tonight."

"Mother. Mother. What's going on up there?"

With that they opened the inner and then outer door of the chamber.

There was Bowden in the dim, holding a light. In a loud, commanding voice he told the men to give way as he was coming through in the name of the King and with his commission that entitled him to search. "I said bugger your commission and the King's shillings. Didn't you hear me?"

With that as Bowden forced open the inner door with his foot the men held him out. Suddenly Bowden could feel the outer door pressing on him. The doors were not much apart but gave that extra bit of security to the traders as they went about their work. He could hear old Mrs. Spriddle's voice, as gnarled as she was in her hands, saying,

"Go on, press the bugger, press him like a cider press squeezes out the last bit of juice from the apple .... rats and all stuck in the straws. This is the rat. Squeeze out the last pip. Flatten the bugger, Your Ma will get rid of him after."

She was banging her stick on the boards above. All Bowden could hear was this and her rasping tongue, set at a volume slightly above the steady thump of her stick, both of which were relentless.

He had wondered why there had been a pause in the beat of her stick. She had let in someone else who had rushed down the stairs and taken the outer door and pressed it hard on him from the other side.

He hadn't quite seen any of them in the dark, candle lit shadows. So, this is where he was going to meet his end. Here in this hell hole. He could see the future in the instant. Taken out before the alarm was raised, weighted down at the reef. So, this was it. At the hands of these lawbreakers. These schemers. These ..... he started to fail..... The pain was excruciating. He felt a crack in his chest area, then more in his arms by the joints. The little air he managed to get in was foul.

Was this to be the last thing he smelt on this earth.

The smell of the illicit trade he had earned his living trying to stamp out?

The smell of the damp, drink infested, soil.

The sweet smell of the flavouring used to colour the drink, the undiluted alcohol.

These were all mixed with the unwashed smells of his captors and the dank, damp air.

This is not the glory he had envisaged would accompany his leaving the service.

Glinn may have met a cruel end in the Lottery incident but he went with some glory that would not be forgotten as the tunnels of time were travelled by future generations. But this. This smacked of nothing but humiliation. Humiliation at the hands of these creatures with that woman, Spriddle chanting her taunts.

That other son of hers, Joe, he hadn't been seen for a while. Was he there? Was he anything to do with this? This wasn't Joe's style. The others though pushed on by that mother of theirs.

Now she bore a grudge against Ambrose Bowden. She could really do it. Cutting him up and feeding him to the crabs and fish or sinking him head first at the Eddystone reef would give her great pleasure. It would be her revenge, yes revenge ..... He could feel himself leaving consciousness to the sound of that woman's taunts, her stick banging incessantly and the stench of their trade.

Next thing he knew he had woken up to agonies of pain, massaged a little by the sound of the sea lapping the hull of a boat. This was what it was like to be dead? There was still pain though and where was his God and Saviour? Where were those who had gone before? There were none here for him today. None to comfort him in his hour of need. Was his work not wanted by the Lord?

He questioned for the first time that which he laboured on and gave his life to day after day. Where was he now? Where was his reward for doing the work of the King?

He rose up slightly, excruciating pain in his chest, unable to move his arms much at all. He started to take in his surroundings. He was in a small punt. It was pitch black. There was Drake's Island and the mouth of the Tamar. He was drifting towards the beach of the Devon side.

"How have I got here?"

There was no one, no boat to shout to for help or any soul to whom he could command help. He could see that soon he would be landed on the Jenny Cliff beach. Ambrose tried to position himself over the gunwales of the boat but the agony coming from his chest wall prevented him. He could not outstretch his arms. They had no strength in them. He could not assist the boat. He relied on the drift. As good fortune would have it, the seas were kind, the big rollers lifted and dropped the small boat with relative gentleness.

He would not now be able to save himself he thought, should he be thrown into the water. He settled into the drift, waiting to see where the punt would take him.

Slumber came once more and that eased the physical pain. He would surely be missed by now?

Ambrose was awoken by the jolt of the punt coming up onto the beach.

As his eyes opened, he saw the sand and shingle of the beach below the cliff ahead. With some difficulty he got himself out and onto the beach.

The swelling all around his chest and arms disguised some of the worst of the pain. He made his way up the cliff paths. He would have to arouse one of the farmers here or head into Plymouth town and the Barbican where at first light he would report these happenings at Customs House.

But there had been no one else there. Evidence would be needed. Whether they had it or not he would have the Spriddles turned over. Every stone of that house would be turned over. And again, the next day. Next hour if needs be. Oh yes, he would see to it that they didn't rest. Turn them over. They would have his very special treatment. The memory of the jolt of the boat's bow hitting the shoreline at the Cliff brought him back to his conversation with the Surveyor.

They drank to the success of the night but also to the work yet to be done. The Surveyor left, knowing that it was not to be long now before Ambrose would be leaving the service. He reflected to himself as he went,

"Ambrose has been a good servant, but the time is drawing nigh. We must let him go soon."

It would be difficult to replace a man of that dedication who knows the area so well. But the boatmen did, and a replacement for Ambrose would get used to it, with their help, soon enough ... or maybe one of the boatmen could step up .... He would ask Ambrose. Another day. For now, he would savour in the success of their catch. But what of the fish that got away? What of that Hannibal Marks and his gang of unworthies? Yes, what about them? What was he doing there? At Church ! At the Church!

Chapter 26

Hannibal 2nd Takes to Cherbourg

Squinting hard on board the Marks' Smuggler, the Captain and crew were straining to see through the heavy sea mists that had completely enveloped them. "I can see fire Hannibal. Look, over there!"

"That's up on Whitsand cliffs alright, although in this mist ……. hard to be sure exactly where."

"We'd better go safe, there's a good deal to unload tonight." The mist which had given them cover as they had approached the beaches with the cliffs of Whitsand Bay rising behind them had also given cover to the preventative officers. That is if they were there at all that night. First light would arrive soon.

The mist had started to transform itself from an all-pervading blanket covering the sea, which was accompanied by an eerie silence, into a shape more akin to a rolled carpet, that was gradually unravelling as it hit the bottom of the cliffs. As it unfurled, reaching the top of the cliffs in a vertical ascent, it spilled out onto the fields above where it continued to unfold, laying low and dense as it went. Was the fire a warning signal to them? Why else would a fire have been lit in the open on the cliffs at Whitsand Bay at this time of night in these conditions?

The young Hannibal 3rd, nineteen years of age now, was on the Smuggler that night with his father and crew.

He answered to those addressing him as Hannibal, Hannibal 3rd or Boy Hannibal as had other Hannibal Marks offspring before him.

His mother had wished for him to take to the Navy rather than take to work with his father in the smuggling business. He could have had a midshipman's life. They had him well educated. He was proficient in mathematics, reading and writing.

There had been no pressure on him to join the family firm. It had been the free choice of Hannibal 3rd to follow his father into the trade. Despite the increased risks and losses, it carried, there was also a sense of adventure and self-reliance that accompanied the danger. This made for an intoxicating cocktail that the youthful and headstrong Hannibal found irresistible.

Susannah Spriddle of Cawsand and Hannibal 3rd had been childhood friends and were on course to marry. Her father had warned her about the possible changes he could foresee coming to the trade that his future son in law was pursuing. Mr. Spriddle expressed his concerns clearly with no doubt as to his feelings on the matter.

"He might not go on for long in this business, Susannah. The tide is starting to turn on smuggling. The signs have been there for a while. More difficult day by day. If that goes, much of the boatbuilding work will go with it. You mark my words. It could happen in my lifetime. They want to look around do those Marks for something else to do with their money. Don't wait to lose it.

As for the business the village gets from the safe anchorage we can provide, well it gives a fine income from the Navy and her ships' crews, but it's been too easy for years and now the time of reckoning is coming fast.

Change is here. You look at that new breakwater finishing up. The ships will off to Plymouth then. Yes, they will and with them will go some of the good trade the Marks have in their drinking houses. That young man of yours, Hannibal, wants to look to the Navy for his living if you're going to be with him. He wants to join up before it's too late. Don't want him dying young with all the dangers in that smuggling now. Look how many have died. No, don't want him dying before his rightful time.

They want to do something else with that money of theirs, while there's still time. They could set up in trade in Plymouth perhaps. That's where it's all going to go. You haven't got to leave here to do that. Where is young Hannibal now?" Mr. Spriddle had asked the question almost knowing the answer.

"I don't know, Father. The boat's been gone a few days and I am expecting him to return any time now."

The crew on board Hannibal 2nd's Smuggler were looking to the shore intently.

"I say we go now Hannibal. Your boy's right. Look the fire is out! It barely burnt, just a bit of smoke now amongst that mist. What's happening there? Maybe they've been caught and it's the revenue men who have put that fire out. I say they're waiting there for us. They won't see us much yet though. Let's turn and get back out, sow the crop if needs be or keep it with us and return tonight."

"Father, I'm with this and think we should make out to sea. The alarm might have been raised and they will be looking for a boat offloading tonight."

"Let's make back out to sea. We'll think on what we should do on the way."

"We could do with knowing what happened back there. Who lit the fire and what for? We could be going out for nothing. We might wish later when we know what this fire has all been about that we'd carried on and waited to unload."

"There were no small boats in the water for us though. Maybe we were too early. They'd done the wink, so we know they're there."

"They would have seen the fire, or, started it."

"No, we are doing the right thing. Make sail."

One of the crew interrupted them.

"What in hell's name is that?"

Out of the mist they saw the bow of a boat. It was a cutter.

"It's the bloody Hind. Quiet. They may not have seen us in this mist."

The familiar voice, tone and shout came out of the murky mist, draining the blood from their faces, sending adrenalin shooting through their veins, soaking them with a state of readiness for what might now come.

"This is a King's boat. Who's there? Declare yourselves!"

"That's Davy Williams and his men. It must be the Wolf not the Hind.

"Keep quiet and keep moving."

With that the noise of the tide splashing against the hull could be heard and the cry went out again from the Revenue Cutter,

"This is a King's Boat. Declare yourselves or we will come over to board you with armed men."

The cover the mist gave continued, but it could not hide the noise of the sea against the hull or the creaking of the planks and masts against the sails as they were being prepared. They knew now they were there and close. But where were they exactly. The boat must be still and holding water close by.

There was no sound apart from the voice and its direction to gauge where they might be. How had they seen through this dense mist and they not seen them? They must have caught a glimpse of them in amongst the changing thickness of the mist as it swirled around. But they must be still. The Smuggler was slowly moving.

In this uncertainty, all options carried risks. They decided to carry on and head south. They heard no more shouts from the Preventatives.

"What in the Devil's name is that now?" Colliding with them on the port side was the bow of the Wolf.

As the boats shook and faltered, but suffering no damage of any consequence, they saw Customs men, Williams and Foot, pulling alongside them in a small boat. They must have left the main Customs Cutter for this one after their last call. A shot fired into the air. They were armed.

The senior Hannibal did not want to risk the lives of his son and crew. Their weapons were stowed below. He needed to buy some time.

"Let them on board."

The two Customs Officers tied up to the Smuggler and boarded.

Elisha, blunderbuss gun held ready, crept up from below, stealing behind Williams and Foot. Holding the weapon to Williams' back he whispered "shhh..." Both Preventative men did as they were told and fell silent, passing over their firearms.

Whispering in the ear of Williams, with a sinister tone, Hannibal demanded information.

"How many more of you?"

"Three" responded Williams nervously, under his breath.

Elisha had two blunderbuss guns he took with him when on the Smugglers. He had brought the blunderbuss pistol up from the bowels of the boat. Light and lethal at short range, with the ability to scatter its shot, this was an old weapon that he nursed. Good enough for his father when he was smuggling. Good enough for Elisha now.

Popularly nicknamed, "The Dragon," this type of gun and its nickname heralded in the name of the land-based force of mounted officers that appeared, with good reason, in the nightmares of smugglers, the "Dragoons." Dragoons also carried the Dragon blunderbuss.

Elisha's Dragon was special to him. This was his symbol of good luck as well as good fortune. He kept it polished, greased well, always at the ready. As he drew it ready, he had kissed the barrel and slowly stroked it. "This may have a job to do tonight," he whispered.

The voice of the Preventative men came again from the Wolf.

"Tell your men to lower their sails and prepare to anchor up. We will be boarding with more of us."

Hannibal looked to his crew, whispering, "There are only a few more on the Preventative boat tonight." Turning towards his captives he snarled quietly through his clenched teeth, "Tell them to ship over and board with all hands. Tell them you have control of the boat, the Captain and crew."

The senior Hannibal had pressed his mouth against the ear of one of the men to give the clear instruction. It was the ear that did not have the barrel of Elisha's blunderbuss pressed against it. One of the other crew had made sure the Preventatives were bound and tightened the ropes just a bit more.

The Preventatives shouted to their men that they held control, the boat was ready to board and search further and called for all hands to come aboard and assist.

As the preventative rowing boat emerged from the mist, the Captain of the Wolf and his boatman had been put away below, tied and gagged. The same fate awaited them. Hannibal 2nd gave a further instruction quietly to his men, "Go and check that boat. Make sure there are no others there. Take your pistols and knives."

There was no struggle. The Preventative officers and their boatmen knew that these were desperate men. They valued their lives and the chance to fight again another day. The ropes cut into their wrists as they were tied tightly behind their backs. They were then chained together below deck.

The same rope had been used to gag the latest arrivals. It was Elisha who wanted them dead. It was he that had tightened the rope into their mouths and behind their necks. The gaps in the teeth of the older boatmen had made perfect anchoring for the rope as it passed through from one side of a mouth to the other. The smell of the hemp that had been through the barkhouse to help preserve it mixed with the sea water almost choked them as it pressed hard against their tongues. It forced them to take in the taste, as well as the smell, of the ropes.

"I'd choke the lot of you here and now. I'd use the same rope to truss you up. Yes, all together you'd be tied. Wouldn't want to waste too much good rope on you lot. Then I'd tie in our sinking stones to send you down to your graves."

Elisha could barely contain his anger at the prospect of taking these men prisoner. Hannibal was the Captain and owner of the boat. His word went. If he hadn't been there this night, these men would have gone. The evidence would have gone. Maybe their boat too.

Hannibal 2nd hadn't often been wrong in his judgement, but there was always a first time. They could only make a big mistake once. One big mistake and it might end with them on the end of a rope, the Navy without pay or transportation. None of the choices were for these men. Not tonight. Not any night if they could help it.

"We could still do it Hannibal. Sink them, and their boat. Take their boat out with them and get rid of both. Hole it further out with them in it. Strangle them, put them in the boat and hole her, watch a while to make sure no one comes back up. If they were washed up it'll look like they have met their fate, natural like. No bloodshed."

Elisha could only see trouble of these men ever made it back or their boat.

“I’ll think on this as we sail.”

“Glinn would be none the wiser,” he thought. He had promised Glinn. There were also the lives of the men, his loyal men and their families, to weigh up in the decision that might seal their fate.

“We need to kill all these men.” Elisha would not let up. “No one must return now to tell the tale. They have seen us.”

“Not all of us.” The young Hannibal had not been seen by the Preventatives and neither had his friend, Daniel.

“We are going to set for Cherbourg.”

“You.” Hannibal looked to his son and Daniel. “You, both go back to the village. Take cover in the mist while you can. Take our landing boat, say nothing to anyone other than your mother. Just tell her I will get a message to her soon.”

The Smuggler would have fewer hands to sail her and complete their business.

“What are we going to do now Hannibal?” The other men on board started to voice their feelings as well as Elisha.

“These men know who we are. They have seen us. What about the Wolf?”

“Let her go, Hannibal, she will go where she wants. Maybe she'll wreck, or we could scuttle her.”

“Yes Hannibal, they will think she went down or there was an accident.

"There's no time to spare and we want little noise. Remember the land officers may be out looking and when the mist clears the Wolf may be seen. Best there's no noise. It would travel in this air."

Hannibal ordered his son to leave and quickly.

"Pull up her anchor and get back as if nothing had happened.

With that Hannibal, his crewmates and captives, set off to Cherbourg.

"Come on Hannibal, these men have got to sink to the bottom. We can shoot them when we get out of hearing and weigh them down. The fish will soon have them. Won't be much left in a few days by that time the ropes may break free and they will wash up. Kill them, strip them naked as the day they were born, tie them down to anchor them up, deep like we sink the ankers. We've got plenty of sinking stones on board at the ready."

The other men joined Elisha in pushing to kill the men.

Hannibal said nothing, contemplating the options. He had promised Glinn no more bloodshed like this and here they were with little choice if they valued their own necks.

He kept going around and around in circles, contemplating the same issues, the same choices. This was not a decision that would come easily.

They had left the Wolf behind so there was now no taking her out and scuttling her with the men on board. The only option left seemed to be that they should kill the lot of them and send them down. Then they would have to hope they didn't get washed in whilst they could still be recognised.

The seasoned smugglers were men who had killed before, and for less, but he had made a vow to Glinn, even if the men did the deed, even if Glinn never knew how they had died, even if he did believe that it had been an accident at sea.

Whatever Glinn believed, he, Hannibal Marks, would know the truth. He would know it and of his pledge to Glinn. That was enough for him. No. There must be another way.

A full day's sail would decide the matter one way or another. He was just hoping now that they didn't come across any other revenue cutters or the choice would be made for them. The game would be up and there would be no way out. It would be over the side with them and sink them right away before they could be seen. They had hauled the cutter's rowing boat up on deck for now but maybe they should get rid of it. A distinctively built boat, it might be recognised from a reasonable distance as a revenue class boat. No, not quite yet. Shame to see good wood go to waste and beside it might yet be needed.

As the mist started to give way to the light of the sun, the seas remained calm. Hannibal continued to stay his course and pacify his men. He knew things might explode soon. A decision needed to be made.

Young Hannibal and his crew mates had returned to the Wolf. They tied up on the seaward side planning to get the anchor up if they could, without boarding her.

“Perhaps we should fill her with some ankers and tubs and mark the sides with the name Foot rather than leave her to run aground. When she’s found they will wonder where the men have gone. Suspicions will run. At the moment we don’t know what father is doing with them.”

“He’ll kill them for sure.”

“We don’t know that. His word has meant everything and whatever he means by his vow, no more bloodshed on his boats, he might keep to that even if it comes at his peril.”

“But he won’t put any of us on danger because of them.”

“No, but if we do this it might be that when she’s found and boarded, they think Foot and his men were in on our trade as well.”

“Well we’d better be quick and quiet about it. There’s not much time until full light and the cover of this mist will lift.”

“We’ve got some goods nearby here. The Preventatives may still be around. The fire went out quick. If they were there, and they saw the fire, they know tonight is a landing night.”

“Yes, but they will think that the boat was probably warned off and they’ve gone back.”

"But if they knew the Wolf was out as well, waiting for us, they may be looking to help her.”

“I reckon they’ve gone. They will have seen no boats and if they could see Five Brothers, they’d see her heading out.”

"Let's load her up then with some ankers but quick and quiet, quick and quiet."

They crept up a string of ankers and towed it slowly and deftly to the Wolf using her rope fenders to slide them up on to her deck.

Hannibal's knife engraved into the side the name Foot and the name of a Guernsey merchant. Thinking quickly, he would see if he could get a document made out to Foot for payment from the merchant. This might look as if Williams and Foot had purchased from a merchant ship off the Reef. Anything could have then happened to the men. There might have been a skirmish with the traders. Maybe, maybe.

Either way, it might cause suspicion about why Foot and his men were carrying goods with their marking. Besides, what was a bill doing there on the ship?

The Customs in Plymouth nor Bowden in Cawsand would believe that the traders had tried to do this to cast off suspicion from themselves. Why waste good spirit and why risk it? No, this would be thought of as the Preventatives doing some free trade. Not unknown, although less of it nowadays. Make them doubt their own people.

They carefully set back to shore. Was there enough time? Should they wait? If the Wolf was left where she lay, he would return with the bill and then wait for news.

They would hopefully learn about the fire later on. Who lit it and what had happened? Hannibal went home.

"Where is your father?"

"I'll tell you later mother. I just need to do one more thing."

He went to the back rooms and searched for a bill he could use or paper and quill. Very little was kept there. They wanted nothing that could be easily found that would tie them to the trade.

He hurriedly took his quill, preparing a bill in his best hand as if he were the merchant. His hand was swift and accurate. The ink flowed well, and he took it. Returning he took out his own small boat equipped with nets.

"Off for the early catch Hann?" More were getting down to the beach. There were still curtains of mist though. The sun was just starting to burn its way through.

"Yes, do a bit to bait up." With that he pushed off, heading out towards the spot the Wolf was anchored. She lay out of sight of the beaches, but folk were stirring everywhere. He had to be quick. Clambering aboard on the seaward side it seemed no one was yet around. If he was seen he would explain he had seen her, wondered what she was doing there and called. On hearing nothing, smelling the spirit, he thought the men may have had a good night and he left the boat alone. Stealing onto a revenue boat alone like this sent a chill from the base of his neck to the base of his back. It was now light, and he could see clearly. So, this is what they were like. He started to let time drift as he went through the vessel.

Coming to his senses he positioned the document in the Captain's section of the vessel under a weight with some other papers. He took his leave of the boat and was away. He saw no one. No boats in the immediate area. No one was there, not in the fields not in the copses above the rocks. No one. Time for some fishing and pots to be laid. He would get back and see if he could find out what had happened on the cliffs that night and wait for word from his father. Best see mother soon to explain.

***

"I said no good would come out of this trade for you. You could have taken any trade or following you had wanted."

Hannibal's mother had not been told the full story, but he had told her that father had continued back to Roscoff. "I hear that boy Richard Cock has been taken in."

"What mother? When did you hear that?"

"The others were with him last night but managed to escape. Richard held back and got the furze blazing. That's what brought them to him. He waited too long until it blazed high."

"Did he know that the boat out there was ours?"

"The boys weren't sure. They couldn't see clearly, no further than the end of their noses but saw the light."

"So, Richard won't be able to say what boat he was warning."

"No and besides he would make one up if he had to, knowing him."

Chapter 27

Fires and Fireforks

"Look what we've got here. Another one from Cawsand or is it Kingsand. As bad as each other. Been spending the King's money, have we? What are you here for? Up to no good out in that Bay of yours? Come on spill the beans. What's it all about? To what do we owe the pleasure of your fine company?"

"Won't be here long. Expect they'll be moving me to Bodmin."

"No one much gets out of Bodmin gaol. You're better off in here with us boys from over this side of the water. So, come on what have you done to deserve a lovely Inn like this to stay and feast in? A few nights here come with all the trimmings."

Richard Cock from Cawsand looked around at the faces of his fellow prisoners who were detained in the Plymouth lock up with him. The array of broken, missing teeth, unkempt, matted beards that provided shelter and sustenance for those small insects unfortunate enough to be incarcerated in this place with their hosts.

"I was trying to put a fire out up on the cliffs at Whitsand."

"Keeping warm, were we? Bit cold this time of year?"

"No home to go to over there in Cawsand?"

"We boys thought you boys were all making the good livings and had houses to go to?"

The iron doors slammed shut as the turnkey left. They heard him go up the stairs, then the scraping of his chair along the floor. The final noise that descended came from the joints in the chair as they strained under his weight. Upstairs then fell silent as the turnkey slumbered.

No more noise was to make its way down to the filthy hole below, into which they were all crammed. For Richard Cock it was to be a temporary stay in the Plymouth lock up. He expected that he would be questioned by the Preventative officers about what he was doing that night on Whitsand cliffs and what he knew. After that ordeal he thought he would be taken off to Bodmin or Truro gaol until his time came up for trial.

The boys who escaped from the first warning fire they lit that night on the cliffs would have guessed or known what had happened to him. It would only be a matter of time before some help or good food arrived. Maybe not today. Today would not be a good day.

Richard may not have had the speed to escape when the Preventatives saw the fires, crept up and caught him. He had never been a fast runner, but he could light a good fire quickly.

It would be a few months in these sorts of conditions before the next Assize Courts, quicker if it was going to go before the Justices. The smugglers were held in good regard in the gaols. His time was less likely to be a rough one. It would be seen to that he had a lawyer and his family were looked out for. Hours passed until the putrid, airless smells of the damp stone walls and inmates, contained several feet underground, finally gave way to the less putrid odour of the gruel that was sloshed in through the gaol door.

The smell of the unwashed bodies of the inmates competed with that of the filthy rags that covered them as clothes. Most had accustomed themselves to the smells, but they had hit Richard like a stone wall. The smell of smoke from the fire earlier that had permeated his clothing gave some relief, as well as a reminder of the events that night on the cliffs.

Chained and manacled they had to either fight to get to the gruel or come to some arrangement where they would all get their turn. Many had been the time, in a fight to get the apology for food that the turnkeys sent down, that the pot had fallen only for the contents to be soaked up by the hungry sandy ground below. The rush that followed to slurp any remains up from the ground saw them appear more like the rats on the stinking hulks that were not far from the gaol. Many of them had a fate of imprisonment on the hulks, with hard labour, to look forward to after their trial. It was that, deportation, or maybe mercilessly, the gallows. The relief of the gallows could not come too soon for some who were maimed, ill or old. Richard had life to live yet. A fine one maybe? He couldn't though see his defence setting him free of any punishment. Juries were usually especially picked now to ensure they wouldn't comprise solely of sympathisers with the free traders. There was a time they would acquit, no matter what the evidence. Less so now. Maybe they would send him away for trial.

After he took some of the gruel and succumbed to slumber, there was a crash at the gate. Three big men came in to unchain him and march him off. He was taken further down into the town to the Customs House. He knew what was likely to come next.

* * *

"So, what were you doing up there. Making bread. Preparing your fire to cook your meal. Cooking up fish?" The Surveyor, as usual, pleased with his own jokes poked him with the fire fork that had been taken as evidence. Firstly, he poked him with the wood handle end and, not having a sensible reply, turned it by spinning it in his hand and re-catching it. The success of this manoeuvre inspired the Surveyor to continue his unnerving party trick. He now threw it into the air above with enough force, dexterity and accuracy, to have its prongs pierce the ceiling. Just a tadge, the prongs entered the ceiling plasters, and the fork fell. It descended, more slowly than it had risen to the ceiling, neatly falling to his hand. He then again twirled the fork before finally somersaulting it, fork to handle end, like a cartwheel in front of him. Bringing it to an abrupt stop, forked end towards Richard, he momentarily pushed the sharp points onto Richard's chest. He released them again quickly as if this next move was happening out of its proper sequence in his interrogation.

Richard was impressed by his deftness. He knew of this man by reputation. He would not push him too far.

"I saw the fires blazing in the distance from the farm where I labour and made my way there to see what was amiss, just in case any of the animals or buildings were in danger. When I got there, I saw the fork and fire. I started to use the fork to try and put it out. It was all I had there to do the job."

"Oh yes, and who else did you see there, or did you go with some others to help put the fires out."

"No, it was just me, but I did see some folk in the distance who shouted at me and then the Preventative arrived."

The Surveyor did his usual walk of intimidation walking slowly around the back of the chair to which Richard had been secured. Without warning, he felt a sharp pain in his shoulder. It was the end of the firefork.

"A little bit of that precious free trader blood has dripped onto my floor Mr Cock. Maybe I should loosen your rope a little, so you might lick it up?"

With that he summonsed one of his men who was listening outside. "Untie him from the chair. Mind to keep his hands tied behind his back." His man did as he was told and stood back. "That's all. Go." The Surveyor started to walk around Richard once more. He did not dare follow him with his eyes or head. Suddenly he felt a sharp pain at the back of his legs as the wooden pole of the firefork was smashed into them. This brought Richard to his knees on the floor with the chair close behind, hitting him in the back as it caught up with him.

"Now, lick up your bloody blood from my bloody floor." The slightest of hesitation from Richard was enough to agitate the Surveyor, his mood changing by the second and voice turning to more of a shout.

"Lick it I said!" The Surveyor leant towards him, speaking now in a slower, snarling tone. "What are you waiting for man? We don't want this staining my lovely floor, do we?"

Richard could hardly reach the blood on the floor but as best he could he did as he was told to do. As he bent down, he felt the prongs of the fork go into his arse. He flinched and felt blood drain onto his trousers. It was the Surveyor's party piece with fireforks. He wouldn't normally devote his time to step in on these cases. This one was, though, involving Cawsand, yes Cawsand and Kingsand too. He had his eye on these people. One recent success under his belt. He now wanted more and better. He wanted the people and especially those controlling the smuggling from the villages. This man was unlikely to be one of them, but he might know more, more that would take him to them. He wanted the chiefs.

"You're dripping again, Cock, Richard Cock. Lick it up and clean off my floor. I don't want to see a drop of it there. None, hear me." The Surveyor was clearly losing any patience with Richard Cock. "The more you drip the more you will lick. Stop bleeding. Look at you, you're bleeding now from head to arse. Maybe I should get a light to seal this blood. There's nothing like a little fire to stop blood flowing.

We know all about fires don't we, Mr Cock. Maybe we also know who starts them and what boats are waiting for them?" Richard turned in agonising pain. The Surveyor, now getting his full attention, continued. "I'll ask you again about the boats you were expecting."

"I don't know of any boats. Boats are coming and going all the time." The fork went in again, was twisted twice, and removed. Nothing further being gained and with other pressing matters to attend to, the Surveyor started to lose interest in him. He kicked him downwards, face flat onto the floor again and left him. He called for his men to get rid of him to Bodmin and clean up.

Richard spent another three nights in the hell hole at Stonehouse near Plymouth before he was thrown into a cart bound for Bodmin Gaol. The cart was surrounded by Dragoons. It had several other prisoners in it bound for the same fate.

The journey down jolted every bone to a new position. Trussed with the other prisoners for company gave him little comfort. He was there with murderers, thieves and vagabonds who would slit his throat if they thought there was a coin or two in it for them.

Eventually they had travelled the thirty miles or so to the gaol where they were greeted yet again with the familiar sound of the iron gates closing over the entrances to the dank and overcrowded cells. Here was home until his case came up.

After a few days he saw a lawyer, sent down and paid for by the traders, who arranged for better conditions. This made things just a bit more bearable. Fresh clothes were brought, and he could keep himself cleaner, shaven and adequately fed. Now he just had to wait.

Chapter 28

Hannibal 2nd Decides

"Bring Williams and Foot up here, ungag them. Go down and keep eyes on the others." The senior captives were dragged up and placed before Hannibal. Humiliation and fear combined to produce a false bravery. Humiliated, as there they were, Officers of the Preventative Customs service, being forced to answer to these men, these smugglers. Fear, because they knew that the next few minutes would decide their fate.

The men's eyes told the fear that lurked behind them. On deck, Hannibal spoke quietly to the two Preventative officers. "Now then, what are we going to do with you? My men want to see you sink to the bottom. They want you to stay there until there's nothing much left of you, until the few bones that are left, escape the knots holding you together and get dragged away, dashed on the rocks. Maybe they will get washed up on the beaches.

No one will then know who those old bones belong to, man or beast. They won't end up in the church yard, that's for sure. Now me. I am a man of more gentle persuasions but need to be persuaded why I should let you live, and at the same time, save our skins. Tell me. Why should I let you live? The King's flag doesn't fly for you out here, so tell me and make it good."

Williams, nursing his chaffed mouth started. "When they find our boat all the Preventative service and the Navy will be looking for us. They will make enquiries to find out what boats were in and out that night. As for that fire that went out on the Cliffs, well, if they were caught, they will try and find out what boats were expected. That will start to pin our disappearance on you and your boat."

Hannibal started to pace the deck looking increasingly angered. These men were not providing any answers, just sealing their own fate. They were leaving him no room for manoeuvre. "Not good enough. You're at the bottom, there is nothing to say this had anything to do with anyone but yourselves. You could have gone in your small boat and got lost in the fog. A high sea could have taken you in a small boat further out. Anything could have happened."

"You don't know who was watching from the shores or the fields and copses."

"No, but in that weather where a man at sea can only see a few yards ...."

A call came from below. It was Elisha asking if he should get the men ready to say goodbye. Hannibal finally relented and accepted these men must go. "Alright, get them all ready. No good is coming of this. We may as well get it over and make sail back."

"Wait. There is a way."

"I'm waiting but make it lively. My men want their room on board back."

"You save us now and we will report that back. That you could have killed us here but didn't. They will go lightly with you."

"Ha! We have freedom now. Why should we want to sacrifice that, putting freedom to the chance? Rely on your word? Truss them up ready."

Elisha started to drag the other men up on deck. He needed no persuasion.

"No. Stop. This will bring all of us ill if not in this world, the next." Williams could see that his captors' patience was now ebbing fast.

Hannibal lifted his hand as Elisha 's head and shoulders rose up onto the deck. He waved it down beckoning him to wait below. With an expression on his face that showed his impatience, Elisha went back down, kicking the man just behind him in the chest as he let go of his rope. The rope was attached to the man, haltering him, just like the animals on the farm he sometimes worked on.

The man fell backwards onto the other man and they both crumpled to the boards below. Elisha continued his watch over them as they resumed their sitting positions on the floor, bound together. The odd gurgling sound came from them, the rope dripping saliva and blood, mixed together, as they struggled to get air into their lungs past the rope.

"Go on Mr Williams … and Mr Foot. What else have you for me?"

The two men knew this must be their final chance to save their skins and those of their two fellow workers below from a dreadful death. They did not yet feel like condemned men with nothing to lose. They felt a chance with this man but only a slim one. Was duty and service to the Crown coffers worth losing their lives for? They thought quickly. If they were gone, they couldn't then continue to fight against the illegal trade, not as a bag of bones down in the deep. They would be a memory for others, for a while, perhaps? Maybe some pension for their families or maybe not?

"You have it in your power to take our lives but if you now show mercy, take us back, or at the least, close to our shores. We can then row the boats back. We will say that you saw us, lost in the fogs, when preparing your nets. You were going to your pots, took us in tow and brought us safely back."

"How can we trust you, all of you to keep to this?"

"I will tell you a secret that if told would finish all four with the Preventative service. A secret that can be proved to be true. If told, a secret that maybe would see us all to the Gallows."

"Alright tell me. You have nothing to lose by telling me now. You can save your skins if this is good. But good, very good it has to be. No, more than good it must compel me to change my mind on your fate. Speak."

"This is for no one else to know. Come…" With that Williams spoke softly in the ear of Hannibal who leant towards him, ear to one side" He told their story in just a few minutes."

"And how will I be able to evidence that this is true?"

"I will give you the places. I will give you the keys, so you might get to them before us. We will swear, all of us, that we will keep to this, our oath, but after today we speak no more of it. We will try to keep out of your way and extend you favour on the seas but will need to carry on and do our duty to the service as if you knew nothing of our secret."

Hannibal paced the deck alone. His men trusted him to decide in the right way. A way that kept them and their families safe and fed. For the first time they were doubting him. To avoid them taking control of this situation he had to persuade them that this was the right thing to do. The secret and evidence were compelling and would condemn these men if revealed. Yes, he would do this.

"How can you trust these men, Hannibal? How can you put our fate in with them?" Elisha had calmed. He was god-fearing despite it all. Although he would have killed that night, he knew that it was better to let the Preventatives go, provided that no harm should come to him and his shipmates from that decision.

Having something held against them that was so bad it would seal their doom, if revealed, would make them all even in this matter.

The boat turned, idling off the reef where the men were released and put back into their small boats. The instruction was that they would, in better visibility now, head back to their Cutter and carry on their business.

"A deal with Preventatives these days." Who would believe it? Well, it was not so different from the common practices of the past."

The men were duly released and dropped into their boats. "It's no different from keeping our secret to ourselves. It is just another one." As they neared the place where their Cutter had been at anchor, they could not see it.

"It may have dragged anchor. Let's go further in." There was no Cutter. "What do we do?"

"We head to Plymouth and the Customs' House. We will have to tell them that two of us were creeping up smuggled, sunken tubs out in the boat. We shouted for help to get them up and that is when the second boat was launched, leaving the Cutter on anchor. The weather was so bad we became lost. We were picked up by the Five Brothers, returned to a place we could row back from. When the weather abated the Cutter was nowhere to be found."

"A likely story this is. We 're all for it."

"Better to take the reprimand than lose our lives."

As they approached Plymouth Barbican and the Customs House, sore and bruised, , they could see the Wolf. "What's that coming off her?" "She's being unloaded of ankers of spirit by looks of it."

The Surveyor was there. He was pacing the harbour where the Wolf was tied. He was with the appointed Deputy Collector of Customs. "This is a mystery if ever I saw one. Where are they? Is this to be a ghost ship? What are the markings on these tubs? The owners' marks no doubt."

"There they are. What are they doing?" The men stepped ashore and walked the cobbled streets to the Customs House adjacent.

"Your boat was seen dragging anchor and close to the Drake's Island. She could have gone onto the rocks there and smashed to firewood. What is this all about?"

"We were creeping when we called for help and the second boat came. We were lightly manned that night but thought the conditions were such that the smugglers would be out. It was very still. We expected the anchor to hold. The mist was so bad that we could not see well. Next thing we are a long way off and don't know where we are. A fishing vessel picked us up and returned us to where the Cutter had been put at anchor. We saw the Cutter gone and couldn't find her so rowed on in."

The Surveyor and Collector looked at each other. "What are these tubs and what are the markings on them?"

"We crept them up and were storing them. We don't know the markings."

With that, Williams clambered on board the Cutter and, on going down, saw the bill. Wondering what it was he took it, crumpled it and put it is his pocket. What was going on?

"Well, get back to your duties. Be ready to sail soon. You've work to do. You'd have been in trouble if this one had run ashore whilst you'd been snug in a rowing boat."

Seemingly satisfied, albeit annoyed, at the incompetence of the men, the Surveyor and Collector went back into the Customs' House. They hadn't been sufficiently close to them to wonder at the rope and skin burn marks the men had on their bodies. Williams and crew got on the Cutter, setting off as soon as all the tubs were offloaded.

"What had that been about ? How did they get there?"

"Let's hope that they don't think these markings indicate they are something to do with us, but believe they are the results of our creeping before we got lost. Out of sight, Williams looked at the bill and realised what had happened. They were ripe to be accused of smuggling or working with the smugglers. This made it look as if they had been involved in using the Cutter as a Smuggler ... and under his command. This bill. These tub markings. There could be others. This could spell the end for them, without any work from Hannibal and his crew. How did this happen? The incident went off with little further note and the Wolf was back in action with the same crew that day.

Chapter 29

Laying Low in Cherbourg

"Well, I hope this pays off Hannibal." The small crew were back en route to Cherbourg, guessing at what had become of the Preventatives they had left at Eddystone reef.

"I think it will," Hannibal smirked. "We have won ourselves some favour from these men if they see us on future runs."

"Even so, I think we should keep below decks for a while until this is settled. Nothing like a bit of time to heal a wound. We'll get message back on one of the boats at Cherbourg that is bound for Cawsand that we are well and over here doing a bit of trading for a while."

"We can make a start selling what we've got here on board and make a profit. The Polperro boys use Cherbourg a lot, we can give them a quick turnaround."

After a few days in Cherbourg, news came of Richard Cock, what had happened on the cliffs and that he was in Bodmin gaol. Hannibal's son had arrived in the port to give his father the news first hand, meeting with him while his boat, Arethusa, was loaded for a return trip. He had already started to step into his father's shoes back home. Richard received help and privilege arranged by him which would continue while he was waiting for the court to sit and hear his case. He had been to see Richard to get the story direct if he could. The turnkeys and others had been bribed to provide somewhere quiet for them to talk.

Richard and the others who lit the fires on Whitsand cliffs had not known for sure which of the smuggling boats were out there that night. They couldn't see much through the thick mists. When they knew the Preventatives were out in force, backed by Dragoons on horseback they decided to light the fires to warn any boats from landing there.

As son gave father the news, the rest of the crew were listening hard. The treatment Richard had been subjected to from the Surveyor fuelled their thirst for revenge.

"That bloody Surveyor. I'd like to meet him up on the cliffs one night. He can be on horseback or be however he likes. I'd make sure he went down the cliffs. Straight to the bottom he would go. Horse and all would follow him. I'd keep his weapons though." Elisha's threats were followed by actions. Coming from him they sent a comforting chill. He saw things in black and white, there was no middle ground for Elisha. It was about their survival, whatever. If that meant taking lives, he would do it and think no more on it afterwards.

Boy Hannibal had no news of anything else untoward. No extra activity by the Preventatives. No one had seen anything. No one had heard anything. It looked as if all was well. They could only speculate however over what happened when they returned and realised their boat was missing.

"They would have had a knock over that ... and then when they find the bugger, she's laden with marked tubs. They would have had some explaining to do over where they came from."

The quiet corner of the Cherbourg Inn witnessed a measure of humour over this, smugglers' justice. "Mother asks when you will back. She says she will be on one of the next boats to join you here for a while if you don't get back soon. What shall I tell her father?"

"I think we should continue to lie low for some time. We don't know for sure what happened when they got in. The marked tubs and bill would have taken some explaining by Williams and his crew, if indeed they were found. If they connected them with a bit of smuggling or if they talked their way out of it. If, if, if and more ifs. We just don't know enough right now.

Should they have dared tell the truth, I would be surprised if they would have been believed. The only believable thing is that they were up to no good themselves. No, I expect they have found some other way to talk themselves out of it. That's of course if the most difficult thing to explain away was found, the bill. I could see they could explain away the tub markings, a mere chance they stood for Williams, but with the bill as well made out to him. Now that would be a bugger for them to wriggle out of."

Just the thought of Williams struggling over his words. The thought of him and his struggling to explain the markings on the tub. And as for the bill, well ..... To see them explain the bill away would have been a real treat. Better than the treats that lay in store in the whorehouses of Cherbourg, they mused. They needed to know what had happened, to gauge whether it would be safe to return.

"We'll head to Roscoff in a few days, set up there for a while. Tell your mother that is no place for her but if I can get us somewhere to live then maybe she should come for a while. It's nie on time that you took on more of the business anyway. You've got the houses, the boats, the cellars and a stack of coins to be getting on with. Maybe these runs are getting more difficult for me now than I care to own up to. I'll do some trading and take a cut. Make sure you bring me back some of the coin and note to get started here. The merchants will provide funds and the stock on the boat will sell. There's nothing like hard cash, coin, to get everyone really excited."

Hannibal's son had really proven himself. His actions with the Wolf had won him the respect of the crew, not just for mustering the courage to steal back onto the boat, planting the marked tubs and bill. He had come up with the idea in the first place.

With that he was ready to go back. It was his turn now to be more active in running the business.

"I'll be marrying soon he shouted to the crew on board the Arethusa. Come on let's make some money. I'll be needing it more than you soon!"

He, Hannibal 3rd was in charge back home now. Well, that is, for as long as father was happy to run the operation from Cherbourg to Roscoff. And, well yes, and depending on mother .... mother too knew the business inside out. She had organised much of the home storage. Much stock at any time was held in village houses. It was mother who knew where it all was. She kept a strict eye on the stocks. She knew how much they had, where it was, who owed the money, what they were likely to need in the coming weeks. That wasn't to say that there wasn't some stock for all those hiding it, there was. Mother didn't mind what they had for themselves on top of their pay. She drew the line if they sold it. That was different and would not be tolerated. She was the silent force behind the business. If mother decided to join father in France for a while, she would be difficult to replace. Maybe more than father even.

But ... he too was planning on marrying soon. His wife in waiting had grown up too with the business. He, Hannibal 3rd and Susanna could do it on their own. They both knew it and could see changing times. They could change with it. They would be the new face coming in of the Hannibal Marks' enterprises.

Sarah, his younger sister, had married only a few years ago and Elizabeth well before that. There had only been two and five years between them. It was this Hannibal's turn next.

His mind cast a thought to the predecessor siblings of he and his sister Elizabeth. Hannibal and Elizabeth had both taken the names of their brother and sister who had died early. The younger Hannibal had died when he was only five, before he, the later Hannibal had been born, so he had never known him. Mother had never let them all forget him though. Nor was the younger Elizabeth forgotten who had died when she was eleven. He had vague memories of Elizabeth as he was two or so when she died.

Poor mother, she went to their graves, close to where their Grandparents lay. The graves were marked with small stones. She would visit their gravesides on the anniversaries of their deaths, lie and weep there to ponder on what might have been if they had lived. What would they look like now? What would they be doing? She made him, and his sisters promise that they would always remember the location of the graves. They promised her that they would never allow the days of their births and deaths go without being recognised and would always be remembered. She asked the Vicar to offer prayers for them on the nearest service to the anniversaries of their deaths.

He would return to pick up the Five Brothers. His father had said he would buy a French vessel instead to ply the North Coast. The recent gin factory established at Dunkirk was prospering with good Geneva coming from it. There was a buoyant market for gin now at home. Father planned to set up a storage facility in Roscoff to hold stock of the best merchandise at the best prices. He would make sure they obtained the highest proof spirit, so it could be watered and coloured down as necessary when it got back. This would maximise the value in a run. They had considered for some time the value in expanding the business on the French side. Their own facility there would increase their ability to stock safely, catch the producers at the right time, when they had over produced or needed revenues, to get the best prices on the best terms.

They could also sell to some of the other smugglers from Devon and Cornwall. They could deliver off their home shores to reduce their risk, command a better price for this. Increase the Marks' margins of profit, volumes too. Broker money when in short supply. These were all new opportunities he should work on.

A few weeks would give time for Father to sell the existing stock on the boat and refill her. He would also obtain enough stocks in advance to fill the boat he came back out in as well. Perhaps he would bring the Daniel and William back for this. The Daniel as she was known was one of the other Smugglers in which the Marks had shares.

Chapter 30

A Maker Marriage for Hannibal 3rd

The front pews, those immediately in front of the altar, were occupied by the Bride's parents, Mr and Mrs Spriddle who had accompanied the Groom's mother, Mrs. Marks, to the Church of St Mary and St Julian at Maker, in her husband's absence.

The pews around them gradually filled with several Spriddles and Spridells. No one was really too sure how the surname Spriddle should be properly spelt or pronounced, but it didn't really matter as all Spriddles were Spridells and all Spridells were Spriddles. It did, however, matter today. The Vicar had to pronounce and write the Bride's name correctly. Susannah was a Spriddle. Somehow, as the name travelled successfully down the centuries being spelt differently on its way, it settled into the two spellings that were still currently in use. Both had stuck and ended up co-existing over centuries but always in a state of some tension. Which one was the correct pronunciation and spelling of their name? Disagreements would flare up between the two factions from time to time, usually at weddings and funerals. The Spridells had chosen to pronounce their name, Sprid-elle as if the elle at the end were pronounced in the French way for she, elle. The Spriddles, moreover, would pronounce Spriddle exactly as it looks, with each letter quickly following the one coming before it.

The Spriddles had branched out from the Mevagissey Spriddles or Spriddells a long time back. It was so long ago now no-one really knew when, who or how. All they knew was that they had been in the Rame area, residing in all the different villages there, but mostly in Kingsand, Cawsand and Millbrook. This had been the case since at least as far back as the fifteenth century. They had been there to hail the coming of King Henry VII into the Bay that thereafter became known as Kingsand Bay. There had been some disagreement between them over whether it had been the Spriddles or Spridelles that had been in the Rame area from these ancient times but in the end, they agreed it was really both.

They could both provide evidence for their assertions. As the two groups met in the pews the same old discussions started up. Two Spriddles, both John, were listed in a Cornish muster roll in 1569 which had been drawn up for the Monarch, Queen Elizabeth 1. They had been put onto a call up list in the event of skirmish or battle, as they owned bows and arrows with one also owning a Bill. The Bill had been passed down since from one Spriddle to the next, until, eventually, only the metal weapon head remained. Having laid around for some time and with no use, it was eventually rejuvenated with a new pole fitted for use by a Spriddle working in the fields. This was in living memory of the Spriddles.

The hooked blade on the end of its long pole had been a fearsome weapon in its day. In more peaceful times it had been valuably employed as a slasher to cut down crops and clear undergrowth. Besides, there were better weapons that had been invented over all those intervening years. It would be in the Rame fields somewhere, missing a pole again, but no one had ever turned it up.

Even back in the days of the bill, there was some confusion over the spelling and pronunciation of Spriddell or Spriddle. This meant that the argument had probably run for at least three hundred years with no sign of a final resolution.

The two early Johns in the muster were Spindrell and Spradell, but again all Spindrells were Spradells and all Spradells were Spindrells. And both were Spridelles or Spriddles.

The conversation was now raging across the pews. Pews immediately adjacent to those of the Spriddles and Marks were filling. As they did so, more folk chipped in their pennyworth.

"Anyway, what use would a couple of bows and arrows be? For that matter what use would an old bill have been? Especially against some of those ships from Spain and France that would come in here, firing and looting us?"

"You know perfectly well", came the raised voice of Susannah's mother. "Perfectly well that they used to come in here. Those folk with weapons would see them off if they could. You also know perfectly well that John Spriddle came across that Spaniard placing a line of barrels of tar ready to light. All strung together they were. Would have burned the village down if he hadn't shot at him with those arrows and chased him with that Bill."

"That Bill, yes that Bill caught him right between the legs he did. Tore off his Spanish stones he did. No more little Spaniards for him. Made him run all the faster that night. Down to the water and off to his boat. Hanging on to them he was. Oh yes that's what we Spriddles do to those Spanish invaders, and the French invaders. We want to give Susannah a good bill with a long pole and a good sharp blade. She might want him now but, in a few years, when she don't, a good billing will sort out that Hannibal."

The men listening winced and changed the conversation. Interrupting, a later John Spriddle chipped in. "Yes, my wager is that he was a good bowman that Spriddle. I'll wager he didn't just use that Bill. No, he would have fired one of those arrows right into that Spaniard's arse. Then he would have chased him with that bill, arrow stuck right in. That Spaniard would have hollered his Spanish all the way to that beach. Lucky to escape back to his boat. It would have hurt getting that arrow out. I hope they gave it a good pull. Yes, foot on his arse to hold him down and pulled at the arrow. I wish I'd been there to see it."

"Well you weren't, John Spriddle" His wife had heard it all before. "And you mind your language. You are in the Church. And you are at a wedding.

The Vicar will be out here soon. He won't want to hear your language filling his Church."

She was convinced that no one nowadays was too sure about it all anyway. What did it matter to anyone in any case? What did it matter whether he had an arrow in his backside or a bill between his legs, or both, or if none of it happened?

The conversation quickly went back to the name and whether the Spriddles were from Cawsand , Kingsand or Millbrook? Which Church should really be marrying Susannah Spriddle today? Even in the muster rolls they were listed as in the Parish of Rame but with no further information. Later, other Spridells and Spriddles were in Millbrook, Anderton as well as both Cawsand and Kingsand. What did it matter anyway thought some of those listening into the ever-intensifying debate?

As the pews filled with more of them up it would all start. Same ground was gone over, again and again. Finally, the arguments centred fully on the occasion and whether the marriage should have really been at Rame.

They did agree in the end that they were from both Parishes and as Susannah was from Kingsand, Maker it should be. They agreed they were in the right Church and for now the name Susannah had been given, that of Spriddle was indeed, her right name.

Mrs Marks put the final lid on the issue of the name.

"Mrs. Marks she'll be soon and that can end that for their children if they're in Cawsand."

"No, it won't if she's Kingsand, they'll be Kingsand". A Spridelle and Spriddle had started it up again for the generations not yet born.

Fortunately, the discussion, that had started to migrate backwards two pews from the parents of the bride and groom was drawn to a halt as Hannibal and Susannah joined each other at the altar with their parents to each side.

The conversations ceased abruptly as the Vicar entered and loudly cleared his throat. The wedding ceremony began, not to last long.

The Vicar made his last call for anyone who knew of any just impediment to the marriage to make it known now. It was the bit of the marriage ceremony he enjoyed the most. He could stand aside whilst making the call, hoping that one day there might be the spectacle of someone coming forward. Not that he would know then what to do, other than to suspend the ceremony whilst the matter was investigated.

No one did, this day, make any last-minute objections. Nor had they before in any service over which he officiated. The ceremony over and the couple making their departure saw the conversations about surnames, events of long ago, all swept aside, awaiting another occasion to ignite them once more. There was nothing quite like a wedding or a funeral to bring out old chestnuts. As the couple started off on their slow walk down the central aisle through the Church towards the main doors at the front of the tower, they could hear the side doors opening as well. The side doors were opened to clear the people attending more quickly than they otherwise would have been able to from the main doors alone. The main entrance went through the tower. The bell ringing chamber and the bell room were further up again, the smugglers' space, sandwiched, hidden, between the two. The bells were peeling well. The smugglers' bell ringing skills had become increasingly well-honed since the Church tower had been commandeered by them. Bell ringing as well as bell maintenance were now duties they had to fulfil well if they wanted to maintain a complete dominance of those upper floors. That meant the roof, walls and essentially the entire tower fell to them to repair and maintain as well as provide trusted ringers for the bells.

"It's a pity that father and Joe aren't here but we couldn't delay this any longer..... a missing Spriddle and a missing Marks." Hannibal was silenced as Susannah took advantage of the short time they would have outside alone before the throng attending arrived and they went off to start the celebrations.

Pushing the massive Church doors closed and hiding them from view, she silenced him in the best way she could think. Her slender arms slinked up his back as she faced him, elbows bending to grip his shoulder, he was pulled in towards her. A deep breath swelled her bosom and as he stared down at the treats that would soon be his all thoughts of absent friends disappeared fast.

"I wish we could lock them all in there for a while Susannah."

"Do you think we would be missed for a while if we took a quick walk down to the copse in the valley?" The valley lay on the downside of churchyard. It was steep. Few folks took the trouble to clamber down there or use the land, which gave rough grazing only. They could probably get out of sight before anyone left the Church. No more said, they ran.

Susannah picked up her dress and cast off her shoes. As they went over the steep valley side, they knew they would be out of sight. Down they went into the valley to the little copse below. As they stood on the soft ground outside of the outer boundary of the copse, Susannah replaced her shoes and in amongst it they went. There was, as they expected, no one around. There was little noise other than produced by the occasional squirrel or bird as they went leaping or flying from tree to tree.

They went in a short way. Much of the sun was lost as it was caught by successive layers of branches and leaves on their way earthward. Speckles of light bobbed about on the sides of the trees, falling onto the ground below as the branches and leaves above moved with the wind.

The young Hannibal sat her on a fallen tree where the sun shone through, kneeling in front of her. He pulled up her dress and opened her legs wide. Her legs were pure white. Looking around with some reserve, Susannah ran her hands up both of his legs from as far down as she could reach gripping him more tightly and digging into him as her grip rose higher and higher towards his buttocks. She looked down and knew what was coming next. Oblivious to their surroundings, she grabbed his belt and roughly unhinged it. The loose-fitting trousers, held in place only by the excitement she was causing him, gave way easily to her short tug. His closeness to her made him unable to hold back any longer. As she pulled him closer, his legs came close against the tree. She slid further across it, the rough bark scraped the whiteness of her flesh as the dress pulled up a little behind. A short rasping tear could be heard as the inner skin of the dress caught on a protruding piece of bark. She controlled her gasps as she was filled with him and the two writhed with an increasing speed on the top of the fallen tree. They ignored the scraping of the bark that was scratching and making their legs raw. The bark was unforgiving and unyielding in its adhesion to the underlying wood of the tree trunk it covered.

"I wish we could go home and start again."

Susannah nodded in agreement. The two knew they could not be much longer. Drawing back, he felt her grip him tight inside. Was there time to stay a while. Time to start again?

"No, Hannibal Marks. I can see what you're thinking. Getting a taste for this now are we. You'll have to wait until we get back later, that's if you'll be any good later?"

Her voice rose tantalisingly as she reached the last few words. With that she slid back on the tree allowing the wetness to fall onto the trunk. He rose and retied his trousers and belt. Brushing himself down he leant over, outstretching his hand to pull her up.

As he looked down on her all he could think of was what tonight might bring. He couldn't wait for tonight. He wanted her again before that. They would have to find a way of getting away from the celebrations early.

Make some excuse and get back to the woods or maybe one of the quiet beaches. Yes, that's what he wanted. Not where people were, no, the beach or maybe one of the boats.

"You just wait, Hannibal Marks." She spoke in a commanding irritated tone to which he recoiled. This was followed with a teasing, "Yes, You just wait..... Hannibal Marks" The beckoning, but forbidding tone, excited him.

As she started to walk off up the valley ahead of him, he caught up on her from behind. Without warning he grabbed her breasts, thrusting himself towards her through her dress, eagerly anticipating a response as before. Just once more, before they headed back.

She gently went to the ground, protesting weakly that they could not keep folk waiting, whilst staying on her knees, head lifted. She could feel him lift her dress again. The excitement was too much for her as she parted her legs, once again, feeling him position himself between hers.

As he grabbed her hanging breasts, she could feel him once more. It was easier this time. She moved and moved, feeling him pushing harder and harder, as he pulled her breasts back towards him that they stretched tight against her frame. She squirmed around, allowing, encouraging him, to go faster, harder at her.

"This time, Hannibal Marks, I will get my way too." As she felt him shudder, she pulled away thinking what folk may now think if they were any longer. Wait until she got him home. It would be her turn next. She would take control of Hannibal Marks. She would tame him.

As they hurriedly walked the short distance back up to the Church they looked towards its tower. On the top she could see a person in behind one of its decorative corner stones. Could that be the Vicar? No, he never went up there? It looked like his distinctive shape. No, it couldn't be. He found it difficult, nay almost impossible, to climb the tower? Thinking little of it, as the head slinked into the shadows of the leaded roof on top of the tower, they continued onwards. Hannibal thought he would ask the bellringers later if the Vicar had taken what would be an almost unprecedented walk up the tower. He would have had to go past the entrance to the bellringing room a few floors below the exit door that would take him out onto the roof. What a struggle it would have been for him to get up there. As for the journey back down again, he had been known to fall a few steps when attempting the climb before. The treads of the steps were simply not deep enough, nor wide enough, to take both his feet easily. Going down backwards was a safer option for a man of his dimensions, allowing his hands to stabilise him as he descended. He would have had quite a difficult climb to get there. What would he be doing up there anyway?

"I bet whoever it is might have been able to see into the valley, Hannibal."

"Not into the wood where we were."

"I am not so sure as you."

With that they were at the Church.

"Where did you two get to?"

"We took a short walk to look over the sea and get some air."

No one thought much of their departure, spending the time catching up with friends and acquaintances. The conversations had turned to their work and how things were going with absent families. There was much to talk about. Fewer of the Spriddles had been so heavily involved in the trade in the last few years. Some had turned for employment to the new emerging Coastguard services that kept watch on their activities, but not locally. Recruited into the new service that was just setting up, they were being drafted to work elsewhere to avoid the problems of bribery those with local connections faced. The Lobbs were there. They too spoke of some of theirs who had taken to the new services that were taking them away for work. Others had gone to piloting full time with some fishing to supplement it if business was slack. Naval work was also growing in popularity for the Spriddles too. That could bring a pension in due course.

The newlyweds led the way as the procession made its way down to the villages again. Not all the elderly who wanted to be there could be. The traps could only take so many and not all could make the walk up the steep mile towards the gentler level tracks that for another mile or so led to the church.

Hannibal's father had remained in Northern France still uncertain of the safety for return. There had not been a murmur since the incident that would suggest he could face any trouble.

***

It was to be the birth of the latest Hannibal that would see Hannibal Marks senior, return. He did not have long to wait. Susannah was at the Marks' house in the Strand when her first child was born.

"When is that child coming Mother?" the impatient and anxious Hannibal, asked. His mother was downstairs with Susannah's. "You just wait. This baby will come when he or she is ready. That's not long now I can see.

Mrs Edwards has helped to deliver more babies in these parts than I've had hot dinners. If she says it's coming, and all is well then, it's coming .. .and all will be well." Hannibal took a large gulp of the best brandy they kept for themselves and walked to the windows. There were a few more folk outside also waiting for the news. Was it a girl or a boy? None had long to wait as the cry of the latest arrival in the Marks' household made his presence known.

Hannibal 4th had arrived in 1819, one hundred years just about after the birth of Hannibal 1st. It had not been as easy as his mother had assured him it would be. She was though alive, they were both alive.

"I am well Hannibal. Say hello to your son. Hold him." He could almost rest him in the palm of his hand. First born, he would bear his name. They had talked of this. It was to be Hannibal after him and his father or Honor after Susannah's mother.

"He'll be on the boats with me as soon as he can walk. No before, he will be safe crawling around the deck!" Hannibal trod around the walls of the room, talking to him as Susannah was overcome with joy at how she had pleased him so much, as well as herself. This, this, the gift of Hannibal 4th, was her greatest gift, the greatest she could give.

"You must rest," he said in a low and broken voice as he heard the turn of the door and a push made against it. It was Mrs Edwards with the two mothers with fresh cloth and hot water.

"Go now about your work. You've another mouth to feed which will be a hungry one we're sure .... if he's like his father." With that Hannibal left and went up to the Ale House they still ran not far around the corner in Kingsand.

"Have you introduced him to the best of Cognacs in Kingsand yet Hann?"

"Yes, never mind the best in Kingsand. Oh no. The best in the Kingdom!"

The Bay boys enjoyed this banter. Word had already arrived that the boy had been delivered safely.

"Whose name will he take? Another Hannibal? Of Kingsand or Cawsand?" The crowd gathered to hear the news.

***

As he sat in the alehouse celebrating the new arrival his mind wandered a while to business.

The arrival of Hannibal 4th was inspiring him, Hannibal 3rd, to consider further plans to expand the Marks' enterprises. His father, now grandfather, Hannibal 2nd, was plying between Roscoff and Cherbourg, more besides. He was busy setting up arrangements for increased, better buying, the holding of stocks and the like. He needed money and preferably hard cash to take to his father. Real money not credit from the merchants would enable him to get the keenest of deals. Their available cash could go a long way but there simply wasn't enough cash in circulation. The mint would have to be the source for additional money required.

He had strict instructions that the hoard at the bottom of the well was to remain untouched. That was the final reserve, that was required for future generations should they need to start all over again. This was the Marks' insurance policy. He had mainly dealt with the Roscoff merchants, but this time he would be dealing with some of the newer establishments direct that had set up along the coast on Northern France including the recently built new Gin factory at Dunkirk and the Cherbourg Cognac distilleries. To get the best prices they might need to take on the whole risk, paying on delivery for stocks and storage as they were taken.

His father had in fact got to work right away, securing the purchase of a French vessel suitable for the work up and down the coast. He was on the way now to Roscoff to arrange storage or part storage facilities to service the smuggling boats, mainly those of Cawsand, Kingsand and vessels in which the Marks held shares or owned them outright. If they could increase their holdings in Inns and Taverns perhaps further afield, as well, he thought, maybe this could be a new side of the business he could develop for himself and his son. Thoughts of Taverns, Alehouses and Inns, alongside the shouts from his friends who had suddenly noticed him slipping away from them, deep in his thoughts, eyes shut. Slumber was beckoning.

"Hey Marksy, stop your dreaming. Come back down out of those clouds."

"You'll need all the brandy we can get to keep you asleep now."

"Come on boys. Drink to Marksy and the latest Marksy to join us. We'll have him shipshape in no time!"

"Bet he could do with a little sup to get used to testing it?"

"Another Hannibal? We can't be doing with any more on the boats. It's going to have to be Hann, Hannibal and Marksy maybe!"

Eventually the jollities ended, and Hannibal returned home. Their first child born, he already felt differently, about Hannibal 4th, his wife and the life he wanted for them all.

"And where do you think you've been, with a wife just had a young one?" His mother was waiting for him at the door of the house on the Strand in Kingsand.

"The Boys wanted to wish the new Marksy well in the world . Welcome Hannibal 4th, Ma."

"Well you can get in there and welcome him yourself. They didn't come here to welcome him. Wait until I see them. I'll give them a bit of my jaw. You can get in there and up to your wife."

With that Sarah and Mary both ushered the swaggering young Marks up the stairs to where his wife was gently slumbering with the new Hannibal to her side.

"Now don't you go falling on her nor the babe or you'll answer to me and Honor Spriddle. Now get in there." The door shut tight. He crossed the floor to his wife and Hannibal 4th as quietly as he could manage.

"Don't you breathe that liquor over him. He's just entered the world and doesn't want any of your old muck near him. Or to see his Da hardly able to walk."

With that Susannah raised herself up on the bed.

"Hello, Da. Say hello to Hannibal. Hannibal, father Hannibal that is, your son looks more sturdy, stronger by the hour. He came out of me as if he just couldn't wait to meet us all in the end, and here he is. What a boy. He looks like you too."

With that, Hannibal 3rd sobered somewhat and with as much gentleness as he could muster, leant over him, took a deep breath for fear of making him drunk on the fumes exhaling from his mouth and kissed the boy. His pride was exceeded only by the pride he had just felt whilst celebrating with the Bay Boys. He then turned to his wife and lay next to her carefully. The sheets had been changed and there were just traces that indicated that this was the place where Hannibal 4th had taken his first view of the world. Susannah addressed her sleeping son with her steely resolve.

"I vow to you that I will do all in my power and that given to me as a woman, now a mother, to keep you safe and well, bring you happiness, health as best I can, whatever happens."

"And I vow to you bot, to keep you safe and well until my dying breath." There was a lot to live for. A lot to do to secure his future.

Chapter 31

Surprise in Roscoff

"Hannibal, Hannibal. Come on. You wanted to go on the next run. The Friends is ready to leave and a boat's waiting for you over at Widdy Cove to take you out to her. I know you wanted the Daniel to take back but she's not here yet." Hannibal had sobered up and was ready to leave. He grabbed the bags and locked trunk. They were both crammed with coin and notes, much from the Mint, all ready to take to his father.

Friends slipped away within minutes of Hannibal getting on deck with the money. "The wind's right for a good crossing, Hannibal. How's that wife and the new one."

All is well. More's the reason I am sad to be heading off so quickly after he's arrived."

"You won't be saying that when he hollers louder than the screeching of those Preventatives when they see a smuggler on their waters."

Hannibal knew where his father's storage and nearby home were located in Roscoff. News of such things travelled fast with the boats. Friends moored upon the quay close by. Hannibal jumped onto the cobbles of the quayside.

"Look who it is with father at the end over there!" Hannibal pointed to the end of the harbour wall where two men were talking and looking out.

"It's Joe. Bonjour Joe." they shouted. Joe turned and ran to them followed more slowly by Hannibal 2nd. As they met, Joe faced a barrage of questions.

"How's Marie?"

"Where are you now?"

"Well I had a bit of a surprise. Marie wasn't quite who we all expected her to be."

"And.....?"

"Enough of that for now," interrupted Hannibal senior. "We have got bags of money to get safely back. No hanging around. Get some of your men here, armed. Quickly. Just in case. There will be time enough when we have done our work to exchange the news. God knows for sure there is enough of it I do suppose."

What was effectively an armed guard for the Marks' money accompanied father and son to his father's residence. Safe keeping arranged for the money, the conversation resumed.

"Well, when we arrived, she said we should go south for a bit. She took me to see her family near Morlaix. I was expecting that Marie's family were amongst the poorer of the area. We've always been given to believe she was in England to start a new life.

It was true that she had come to start that life but not that she was from a poor family there. No, she had run away from an ancient, well known merchant family of great wealth and nobility in France."

"So why end up in Roscoff in the Taverns? Why mix with the smugglers? Why come to a Vicar's house in England?"

"She had run away from their house and lands, escaping from the life that had constrained her even though it gave her security, comfort with no need to want for anything. Joe went as far as to say it had made a prisoner of her. Her family had at that time then disowned her. Coming back with me she felt she had not only made a new beginning but a new start that could be a happy one. She felt she was ready to face them again but this time, not alone. They would have to take of us what they would."

"And what then Joe? What did they do when you called there?"

"She thought the door would be shut, especially turning up with an Englishman. A Cornishman as well ... not even a pure Englishman, and of the free trading type, with nothing much back home to offer that befitted her birth and station. They were right. I had nothing to offer that could match what she had left behind there. Nothing at all."

"Come on Jo. What happened then?"

"Turns out that her father had died. Her brothers were running the family affairs."

"And. And. What of it?"

"Well, amongst those affairs they are involved widely in lending money. They also own much of the harbour areas and buildings around here. They welcomed Marie back and took me in with her. We married."

"Thought you were dressed better than we have seen you ever dressed. And smelling nice too! Have you smelt Joe, father?"

Joe laughed. "Well we have a little business going on now. Your father is buying well up and down the coast. He buys more besides the spirits. With big storage, close to the harbour, we can buy keenly, store and distribute from here. We are looking at more boats, big boats as well. These could come over to you for unloading. Like a lot of them used to. You know the days when the boats would bring the stock and moor off Cawsand and Kingsand. They would sell to our traders direct from their boats. Went well in those days. They'd be in trouble if caught doing it now. But we can learn from their ways. This time they could bring it across and sink for us if it is too dangerous to land. As long as they do it well, we could then get it when we are ready for it."

"How about the reef or the Islands. Maybe a bit further out. We can then do less runs over with a much-reduced risk if they are French boats. They won't want to be starting up the wars again by taking in Frenchy boats and men."

"They could sink them as we would, off the reef, near the inshore rocks, when the coast is clear, at night. They could then come closer to signal. Joe and I know the reef and the Islands like we know the backs of our hands. We can teach the Frenchies how to get to the Islands too, the best direction to come in and on what winds and tides. Teach them our signals and make sure our decoys know about them and our decoys."

"Don't give them too much too soon," Hannibal 2nd interrupted. "A little bit and see how they get on. Something to start with that we can afford to lose."

"Our boats could be tied up at home when the Frenchies come in. Nothing for the Preventatives to think is happening, or we can send them off, chasing us up river only to get a pile of fish maybe. Say we're after an honest living now and then wait our time to go out and collect. We could signal or get messages in a different way as well. These winking and flashing lights are there for all to see and get used to. Could be we and they put down pots with a certain stone in to say where things are and get other messages to each other. No one would see that. We need to think of new ways again. This new way of doing things could come with a new way of sending and receiving messages, with less risk of them being seen or found, if they are found, there would be no obvious sign of any message going to and fro. We would be seen hauling pots in. The weighting stones could be different colours in different ones to tell us how much and where. If the Preventatives see us, they can come and check us and the pots and all they'll see will be a bunch of stones holding down the pots and a load of crabs in them coming aboard. We could place our orders in the pots in the same way."

"They won't want to take out the congers from the pots to have a closer look, I don't expect." Hannibal 2nd looked mischievously at the others.

The sight of the Preventatives pulling out a six-foot-long conger curled around inside a pot with a load of big pincer crabs, appealed to them.

"We can easily arrange credit for your father here and build a stock of money to make our payments. Marie's family will let us operate some of the harbour sections by the buildings and there will be storage fees and other fees we can make an income from here that will help to reduce the need for cash to come over. Money made here and invested here in stock. We then bank the money from sales back home. Money stays in England. This will reduce our needs from the Mint and give us the money we need at home to invest."

"What will Marie's family get from this?" asked Hannibal 3rd.

"They will get a cut and their cut will be banked for them in England."

"There could be easier ways for them."

"Yes, maybe," said Joe pensively, "but they are content with this. It spreads things for them should anything happen in France that could take their wealth away. This way money will start to accrue away from France for them, should anything go wrong."

The two Hannibals agreed to meet with Joe that night. They would meet alone to establish how this way of operating might work. It was a long night with Joe and Marie. The Vicar's exploits with Marie had not bred resentment of him in the end. If it had not been for the Vicar she would not have gone to England. If she hadn't gone to England, she would not have met Joe. If she hadn't met Joe, her life would not be as happy as it had become now. Joe, however, felt matters had been left unsettled with the Vicar. He had a score to settle. Man of God or not, he had a score to settle, and settle it he would. Somehow, sometime, he would be settling this alright. He had time. Wait he would if he had to.

Chapter 32

The Surveyor Suspects

"No information, Mr Glinn? Nothing much coming out of your Cawsand Mint?" The Surveyor had Glinn in his usual place at Plymouth. Since the major haul they had won at the Mewstone, all down to Glinn's information, the Surveyor had lightened up on him. There had, though, not since, been much information coming forth that was of any great value to the Surveyor.

"No Sir. They don't use me much now and I don't hear so much either. It looks as if they are turning to a more God-fearing life. We haven't seen that older Hannibal Marks for a while. Talk is he may have died out at sea. One or two of the boats have been missing too."

'That's justice served if he has."

"Seems like maybe the tightening up has turned them from their old ways, Sir. The boy Hannibal doesn't put off to sea so much and when he does it looks as if it is fishing and potting, he does. Mind, they still have the alehouses."

"I know, but it is the smuggling from France, the bigger fish, that we are out for. Maybe your services won't be needed for much longer after all, Mr Glinn."

"I am thinking, Sir, of joining some of my people at Turnchapel. Might turn to helping with the piloting that runs from there."

"Yes, these pilots won't get wound up in the smuggling that we know of. If they do, it is trifling. Perhaps for the odd keg for themselves. We do not believe nowadays that they are part of these well organised bands of smugglers. They have a good living to make from the pilotage. Plenty of good work without soiling themselves with the dirt of the devil I say." He was pleased as usual at his own joke.

Despite what seemed to be a newfound favour with the Surveyor, Glinn laughed cautiously with him. He had learnt this was the way with the Surveyor. Take no chances on his mood. Take no chances on it being the same for very long. He could change like the wind. Glinn was now really planning to leave the villages and head for Turnchapel whilst his luck was still in. Or at the very least to let the bakehouse and its secrets go to someone else.

"Get out then." The Surveyor beckoned him to leave waiving his hand in such an erratic way as if he were shooing away a rabid dog. They had received some information that had led to the capture of goods since the big haul at the Mewstone. No boats had been taken in from his tip offs at any time. No people captured either ... yet. The tip offs Glinn made to the Surveyor had all been planned with one of the Hannibals. The goods captured always spoiled, always waste to the smugglers, representing no real loss to them. Surprisingly the Customs had never tested the contents of the barrels. They looked good on the outside. Those opened and discarded were indeed full of spirit. There was no reason to suspect these were anything than smuggled merchandise destined for sale. Should the odd keg have found its way to the home of a Preventative man it was unlikely they would have complained. It was also unlikely that it would have aroused suspicion. Anything could have happened to the kegs up to the point when they got them. They usually retrieved them from the sea. The tip offs had never enabled them to recover contraband from a boat. This way it was quite possible goods had been spoiled in the sea from seepage of sea water into the keg or from damage as they washed ashore or onto rocks.

The Surveyor and Chief Preventative Officer mulled over together what seemed to be a change of direction for the Marks' smuggling operation in Cawsand. "What is going on? Several of the Cawsand boats don't seem to leave moorings and when they do, all they appear to be doing is fishing and supplying markets up and down the Tamar. We've searched them. Nothing. Could it be they have turned over a new leaf?"

"Stinks! We are still getting other boats. It seems that those in which the Marks have an interest, at least those that we know of, are all used for lawful purposes. I doubt very much that these are all lawful. Stuff and nonsense, Burke. Stuff and nonsense. We don't know what is going on. Try all the informers again. Again, I say. Someone, somewhere, will talk, sometime. Let's get the truth out about this. Oh, and follow that young Marks."

With that the Chief Preventative Officer left to return to his vessels and station. The Surveyor stayed, continuing to pace the room, talking to himself out loud as he went, working through the various scenarios and possibilities.

"The older Marks has just about disappeared. The younger one spends time on fishing. He spends time with that new born of his. He works their alehouses too. But no sign of anything much there either. Hmmm. I don't believe it. Why aren't the others there doing the same? There had been several hauls, captures and jailings of them. Maybe that new boy Hannibal has softened his father up? Maybe his father had indeed died at sea, just not come back. It would explain a lot. Still find it hard to believe. A man like that doesn't just die. He comes back, time and time and time again. We'll see about all of this."

Chapter 33

A Heart Rules a Head

Joe and his French crew were nearing the Eddystone reef in his boat, the Joe Marie. Hannibal 2nd and his wife, Sarah, were passengers for this journey. They were heading homeward. Sarah's time in Roscoff had been relatively short lived. Her desire was to be with her husband. The risks of Roscoff seemed a small price to pay for that. Any possible danger there might have been in returning for her husband seemed to have passed. The undertaking with Williams had been kept. It was time to return. The relationship with Joe had strengthened and they had established their own facility in Roscoff.

They could not resist taking with them a boat full of kegs. An empty boat would have been a missed opportunity. Old habits were to die hard for these traders. They could have made a start at transferring their lives to that of the lower gentry, using the profits they had made from the trade to invest in land and property. But not these men. These men were traders, free traders at that. They had property with their stores, taverns but all they had was linked to the trade. They would continue to do what they knew and do it well.

They had intended to make the journey as a passenger boat only to take any risks out of the journey for Hannibal and his wife. The combined attraction of the empty Joe Marie tied up next to their well-stocked warehouses on the quayside at Roscoff had proved too much for them as they stood ready to board. The Joe Marie was filled from the warehouse.

As they approached English waters, they had been conscious of a vessel way off in the distance, the outline of which resembled that of a revenue cutter. Their vision improved only by the occasional sweep of moonlight, it remained too far off and too dim to be certain.

If she were, she was a long way out for a Customs boat. In any event it wasn't thought that the English Customs would be seeking to cause trouble for a French vessel that far out.

Nonetheless they had been sobered by its presence and felt they were being followed, although there was a long distance being kept between them. It might be the boy Hannibal that they were following. The two boats had left together.

The Joe Marie was not a light, nimble vessel, she was more of a working, lumbering boat capable of riding out the worst of storms, capable of taking a large payload. Dependability and strength were the characteristics of the Joe Marie rather than a boat ready to take on a chase with the Preventative boats.
They neared the Lighthouse on the reef, the Eddystone Light, the Stone as it was often abbreviated.

This was the fourth lighthouse that had been erected at this site on the reef. Chosen for its location on the reef with its rocky outcrop that made it possible to build a lighthouse there at most tides There was enough prominent rock to build. The current lighthouse was, without question, the best yet. Built by John Smeaton, it was of local granite, finally offering a more permanent solution.
This was a lighthouse that had become part of the very rocks that it stood on, rocks that had survived as far back as anyone could remember. These rocks had neither moved nor broken despite the best attempts of the seas. Day after day the seas would at best rub against them and at worst, pound them mercilessly. A successful lighthouse would be one that could merge in with these rocks, become part of them.

A circular, tapered structure, its design taken from the shape of the oak tree, the solid lower section rose from its foundation to over thirty feet in height, consisting of large hewn and smoothed pieces of the hard stone. These were keyed together and pinned with marble dowels. The lighthouse then rose to a height nearing one hundred feet up from this foundation of rocks and seas below.

This lighthouse was not going to be blown down in the winds that assaulted its circumference from all directions. Neither would it be broken up and washed away from the lashings it took from the tons of heavy storm water that crashed against it. These were seas that could send waves and water crashing high near her peak and send heavy sprays of water over her lantern.

Nor would it succumb to nature's last resort to end man's invasion of this reef, fire. The last wooden lighthouse had stood robustly for fifty years but in the end caught fire. The Keeper escaped to the rocks and it was a Cawsand man who saw the fire and sent help to collect the survivors. The story had travelled down with the succession of Keepers and their families. It had formed an affection with them for the people of the villages.

Nothing, nay nothing, short of the divine intervention of the Almighty, was going to see this light extinguished on the mariners of the English Channel. Mariners who relied on this beacon to warn them of the treacherous rocks on which she rested and that lay around her.

"When the second lighthouse to stand here burnt down, a piece of molten lead from the roof went down the throat of one of the lighthouse men. He died of it in the end but seemed alright for a while. Didn't kill him right away, not for days. What a thing, to swallow molten lead. Right down the hatch it went without stopping. Then carries on as normal for a while, until..... until that is, he started urging and retching. Then, finally he goes, in agonies of pain. Nothing anyone could do for him my Grandfather said. Just had to watch him. Couldn't even take a good strong bottle of brandy to take the pain away. Couldn't hold it down he couldn't."

"That's a tall one Hannibal, expect us to believe that? You'd die of it right away if that went down in to your guts. Go on with you with that one. You've been swallowing too much of that salt water. Turning you mazed."

"It's true. My grandfather said no one believed the Keeper at the time but when he died, they found it inside him. The doctor, he said, not able to satisfy folk it was true, wanted to prove a man could live for a good while after swallowing molten lead. He tried to prove it by putting molten lead down the throats of different animals. Dogs, cats, chickens. You name the animal, he tried to put some down it."

"Go on, did any live?"

"Never mind all that now. Keep your eyes skinned. That boat we thought was a cutter is still out there. I don't suppose it can make out much of us in this light, if anything, but I'll wager it's been keeping an eye best it can at a distance. I reckon it knows us for some reason. It's waiting, waiting for something."

Maybe it's the boy's boat he's eying?"

"If it is, it will be faster than this old tub, maybe faster than that boat the boy's in with a full load like he's got. I say let's offload what we have out here somewhere off the reef. The boys can get it a little bit later on. We will be lighter to take on a chase and help the boy then if we must. Better to be ready. We could ask the Keeper to keep an eye on it for us, maybe take some in if that boat stays out of sight a while. Take it while its dark?

It'll lighten us up and if searched we have nothing here."

"Trouble is with the Keepers these days is they've all got sleepy now that set up, Trinity House, is taking them under its wing more and more. Get a pension some do."

"They still like a little something to keep them warm ... especially out on this one. Stuck out here, sometimes week after week, without a soul to talk to if the weather's bad and he's on his own. No wife, children out there or helper. Bit of silver to help that pension would go down well. They've all been bribed. That's what's worrying them. Losing that bloody pension."

Father had been to see the lighthouse keeper to sound him out about help for the trade here and there. Turn a blind eye even. That's worth something. Got to be careful, now it's part of Trinity they all think they are better than they were. Some of them are known to be in league with the Preventatives now even. What do you make of that?"

Storage at the lighthouse or sinking tubs at the reef was a last resort. It was far from being a suitable location due to the savage weather that could quickly arise. There was also the distance, the double handling, poor accessibility and so the list went on.

But there were moments when needs must and some help from the Keepers was a safer option than running the goods in to shore or sinking them closer in. The old Keepers had been a different breed to some of the ones that were starting to come through with the new service. Usually fishermen and sometimes former smugglers, they often worked for wealthy families who leased the rocks, built a lighthouse and took tolls from passing ships. The lease of the rocks off shore gave them this right to tolls. Some of these wealthy families were known to have made the money to lease the rocks from the smuggling trade. The Killigrews were just one further down in Cornwall that everyone in the trade knew of.

Nine miles offshore from Rame Head, often providing not only a home for the Keepers but helpers, wives and children.

The present Keeper had it a bit easier than his forebearer Keepers. Now fitted with reflectors and lit by oil, those who held the job before him would need to light and change twenty-four large tallow candles. It was a better light now, more reliable, more intense, more visible for the ships that relied on it to keep them safe from the Eddystone rocks.

To keep the Keeper on their side the odd tub had been passed to him when a Marks boat had been passing and the conditions were suitable. It was always awkward manoeuvring the boat in close enough to the lighthouse or taking in a smaller shallower draft boat. Boats could tie up on the ring that was at the edge near the Lighthouse steps that meandered around to a door, high up and away from the biggest of tides. There were also iron rungs set into its side.

Some said there were ninety-two steps to get up to the door and others ninety-four. It depended on who you spoke to and how they counted the first and last steps. Both were right, and both were wrong. There were less if they went up the treacherous, vertical, iron steps.

Pulling up a string of tubs using the gantry and its pulleys was sometimes the easiest way of getting provisions up into the body of the lighthouse when there were small numbers of helpers or a storm was brewing and the boats wanted to return to safer waters rather than delay and face a gruelling, dangerous, return journey of in between nine and twelve miles rowing or sailing.

The keeper had some stow away area but not much. The area at the bottom underneath the main living areas was used as a store. This was safe enough and a good deal of stock could be successfully covered over there. The Preventatives would rarely go there due to the difficulties with landing and the need for good weather conditions.

The Joe Marie's rowing boat was dropped down and paddled the short distance towards the lighthouse.

"Joe Spriddle? Joe? Come on, speak, won't you? I'd recognise that shape anywhere. You ugly bugger. What business have you got out here on the stone? At this time of night as well, when most folks are turned in."

"I've got a full load, Jamie and I don't know. Got a funny feeling about it tonight. I don't want to risk taking it in. I want to lighten the boat up. Can you take care of a load for a day or two perhaps?"

"How do you think I can take a boat load the size of that Joe? Can't you sink some nearby? How long will it take you to get it in here? I don't want to chance much these days. Don't want you hanging around still unloading here at first light or be seen. How would I explain that? You tell me. How would I explain that, eh? Lose this and I lose my home. And my missus' home. And my little ones. And ... well everything. You'd see me end up on the parish, worse ... worse you would. Anyhow, what's it worth to do it? Come on Joe, what's it worth? Jamie here, the Keeper, what'll be in his pay packet? What's for the Keeper Joe?"

Jamie, the lighthouse Keeper was a man in his thirties, but looked older than his years. The exposure to sun and salt had given him a leather like appearance. Hands were tough like the soles of his shoes. Callous after callous had formed making his skin thicker than most. He was able to withstand the ropes burning his skin, as he gripped and hauled on them, tied them, untied them, over and over again. He had managed to keep his hands intact. No lost fingers.

Not a tall man, he was though wide, very wide, packed tightly with muscle and brawn that tried, without success, to burst free from the skin that kept it locked in and taut. Outwardly, this made Jamie a shapely, well-muscled, individual, one that carried little surplus weight.

This was beneficial to him in his job as Keeper, providing him with a strength, held taut within an outer frame, capable of negotiating the narrow, keystone staircasing that took him floor to floor in the lighthouse. Walking the almost vertical steps that wound their way up and down the lighthouse, joining each of his rooms, almost vertical, often carrying heavy weights, had given him an uncommon strength in his legs with muscles standing proud and shapely.

His mind was as steely strong as his body. It took a rare breed of resilience to live in this isolation, sometimes cut off from land and other human contact for weeks in the winter.

"You know how it is Joe. I've got a good job here, somewhere to live for me and the family. A pension ....

"Oh, come on Jamie. How about a cut for you? And as many tubs as you want for yourself. Bill too. Is he here as well? How about some nice French cloth for your good lady on the next run as well? They'll not come here. A bit in with you and a bit off the rocks, maybe. Just take them all in if it cuts up really rough?"

"Bill's not here. It's just me. Maria and the youngsters went ashore for a few days. They are all back tomorrow on the supply boat."

"Well then Jamie. It's only us that'll know about this. Have they ever gone down into that bear pit of yours?"

“That stinking hole! No! We just keep the oil and other stuff down there. The Customs don’t go there if they come here for a warm up and glass of spirit.”
“I’ve got a good crew here. They’ll off load it all, get it up into that store nicely covered, hidden and put to bed in no time.”

“I saw quite a few of the Preventative boats out here Joe in the last couple of days. Not just the one you’d expect but three spread out as if they were working the seas like a navy fleet. Making messages with flags to each other they were. I could see them up high up there, up by the lantern like no other. As if they were expecting something.
Never come here. Usually just shout up, ask if everything is well and if anything is needed.
Have been known to bring things out here and there but never do searches.
They think we’re one of them these days, now Trinity are running so much.”

“We thought we saw one tailing us from afar Jamie. Won’t see us now it’s dark.”

“I thought I saw the shape of one just now. Saw it from the top. You can see much further from up there. Just hanging around it was. Unless they know about something. Have some information.”

"Come on Jamie. Will you do it. Lighten us up. Go on. We haven't much time. Light will be on us before we know where we are."

"Bring it in you buggers. Bring the bloody lot in if you can. Better pay well. Some tonight, some when you collect. You'd better collect it soon or it'll be out that lighthouse opening into the next heavy sea. Less a few for me. So, you had better get it in soon Joe Spriddle. Hear me, get it in soon or into the briny it goes. Let it wash up anywhere on the seven seas, anywhere. Do you hear me? Not again Joe. Not again, I say."

With that, Joe returned to the Joe Marie. The men were quick about their task and they were again gone.

The Friends with the boy Hannibal and his crew were further ahead of the Joe Marie. A faster boat, they were now preparing the cargo of contraband on deck ready to unload at Looe Island. They had paused as they saw the Joe Marie stall near the lighthouse, unsure of what they were doing there.

Not too far off, Hannibal decided to head back to the Lighthouse. Had something gone wrong? Did they need help? They didn't want to lose time, but his father and mother were on board and they too had been conscious of the unconfirmed, occasional sighting of the Customs cutter on the horizon He was not going to see any risks taken with their safe passage homeward.

“Here she comes. She’s sitting higher in the water. She’s got rid of her load. Come on let’s turn and head to the Island. She is following us again now. We’ll find out what went on later.”

They could see the outline of the cutter in the distance again and it looked as if it were making a course towards them.

“Look there’s another on the other side. I’m sure of it. What are the two doing?”

Eventually as the boats started to close in, their silhouettes were confirmed as revenue boats.

They made their decision to make a run for it.

“Don’t cut the cargo free. Let’s not lose what we’ve worked for because of these thieving buggers. We can outrun them. Joe and father will sort theirs out later I am sure. They probably won’t interfere with them. Their boat looks French, is French and is a bit of a tub for a Smuggler. It’ll be us they’re after.”

“Look there’s the second cutter. What in Davy’s name is that doing out here?” The Joe Marie, now a lighter, more responsive boat to sail, was heading straight towards the boy’s boat. Although still a way off they were gaining now on the Friends.

Joe and Hannibal the elder had hoped they would see them and follow them. They had strung some remaining tubs, that they had not offloaded at the Lighthouse, along their side in attempt to divert their attention and provoke them away from the boy's boat. As they neared, they would see them through the dark.

One of the boats changed course making towards them. "Now the other one. Come on." The other one stayed the course to follow Boy Hannibal's boat. They could see she was gaining on it.

Hannibal 2nd was beginning to get concerned for his son. "It's no good Joe, unless he gets rid of those ankers quickly he isn't going to lose enough weight and gain enough time to get away. We'll have to follow him and get ready for some troubles."

"But that'll take the second boat to him as well."

"Whatever we do is wrong now Joe. We might get in the way, slow them up a bit. Give him a chance. Difficult with two of the buggers though. Look, is that the outline of another of them, way off. Not three! What's going on. I didn't think they had that many here? Here, at night, three of them?"

"Wish he'd get rid of those ankers."

"Maybe he has."

"No, I can see the way the boat is working. It's working hard to gain the ground they need."

The chase went west, past Looe Island in the distance and towards the seas off Mevagissey.

"What in the name of the Almighty is that?"

A loud boom had shattered the relative quiet of the open expanses. "That cutter's taken their main mast. She's taken a shot in the dark. They don't do that. "

"Pray no one has been hurt from that fallen top section."
"Head down and prepare our arms." As they approached, they could hear a further boom, then another and another. They were attacking the boy's boat. The shot had missed but the damage done. As they neared, the boat was coming along them.

On board the boy and crew were at the ready and some shots were fired across the bows of the Preventative boat as it came nearby and into better view. The fire had ripped into the sail-cloth, shredding much of it and raining firepower everywhere they could. They would take the Preventative men now if they could.

The mast came down under the strain with a loud crack. Making the boat lurch to the lee side and gulping down some seawater before it righted itself. The boats were now stricken. The others they had spotted were on their way to join the scene.

Suddenly Hannibal 3rd saw the bow of the Joe Marie, coming right across to his. He was going to ram the Preventative boat, the first to confront them? Why? Without warning, the Joe Marie moved hard away and turned in against the Revenue cutter. The heavy, tough, resilient, beamy, Joe Marie. This tough, gnarled old girl of the sea would go down fighting if she had to.

She was capable of battering and ramming vessels much larger than herself, inflicting much damage if she struck them at their weakest point.

The Joe Marie had been adapted, when Joe acquired her, to take a figurehead placed proud of the bow. Fixed well back into the boat structure, this not only served as a symbol of recognition with the trades folk as she arrived in French ports, but as a battering ram against unwelcome intruders and invaders on the seas. For this figurehead was designed and fixed to stand out proud of the vessel's vertical bow line. The rest of her, bulky, weighty, was able to take the additional bow weight without the additional spars and sails.

The figurehead was at Joe's request. Bearing the symbol of Marie's family, combined with the Cornish fifteen bezants and Breton symbol of a black tipped tail. The black tipped tail against the pure white paint represented ermine, a fur, taken from the white winter fur of the stoat.

The bow of the craft gleamed with pride. This was the Joe Marie, the vessel that enshrined the union and love forged between Joseph Spriddle of Cawsand, Cornwall and Marie Antoinette of Morlaix, Brittany. The Celtic spirit of adventure, trade and love was celebrated in this figurehead. The figurehead tapered at its furthermost point giving it the appearance, at a distance, of a javelin.

Without a bow sprit and sail, it was this figurehead that now stood proud of the boat at its bow end. It faced the oncoming seas eye to eye daring them to do their worst.

Both the Cornish smugglers and the Breton traders were at first bemused with the figurehead. Normally seen on those ships of the high seas, the Joe Marie did not fit into this category of vessel.

Joe's rise to influence and wealth was sudden, abrupt and without time for him to ease into it. The Joe Marie was his pride. Now it had a job to do.

The Breton symbolism was still used in a guarded fashion by Marie's family. They had been close to the Dukes of Breton but had seen their power decline for centuries, only to be decimated from its former glory in the 1790's, following the French revolution.

It seemed odd that this symbol, used so sparingly, not overtly, for fear of provoking attack on the family by the French departments, should find its way onto a vessel used in furtherance of smuggling.

But this was a prodigal ship, befitting a prodigal daughter and her prodigal husband. Here it was, mid seas, with all that symbolised the lands of Cornwall and Brittany, those pioneers of the free trading spirit. They were, together, launching a head on attack against a Preventative boat. A boat, with a Captain and crew that sought to stop this freedom. They were, though, doing so against all odds of success. The crack of wood on wood, the splitting of the planking to the side, surprised, indeed shocked, all on the revenue boat. It threw the Captain and crew almost completely off their guard. It happened quickly and unexpectedly. They were unprepared. This sort of attack in this area was without precedent. They were certain now that this was a Smuggler, French boat or not.

The other Preventative boat was gaining ground. It must have seen what had happened, or had it? Hannibal 3rd knew it was time to leave his boat. With great reluctance and despair, the decision was taken to abandon her. In the ensuing mayhem he and the crew all managed to get to the Joe Marie. Dragged up on decks they were exhausted. The Joe Marie sat, almost becalmed, in between what were now two Revenue boats at the scene.

The crew on the stricken Preventative boat lay on the deck as gunfire continued to ricochet all around them. Their lives were spared, including those of Williams and Foot, who were present on one of the boats once again. The intense gunfire kept them held down, preventing them from returning it.

The Joe Marie had given itself the advantage of surprise and she quickly prepared to leave under the protection of the continuing gun fire. As they left, the other boat, the undamaged Revenue cutter, was watched closely. Its Captain and crew were for now keeping themselves below deck.

They had realised the Smuggler was to some extent armed. They also knew that these were men that held few scruples that prevented them from using their firepower to kill if they saw no other way out of a predicament. The boat was French, or so it seemed. The other boat had no markings to identify it. Was this part of a small flotilla of boats connected with a smuggling run? Might more arrive at this scene soon?

The Customs boat waited until the Joe Marie was out of sight and out of firing range. They would not follow them for now but would go to the stricken vessels. The Smuggler and the Customs boat had moved closer together, damaged and clinging together. Although unlikely bedfellows, they resembled war injured, holding on for dear life to each other, not caring which side of the conflict they were on.

As the Joe Marie parted company with the revenue boats, leaving the carnage behind, they felt more confident to head back under cover of the low light of night time that remained. They would take Hannibal and Sarah to Looe Island, rather than to return to France. It was uncertain who had been seen on the Friends or the Joe Marie. Back at the scene, the Preventative officers felt the most likely occupants were the boy Hannibal and his crew.

Pulling into Looe Island, what kegs remained on the Joe Marie were unloaded, and they prepared to sail off again. Hannibal and his wife waved them off and went with Fyn and Joan to a safe place to stay on the Island until it was worked through what should happen next.

Fyn and Joan had got to know Looe Island well since arriving from the Mewstone. Save an inch by inch search of the Island they could give the couple safe sanctuary.

* * *

The Joe Marie, now lightened, was ploughing her way through the waves with Hannibal 3rd, making better speed than she had.

"It's no good Joe, I have to return to see Susannah and the little Hannibal."

“You can take a boat from Roscoff when we know what has happened back there. Did anyone die? Was anyone seen that could be identified? We can then work out the best way to get you back and when.”

“No, it has to be now. I can’t wait. Who knows, the next few nights may be my last. I need to return. The Bay Boys will hide me well until we know. I shall leave you at Rame Head and make my way back from there.

“This is dangerous Hannibal. We don’t know what is going on, what alarms have been sent out. Who is now patrolling the coast? Nothing. We know nothing. We need to wait and get you back to France.”

“They won’t be expecting anything tonight other than whoever was on Friends to be well gone and most likely with the French boat they saw.”

“Alright but make swift. We can’t wait.”

"I’ll take my chances, swim in and go from there. They won’t see me, and you’ll be well away time they raise the alarm. That’s if they are there and if they suspect.”

“We’ll head in, but you watch yourself Hannibal Marks. Remember I will have your father to answer to over this if anything happens to you.” With that the Joe Marie tacked around and they headed back shorewards, Rame Head in their sight.

The Joe Marie had barely stopped when Hannibal slipped over the side and swam in to the shore. He knew the place he would go to. It wasn’t far, but the currents ran strong there. Unnoticed, he clambered onto the rocky face in the lee of Rame where he knew the path and steps, up the almost vertical section of face and then onto Rame and back to the villages. He stole down through the paths, fields and hedgerows until he was home again.

Entering through the rear access which was up a small bank, into the courtyard area he was relieved to shed his wet clothing and grab fresh that was waiting just inside. Gently and quietly he went first into his boy's room. The troubles he knew might yet face him, melted from his mind.

He soothed and calmed his son's murmuring and gurgles with softly whispered words. As a slight cry came from him, he took the babe, cradled him. He wanted him to always have his touch, his smell, his presence, his all. He would remember these, his father's features, for ever.

Placing the babe back with the tenderness at least the equal of his mother he gently stroked his forehead, rocking the cradle into which he had been placed. The cradle had been made especially for him by his father, part of whose early training had been in the craft of boatbuilding. In the shape of a boat, the cradle defined his future. He was rocked as gently as the waves could rock him on a peaceful day in the bay of his birth.

Satisfied that the babe had fallen into a deeper slumber he turned to go into the bedroom he shared with his wife. "Shhh .... Shhh," he whispered softly in her ear, to stir, but not alarm her. Susannah stirred. She had slept lightly since the babe had been born. This night was no exception.

Through the blur of sleep, which in these dangerous times sat uncomfortably between this world and the next, she opened her eyes, picking out the face of her husband. He saw her eyes move and in response held up his forefinger, pressing it tightly against his lips. He was beckoning her not to be alarmed, not to make a noise. As she rose up the bed, a smile breaking widely across her face, he parted the bedclothes and she waited for him, welcoming him to come further.

No words needed to be spoken, as Hannibal slowly, quietly undressed placing his clothes over the chair that sat in the corner. He was no longer dripping with a mixture of sea and sweat. The heat of his skin evaporated the last sheen of the moisture that ran across his back. It produced the odd bead of liquid that travelled to the central valley of his back falling swiftly downwards. It followed, almost with plumb line accuracy, a line vertically down and down to his coccyx laying pronounced at the bottom his spine.

She sunk her fingers into the sides of his back with her fingers, the nails of her four fingers digging into his spine following its uppermost inches down to its base where she took hold of each of his buttocks, squeezing hard as she felt him ease his way into her. Rising and falling with a quiet grace that was to maintain a rhythm which they fell into together she could feel herself losing control.

Together they went into a place that was theirs and theirs alone. He savoured the moment knowing it would unlikely be repeated for some time.

"What are you doing back here now? Did Ma and Da get back alright. Did the run go to plan?"

"Not quite, but hush now we'll speak on it more in the morning after some sleep. I will need to hide for a few days below. You will need to be my ears and eyes to find out what is happening. We may have prices on our heads. We need to know. I will need to know. It will decide everything."

She could not sleep with half a story left to tell. She rose to question him further. As the truth outed about the events, Susannah could not rest.

"Come. There is no time to spare. You cannot stay here like this. If they know it was you, this will be one of the first places they will come.

They will know the Friends has a connection with Marks. They will know your father has not been here for a while, maybe dead. Who else might have been on that boat? Ask yourself. Ask yourself, Hannibal."

With that she rose and implored him to talk softly with her about the choices and which should be taken now, without delay, for the sake of her and their son.

"If this is bad and they have seen that you were one on board they will come and tear our houses and cellars down to try and find you, especially if one of theirs has been killed.

Let's find another place for you, just for now, where they would not think of going to." With that the mists in her mind that had been created from a wave of panic, cleared like the rising curtain of a stage. She could with a clarity, see the options and odds laid out before her. Sharing these with her exhausted husband, she would not allow him to slumber.

"There is no time for sleep, slumber or rest of any kind. This is not the time to slow. You are my husband and next door is our babe, our first born. He will be grown with his father. You will teach him and nurture him. Nay he will be in your image. Come we will prepare for the worst."

With that Hannibal got his second wind and the pair plotted his movements for the next days.

"They will not do anything to Glinn's. They never do. We have seen, we have noticed."

"Whatever it is going on, you must go there, ask for help. We know he has places around, under and over the bakehouse that are never disturbed. Glinn is alone there now. The bakehouse tunnels also lead up in behind the chimneys of the houses further over Cawsand and join into the larger ones. Airless and hot they become ……… and dark. They won't want to delay there nor go further in than they have to."

"Glinn's it is. I will go the back of it now before all awake and see if I can quietly disturb him."

Glinn was up in the room on the first-floor level. Warm and comforted from the chimney of the bakehouse fire he remained fast asleep. Hannibal crept in and stirring him held his hand over his mouth until he could identify him. He and Glinn poured a glass of strong spirit and spoke. Hannibal had to tell Glinn of the events and why he wanted cover.

"You have profited well from us. If you want to continue, I will need you to do this for me." Glinn knew the Preventatives were unlikely to search the bakehouse. There was an agreement with the Surveyor, and they had kept to it, as he had, well, at least to an extent, sufficiently so to keep them happy with the arrangement.

They understood there was no love lost on Glinn's part for the smugglers after the death of his cousin. He knew he had to provide some information to keep them off the scent but could not share more detail with the young Hannibal, even now.

He did owe the Marks. Were it not this man's father who had kept his word, to this day? If he had done otherwise matters may not have turned out as well as they had.

Glinn was resolved to help. He would hide him in the tunnels and chambers beneath. He would, with haste, see the Surveyor with some more information that would keep favour. This would avoid suspicion. He would need to know more from Hannibal. Give something that would keep them off him and his hides.

He could not disclose much of his dealings with the Surveyor to this Hannibal, but he could ask him for some information that he could pass on to throw them off the scent of the bakehouse. Give them something to occupy them, something that would divert their attention.

For now, though, the priority was to conceal Hannibal, ensuring that no suspicion lay at the door of the mint. They had never searched it whilst his arrangement with the Surveyor was running. He didn't want them to start thinking of it now.

Some titbits for the Surveyor were needed. They were needed now. They had to be good. Hannibal gave the location of some of the equipment used by the Marks. Colourings for spirits too, in large tubs. They chose the hides that were in any case the most vulnerable. Those that had not previously been uncovered. That would interest them. No old ground. Something new. Something they would not have expected. The information must lead to a good haul. It must retain their faith in the arrangement with Glinn.

As morning broke, the baker went around the villages to see what he might find out. Notices were being nailed up offering reward for information leading to the identification, arrest and successful bringing before the Justices of those on a boat named as the Friends who were responsible for shooting at the Preventative boat, her Captain and crew, causing serious damage.

Descriptions were too loose to identify Hannibal precisely and the naming of the boat did not necessarily lead back to him.

On his return the enormity of the situation descended on the young Hannibal

"I must go until memory of this has weakened. I will need money and quick. Cash is the best. A mixture of note and coin. I may need to pay some people and have enough to set up. It may not be Roscoff.

What cash have we at the mint that has been paid for?"

"There is about £5,000 in coin and £8,000 in notes."

"That will be enough, but notes would be light to travel with. Can we do more, much more, for tomorrow. I dare not leave it longer."

"If it is to be that soon I will have to use others as well as myself to do the copying. I go to the prison ships where I know people if we need more notes in a hurry. I will row out today and get the signal to them that we will buy as much as they have and can make. The Temeraire hulk has the best on board. I have given them stocks of paper, inks and all else they need for when we require more in a hurry."

The Temeraire was, in origin, a second-rate ship of the line, well equipped, she had ninety-eight guns spread along her one hundred and eight-foot-long gun deck. Now all taken off, her fine rigging gone as well, she was a comparatively forlorn looking specimen. One of several ships lining the river Tamar near the Hamoaze, she was alongside other temporary prison ships. These were used mainly to house the prisoners of war that had been taken in the wars with France and Spain. She had only seen one real fleet action in war when she was part of the Channel fleet. At Trafalgar she came to the support of the Victory when Nelson was escorting two French fighter ships back to England. When they arrived, they would be plundered, refitted and re-used. Coming into Plymouth she was met with thousands of townsfolk wishing her good speed. Everyone had heard of Temeraire after Trafalgar.

"I will go now." Glinn headed to the modest and quiet harbour just up river from Cremyll where his small boat was kept, conveniently, almost opposite the berthing of the hulks. He would go by the Temeraire and round her once to indicate a purchase was needed and then around the other way to indicate how much and then the other way again for the night he would be coming, starting from tonight. A familiar face appeared at the usual place. The hand signal was given to accept. This was a big order and with little time. They must have stocks to have taken it.

He would return the following night and be positioned as usual at the end of the main cable and wait for the signal. He would then prepare his bag in exchange for theirs.

The Temeraire was just one of many hulks now holding prisoners of war, some of whom had become expert in the art of forging the notes, especially some of the newer notes. They needed the equipment but that was all. He could get a deal for twenty to one, sometimes. They wanted coin usually, but would accept real, genuine notes. The Tremeraire really did have the best forgers on board and were costlier than some for the notes, but the Marks always wanted the best available. When Glinn could not come up with the quantity needed he had to buy on the local open market. The marketplace of the hulks.

Glinn was always cautious, never over confident. It might only take one false move, one error of judgement or suspicion lying on him and this business could be brought to an abrupt end ... an end, at the end of a rope.

He was always a bit unsure of how far the Surveyor's powers would stretch to protect him and for that matter how far his good will could be stretched. This relationship had not yet been put to the test. What might he do if he suspected Glinn had been only part true to his word?

The night came, and the transaction was, as usual, successfully completed. Bags were exchanged by sliding them up and down the rope. A smaller rope went around the main cable tied to a thin but strong line that would be coiled at the top and lowered and then hauled up again when the bag was fixed the other end. Trust was paramount as there was no time to risk the checking of the coin and note on the spot for their authenticity, quality, nor indeed, the quantity supplied .

Chapter 34

Bodmin Gaol

"This is too risky my love. Too risky. Say goodbye to us now. We will see you before long." As she said these words, her muscles tensed. She felt a vice like grip inside her chest. Her intuition was telling her that he could not stay anywhere in the area now. He might not still take this decision. She had to re-enforce it, make it for him if needs be.

He was a hunted man. This time the risk was just too great.

"I will get word to you that I am well and return when the time is right. Mother and father will come as soon as the heat is off. They are getting old for this. Few would suspect him now of any active part in the running of the boats."

Their hard grip on each other sent messages of both desperation and comfort. Messages that they had no true will to let each other go. Fortified, despite his sadness, Hannibal prepared for his journey. He had changed his plans last minute, telling Glinn one thing and planning another. The fewer that knew anything about his movements from here on the better He had not even told his wife for fear she would be placed under any duress.

As he approached the stables at Rame Farm he could see some activity. As he drew nearer, taking cover on the side of the stable, he saw the boys preparing the horses. He would take his chance.

"Hannibal. What are you doing here? They have been everywhere for you. They want to talk to you alright."

"I have to go now. Get away from here."

"Where do you plan to go from? There is a boat heading back tonight, why not go with it. She's being unloaded now from inside Rame Head, the steep side to the East. You know the way in the dark. You could be there if you hurry. Be gone now before it is too late."

It was not the escape he had planned. He was expecting the area to be flooded with the Preventatives and all other forces they could muster. He made a split-second decision to leave this way. His original plan was to get to the north coast and travel by sea from there, maybe to Roscoff via Ireland. He would stop at Jamaica Inn on the way. That would be a safe house for a night or two. He was less well known in those parts. Fewer there would know of the incident and the price on his head. Travelling alone by land was, though, very risky for other reasons. He had money with him. A lot of money. One risk over the next few hours by boat with those he knew and trusted was all it would take to get to safety. Safe for the time being until things had died down and memories faded. No one had died. He would have heard. The damage to the Revenue boats would be repaired or they would be replaced. Memory of this would fade and it would be less likely anything could be proven against him.

He left and got to the path leading sharply down to the beach. This beach was only exposed at low water The Smuggler was offshore surrounded by the unloading boats that were going to and fro the beach. As he neared, he felt a hand grab him. It held his mouth tightly. Who was this?

"And who might you be?" As his head turned into some light he was immediately recognised.

"I need to get away now Jim."

"It was you! I thought so. You were something to do with that incident with the two Preventative boats?"

"That's for me to know Jim but I must go and go now."

"Go then, the boats are there, and we have watchers out."

Hannibal clambered into one of the boats as it was leaving the shore to get to the smuggler.

"What's that?"

Their eyes followed the trail of smoke best they could They needed to see its source. Where was the warning fire? There it was. In the fields further over to the east of them, below where the Church at Rame stood.

The crack of gunshot went through the still night, echoing repeatedly around the partly enclosed area they were in. The rock face, almost sheer, towered above them. This led up to the track that went to the small chapel on the top of the Rame Head on one side and inland towards the farms and Church on the other.

"Pull the boat back and take cover. There must be a lot of them or the boys would have seen to them. They must have gone past the boys, and not seen them, to have had a chance to light the fires."

With that the boats were hauled into the rock crevices behind the beach. The smugglers scrambled into the recesses and small caves. They waited. The Smuggler must have been seen. It was unlikely that the Preventatives would clamber down the dangerous paths, should they know where to find them.

They were exposed here. Maybe they should swim for it? Get further down. Chances where they wouldn't be seen in the water especially if they went in different directions and then would have to sit it out until next day.

The Smuggler was leaving part unloaded but had little choice. The boys that were stationed at the top waiting may be gone by now. They would think that those on the beach would sit it out down there rather than try to get back up the cliff. Suddenly they heard a cry. What was it? Had one of theirs been caught, injured perhaps? Or had the smugglers got one of them. The officers could be on foot which would make it easier for them to be taken. That night there were about a dozen of the smugglers on the beach and the surrounding rocks with a further two dozen above on the cliff top. Those at the top had been ready to take the goods to safe places in and around Rame.

There would have to be a lot of officers, well-armed too, for them to think they could take on that number of smugglers. Chances were, it was the Preventatives that had come off the worse.

More cries and shouts from above followed. A shout filled the air. It was intended for those below.

"There's a pack of them! Too many!"

They recognised the voice as one of theirs.

"Let's go now while we can down here." With that some of the men took to the sea to get further away. They scattered into deeper coves where the sea would rush in almost filling them at the higher tides.

They could wait until the next day to make their way back if need be. Brave out the cold and wet of the sea rushing in. Dark, cold, dripping caves with water starting to rush around their feet, some would fill for an hour or two to waist height. If they went further back into some, they could clamber up onto rock that had been carved into flat areas above for storage and as an emergency hide away.

Tonight, it was used as the emergency hide. Getting back into these areas was treacherous as the tide rose. Well back into the caves through narrow areas, no light came here.

Hannibal decided that he would try to get further down, away from this beach. He could swim and strongly. He would swim around Rame Head and sleep near the Polhawn cellars. He would wait there and work out what to do when all was quiet.

As he went past the Queener Point, he got out onto the rocks and took the narrow steps and pathways to a small hut near the cellars. Starting to shiver now, he would have to try to dry off. Removing his clothes, he wrung them to take out the sea water. He had tied some of the lighter bags to his legs and brought them. The notes inside were wrapped to protect against damage from water. After a while, sheltered, but dangerously cold, he fell into a light, broken sleep, starting continually at every sound. He had some cover from the rags of old sails left there.

Morning came and with sun his clothes dried, alongside any wet notes. He would stay here, hoping he wouldn't be disturbed. He would take his chance at escape again, that night. As the sun bathed the rough walls of the hut he began to warm through, finally giving way to a much needed, deep sleep.

* * *

"Well, well, well. It's the young Hannibal Marks."

With a start, he awoke. Above him were armed Preventatives.

"We'll be taking you in Mr Marks. The Friends is to do with you."

Little could be done to resist. The men were armed and there were three of them.

"This is a lot of money for a fisherman to be walking around with. A lot of money."

With that, Hannibal was tied onto a long rope. When they reached the fields above, the rope was secured to one of the horses tethered there.

"You've got a long walk to Plymouth you can look forward to. They will decide what to do with you in there." As they neared the top of the path there were more of them. The area must be festooned with them. What was going on? They knew his name, his connection with the Friends. What more. Who else had been taken in?

He pulled at the ropes that held him like an animal on the way to the slaughter. Where were the other boys? To free him now would mean a major attack had to be made on these Preventative men. He could not now see how he would now be broken free from being taken in. When would father know about this? Where was he?

As they passed close by the farms, he glimpsed one of the Edwards boys who nodded to acknowledge he had been seen. There was little they would be able to do now but at least his wife and family would know soon what had happened.

Word did get back quickly that Hannibal had been caught. There was speculation over where he would be taken. Susannah was beside herself.

"What do they know? What is the charge? What will become of him? The baby is barely one year!"

Glinn heard the news too. He guessed the money, some fresh, would have been found with him. This, coupled with Glinn's failure to provide any advance information, could spell disastrous consequences for him.

These events confirmed the need to expedite his plans to get out of this business. He had put them on the table to the Surveyor. It was about time they were put into action. Glinns had boats in Turnchapel now. They had shares with the Skiltons in Drift, the pilot boat. He could use some of his money to buy shares and a house in Turnchapel. He had been quietly planning for this day. The time for waiting was over. He just needed to finally get out of the clutches of the Preventatives, smugglers too for that matter.

Ann Bath from Kingsand was marrying Henry Skilton from Turnchapel. Henry and the other Skiltons had well-built pilot boats. Glinn was friendly with the Baths. Ann was leaving to make her life with her new husband in Turnchapel. He would speak with them again about a move and investing in their ventures.

He still needed to cut the final chains the Surveyor held him in. He would also need to make a break from the smugglers although this would be less difficult. It was the Surveyor he needed to convince. How could he finally free himself?

He went over and over this, again and again. Whatever his choice, he had better see the Surveyor. Once more, once more only he hoped. Maybe if he said that information was drying up. Maybe if he said that he felt as though they were now more suspicious of him. That was it. Get in first to explain why nothing much had been divulged to him. Explain how he was sure that they were going elsewhere for the currency now, especially all the new notes the forgery of which he was less proficient with.

Yes, he could provide information on the forging activity in the hulks if he was getting out of the business. Besides they were only prisoners of war for the main-part. Another, hopefully final meeting with the Surveyor was needed and needed now.

***

"You have no real information for me?"

"No, Sir. I think they are getting their currency elsewhere now. I believe I know where."

"Oh, and where might that be?"

"The hulks Sir. I have been there when we can't make note quickly enough. They seem to get what they need to do the work. They do a good job."

"Well we could look at how we finish that little game. A Mint on a Hulk, eh!"

"Also, I am finding it difficult now with swollen hands to do this work as well as I used to, which may be causing them to go there instead of using me."

"What you mean you may not be able to do it?"

"Yes Sir. Look."

Glinn showed his gnarled hands. He did have something wrong with them but could still use them to good effect. They looked dysfunctional and impaired.

"Mmm. What damned use is a forger who has bad hands?"

With that he laughed, enquiring what he planned to do about it.

"It is probably time for me to consider giving it up, Sir. Either just do some baking or help on the pilot boats to earn my way."

"You have spoken of these plans before, but not your hands. Get out and do what you will. Never speak of our dealings or I will see to it that those words are your last. No need for hands then."

With that, Glinn hurriedly left to return. Feeling awkwardly dispensable, but relieved to be so, he would plan his departure now. The Surveyor clearly believed Glinn's increasingly poor dexterity had rendered him useless to the smugglers. He was now also useless to him. He would go to Turnchapel, ask the Glinns there about work on their boats and the boats they had shares in with the Skiltons. He had money to invest as well. He hoped to start again. There were several who would like to take on the Bakehouse who knew nothing about the mint and he was expecting no difficulty in transferring the bakehouse and its accommodation.

***

"What! He's where? Bodmin! In Plymouth being questioned? What has he been doing to get there? I thought he would be in Roscoff and doing some business by now."

"Now, Now, Hannibal. Let's hear what he has to say."

Fyn had been to the mainland, picked up news and was now telling Hannibal what he had heard. Hannibal and Sarah had decided to lay low there for a while. They would return by sea or land to the towns in due course. "Talk is he went back and got picked up in between Rame and Penlee in the hut there."

"What in God's name was he doing there?"

"They say he had come to take a boat back to Roscoff when they came. He couldn't get on the boat and took off to the hut."

"Where was the offloading?"

"Other side of Rame"

"So, is the Joe Marie safe?"

"The Joe Marie?"

"It wasn't the Joe Marie."

It dawned on him that his son must have left the Joe Marie, returned and was to re-join another boat that was unloading and making for Roscoff. The Joe Marie shouldn't have been unloading, she had been emptied before. Hadn't she? What was going on?

"There's notices everywhere they say wanting information about the Friends."

His father speculated that this was it. He had returned to see his wife and child. Then he had taken off again.

"Damned fool! He was meant to be going right back with the Joe Marie until we knew exactly what was going on and if there was any risk to any of us returning."

"There is no talk about anyone looking for you. It is all about the Friends and the crew."

"Well there's more than just him with a stake in The Friends. Anyway, what now? We need to know what he's charged with and make sure he is looked out for as best as possible until we know more and can work out what to do."

Sarah's face was ashen. "I knew this day would come. I knew this day would come with one of you."

Chapter 35

Plans to Free Hannibal 3rd

"Fyn, can you have me here until such time as it is right to return? I can make arrangements from here to see what we can do for the boy. Sarah, you must return and leave me to this. Go, see to the new Hannibal. Susannah will need all the help she can have now. They may be looking to question me. It is best I am not around. It is possible right now that they don't know if I am dead or alive. Whether I am still in France or have returned. Tell our most trusted where I am. Say that I will need help to do something for the boy. I will devise a plan in the next day or so to get him out."

With that, Sarah spent a restless last night on the Island. Both Hannibals in her life were now in jeopardy. Sarah returned to Cawsand the next day.

Fyn rowed her to the Three Doves, a Smuggler boat that would take her to the village after he had helped to unload her. Emptied and en route again to Roscoff, the Three Doves diverted safely to a short distance off the Coves near the Cellars east of Kingsand. Here, Sarah was carefully lowered onto the smallest boat kept on deck and taken to the little harbour hewn out of the red rocks of the area. A short walk from the towns she made her way back as the Smuggler continued on its journey.

***

"Where have you been? What has been going on? Have you heard any more about my Hannibal?"

A perplexed Susannah almost appealed to Sarah for comforting news. It suddenly dawned on Sarah that she was the head of things now. Her Hannibal was not here, neither was her son. She could not now show her weakness in this and how vulnerable and alone she really felt without him. Being alone this time was very different. One of her children was incarcerated with a charge hanging over his head, the detail of which they did not yet know. He was the main child involved in the business. It was he who had taken her husband's name. It was he who had been prepared to take over. Her husband was on a mission to help their son with risks the like of which they had never seen before. And then, there was a new arrival and his mother. One without a husband and the other without a father. Susannah felt she should go to her husband. But how could she get there and how would she be able to see him? One thing was certain, she could not comfort him from here? Yes, she needed to give him comfort whatever was to happen.

"He could face the gallows if things go wrong. And I .... I would not be able to be with him. To help him. To bring him solace."

She imploringly looked at her mother and mother in law. "How, how do I get to him? How can I be a wife to him when he needs me most of all?"

The two older women looked briefly at each other. This was not the first time they had faced the prospect that one day their men would not return home. Almost daily their husbands had gone to sea in the Smugglers, unloaded the boats, conducted risky business of one kind or another in furtherance of their well-being. Even as the enterprises grew the dangers were ever present. They were not above it like some of the investors were. They were both investors and the doers now. They had some of the best cuts of the meat but remained close to the knife when it fell. Smuggling had taken them, the towns and villages around too, out of the poverty they had known before, but would that previous, more menial, life of subsistence, day after day, be a better one than this?

"Come dear. Hannibal would not want you to fret like this. His father is on the Island now working, gathering support to find him, to free him. This talk must stay between us. We must be strong. Let him be free to work out help for his son. He will get word to us soon enough."

***

The Island had been a busy place.

"Well are you in or out on this. You are the most loyal and trusted of all our people. This is your brother and your cousin ... all of you here. His blood is your blood and your blood is his blood."

Addressing the faithful after they had shared everything they could about the gaol, Hannibal implored them to now help put a plan into action.

"He would do this for you. It is now that you must do this for him. If you can .... Well?"

"Ay, I'm in," was the call from the select group that Hannibal had mustered onto the Looe Island headquarters. First one, then another and then all.

"But this is going to be near on impossible. It's like a fortress down there in that damned new gaol."

"Come on what's wrong with you? We have bust down fortresses before, faced the tides, winds, storms. Bodmin gaol and its gaolers have never faced the likes of us when we are determined. We have beaten authority before. Time and time again we have done it. We can do it now. We have been against all the odds of wager. Told that our plans cannot succeed. We have made them succeed. That is what we are."

Sober faced, with a hearty meal in front them, tankards full of the best kept back by Fyn and Joan, they perused various maps of the gaol and its surrounds. These were amongst the most hardened of men, the most cunning of Cornwall. Brains and brawn were amongst the group in equal measure.

The map had come from the Polperro boys, through a message to Zephania from Hannibal. If anyone had knowledge of it, he would. If he didn't, he would soon obtain it.

There was a long night of debate, airing potential plans. They pooled their knowledge over and over. They brought smugglers before them who had been inside the gaol. They tapped their knowledge and memories. These former gaoled smugglers were brought to the Island blindfolded. They would have known they were in a boat and taken to dry land but that was it. They could have been anywhere.

"This will be impossible unless we can find and get to Hannibal, release him without attracting attention That is not the end but the beginning. He then has to be away to a safe house with perils all the way. We need a Trojan Horse."

"What's a Trojan horse?"

"We need to innocently get in there as if on normal business, with enough of us to deal with any situation that arises, pick our moment to get to him, then out of there .... fast."

"Sounds easy, but there will be turnkeys at every corner, other prisoners and workers. Where would he be, and how about all the keys? So many questions. How do we then get out and get him away to safety that night? Out of Cornwall. Out of England?"

"Well, I say we do it and it has to happen right away with no delay. No rest here until we find a way." They acted quickly. The next day all manner of folk from the area who had stayed in the gaol and survived it to get out again were brought to Hannibal. This time not just the smugglers. These were all sorts of people. Men, women, thieves, vagabonds. Well treated, but blindfolded they came. Kept apart, they were brought in to enquire of them what they knew, who they knew and how a person or few persons could get in and out as safely as possible. How might they blend in with the daily work of the prison.

These men, these dubious men, were not to leave the Island again until this was over. Fed, watered and kept comfortable in the secure areas in the caves where the stock was kept, any knowledge of what might be afoot had to stay on the Island apart from the trusted few.

"We've been painted a picture of the gaol. How we can get in, where things are, who stands where and does what where, so now what?"

"Even if we get in then we need keys. We need to leave without causing alarm if we can. We will need time to get away with Hannibal without interruption."

Hannibal asked Fyn for a boat small enough for him to handle alone to get him across to Polperro. As he entered the area outside the Polperro harbour, he pulled the boat up as quietly as he could. The tide was nearly full. He took the sweeps, leaving them further up in the hedge to collect on his return.

Clambering through the scrub and rock around the village, he emerged near Job's house. He could not alarm Job at this time. Creeping, stealth like, around the rear of the house to the room he knew Job would be in, he scratched lightly on the pane. Job started and came to the window, pistol in hand. Hannibal had grown a full beard in the last few weeks, but his features were quickly assimilated and recognised by Job, who promptly put his pistol away.

Opening the window to let in his friend, his accomplice from Cawsand, he turned, looked around to check all was clear.

"What are you doing here? Get in." Hannibal crawled through. "I have heard about the boy but there seems to be nothing on you, nor talk of the Joe Marie associated with you in any way. It looks as if the two have not been connected."

"I want to get the boy out of there, Zephania."

"And you're here to ask to see what I can do? Maps alone not good enough?"

"That place is a fortress."

"You can say that again. And there are few in the pocket like there used to be. I have arranged lawyers, got people in to see the condemned, arranged good food, drink as best as can, doctors too… but to get someone out… now that .. well that, Hannibal Marks is a different thing altogether."

"I want to get in with some of the boys, Zephania. Then walk out with him."

"Fat chance of that. If they were to move the boy, well then, then we might have a chance on the highway …. a slim one at that mind you …. but from the gaol?"

"Yes, from the gaol. I cannot leave him there. He's just had a son as well."

"I heard, also how you have set up in France, of course. Smart move. And Joe. Who would have thought it? Quite the businessman now and with assets. A fine woman behind him. Deceived us all she did! So, what is your plan?"

"Trojan Horse."

"Again!"

"Well. A few of us need to get in under some guise. Workers maybe? If we could get keys in advance, I could get them copied."

"But how do you think you will do this without the alarm being raised. You would never get to the main door before they were all there, rifles, pistols, the lot at the ready."

"We would have to fight our way out if need be and were hoping that outside there would be horses waiting."

"The only way is if you had a distraction outside or something that might make them clear the jail or would cause a great disruption and panic."

"Fire. Fire of course."

"What will catch fire in that God forsaken hole, Hannibal. The roof timbers or floor timbers, that's about all that can catch fire there."

"We take our own timber in."

"Or how about outside?"

"Well, if it could be done just outside, where it would threaten the inside of the jail, it might just create the distraction that's needed. You would need the keys. That map too. Memorise it as best you can. No fumbling, reading it wrong. No panic. Remember they will know that rabbit warren better than you. If you get in, if you get to him. If all these things inside go well. If, if, if.... if, if .... You still have to get out of there, best in one piece as well. Then you have to get him before you even have a chance of getting away. Risks all along the way, Hannibal. Risks all the way, I say. Could it do the boy more harm than good? And if you are caught.... Arson .. the gallows for you to be sure."

"I can't sit back Zephania. I just can't sit back."

"What do you want of me?"

"If we could get the keys we will need. Get them copied. I can probably arrange the copying and quick, so they are returned to their keeper before there is suspicion.

And .. to talk more with those who have been in there and got out. Most of ours are in the Navy or with the Lord now. We have spoken to a lot of folk who have been in there. But reliable folk and some stories are different."

"I might be able to do one better. We have one in our pocket ..... well a bit as it were. Yes, in our pocket ..... a little way down in our pocket in fact. He has let us come through. When we have, it isn't for long, mind. Not for long. You would need to make it longer. Much longer. Maybe you would need to give him a little draft of something? Make him sleep like a baby. Or you may need to make him sleep like a baby, forever. If we could get to him and find out the best time for you. ...Yes, the best time for you. Maybe distractions will not be needed on a grand scale. It would be the other turnkeys, the others working there. How could you get off and away? How about those on watch. May not be able to bribe them all. But once you're in and the boy's out, well, well, maybe, just maybe, mind you ... maybe you could get to the yard but then there are the others there."

"If there are others, do you think they could be got rid of from the outside?"

"That is where your disruption might come in. If you could get them all out to the gate? If you were behind, unseen ... or just un-noticed, just maybe it could be you that finishes them off first before they realise and come for you. But you are older now and your boy may be weaker. Maybe we should make sure he has the best food that can be arranged, get his spirits and strength up. Do the rest by bribing the turnkey we have in our pocket. Get them ready for this."

"Will you help, Zephania Job?"

"I may not have long to go. He has a long way to go. I will get to our turnkey. We need his keys, others as well if we can. Some money is needed for him. Perhaps enough for him to start again somewhere else?"

"Thank you, Zephania Job, my friend. I can get keys crafted back in Cawsand."

"You cannot stay here though. It is safest you return to the Island.. just in case I would say. Or you know the Mark family in Looe. Why not stay there for now? They have a hide there that has never been uncovered."

"I know the one. I'll to there now."

Job, ever the cautious, bade good bye to Hannibal and set to with his plans. He would, in the morning, send an envoy to the turnkey with a little money with the promise of more to come. Not too much, not too little.

"I will settle up with you as soon as I can get to send a draft or provide the cash."

"No need to do that now Hannibal. If you are determined to do this, let us see that you have the best chance that is possible to succeed even if that chance is small. Small indeed it is. But you and your father before you were always ready to take a chance. This might be the biggest ever though. The biggest ever, I say."

With that, a wry grin, fed by the anxiety in the atmosphere, Hannibal left as he came, heading through the dim streets and opes to the home of Mrs Mark.

Mrs Mark couldn't hear him to begin with. Hannibal resigned himself to sleeping in a gap behind the woodpile that rested in a heap on the cobbles at the rear. The pile had grown higher and higher as more wood came. It arrived at a rate that grew more quickly than it could be used. This was a mixture of timber cut from the woods above the village with that taken from the remnants of boats. Wreckage generally provided a weekly supply after whatever could be salvaged for other purposes had been taken.

He wasn't to be there long, as the sound of the odd falling log had awoken Mrs. Mark who rose and came out through the passageway of the cottage. Not sharp of sight in the dim, she stared out. As her vision became clearer, she could make out the shape of Hannibal Marks. "I know that figure of a man," she rasped in a whisper. "Come on out you, come and get inside here." Hannibal didn't need much of a prompt. He took himself inside where the shutters hid them from the shadows cast by the candle Mrs Mark lit. The remnants of yesterday's fire cast light on him from its glow. A slit in the shutters allowed light out and for a keen eye close up to the shutters, offered up the sight of Mrs Mark and Hannibal. Wary of this she closed the shutters even tighter, jamming them tightly in the shut position against a large stone that had been placed in front them for the purpose. They could not be seen nor heard now.

"News travelled fast about the boy. How he is he?"

"Not much news yet, but we're hoping there will be soon. It looks like Bodmin, but we don't know the charge."

"No one killed?"

"Not that we know."

"That's good. Only thing better is if you could have killed the lot of them. The whole bloody stinking lot of them. Worst might be five years of punishment now, or Australia. He would have a few friends out there."

Hannibal didn't see the lighter side that Mrs Mark was trying to bring in to the conversation, so he continued.

"He's only just had a son, Hannibal, who is about a year old."

"I did hear. How are they getting on?"

"Feeling helpless. Like I am."

The flame made shadows of the lines of Hannibal's face extenuating them. "I can't let that happen. I have got to at least try to get him out of there or off the charge."

"What do you think the charge might be?" Damage to the Customs Cutters, obstructing the Officers? If there's been a death ..... murder even?"

“You’re getting old to do all of this, Hannibal. You cannot do it alone and others may shirk at this when it cuts to the quick. If they’re caught, they will face the gallows too for it.”

“Our boys all take risks every night they go out as do yours. This will be a risk like all the others.”

“But in the boats, you have a chance. If anything goes wrong in Bodmin you’re like the rats caught on the rat-catcher’s pole. Just stuck and waiting to take your last breath. Now, go on with you. Down in the hide, you know where to go. It’ll still take you. Though looks as if you have fed on the fat of the land since I saw you last.”

A smile broke through at this and nodding he went down through the cupboard that led into the passageway, then onto the hideaway.

“We’ll let you know when it is completely safe to come out." With that he slipped into the dark, waited, slept and waited.

Knock, knock, knock knock, was heard. The knocks in sequence startled him and then they came again. Music to his ears though as It was the signal to go back into the area under the cupboard. “This has been brought for you. It must be back here tonight.” Hannibal took the small package and opened it. No letter with it came, just the contents. Heavy, blackened keys. These must be them.

“How had Job done it?” He maybe would never know. Job was in many ways secretive about his means and contacts. They often worked through third parties ensuring that Job was not directly implicated in anything that could bring down the empire he had created.

"Your boat's waiting to go. It's the fisher not far out from where your punt lies. Go now. The coast is clear but take the quiet way to it. You know how to get there. Tonight remember."

'Tonight, is the only message that came with the keys."

Hannibal shook off the cramps and pains he had endured stuck in the hide. He hurried to his boat. He saw the fisher not far out and headed to it. He knew most of the men on her. Helping him on board, they were gone.

Passing as swiftly as the craft could take them, on they went, to the south of the Island, Seaton, Downderry, Portwrinkle and were soon rounding Rame Head without interruptions. Hannibal once more took to the small punt and went into the soft sands of Widdey Cove, hugging the rocks to the side of Cawsand Bay as he went, unnoticed. Glinn was already up and preparing the fires. He was counting down the days. How many more fires? How many more jobs before he could in an orderly way simply leave here?

"Have a little smithying for you if you can?"

"What's all this?"

"Ask nothing. You have seen nothing and have done nothing. Maybe, just maybe, your last job?"

"You might have been best off to take this to the Blacky rather than me. This type of work …… it's been a while ….. I'm a bit rusty."

The jest was lost on Hannibal who could only concentrate on the job in hand at the moment. "Sorry for the jest. What's up with you? What are you doing here anyway? We haven't seen you for a while. Hear that boy of yours is in a spot of trouble."

"Best you haven't seen me. Quicker this one is done, quicker I am gone." With that, not a further word was spoken. Glinn would be glad to finish and be out of here. He owed Hannibal this one last job. He hadn't told anyone his plans but had simply started to make his arrangements for his move to Turnchapel and a new life.

* * *

"Perfect." Hannibal inspected the work on the keys, promised Glinn favour in return and left as he had come. The arrangement with the fisher was that it would return by noon for him and would leave without delay. He had thought of daring to see his wife and grandson. But no, he must concentrate on the job in hand and leave. He had to think of the boy, incarcerated in that Bodmin hellhole. That and only that. There was no room now for any other thoughts or emotions.

As the boat approached Polperro it was met, and the package taken. Job was as usual, one step ahead.

"Mr Job has asked us to land you a bit further up. We'll take you back to the Island after you have seen him."

They pulled up against the boat and Hannibal went with two of the boatmen. The Inn was too busy to take much note of the new arrivals, all of whom went into an upstairs small room. Job welcomed his friend and they sat as the other men left.

"The keys are on their way back now. Did you get copies of all of them?"

"It is done, but which opens which?"

"You had the master keys that will give you ease of entry throughout the gaol. You will need to work them out at the time when you face a door. Now. When will you do this and how? I hear that there is going to be a hanging in a few days. The gaol will go quieter than usual. The Governor and many of his workers will want to be there as the nooses are being tightened. The town will be very busy. All Inns will be fully occupied. There will be a fairground set up too with all the frivolity that brings. Noise, Hannibal. Noise and more noise. Noise is what you will want. Provided the hanging is at noon or thereabouts, as usual, jollity and breaches of the peace will most likely occur, busying the gaol afterwards by a few hours. There will be a chance, a small chance, for you and your boys to get in. A chance for you to get to the cell where he is while most are occupied with the hanging. A chance before the gaol fills with those who have allowed the jollity of the event to cloud their thinking and good judgement. Chance, chance and more chance. You need a lot of good cards in your hand for this Hannibal."

"When is the hanging day?"

"It has already been announced to give the town time to get ready. A hanging always attracts a good crowd. A very good crowd. Very good for the business of Bodmin."

"How will the boy know we are coming and be prepared?"

"I don't think we can risk a message to him about it. Things can be tough in there and some folk become quite mad. You don't know if the boy may let something out or whispers go around. Surprise is the thing. When they are not on their guard so much. At the moment there is not even anything to connect the keys to us. Nothing I say. Nothing at all. Nothing to connect us to keys, nothing to suggest what will happen there. Not that day or any day. It must be kept like that. Besides the source of the keys won't say anything. If he does, well, he will be on the other side of the prison doors. Not so good for him on the other side. Not by far it isn't."

"We've still got to get in to do this and know where he is ... and then be out .... and then get away?" Zephania had already considered this now he was fully on the case.

"Here is the plan of the gaol including where Hannibal will be that day. The gaol is packed like sardines in a tub at the moment, but he will be in the end cell, closest to the women's side. To get in to the gaol you will take provisions to the side entrance with two others. You will say you are from

Trethewey's. Some spirit will also be beneath the provisions which, with luck, the turnkeys left at the prison that day will start to consume. consume it all we want. Dull their senses. It is full proof. No dilution. Sleep like babies they should. The clothes they wear will be waiting for you, stowed under the cart itself.

When they leave, you will stay. Now look. The store is not far from the judging area which is where you need to get to. It will not be in use that day and the tunnel goes deep under. Most have forgotten this tunnel now. It hasn't been used almost since the prison was built, I am told. Enter it and go right through. When you exit you will be by the women's section. You will need to get across to where Hannibal will be. All prisoners will be locked away but the gate between the men's and women's sections will not. You must then get to him. That is your chance. Get him out and back through into the judging area. Out you both will go. There will be new clothing stowed under the cart. You can both then appear what you are not when you travel away. You will as a turnkey rough handle him out and take him to the women's side where you will again take him through the tunnel that leads to the judging area. Once there, out you must go again to rejoin the cart. Not much further on there will be horses for you ready prepared. You will then go with the boy to the Camel River where it is deep enough to take the small boat waiting for you. From there you will travel down through the estuary to a point off the disused quarries close to Hawker's cove. Small boat, oars and sail. It's on the east side of the estuary as you meet the open waters but around the point. Can be dangerous water there. You may not have long to do this. The cart will be unloaded into the store area. This is to be done just before the hanging is set so all will be watching that. Few will have their minds on the security of the gaol. We expect you will be undisturbed but if you are, or the cart is examined, there will be knives there, pistols too. Let us hope they will not need to be used. Trust they are all watching the hanging from the vantage point. You will be heading in the opposite direction. But if there is any interference with the unloading and loading you will need to deal with those doing the interfering. Pray God there are none. A boat will be waiting off Hawkers bound for Roscoff. Then lay low with the boy when you get to Roscoff until I make contact again. Trade there but do not return until we know what is known, if indeed anything is ever known."

***

The return to the Island was made with a real hope that he could get his son out of there. As he stared out from the bow as it cut through the seas, the salt and spray that moistened and encrusted his beard was welcomed as auspicious of freedom and hope. The two chosen men for this deed clasped hands as a sign of their resolve to do this together, whatever it took. The hanging was planned for the coming Saturday, only a few days away.

There was an excitement in the town, the surrounding area too. Notices were everywhere and much further afield in the county as well. The news travelled far into Devon. It was the talk of Bodmin. As the scaffold was erected a few days before, the atmosphere in the town was climbing to a fever pitch of excitement. This was entertainment on a grand scale.

The convicted miscreant was a poisoner and murderer. The rumour was that there might be more going to the gibbet on the same day. A multiple hanging would attract even more and from further afield.

The scaffold was erected using three large poles at the Five Lanes where the Turnpike roads met for Truro to the west, Liskeard to the east and Wadebridge to the north. Positioned so it could be seen from the gaol, it also gave a view of the prison to those watching the hanging. This was a salutary reminder of the fate that would meet wrongdoers.

The three- legged mare, as the scaffold was called with affection, trepidation and fear, could hold twenty-four poor souls condemned to hang by the neck until dead. The design of the three-legged mare also provided a much-enhanced viewing experience for the crowd. People could wrap themselves around the scaffold in order that they might take in the front, rear and side views of the unfortunate condemned.

Much publicised, it was the hanging of Sarah Polgrean of Polgrean that was providing the crowd with their star showing.

She had been convicted of murdering her husband by poisoning him with arsenic on 5th September.

"Thirty-four years old and hated her husband so much she chose to flavour his food with a good dose of arsenic the story goes!"

"Better watch what we eat here then."

Talking was difficult in the prison, but prisoners managed to exchange some words. Sarah's story was topical as she was destined to make her last journey the Saturday coming, and a husband poisoning was unusual in the County. She would not be taking the journey to the scaffold alone. There were others coming to the gaol that would have their last night at Bodmin. Prisoners in most cells could see the hanging from the gaol. They were encouraged to watch, taking heed of what could happen in return for their misdeeds. The sobbing from the women's section had continued all night. Fellow inmates who couldn't sleep showed little sympathy for her plight.

"It'll all be over for you soon. But us, no, some of us have got to wait here and listen to the likes of you wailing your fate. Get to the gibbet. Sooner the better and take this squalling with you."

"It'll be worse to hang by that rope, worse than what your poor husband of yours had to put up with. He wouldn't have known what was coming. Tasteless it is, no smell. He didn't have a chance. Put it in his ale, did you? Maybe on his dinner if you had no seasoning for it? Go on, tell us. Watched him retch all over the place? Did you tell him when he was retching why it was? Why his wife should want to put him away with the poison?"

"As he choked on his sick you'll be choking. Choking from the smell. Yes, choking from the smell and the tightening of that rope. Might be an old ship's rope. Smell the ochre like we smell it when we pick it!" "It'll cut slowly into your neck stripping off bits of skin until it gets under and then to your bone. Then it'll start choking you. You'll feel it go through your skin, gradual like. Maybe you'll smell the flesh and blood it has soaked up on those hung before you. Your blood will join theirs on that rope. The blood of murderers, thieves, those damaging the property of other innocent folk. Then there's those taking pleasure from having the sheep, the goats and more. Poor things. They should take the sheep, goats, sometimes the cattle along to the hanging who've been shafted. Let them watch them swing too. Those bloody bestiality folks. Who'd want a cow or goat anyway when there's good women up on Bodmin moor?"

Summoning up her strength she hurled the final abuse at them, "Bet the men of Bodmin moor would prefer a good bullock even to the likes of you."

With that outburst they laughed and laughed waiting for a turnkey if one was awake to come and silence them. Too much if any noise or talking by day could mean tougher punishment. The gaol was equipped with a small treadmill and crank which drove those on it mad if they did not collapse and die before. Governor Chappell had been wanting new ones, so they had heard. He had seen the latest invention of a treadmill that could take many more people treading it for hours, with no purpose. No purpose, that was, other than to tread it. Folk couldn't see each other to talk or exchange expressions. The watchers would be close by making sure they trod, trod and trod it, over and over and over again. Sometimes hours would pass on the treadmill. For those who survived the ordeal, great strength would build in their legs. The crank was just a handle they would have to push around and around with sand on the other side of a wall through which the cranking handle passed to paddles and sand. The sand being paddled up and down, up and down, getting heavier, lighter, heavier and heavier. Folk using the crank might have the tightening screw turned up making the turning even more difficult. Some folk say impossible for those of lighter build.

Sarah was heading to the condemned cell where there were others awaiting the same fate. They were all to be strung up on the gibbet that day. The gibbet, that section of the hanging scaffold that would hold the bodies for weeks after they had been hung. She would have company up there on the scaffold, to die exactly at the same time and they would be with her on the final journey, as well. These others would take the attention off just her as they made the journey in the back of the cart to the hanging scaffold. Wouldn't just be women. She would be sharing the scaffold, much to the delight of the crowd, with some others, of all types and deeds. There was a young lad who had stolen from one of the big houses near Launceston. Then there was the farm worker who had his way with the sheep. He had been seen by one of the Ladies of the nearby Manor who said she had nearly feinted at the sight. The ladies in her company had to be shielded from the view as quickly as could be arranged. Some of them had said they would never recover from the glimpses they had been forced to take of the poor struggling sheep and the leering, determined face of their human attacker. The offender had been rounded up and brought to trial with all the accompanying mirth of the Court.

The Judge had to clear the Court that day many times. The crowd gathered in the courtroom mimicked the bleat a sheep might make as it was unceremoniously grabbed by its attacker from behind.

"Get out of this courtroom. The next person to take on the guise of an innocent sheep will face thirty days in Bodmin themselves. Maybe then they might spend time thinking on this and the crime of buggering a sheep or any other animal. They can practice there the noises and cries of help a sheep subjected to these dire acts may be forced to bleat. Not here in my courtroom. They can spend that time thinking whilst pushing the treadmill. A bigger treadmill is needed for folk down here."

The Assize Judge had enough of the mocking crowd.

"Come on Judge ask for evidence from the sheep. Round her up. Put her on the stand. Ask her what happened. Have to find the right one Judge. Reckon she'll be the horny one!"

The man shouting had not thought, with the volume of courtroom spectators present on this occasion, that either the Judge or the Court officials, would be able to pick him or his voice and shouts out.

He had, however, mis-judged the judge. Equipped with sharp and fully attuned ears, he could without difficulty pick out who said what in his courtroom.

As the crowds roared, the Judge sent down the man shouting. "Send him for correction. Thirty days hard labour at Bodmin." The Court had quietened.

Sarah was to share her scaffold with all of these and more. They were to be the very distraction Hannibal had wished for to get his Trojan Horse into the gaol. As the day approached, the town was filling rapidly with folk from near and far afield including the travelling entertainers, market traders and vendors of all types of products. Quackery fuelled by the illnesses of the day would rarely find a cure from the products peddled at these sorts of events, but they were there in great numbers looking for the ill and infirm to whom they may offer a cure ..... at a price.

The brewers too prepared well in advance, upping their production and stocks to take full advantage of the marketplace that was coming to them.

No tradesperson, vendor nor spectator were to be disappointed.

Chapter 36

The Vicar Does Some Visiting

Unbeknown to Hannibal 3rd his case had also been discussed in advance of the hearing. Not only the Preventative service with Williams fighting his corner, but also by the Justice who would be hearing the case ……. and his cousin.

"Cousin, how good to see you. Pray what brings you here?" enquired Tremayne.

"Well," said the Vicar from Maker, with a drawn-out sigh in his voice. "It is a matter of some delicacy. It is a matter of some, shall we say, not only delicacy, but sensitivity. Sensitivity for my office, cousin. Could we …walk perhaps?"

The estate was not now the size it was, but the Manor House and farms had been retained in a delightful spot close to Bodmin moor.

The Vicar had travelled alone on his horse. Still of mighty girth, the horse looked relieved as he was taken off for water and feed.

"You'll stay, cousin?"

"Yes. It was a slow ride down. I ache more these days than I used to." "Prepare a room for my cousin," yelled Tremayne into thin air, for no one was there. Predictably, there was no response.

"Prepare a room for my cousin, girl," he shouted louder. With that a girl rushed through into the writing room of the Justice.

The role of Justice was one of his prominent duties in the area. As Justice he could make a public display of his worth, reminding them of the status that still pervaded from the family seat. Not known for his generosity of spirit to either people in his employ or to tenants on some of the more difficult to farm parts of his land, Tremayne barked at the household maid impatiently, even though the girl had not had a chance to hear the command until its second utterance.

"Come, take a drink and we'll walk." A gentle walk through the gardens was a delight indeed. Many of the plants chosen by successive generations were coming into bloom with their accompanying scents. These brought calm, indeed, some peace to the consternations of the Vicar.

"You may know that I have had a French girl staying. Indeed, I have two so far that have come from the French area of Roscoff. They have been here to help me to improve in the use of their written language and my competency in the spoken French language."

"Why on earth do you need to be more competent in the French language? You are a Parish priest, albeit one who holds a highly esteemed role in your Parish and holds the freeholds and Rectory of another. A good living you obtain, let alone status and income by marriage. And there is the settlement paid to you by the estate annually to ensure you do not starve. Well, I can't see that happening for some years, even if you ate nothing, cousin."

With that he faced his cousin, his eyes gradually and slowly peering downwards. Giving the protruding fat that faced him a good slap, he counted its wobble time in seconds and continued. "But you are hardly likely to be travelling to France to spread the word of God or join a crusade in the nineteenth century are you or are you not?"

"No ... but we do get some French spoken there now and amongst some of the parishioners."

"Ha, Ha," Tremayne exploded with disbelief. "You mean, you like a little bit of L'amour de la France, you old Dog."

With that Tremayne slapped him across the back with such loving force and hard of hand that the Vicar very nearly toppled over. Spluttering and taking time to recover, he retorted, "It's no laughing matter, Tremayne. This, this whole thing .. ..why it gets worse and worse."

"What could be worse about a little Francais al la tarte?"

"Shhhhhh Tremayne. These hedges and shrubs may well have ears."

"No, no ears here. Now then what do you want me to do about it. Help you out with her? Too much girth and not enough gait eh? Ha! Or maybe provide her a little allowance. Fat chance of that, the coffers need to be a bit fuller. Help you if there's a bastardy hearing. Ha ! Now that wouldn't do. Couldn't have you with a bastard, could we? Wouldn't be the first clergyman, man of the ecclesiastical cloth to have a bastard. A bastard, yes, a bastard. Plenty of bastards out there belonging to men, just like you. Men who were caught up with their indiscretions. Oh no. You would most certainly not be the first to have a bastard. Perhaps you should see that as an asset. A fertile Vicar amongst his flock. A provenly fertile one at that."

"Nothing like that at all. I need a little judicial help shall we say."

"And how could a member of the judiciary be of assistance?"

"It's more to make you aware of a few things that may help you pass an appropriate punishment or exercise similar good sense when dealing with an offender, Tremayne."

"Now we have it! Didn't think you had come all this way down on your own, to give yourself a sore arse, that you might see the Camelias and other plants coming along!

Who is this that is coming up before me or is it at the Quarters or the Assizes? Maybe in such instance, cousin, you would want me to have a quiet word with the other Justices or the Judge maybe?"

"Well it concerns one Hannibal Marks...... he is likely to come forward on a smuggling charge, I am given to understand. Good family. Good family and becoming quite prosperous from the fishing of the town, I gather.

His father, God rest his soul, helped arrange the French maids. I would remind you, Tremayne, that, as a consequence of him arranging these appointments, my French has come on well, very well as it were. You might think listening to me that I was indeed a Frenchman. Although a few indiscretions have arisen along the way, Tremayne. Indiscretions, no more, Tremayne. Indiscretions. Do you hear me?"

"Indiscretions, of course, my dear Algernon. We all, good creatures of God, his servants on earth, have these at some time or another."

"So, this man of good family and very remorseful over his deeds may come before you to plead his case or by the representation of one, Mr Yonge."

"I know Yonge. The man is alright, but he can take up my time in a busy Courtroom. Mind, I cannot find innocence when clearly there is none, Algernon. I cannot."

"I know you can't do that, but you can ensure a fit and proper punishment is delivered. A fit and proper punishment, no more no less, Tremayne. That is what is called for. As Mr. Yonge knows him best I wondered if it might be prudent to hear him on any punishment he may recommend."

"Very well. I will hear no more now. I understand that you could well do for this to end better than it otherwise might for this Hannibal Marks, for some reason. But not so much as an acquittal?"

"I would not dare say such a thing."

"Well no these days I cannot, but there is the power Algernon, there is the power."

"Naval service will do him no harm to break his ways for a few years. His wife will not starve, far from it. What do you think Tremayne? I am only doing my duty as a man of God to ensure an appropriate and Godly punishment is delivered. Justice, Tremayne, is my interest. Justice. No doubt I could arrange a little gift here and there of some fine spirits... mm."

"Don't be preposterous Algernon. Should you have some to spare, mind. If you have some to spare which finds its way to the area outside of my drawing room, I could do something with it!"

With that the two cousins made their way around the delights of the garden, talking of the blooms, life back in the parishes, before heading back into the house to make way for food and drink.

Chapter 37

Freedom is Short Lived

"Who are you? When did you start?"

"Only today. Just getting used to it. Big place?"

"No one said anything about a new person. Mind here no one tells me anything. Where do you come from?"

"Here I've got a drawing of it to find my way around."

The turnkey saw the drawing come out of Hannibal' 2nd's pocket, followed by a container. "And a little drink to quench my thirst in the day." A broad grin swept across the turnkey's face, creasing the skin on his forehead into large horizontal flaps. He was not a young man, similar in years to Hannibal. He had been working there from almost the day the gaol opened.

The turnkey took the container of the best spirit to which his gullet had ever been treated. Taking a slurp, then a gulp from it, his eyes popped from their sockets as he savoured not only the taste, but the smell, then its effect. It was just as well that Hannibal had more with him, as the greedy turnkey took an instant liking to it. Recognising his luck was in with this new work fellow he took another, then another.

"Where did you get this?" With that, the impatient Hannibal grabbed him at the rear of his head bringing it crashing down to his knee and continued to bludgeon the man until he lay senseless, but neither dead nor maimed.

Hannibal had little time available for niceties and politeness this day. Taking the keys and opening the nearest cell door, he pushed the turnkey into it. The container of drink was put into his pocket as both medicine and compensation for his discomfort. The three women in the cell went to make a hurried escape. Hannibal pushed them back in. One had not even tried to escape but had cowered in the corner near the slop bucket. In the scuffle it fell over, the stench of excrement from different souls pre-occupying them all for a few seconds.

He turned the key on the cell, departing hurriedly to the shouts of the women. He hoped that there would be few others listening or caring at this time to be attracted to the commotion. Job thought he had made sure that this section of the gaol would be unattended by the turnkeys at this time. Most would be watching the hangings from the vantage point outside, rather than through the slits positioned at waist height throughout this area which offered a more restricted view. The slits provided windows of sort for the occupants. They would huddle, push and jostle in front of them. There were simply too many of the women prisoners to settle into any order that would make the spectacle acceptable to them all. It was a scramble for those wishing to watch it. For those expecting to meet the same fate there was a reluctance to live it twice. They kept away.

Hannibal had not therefore expected to see anyone in this section of the gaol, let alone have the need to make conversation or take any action against any person. He had successfully entered the gaol with the others in the back of the cart. They were stocked well with provisions, arousing no suspicion. Nothing on or inside the cart had been checked. Without much ado they had been waved in. The massive service doors had yawned open, as if swallowing them up. As Job had said, there was thereafter, no one to interfere.

The map had been true to its markings. With the Court not in session, most folk off to the hanging, Hannibal had been able to access the tunnel. He had got through to the women's section without any great difficulty. The noise from some of the cells, the stench of excrement laying in buckets, urine that had long soaked away into the gaps of the floor slabs, had combined, producing an unwelcome cocktail. It seemed to soak into his clothing, begging to be wrung out.

He knew now he had not long. Going to the cell he believed Hannibal to be in, he could not find him. In the end he raised his voice, sufficiently to be heard. "Hannibal, Hannibal", he called as he passed each cell.

With that, there was soon a chorus of people shouting, I'm Hannibal, I'm Hannibal." Running along the outsides of the cells he listened intently, filtering unwanted sound, listening only for the sound and pitch of his son's voice. Even if this place of human squalor and despair had crushed his son's spirit, crushed the sound of him even, he would know if he was there. Then he heard it, "Hannibal the third is here."

As the noise escalated, he feared more and more that the window of time available to get him out was starting to whine shut. For how much longer could he rely on the disguise afforded him by the commotion of the fair?

As the banging on doors gave way to the chorus of "I'm Hannibal the third", from the other cells, his father got to his son's. He fumbled with the keys. After a short while he hit on the right key. He was there. He was in. There were a few others there with him. As his son left, the others started to run too, father and son put their weight behind the large oak door and locked it tight again. Poor souls maybe, but they could not chance a riot and more escapes. This was about his son, no-one else. "No questions. Come."

They got back to the area where the turnkey was in the cell, only to hear murmuring from him and shouting from the women.

"Come on let's have him. Have the turnkey. This is your chance."

"I'll have him. Ugly old bastard, but there's been no men here for a while. Even this one will do." In amongst their laughter, he could hear them, taunting him, mercilessly exacting revenge for the years he had tormented some of them. It was their turn now.

As they went through the tunnel their light failed. They groped their way through until there was light at the end with hardly a word passing between them.

It didn't need to. Running through the mind of his son was, how on this earth had his father done this. A fit and strong man for his years, he was now dogged with some pain in his joints. He couldn't move as he used to. This was a man driven, a man for whom strength had come in this, this his hour. Nothing else mattered now. Hannibal 2nd was unstoppable. He had gained that strength, that depth of calm that can only come with desperation and love. This was such an occasion. He had one chance, one chance only to succeed in this. They both knew a safe ending was not yet upon them. It could be both father and son strung up on the three-legged mare for this, or transported after hard labour for years, if they were very lucky. As they emerged from the tunnel and climbed back through to the judging rooms, they had to re-join the cart.

Hannibal 2nd had disguised his fear that it was this moment, this very moment, time and place, when they reached the cart, that they would all be there, waiting for them. They, the Gaolers, the Dragoons, the Constables from the town, and so the list could go on. But no, there were none of them. Job was right again.

Leaving through the window, they re-joined the cart. It was simply waved through when they re-appeared at the exit gate.

Trundling down the track until the quiet of the farms was reached, they spotted an open cattle barn, waiting with two horses ready to leave. Changed, armed, ready, they could hardly speak with their accomplices, but an embrace said it all for them. There was a note waiting for them with a map of how to get to the meeting place where a boat lay waiting on the Camel River.

The jollities continued in the town. The fairground and Inns were full of the same talk. "Did you hear her repent for her actions in killing her husband? Poor soul. She recounted the Lord's prayer exactly so. Didn't hear a prayer from the others."

Mind, she was the one they had mainly come to see. There were not so many hangings of women, less again murderesses of husbands. Others facing the rope that day were being punished for crimes more common, and were for the mostpart, men.

The cart with the condemned laying and sitting on the back went through the town first, on a circular route. The Gallows finally came into sight with the space where the cart pulled underneath. Their humiliation was nearly complete.

The ropes were seen by them in the distance, swaying in the slight wind. As they came underneath, they were placed around their necks. Sarah on whom most of the eyes of the crowd were transfixed asked, begged, for forgiveness. It was then that amidst the noise, the smells and all else that assaulted her senses, that she made her final call to her God and gave her recital:

"Our father who art in heaven, Hallowed be thy name, Thy kingdom come, Thy will be done, On earth as it is in heaven. Give us this day our daily bread, And forgive us our trespasses, As we forgive those that trespass against us. And lead us not into temptation, But deliver us from evil. For thine is the Kingdom, the power and the glory. For ever and ever, Amen."

An acknowledgement that she was ready, and an "Ay" from the rest on the three sides of the gallows, saw the cart pulled sharply away by its mule. With that, the dangling, writhing bodies of the condemned remained. All were then still. All were then quiet. Their final silence.

They were to be left for two months, to be eaten and pecked at by birds who could reach. Some would be buried at the end, in consecrated ground. Others, like Sarah, condemned for heinously taking the life of another, without mitigation, would not.

Sarah was to be dissected by order of the court. Her body would be used for experimentation and medical research. She was the only one to be cut down and carted off quickly after the hanging.

"They will want her while she's still warm."

"Look at her, poor thing. She did wrong but who hasn't. Anyway, come on, let's be having her."

With that, the cart that had brought her, also took her away to the eagerly awaiting doctors and physics.

The revelling in the town had reached a fever pitch. The talk of the Taverns was about the hangings. Who had been hanged, what they had done, and how they met their end.

"Birds came quick this time. Must have been the heat. See how their eyes popped. Them birds knew. They came swooping and fighting for them? They go for the soft bits first."

"I thought it was to be the hanging that was our fun today, but it has been that old man and his wife that made me laugh the most."

"I missed that. What was that?"

"Well he brings her in on that Liskeard road. Walking with her he was."

"What's so unusual about that?"

"Patience, patience when I'm talking.

He's bringing her into town on a halter. Just like he would his prize beast. He's a farmer up on the lower part of the moor. Up a couple of miles, short of St. Neot. Poor thing, he's walked her some way. Anyways, he takes her up to the stand after the hanging, stands under the bodies. Hangman's gone, so anyone can go there before they takes it all down to leave them swinging.

He starts to auction her, saying she's his wife. Saying she is for sale because he has tired of her."

"Did anyone buy her? What was she like?"

"Well", he says, "she has plenty of life in her, but snorts and hollers more than his pigs."

"Did anyone buy her?"

"Quiet! I am coming now to that. Two folks come forward, two brothers, I think, and they say that they will share a wife, and half the cost. Neither of them had ever had a wife before.

They agree on a price. Two pounds it were, with no comeback on the farmer. He promises a sack of feed to go with her, along with turnips and potatoes from his farm for a year after the purchase, to feed her as well as themselves.

Next thing, we see the two men with her on the grass close by. We see her shouting to her husband from across the way, that it was the best thing he'd ever done. These two men who bought her were twice the man he was she said, and she had two now, not just one miserable, tired out, mean old man."

"And that's it?"

"No, it doesn't stop there. Suddenly the man who is the cattle auctioneer arrives. He asks for money. He says this is due because the farmer has auctioned, and sold, in the town area of Bodmin. That meant a fee is due."

"What's the fee? What can the fee be to sell a wife? I have never seen that posted up, only the fees for the animals like, sheep, bullocks, lambs."

"Well they had an argument about how he should be charged and what she was. The auctioneer says the farmer should pay as if it were a milking cow he had sold. The farmer says she is too small but has the size and snout of a pig. Auctioneer then charges him the rate for selling a pig. The farmer pays, and they are all happy.

Meantime, the wife is watching. She yells at the husband that she couldn't even sell him at any price as he was a miserable old bastard of a bore that hadn't been seen mating for many a year, so was worthless now!"

"Better than the hanging that."

***

The dead, hanging on the gantry, left to rot, retained the stench of decaying flesh as the weeks passed. Interest always waned amongst the townsfolk, who ended up being glad to see them removed. Those travelling to or through Bodmin could scarce fail to see the bodies hanging there as a stark warning to anyone who came to the town that Bodmin would not be tolerant of miscreants.

The two Hannibals were oblivious to all the mirth of the fair and the hangings.

They had served their purpose. They had provided the much-needed distraction. This distraction had allowed them the opportunity to get into the gaol. It had then allowed them the chance to get out of it again.

They had been given their window of opportunity. They had seized it. The opportunity had been taken it for all it was worth. They had been led to the point where a small boat lay. The river was navigable down to the open sea from here.

They had stayed at the farm and hid, waiting for dark to make a move. They had a long wait but eventually the curtain of the night fell. They were away.

"There'll be a sail boat further down. Keep going. With that he took the horses, waited for them to dismount, watching them walk the short distance down.

"They will be waiting and will know this boat. You'll know them when you see them. Go quick. Don't stop for anyone. Use the arms if you feel you need to. Don't wait to use them. The Preventatives are everywhere now. Word may have got further out by now about an escape, so have your reasons, who you are, why you are there and where you have come from. Have them at the ready. They had better be good. They won't know what you look like and may not be expecting anyone that has got out to come here to this place, let alone you. They will most likely expect you to take the south coast. With that he turned and left.

They were alone, with money and arms, on a strange bit of the north coast to navigate. It would be easy to follow the river downstream in the boat until they reached higher water. The river and outflowing tide took them down with an effortless speed, but they rowed for all they were worth regardless.

"Where is this sail-boat? We are in deeper water now. There is the old bridge ahead."

"Keep going and keep to the east and away from the bars as we get into the mouth. It's a fair way to go yet. If there's no sail boat here we'll have to get out in this to open waters, and hope we can see the Smuggler that is for us. Pull hard. We want to clear the harbours as quickly and as un-noticed as we can."

Sand bars were everywhere. Nothing must delay them. Tide, river and brawn took them down past Padstow and into the open seas. The swells were very high, the wind creeping up. They had to bear east again, then around the point. There the Smuggler was meant to be waiting. "

What's happened to the sail-boat? Where is she?"

"There! There!"

Their small boat tossed and turned as they pulled as hard as they were able against the swells and slop of the open seas nearing the Smuggler.

A line was thrown down as they approached and on they climbed.

"Welcome aboard. You must be Hannibal Marks," a man said, addressing the young Hannibal.

He looked at this man, and the men in the background, who quickly came forward.

“The Preventatives.” Then realising, things had gone badly wrong, and no word of this had got to them. How could it? This was the Smuggler. Her name as they approached had been the name they were expecting. The North Star. But who was this? An accomplice no doubt.”

With that, as the men coming forward lurched at them, Hannibal 2nd drew from his back belt the pistol he had hoped would have no use.

The Preventative men could not have seen nor expected that. He, Hannibal 2nd, had not come thus far to give up his son without a fight. The crack of the pistol shattered the night air. The Preventative who greeted them fell. He stood in front of his son, protecting him. He faced the rest, one of whom drew a pistol. Hannibal tore into him as well, shooting the weapon right out of his hand, blowing off his right arm. The others appeared to have no weapons.

They retreated, turning to go below, leaving their wounded, fallen and unable to defend themselves or any of the others, on deck. Hannibal 3rd collected up their firearms.

“Get back down to that boat boy before they come back all armed and finish us off. I am staying here. I can hold them while you go. Now go.”

“No, I'm not leaving you here. We can finish them all off with luck and take the boat. We can sail her alone."

The Preventatives did not re-appear. The threat was too great. Where had they gone, were they still there? The two Hannibals, with no further words, climbed down into their boat, Hannibal continuing the shooting, hoping the Preventatives would still not yet dare re-appear. They were not to know where they were. Had one gone, both? With some luck they would get away.

Shooting through the planking by the waterline and the sails, anything they thought might disable the boat, the Preventatives heard the shots, choosing not to re-appear. They would not have much of a start and chose to row immediately to the rocky shore to abandon the boat and take their chances on land. Shots rang out, many shots. They picked their way through the rocks and then the undergrowth above. A cry came from Hannibal 2nd who was already starting to slow behind his son.

"They have me," he said in a voice not loud. His son turned and saw his father had been shot through the upper part of his leg. He was bleeding badly. "Go! Go! I will hold them with what I have," he said to the sound of more shots. They did not know if the shots were random or they could see them well. They had probably seen the boat, but had they picked them out against the rocks?

Ignoring his father, the boy took him and curled him around his shoulders. His father was a heavy man to lift and carry. Hannibal 2nd implored his son to leave him there and go while he still could.

"You cannot go with me now. Go alone. Take refuge with the Inns if you can. Travel by night and hide by day. Get to Jamaica and you can plan from there. Now leave me. If I live and they find me I shall say you swam for it or we both got shot and you went in and disappeared under. They may believe me. The seas were high. It is you now that matters. I have had my time. I will die happy if I know I have helped to save you and know you will live to see that child of yours grow up into a fine Hannibal 4th. Now go. I beg you go. I would kill myself to make you go if needs be. But I can better serve you if I stay here, stem the bleed and if they come close, take them. Give you the chance of escape and a life is my last wish."

With that and with a heavy heart he gently placed his father down. The shots appeared random as they were elsewhere now.

"That's it. Keep your shots as they won't now know from whence they come. I will mine now, unless they are on me."

There was little light, but as he grabbed his son's head and pressed it briefly to his, he could feel the cold of tears.

"Do not spend time weeping for me. You have my love my son, whatever. Carry that with you all your days. Pass on our story to your son and him to his. Get to Roscoff and work it from there. Joe is your friend, you will have business. Now go, think only of yourself for now, and not me, as you fly through the winds. Go, and don't look back. I am telling you. He held his father gently but strongly. No words came.

"Now go. Go. You need say nothing. I know it all. It is my last will that you go, and go with all the strength you can muster and that I will pass to you.

When you see them, embrace your brother, sister and mother from me and tell them my dying words were for all of you and tell them of my love and care for them also. Go! Go!"

With that he faked a faint. Hannibal went. The night air, as it rushed past him, cleared the tears from his eyes. He had to leave his dying father. How was he to be buried, where would he end up? He needed to know but for now he must fulfil his father's wishes. He got to the top and headed eastward along a coastal stretch with which he was not familiar.

It was not long before the Preventatives and Constables stumbled over the body of Hannibal 2nd. Rolling him over with a foot, one of them dismissed him as of no interest to them.

"Is this the man who was on the boat and fired the pistol?"

"Can't be certain. He looks as dead as they come though, whoever he is."

"No point in doing anything with him now. The Parish here will deal with the body."

"So where might be this Hannibal Marks who escaped from the gaol at Bodmin. He who then escaped from the Smuggler you apprehended?"

"We thought we saw him climb onto the rocks. It was dark. The boat he must have been on isn't anywhere to be found."

"This man looks as if he was shot by a pistol. Could have been yours, or maybe this Hannibal Marks shot him?"

* * *

He would take his chances in the seas. He needed to get to Roscoff and from there find out what was happening. Joe would help him if he still needed to stay low. Messages could be received back easily from there to his family. How could he now get there?

If he could get further down west on this northern coast, then overland to Prussia Cove he could get a Smuggler from there more easily direct to Roscoff. The Carters who ran the operation at Prussia Cove knew him well. He would have to get down further or face the dangers of travel overland. Maybe keep close to the sea edge as far as he could down the coast until the distance south to Prussia overland could be made one night on foot, quicker if he could take a horse. He had money. If he dared show himself, he could buy one.

He stopped by a stream to wash the blood off his clothes. This was his father's blood. He wanted in so many ways to keep this on him. It gave him a sense of familiarity, from one who cared for him. This was, right now, the symbol, macabre though it was, of his father's memory. The father that had risked all for him. His blood had been spared for him. This meant him no harm. He knew, though, he would be safer if he removed any sign of conflict or armed struggle, so get it off he must, or at the least, dull the colour.

Light had come, and he was in a barren area of the land.

Whilst the heat was on, he would take shelter near the rugged coast. He would wait until dark fell, once more, to move.

"The rocks just offshore must be Gull's Island that the smugglers in these parts use", he thought.

The group of small islands of which Gull was the biggest, showed itself with the light. Difficult and treacherous, the smugglers were untroubled here at nightfall.

His punt, hidden below, would get him there. If there was somewhere he could find to drag up the boat, he could leave it to collect water. There might not be much place to shelter there, but if the boat was hidden, he might stand a better chance than moving on land. His father had told him to head to Jamaica, but this meant going overland and going back over his steps and to the north of Bodmin.

No, he would make to Gull Island for now, hide and see if he could pick up a Smuggler. They would be unlikely to know him in these parts. He would have to exercise great caution and not surprise them. He must get his story right and gain their trust quickly if he could. The Island stank of bird excrement that had formed the earth of the island and given rise to growth. The punt had a few lines and nets stowed in it. If there was some fresh water collected on the Island or he could capture enough in the punt, he could survive a while there if needs be.

Hannibal scrambled down the cliffs to where the punt had been left. There it had remained, small and inconspicuous. He would hide close by until dark fell, then get to the Island. There were plenty of crevices here. He had filled himself with water from the stream but was starting to feel the pangs of hunger strike.

He would see if he could get some rock crab and limpet for later and take wood to smoke them on the island at night. He saw ships and boats pass, but no one came to the rocks. Eventually darkness fell once again. He was able to take in his boat and crawl up the island and into a safe area. He made a fire on the south side to take a meal of limpet. The fire was concealed in a rocky area and he cooked them in salt water.

Two nights passed. He wondered whether he should return. Try to make his way overland to Jamaica as his father had asked him to do. It was on the third night when hunger for proper food and drink was starting to make his decision for him, that he spotted a large boat coming close to the island, and then a small one off that.

He stood on the rocky outcrop of the Island close to where they were coming in. He could see kegs aboard the small boat and knew they must be going to hide them close by. He placed himself where he could easily be seen and heard without the sound travelling far.

"I am your friend. I am your friend. I am one of you. I am from the south and have got stranded here."

"How do we know you are our friend. We don't have any friends on this Island. No one stays here."

"They do if they have no choice and the Preventatives are after them."

"Get rid of him. If he sees us, we don't know who he is."

"Wait, let's hear him. Be quick. What is your tale? What brings you to Gull Island?"

"Caught smuggling when accompanying the Joe Marie from Roscoff on the south coast. Taken to the gaol at Bodmin. From there I escaped and came down river to here."

"Your name?"

Hannibal reluctantly decided he should give his name. "Marks."

"I know the Joe Marie ... and Joe."

One of the smugglers had been involved on the Roscoff runs.

"What's your other name?"

"Hannibal."

"Ha, Hannibal Marks. Which one are you? I have bought from a Hannibal Marks."

"I am his son. I am Hannibal 3rd of that name."

"Let me take a closer look at you?"

"Yes. He's the boy. I haven't seen you there before though, boy Marks."

"I have been on board the Five Brothers and the Friends."

"I know them. Your father and I, our paths have crossed."

"Get out to our boat before we change our minds."

"We'll show you to Captain Coppinger."

The name meant a lot to Hannibal. What smuggler in the country had not heard of Coppinger, the Dane from Ireland? As he approached, he could make out the name. Yes, this was the boat. He had seen it before. It plied near and far but rarely was it seen on the south coast, but it made it to northern France. It was known to run to Ireland. It had traded tobaccos, linens as well as spirits.

This was the Black Prince. He was on the Black Prince.

Coppinger's Black Prince had been built in Denmark, to a Danish design. Coppinger himself had personally overseen the build of his prize boat. Never been captured, armed and stocked for battle if need be, she was left alone by many to ply the seas, uninterrupted by revenue boats. She stood out. She was one of the most feared boats plying the free trade. He would be safe on her for as long as Coppinger would have him. His father too had known Coppinger. He had fearsome tales of him.

"Who is this you've got?"

"Hannibal Marks, Captain."

"A name like that. It must be to do with Roscoff and Cawsand."

"That's true. My father is also Hannibal, but he is now dead."

"Dead. How?"

"Preventatives."

"When was this?"

Hannibal decided he would confide in Coppinger. He and his handpicked gang were no friends of authority. His father had told of his occasional business with the man. Money was never a problem for him. He was a tough man, and no one would argue for long with Coppinger.

"Your father was a fair dealer and did well. Too fair by my book though. I'll get you to somewhere safer for now, so you can get back to Roscoff."

With that they unloaded. They were in sail soon and away. Hannibal was given water and some cognac to warm him. There was little food, but they shared what they had.

It was not long before they were close to Lundy Island further up the coast.

"It's the bloody Harpy over there. Make west. We can outrun her. Better than taking her down and having them all start on us. She might clear from us when she sees who it is. Prepare to fire some canon and shot. Make a noise and let the bastards know who we are."

"What's she doing down here. She normally runs more around Ilfracombe and to the north and east."

"I don't think we need to scuttle the last of goods to outrun the Harpy. We're by the Island. Go to the west of her and then if she follows us, we'll deal with her there. Hannibal, you can stay with us or take the punt onto the Island. If you choose to ashore, go to the small cottage at the south-western end. Say you have been sent by Coppinger, the Dane. Here, take this. They will know it then to be true."

With that, Coppinger gave Hannibal a coin.

"It's a Danish coin. When Black Prince was being built, I took a stock. They will know it has come from me."

As they skewed around the island, they saw the Harpy get closer and then tack away. Coppinger was right. They didn't want to tangle with him, his gang, and the Black Prince, if they could excuse it. With that he sailed south-west a while and then returned to drop off Hannibal and some more tubs to the Island.

Hannibal went to the cottage as directed. When he produced the coin, letting them know he had been sent by Coppinger, he was admitted without further questions. Coppinger and his will were not to be questioned. As he watched the Black Prince sail, he sat with the man and his wife. No names were asked for and no names given. They drank, and he was given a stew to eat.

Eventually the silence was broken.

"You staying a while, or a boat to take?"

"A free trader's boat is what I want. Roscoff or Ireland."

"You won't need to wait long."

"Have no fear, no one of authority will come here. Give the man a bed and some of our stock to take with him. Warm him through."

With that the man's wife took him through some passageways to a small room with a bowl of water, pitcher and tankard.

"The water's good too here. Straight from a deep well."

For the first time in a while Hannibal could breathe easy. The little room had a fire which the man's wife prepared. He lay by it, feeling the warmth go through him, sinking slowly into his very bones, relaxing his exhausted muscles on its way. He washed using the bowl of water with some soaps. The drink and soaps were courtesy of the traders. These people knew Coppinger and his gangs of smugglers. He felt in safe hands. No one asked anything, no one knew anything. He must though be away as soon as he could take a boat.

Slumber came with a rude, premature, awaking.

"What do you want with us? Getting old folk like us up in the night?" The voice of his host was raised. This was so he could hear it. What was going on? Who were these people that had woken the old people in the night?

"You can't come in here like this stirring old people and my poor wife who has not long in this world."

"Make way."

With that Hannibal guessed these were the Preventatives. Maybe the boat Harpy had seen more than they thought as she sailed away. Maybe they were going for the easy meat. Going for a catch of contraband goods without taking on Coppinger and his gang of roughnecks? He heard several footsteps. There were a good number of them. The coals had been lit late. They would not have seen smoke from the chimney at this section of the house. The embers were glowing though. If they come in here and he had taken flight they would know someone had been here. Maybe that didn't matter to them. It might just be a catch of goods was what they wanted.

There was no time to out the fire embers or do anything. He grabbed his bag of money and pistol, threw his boots out of the window and jumped.

"And what have we here?"

Before Hannibal had time to draw his pistol or check his surroundings to see who it was and enquire what they wanted he had been wrestled to the ground by a force of men in uniform. As he struggled to regain his freedom, he knew he would not now be able to get away from their grip. There were four of them. At least the man and his wife knew nothing of him. They would say he was a stray, shipwrecked or rescued, and was staying there a while waiting for a ship.

"So, what are we wanting to get away from then?"

"I was shipwrecked off here and am waiting to join a ship to get back."

"Back to where then?"

"I am from Ireland."

"Don't sound too Irish to me, does he you?" With that the men laughed. Hannibal was still pinned down, but their grip and weight came off him a little, giving him room to take a deep breath.

"I have been there for the last years since my Irish mother went back to live out her days. I was raised in Mevagissey."

"He looks a bit like how they described that man who escaped the gaol."

"What," thought Hannibal, "news couldn't have travelled that quickly and was it really very important?" The sweat in the cold night air came to his forehead on hearing this. News was starting to travel the area and had come to this Island with these men.

"Let's take this one in. A night in the lock up will sober him up and open his mouth."

"How could he have got this far from the gaol and out onto the Island?" chipped in one of the other men.

"Yes unlikely. Do we want to waste our lock up and time on this?"

Hannibal was unshaven, rough looking, with clothes stained, hair unkempt, matted with salt and grime.

"What's this?" The bag and pistol had scattered when they fell to the ground. One of the men not holding him down, walked to the bag and opened it.

"Well, well, well. A poor seaman is doing well for himself."

"It's not mine."

"What a fine pistol."

"Let's take him in."

Hannibal decided not to struggle as he could do no more right now. He would wait his time to see if he could get out of this or pick his moment to see if he could fight his way out of it. As he was tied and taken to

Padstow where he was going to be taken by cart and guard to the gaol, he made his first attempt with just one of his captors.

"There is more money like that if I could get to it. More to share about a bit for a little help here and there." His captors were unmoved. "If you are who we think you are, there's a price on you anyway."

"I could beat it."

"How much?"

"What do you want?" No reply came. He was to get nowhere. Word would get back to Job who would see what help he could provide. Much would depend on what had happened in the last days. Did anyone die from the incidents at sea with the Preventative boats and the smuggler? Could they be nailed onto him? In Padstow he was detained before being rough handled into a cart which took him to Bodmin gaol.

As they entered the gaol, the warder and turnkeys recognised him.

"Hannibal Marks. Wasn't your stay here good enough? Not warm enough for you? No good spirits for you or fine fare? Well we'll have to see what we can do to provide you with better then."

As he was taken through, they cast him into irons and he was put into a solitary cell. Questioned later about what had happened, he managed to glean some of the missing facts. No one seemed to know it was his father who had broken him out. The shooting on the detained smuggler off the headland to the east of Padstow, Hawkers, was also unknown to them. They did know he had been broken out and taken.

"I was broken out of here and taken against my will as my captors thought I had money. That is what they wanted.

They planned to take me to the French banks to get money. It was they who had the muskets and pistols. I could have had none of these here."

"Tell that to the Judges at the Assizes. See if they believe you. That's who'll try you."

Chapter 38

Back in Bodmin

"Hannibal Marks again. You won't be getting out of here this time in a hurry." The cell doors slammed shut with a resonance that was unlikely to ever leave his memory. Hannibal felt that this was the noise he would have to get used to again and again, until the Courts next met. The next Assizes, most like.

He did not yet know the charges against him. He had heard nothing of what became of the Preventative boats and men aboard. Were any dead or injured? What had become of the boats? Days and more days passed. He then heard the cell doors open and a familiar voice.

"We won't need long." It was Job and one other, a lawyer.

"We haven't much time, I thought with your father not here to see to this sorry mess, you could do with a little bit of help. We'll get straight to it. No one has died on the boats from, shall we call it, the unfortunate incident at sea. Any other injuries and deaths in the last weeks are not levied at you. It would seem that you will be charged simply with smuggling. Your escape from here is being taken as an act of abduction. There is a reward out for the capture of those who took you out of the gaol, for the one who shot at the Preventatives, damaged their vessels and caused some injuries Those charges are not levied at you. We are hoping thus to ensure that your case stays with the Justices. Indeed, Mr. Yonge here is expecting, he tells me, for the case to stay with the Justices and go no further. If it were to go further, you might be taken from the Courts here to an Exeter or even London Assize. We don't want that if we can help it. Smuggling as you know can still carry serious punishments. Mr.Yonge believes that he can represent you and persuade the Justices that a light punishment is both appropriate and deserved. Perhaps a fine or a short spell of hard labour here on the Hamoaze ships. Neither is good, but you will survive it and be out, back to that family of yours before you know where you are. Just do what he says. There's my boy."

"Any news of what has happened to father's body. A decent burial for him, Mr. Job. A decent burial back home for him is needed?"

"Nothing, I fear. I am making enquiries. It seems that nothing has been found by the Preventatives nor Constables. Nor anyone else for that matter. No bodies found anywhere in that area that could remotely fit the description of your father, Hannibal. As they have not got your abductor or abductors, I gather there were more than one involved, a reward is on offer. They think this will lead to more smugglers who are at the top of the tree. Yes, those in charge, that is who they are seeking. They want the leaders?

The man who was injured here, then set upon in the women's section, is said to be recovering. He is not suffering from any bad injuries. He must have been given a right whack by one of your abductors?"

But that it not your concern. Mr Yonge will be handling issues of compensation, where it is deserved, as a matter of goodwill shall we say. To compensate for anything that happened. Not as if it were, anything of your doing or fault. Oh no, not of your fault. A mere acceptance, moreover, that these things happened whilst you were there and largely it would seem, well, because of you."

"Yes," piped and chimed Mr Yonge, with an echo, an echo of a judicial authority he did not have, but as one who was nonetheless regarded as an officer of a court.

"Yes, not by you, but because of you. Yes, I will say to the good Justice, it was not by you, but because of you. Moreover, this event consisted of many events, shall we say, events over which you, yes you, had no control. No control I say, no control, whatever. As I understand it Mr Marks you were indeed on the smuggling boat when the first incidents occurred and were present when the shots were fired that damaged the Revenue Cutter, but you did not carry a pistol or other armament. Furthermore, you did not place any shots?"

"Well ...."

"I thought not," interrupted Mr Yonge.

"Well...."

"Well what?" Mr Yonge interrupted again. "As I understand it you were a mere helper with the sailing of the vessel on this occasion."

"Well ..." stammered Hannibal.

Yet again interrupting, Mr Yonge more impatiently, with a voice now slightly raised, "Well nothing. And then on being captured and taken to the jail at Bodmin, you are captured again, albeit this time by men who take you by threat of shooting, stabbing and other mutilation. Then, yes then, they demand money from you. Demand it they did, I shall say to his Justice, with menace.

It would seem that when you left the smuggling vessels you managed to take with you some bags of money. The other men wanted to know what had happened to it and came to get you for it."

"Well now, it wasn't ...."

"Wasn't what .... exactly?" Mr Yonge had had enough of his client's attempted procrastinations. He was, yet again, being paid handsomely as retained lawyer for the Job enterprises and he was paid to achieve results. Results that is where results were possible, and here there could be a result.

"My dear boy, listen to Mr Yonge. For your father too and his father, I want to see this settled. It seems we can see this settled. We can, oh yes we can, if you take my meaning."

"I do Mr Job and Mr Yonge. Thank you."

"There is nothing else really you know. You only know the short names of the others that were with you and you believe them to be mainly from Ireland that night – well you will know these shortened names won't you and could describe them? You could describe them if called to do so. Search your memory, Mr Marks. Should you be questioned. Search your memory to help the Court make the right decision for one who has turned over a new leaf in their behaviour. Don't suppose they would ever be found. All would be forgotten in time. No one killed by you. No murder charges."

"Have you finished in there?"

It was the turnkey. He didn't want to push his luck any further. Hannibal turned to the door and then back to Job and Yonge, "You will make sure my family know?"

"They already do, and they know where to come if any help is needed while you are away." Hannibal lowered his head, nodded, raising it again to show his gratitude and approval.

"Haven't you finished yet?" It was the turnkey.

Job acknowledged they had through the small opening at the front of the door. This meagre opening had streamed in some further light for

Hannibal's fine company at this dismal time of day. Job passed his palm over the hand of the turnkey, a skill he had perfected over his years in the free trade. At the most basic level it was a way of discretely passing over small cash bribes with a measure of subtlety. At a more sophisticated level it was conducted with cheques or drafts drawn on the London and Guernsey banks, or those notes of his own issue, his own promissory notes that were widely accepted. They need only bear the name of Zephania Job and his authenticated hand

"Make sure he receives the best you can, won't you, the very best. I shall be checking. More where that came from for you if you do this, and do it well, very well?" The turnkey said nothing but nodded, turning the key with a well-practiced single flick of the wrist.

Hannibal was left a while contemplating the events of the last minutes. A few days passed before the key again turned on the door of the cell. The wood of the door, swollen with the persistent damp in the atmosphere, competed with the iron cladding confining it. Fat was needed on the hinge posts to stop the noise it made from the friction of metal upon metal, grinding on each other when it opened. Hannibal was pleased to hear this whine of the door when it opened or shut. The movement indicated there was a way out of the cell, of the gaol. It was the door, the door alone that stood in the way of his exit. The door stood for both his incarceration and his freedom. The day came when it opened, and he was bundled towards the courtroom. As he entered, he stood before the Justice. Mr Yonge was there, but no Job.

It had been a surprise that Job had been there before. His business was normally conducted by others in these matters. He didn't know the Justice, but Mr Yonge addressed him as Sir and Justice Tremayne.

This was a single Justice and he knew of Tremayne by reputation. Hannibal looked him cautiously up and down with head slightly bowed. He knew him to be a local landowner, a member of the gentry, one of the old landed families of the area but one who fell short of the ranking of nobility. Nonetheless, he had wealth and status. He was, Hannibal believed, a cousin, by some line of descent, to the Vicar of their Parish at Maker.

He had seen him occasionally at the Church where it was whispered that he too benefitted from the free trade. An investor may be? He had though never raised his head as one, but then, many did not.

Justice Tremayne looked stern. He fitted his office and his office fitted him. Bewigged, but not in such manner that might run the risk of being accused of giving the impression he was a High Court or other senior, qualified member of the judiciary, he still had that aura exuded by the long wig of the Judge. His attire was red and black, his shoes revealed an occasional glimpse of his wealth. Fully adorned, with the finest patterned silver buckles, these buckles shone above the blackness, a feature known only to the finest of footwear. He was an exemplar of his office. Not generally a well-liked man, he held a reputation that preceded him for the harsh punishments that could be meted out in his courtroom. Transportation was the punishment he most relished. The thought of prescribing transportation to those transgressors of his beloved legal system, witnessing the anguish of loved ones present to hear his delivery of the sentence. A delivery that by its sheer eloquence transcended the desperation it imposed for those receiving it, almost, he believed, to the extent that it would make them proud to receive it. Those transgressors that dared to run the risk of appearing before him had this to look forward to.

"Let thee be gone from these shores. Take with you your bad behaviour. Reflect, whilst on your long and treacherous journey to the new worlds."

This became his stock phrase when dispensing this punishment to offendors. Sometimes, he would give a time for the banishment. Two years, five years, life, depending on whether he was sitting alone or with others. Few could afford to appeal against his decisions and would have scarce dare to do so.

There was no one Hannibal knew in the courtroom other than from his brief acquaintance with Mr Yonge. Maybe his family had been advised to keep clear to let Mr Yonge do his job without any distractions, interruptions or any unexpected interference from a gallery. How Hannibal longed to see his wife, brothers, sisters, cousins, friends and accomplices. And what of his newly born? Oh, how he panged to see and hold them all.

He was not the only one being tried before the Justice this day. He did seem to be the only one receiving help from anyone, let alone from a lawyer, in presenting the case.

The charge was read out to the Court. It was one of smuggling, nothing else. The facts provided were scant. He was charged with being on the Smuggler. No one else had been caught from the boat. Hannibal breathed a sigh of relief.

Justice Tremayne sounded impatient. This impatience included that inspired from his audience with Mr Yonge. A known sufferer from the gout, this affliction was known to affect the mood of Justice Tremayne, this mood influencing the punishment he would dole out on a bad gout day.

"What have you to say, Mr Yonge. There is a busy gaol to deliver. A busy court here today." "Are we looking at five years hard labour or five years transportation?"

Yonge looked at Hannibal. "I wonder, Sir, if the Preventative and Naval Services would agree, whether a spell in the Navy would also be a punishment that would pay for his crime. This would benefit our Navy whilst repaying his debt to the government whose coffers have been affected somewhat by the actions of Mr Marks. In the smuggling way I mean, the smuggling or shall we say free trade way. Compensation I say Sir, compensation is called for."

"I cannot determine that as well you know Mr Yonge, but should the accused choose it and it be approved by the Preventative service and Navy, I will stand the case down now. But hurry up man, Hurry up! There's a courtroom full, a gaol full. Full I am saying. This is a full courtroom, a full gaol that I must clear and clear today. Not tomorrow, today. Do you hear?"

He turned his attention to Williams of the Preventative service.

"And you man? Are you content with that? Will the Navy be content with that?" Hannibal had not expected this. The country was now at relative peace. Although life could be tougher in the Navy than gaol at this time, things were better, better than if at war. He would at least have a chance here and there to see his wife and son, without having them travel to the Colonies. That would be no good. No good at all.

"I would choose to serve the Navy if allowed, Sir. If that pleases you and the Navy." Hannibal had to think swiftly. He had made his choice. Greater freedom in these times of peace and he may learn a few new tricks.

* * *

The agreement of the Preventatives to allow their captive, Hannibal Marks, to serve in the Navy rather than accept a sentence of the Court had been determined prior to the trial. Williams of the service attended the trial with the authority of the Surveyor to agree to Naval service should the issue arise.

"We have then, at last, one of the Marks in gaol and implicated in this whole business from start to finish." The Surveyor and Collector spoke together about the forthcoming charges against Hannibal Marks.

"Where is his father in all of this or any other of the Marks and their associates?"

"There is only this one of the same name."

"We have enough evidence for the charge of smuggling against this Marks. Maybe the Navy could be offered as a punishment? Let him pay back over 5 years. No pay for his seafaring skills. Is there no evidence that links him to the damage of our vessels or the escape from the jail?"

"It seems not."

"Any of our boatmen able to identify him as the man who discharged the pistol? No one in the gaol who heard anything or saw anything that would link him to the escape?"

"Again, it seems not. The only evidence is that he was working the boat and was stolen from the gaol by those wanting their money. He may have taken money from their boat?"

"Ha, well serves them all their just deserts, I say. Serves them all that. And no one brought a charge of theft against him? I suppose this will see him before the Justice. Or the session now?"

"Yes, it will most likely be a Justice unless he sends it to the sessions."

"Well, get on with it. Quicker the better if he is to enter into service of his Country. Although, hard labour at Bodmin sounds good to me or send him to those colonies. Not many come back from those."

"Anyway, where is the father and this Joe Marie?"

"We don't know. They say the father is dead, but no one hears why, where or how?"

"Well good riddance I say to any of that family and their free trade dealings. He was at it a long time. Built an empire for them, he did. We get one paltry Marks and the young one at that."

"Alright let him go to the Navy as he so chooses and repay his debt to us all like that. Pity it is not wartime I say. But you never know. Little time passes without a war. Let the Court know. You had better be there. I wonder who will take over their boats if the two Hannibal Marks are not there?"

"There's plenty of other men will do it. The brothers perhaps and cousins."

"I don't suppose we've seen the back of them yet?"

The matter agreed, Williams left. Williams was alone with his thoughts for a while as he walked back along the Plymouth Barbican harbour to his Cutter from the Customs' House. It was a result he felt good conscience with. The debt had properly been repaid now he felt to the accused Hannibal's father. The rest was over to the Justices to do what they all felt best, or for that matter to Hannibal. He would have punishment. Oh yes, he would be doled his punishment, but not as it might have been should more evidence had been forthcoming come from him and his men.

Williams felt that this was a fair exchange for the debt he owed the father of the prisoner, the debt he owed to Hannibal Marks 2nd.

He and his men did owe them their lives. They could have taken them that day. In addition, Williams felt this punishment served King and Country. He, Williams, could live with his conscience. Besides this Hannibal may have a new life with the Navy. He was young, spirited and could handle a boat with the best of them now and who knows ....

He would sleep easy with this tonight. He would be absolved by all involved in the next world for this. Satisfied that he had done the right thing, he went to the Customs' Cutter. It was tied up against the harbour wall, mooring rope hitched around the bollard that once was a canon. The canon was now upturned, a useful life for it resumed by fixing it into the granite and limestone harbour wall that had been built to offer up more land reclaimed from the sea. Williams tapped the side as he were patting a pet dog. "Back to normal. Back to normal.

"You have heard the accused, Mr Yonge. Take him away, Constables. Lock him up until the Navy arrive for him. And I presume Mr Yonge this is the usual, without pay, that is. No pay, but doubtless he will come home to a good living well enough, these 'free traders. Don't let me see you here again in five years or it'll be the Colonies for you or hard labour, worse maybe."

"Yes Sir, no pay and a chance to consider his wrongdoings Sir and make a new life serving England."

"Yes. Next one." With that the trial was over. Hannibal thought again through the events of the last few weeks. As it had turned out he had been fortunate. The rope could easily have been the punishment for all that he had in fact been involved in.

How did he get off, and so lightly? Manhandled back to his cell, he had not to wait there long before the Navy pressgang arrived for him. Bundled unceremoniously onto a cart, secured with others that had taken the King's shilling, there was little chance of escape from this now. The money and influence from free trade would only be of limited good. It would though be waiting for him when the five years had passed.

"Where are we heading?" he shouted to one of his captors?

"Nowhere you need think about?"

"Plymouth first," said one of the others. "Plymouth Dock."

"You'll be taken to join a ship from there."

“Man o War with no war!” The cart rumbled on, jolting every bone he had in his body. The ropes and chains bit sharply into his hands and feet. He nonetheless was able to smell the sweetness of fresh air. He wondered how he might now hear news of home and what had happened.

Chapter 39

Sarah Marks Steps up to the Mark

"Susannah, we must prepare for the worst today." "I keep looking at the latest Hannibal, and wonder what I may have to tell him one day about his father."

"We will hear soon enough what has happened in that Court, within a few days I do suppose. Until then ..."

"Until then we can do nothing."

"Oh yes we can... why we can play with the little Hannibal and take him for some fresh air. I will see how the boats are doing as well. We have done little in the last weeks because of this and your husband and mine would be none too pleased about that. Come on, we women folk can do this as well as the men."

"We may have to get used to it or shut it all down. But there are mouths to feed. Not just ours. We could now live well on what we have and the Inns, even the fishing. But there are many here who rely on us for their livings. There is a young Hannibal to come into this and maybe many more to arrive yet?"

"Maybe, maybe. It's all maybe. I need to know what is happening. Could you look after the little one, as well? I should go to Bodmin, despite the message that came through to do nothing and wait for the result."

"You cannot ride alone. Anyway, where do you think you will be going?"

"The gaol at Bodmin and Courthouse there."

"We were asked to keep away and wait."

"I need to know what has become of him. What is his fate? It's the not knowing what is happening, the knowing he is alone. I can't wait any more."

"Ask your mother to take care of Hannibal and we'll go together."

Sarah took the young Hannibal and spoke gently to him in her arms. "You won't understand yet, but your father is paying for things he has done for us all, in the same way as your grandfather has done. We must go to him now. I will tell you when you are old enough to know." With that the young baby was cradled and rocked. Mrs Spriddle arrived within the hour to look after Hannibal 4th.

"I don't like you going Susannah. Why not send one of the men and let them tell you what has happened."

"I must go to him myself. Maybe I will see him. I should have gone before and been there for this trial."

With that the two women were gone to Rame Barton farm, where they picked up their horses and went. They had seen Bodmin Moor from the high spot of the Peninsula at Tregantle up from the farm where the road to Anthony dropped eastward, overlooking the Lynher, Tiddy and St German's rivers that peeled off the Tamar.

The eastern edge of the Moor could not be missed, with its high hills standing out on the skyline. From the village they could also see the fringes of Dartmoor, the companion moor to Bodmin that lay only a few miles over the river Tamar and was considerably bigger than their native Bodmin Moor.

The two women rode towards the hills knowing they would be close to Bodmin when they got there.

"Let's join the turnpike road at Sheviock. It will take us to Liskeard and then straight onto Bodmin." Neither had travelled much on these roads and Susannah had not been far past Sheviock in this direction. The turnpike road was well-kept. it was not long before Liskeard came, and they saw the Bodmin stone providing directions to major towns and villages.

"We don't want Boconnoc. We don't want Lostwithiel either. There it is, Bodmin."

They took to the Bodmin road, passing some carts and carriages as they did so.

"Look, what is that cart there?"

'There are uniformed people around it. Let's go slower and look."

"There are men in chains and ropes in the back."

"Is that Hannibal?" With that Susannah took her horse right up to its side. The uniformed men warned her to keep her distance and away. Joined by Sarah the two women went either side of the cart. Hannibal was resting as best he could as every jolt of the cart on the potholes pulled on the tightened chains. This disturbed the meagre comfort and slumber he and the others were trying to grab at every opportunity they could. They had got themselves into as comfortable a set of positions on the cart as they could for the journey to a ship at Plymouth. This ship might not be the ship they were joining but would be the start of their time in the English Naval fleet.

"Keep off you women. Get back."

The burly, toothless, unshaven specimens of men with them on the cart did not put them off. Two smartly uniformed mounted men were with them escorting the cart and its pressed men.

"It's him. It's Hannibal." The rush of excitement on their faces as they looked to each other was tempered as their minds turned to how they free him. Should they go back and try to raise their men to ambush them by the side of the road? Was there a chance? Was there time? These men were armed and escorted.

"That's my son."

"That's my husband."

With that they instinctively veered in front of the cart, bringing it to an abrupt halt. Spotting his wife and mother, Hannibal moved and shouted to them, "I'm here. I'm here!"

Standing and pulling one of the other men up with him he showed them he was not done for.

"I am joining the Navy for five years. Do not fear. Look after everything and especially yourselves and the young Hannibal. I'll see you well before the five years is out. I'll get news of where I am. Write. We will arrange for you to come to the ship when in Plymouth. I will be back. It's peacetime. I will be back often I am sure. Visit the ships when in dock."

With that Susannah, who could ride well, rode close to the side on which Hannibal was sat, causing the guard's horse to rear and the pulling horses to start and veer across to one side. Fearing this might signal an attempt at releasing the men, the Guards drew pistols, warning the women to stay back. The Naval men shook their fists and drew their swords.

The two women were undeterred, driven on by seeing Hannibal.

"I will be alright. Do not risk anything now. Go home and look after Hannibal. Keep everything for me when I return."

Breaking through to reach her husband, she managed one last kiss. She then did as she was bid and withdrew.

Sarah shouted well wishing to Hannibal. With that the two women drew back fearing things may turn against them with the Guards. They shadowed them for the rest of their journey to the ferry that crossed to Plymouth from Cremyll. As they discharged their prisoners the women knew it might be a while before they saw Hannibal once more. But no war, the less likelihood of injury or death in service.

They prayed he would be more on the Men o War than the other ships in the fleet. These ships were less likely to end their days floundering. The Men o War had the best fitments and design of any ships in the Royal Navy.

On arriving at the other side of the river they would be put into the care of the Navy pressgang. The pressgang would escort them to the Naval dock to join a ship. This would be their first night on a Naval vessel. If there were not one docked and ready to join, the prison hulks on the Hamoaze would accommodate them until a ship was ready.

"Pledge you will keep the trade for me, for my return. For Hannibal 4th. Pledge?"

"I pledge my love and until we meet again. Write, get a letter through. Let me know your ships and when they are coming. I will be there."

His mother nodded to him. Hannibal knew she would keep the trade running for her husband's memory, for her son Hannibal and for her grandson. She would do this for all the family. Her other children were not so involved. It had been the two Hannibals. Now it was her. She would have to do this and help to rear the next Hannibal. It was only five years. It would pass. With that Susannah rushed towards him pushing past the Navy men who were taken by surprise. They let her go.

"Go on then, it'll be your last for a while. The Navy'll toughen him even more than the bugger is now. Get on that ferry."

With that they parted. She watched every step, every move of the boat as it turned to take him in and out of view. Until she could see him no more.

Chapter 40

Shipwreck and a Fresh Start for Hannibal 4th

"This is a howler. It's not stopping Richard. We're going in."

"She's strong and copper bottomed too. She'll survive this."

" We're not pulling around. She's going to hit the rocks."

The sound and vibration shattered even the crashing sound of the howling gales. The two sounds mixed to give that unearthly sound of a dying ship as the people on her were thrown everywhere, their possessions too.

Most of the crates had been loosened in preparation to get them ashore, despite the poor weather in the previous days. The Regina had held her cables well and it surprised the Captain and crew to think that she should suddenly drag or break them. The Regina had served well since she left Plymouth Sound beginning of April. She had arrived in Port Nicholson towards the end of August, planning to finally arrive at her planned destination in New Plymouth the end of October. She had been greeted on arrival by appalling weather, some of the worst that New Zealand's North Island could supply.

"She's stuck Hann. She's taking in water below but she's riding high above. There's hardly any movement and the tides outing. She'll sit here unless she floats at the next flood tide."

"Look at where she is on the rocks though. Can you see them? She's almost dead centre."

"Just as well the shore boats managed to get out and take most of the settlers' crates ashore. If this storm settles, they could walk the rest ashore from these rocks."

The water receded, with it the ship left high and dry on the rocky outcrop. The few remaining crew took the ladders down on the side against the slight list.

"By God's will we will walk ashore. It could have been different Hann if that storm had caught us and taken us further out. Don't forget to take that barometer case you made on the journey."

"Can you take it for me Richard, I'm going to swim through that channel of water there to the shore."

"You can walk the rocks almost all the way Hann?"

"I want to tell my children and grandchildren I swam to New Zealand!"

"Make sure you tell them the story you have told me of Hannibal 1st to Hannibal 3rd.   You will have to make sure that you,   Hannibal 4th is there as well next time !"

Location maps

The following location maps set out to provide an indication of the approximate and relative positions of the different places referred to in the book.

The River Tamar, its source but a few miles in the north, has provided the natural boundary between the two neighbouring counties of Cornwall and Devon. This has not always, though, been the case. Kingsand and the surrounding area to the east was once in Devon. This was before the river had once again resumed its pre-eminence in providing the boundary. There remain to this day some anomalies and there are still some areas that are classed in Devon and some that are classed in Cornwall that defy the river's passage.

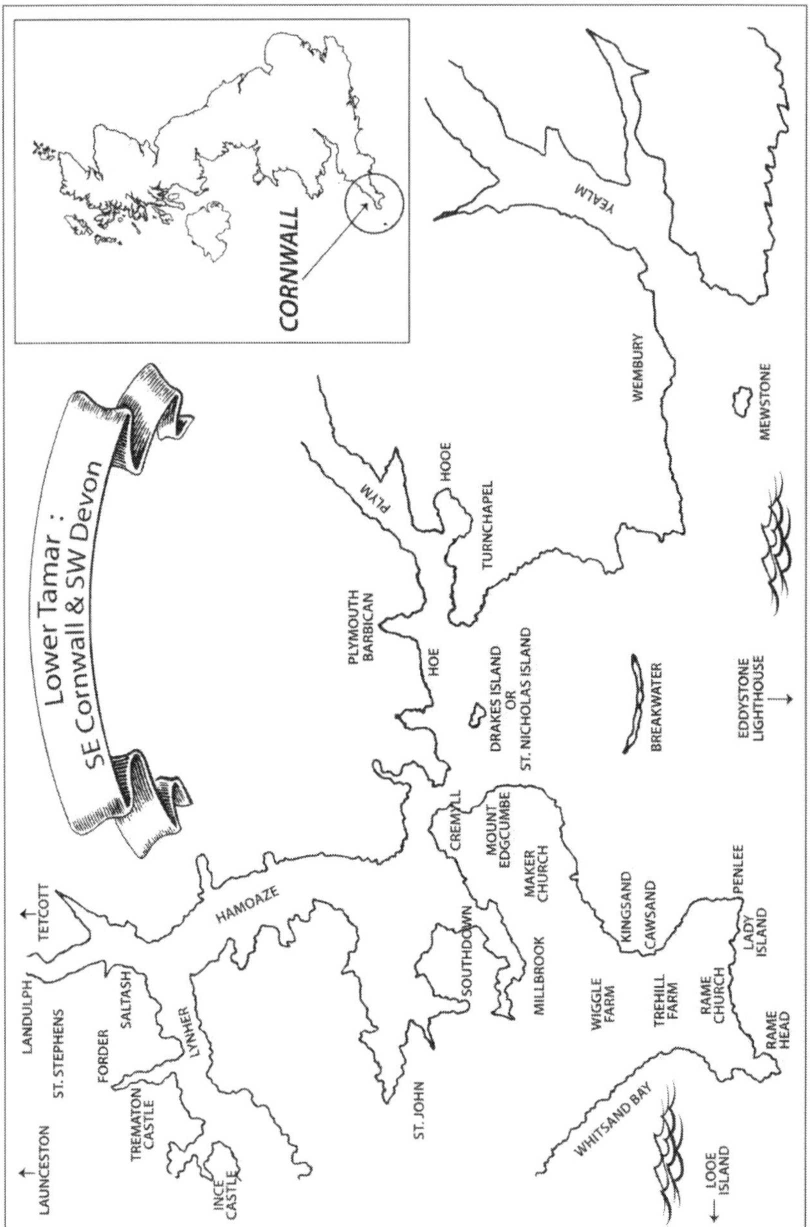
Lower Tamar :
SE Cornwall & SW Devon
CORNWALL
TETCOTT
LAUNCESTON
LANDULPH
ST. STEPHENS
SALTASH
FORDER
TREMATON CASTLE
INCE CASTLE
LYNHER
HAMOAZE
ST. JOHN
SOUTHDOWN
MILLBROOK
CREMYLL
MOUNT EDGCUMBE
MAKER CHURCH
WIGGLE FARM
TREHILL FARM
KINGSAND
CAWSAND
PENLEE
LADY ISLAND
RAME CHURCH
RAME HEAD
WHITSAND BAY
LOOE ISLAND
PLYMOUTH BARBICAN
HOE
DRAKES ISLAND OR ST. NICHOLAS ISLAND
BREAKWATER
EDDYSTONE LIGHTHOUSE
PLYM
HOOE
TURNCHAPEL
WEMBURY
MEWSTONE
YEALM

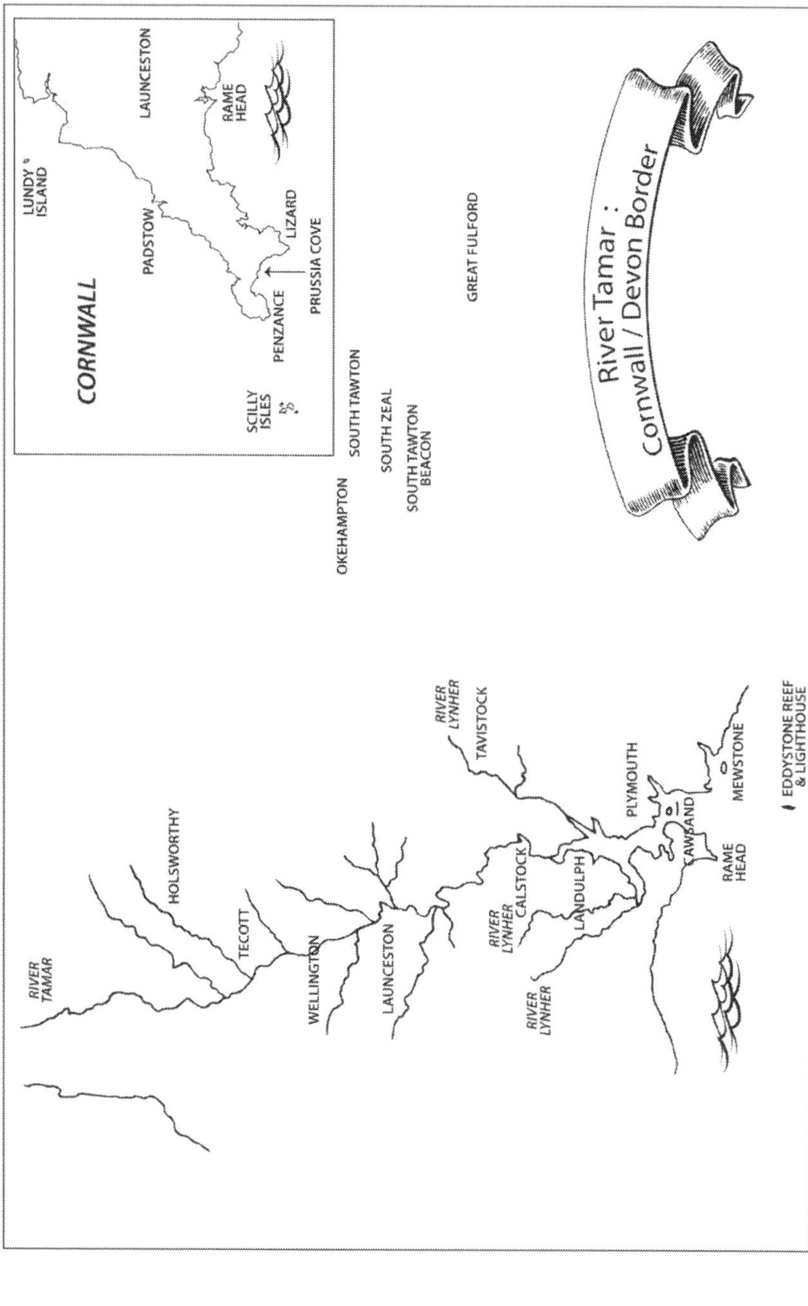

CORNWALL
LUNDY ISLAND
PADSTOW
LAUNCESTON
RAME HEAD
LIZARD
PRUSSIA COVE
PENZANCE
SCILLY ISLES
SOUTH TAWTON
SOUTH ZEAL
SOUTH TAWTON BEACON
OKEHAMPTON
GREAT FULFORD
River Tamar :
Cornwall / Devon Border
RIVER TAMAR
HOLSWORTHY
TECOTT
WELLINGTON
LAUNCESTON
RIVER LYNHER
TAVISTOCK
PLYMOUTH
CALSTOCK
LANDULPH
RIVER LYNHER
RIVER LYNHER
CAWSAND
RAME HEAD
MEWSTONE
EDDYSTONE REEF & LIGHTHOUSE

Sequel

What happened to Hannibal 2nd

Hannibal 3rd's Navy days

Sarah Marks runs the firm

Joe gets justice for Marie

Hannibal 4th starts again in New Zealand

The last of the Smugglers leave a legacy for future generations

A future generation gets a surprise inheritance

Fortunes start to be rebuilt.

Without her husband and son to rely on, Sarah steels herself to honour the pledge they all made to maintain the family firm. She enters the shadowy, twilight existence of the smuggling industry in her own right.

Hannibal 4th is brought up to the smuggling life despite best efforts by many now in the family to persuade him into a different career. He escapes capture in a major raid and heads to New Zealand with an old friend to start again but must leave his childhood sweetheart behind with her not knowing what has become of him.

It is the last straw for Sarah, who decides it is time to wind down their operation, but she is keen to ensure there is an inheritance from it for her future generations.

No more children take the Hannibal name in Cawsand and with the demise of the name comes the gradual demise of the Marks' smuggling firm.

Their legacy though is to live on and a future generation receive a surprise inheritance. With this, the new generation start to rebuild the family fortunes.

It is not, though, this inheritance alone that provides the foundation stone for the rise of the new generation. The hand of fate also delivers them a further surprise inheritance.

This is from a direct branch of their family whose wealth had come from marriages into some of the wealthiest and most influential families in Cornwall.

Coming with strongly forged links to the Crown and nobility of the land their inheritance comes with a high price for the modern generation to pay. They find themselves taken back to the misdeeds and dramas of earlier centuries that the family had since tried to forget.

The past, however, awakens to both haunt and favour the later generation as it did to their predecessors, as they come to terms with the secrets that come to life with it.

This mix of fortunes combines the rough and tumble of the smugglers' legacies with the more genteel face of the fortunes of the British gentry and aristocracy.

Together they combine to form an explosive cocktail for the later generations on whom the legacies fall to rebuild their standing and fortune.

41676547R00390

Printed in Poland
by Amazon Fulfillment
Poland Sp. z o.o., Wrocław